CATHERINE COOKSON

Catherine Cookson is a native of Tyneside
and has told the story of her rugged early life there in an
autobiography *Our Kate**. After tackling a variety
of posts she moved south to Hastings
where she married a grammar school master and
lived for many years, before returning to the
North East. She has published over fifty novels and
became an international bestseller with
*Katie Mulholland** in 1967. *The Round Tower** won
her the Winifred Holtby Award for the best regional
novel of 1968 and more recently
*The Girl** has confirmed her position as one of the most
popular of contemporary women novelists.

THE MALLEN GIRL
The sequel to *The Mallen Streak* and the popular
television series *The Mallens*

*Published by Corgi Books

Catherine Cookson

The Mallen Girl

CORGI BOOKS
A DIVISION OF TRANSWORLD PUBLISHERS LTD

THE MALLEN GIRL

A CORGI BOOK 0 552 11570 3

Originally published in Great Britain
by William Heinemann Ltd.

PRINTING HISTORY
William Heinemann edition published 1974
William Heinemann edition reprinted 1974
Corgi edition published 1975
Corgi edition reprinted 1975
Corgi edition reprinted 1977 (twice)
Corgi edition reprinted 1978
Corgi edition reissued 1979
Corgi edition reprinted 1979 (twice)
Corgi edition reprinted 1980
Corgi edition reissued 1980

This book is set in Intertype Times

Corgi Books are published by
Transworld Publishers Ltd,
Century House, 61–63 Uxbridge Road,
Ealing, London W5 5SA

Set, printed and bound in Great Britain by
Cox and Wyman Ltd, Reading

Contents

BOOK I

YOUNG BARBARA

ONE

The trap had hardly stopped opposite the cottage gate before the lithe figure of the young girl sprang down from it, ran up the back path, across the small court-yard, thrust open the door of the kitchen, and slammed her beaded handbag and the book she was carrying down on the table, which action caused Mary Peel, who was standing at the far end of the table, to space her lips widely apart and mouth her words in a loud voice, crying, "Now Miss Bar-bara you! Now don't you start the minute you're in; keep your tantrums for those who caused them."

The young girl's hand went to the book again, and as she grabbed it up and threw it the door leading from the hall opened and Miss Anna Brigmore entered. The book had missed its target, skimming by Mary Peel's face, but it hit Miss Brigmore's shoulder, bounced off and onto the dresser, knocking a jug onto the stone floor.

After the resounding crash of the jug splintering there was quiet in the kitchen for a moment. Miss Brigmore, staring in pained silence at the young girl who was known as her ward, but whom she thought of as her daughter, cried from her heart, "Oh Barbara! Barbara, my dear." But Mary Peel, looking at the girl, thought, By! If I had me way I'd skelp your back-side for you, I would that. Your neck's been broken, that's your trouble, miss.

And apparently her thinking was endorsed by Jim

3

Waite as he held the door open when Miss Brigmore took hold of Barbara's hand and led her out of the room, for as soon as he closed it he said, "That one wants her ears scudded."

"Aw, don't say that, Jim," said Mary Peel now; "I know she deserves her hammers, but it's her ears an' not being able to hear right that makes her as she is. Sit yourself down, the kettle's just on the boil. How's things been?"

Jim Waite lowered his long length onto the wooden kitchen chair and stretched out his hands toward the fire before saying, "Oh, much as usual. I suppose I'm sayin' it as shouldn't, but I tell you everybody on the farm breathes a sigh of relief when that young monkey steps up into the trap. They do, they do." He nodded at her. "She makes the young master's life hell. She never lets him out of her sight; he can't go to the netty for her, an' that's a fact. And I'm not just usin' that as a sayin', 'cos only this mornin' he was in the closet and there she was standin' in the middle of the yard looking at the doorway waitin' for him coming out. It isn't decent. You'd think Miss Brigmore would be able to do something about it, now wouldn't you? If anybody could you'd think she could. And yet on the other hand, as me da was sayin' just the other night, it's her who's partly to blame for the way Miss Barbara is now. Oh, not her ears, no, but the way she carries on, 'cos she's given into her all along the line."

"Here, drink this." Mary handed him a mug of tea and asked, "Would you like a bit of new fadge, it's just out of the oven?"

"Aye, ta; it'll fill a corner."

"An' you've got some corners to fill." Mary pushed him in the shoulder with the flat of her hand. "You would've thought you'd stopped growin' years ago. . . . How's your ma and da?"

"Oh fine, fine."

"And Lily?"

"Oh, Lily. You'll never believe it but I think she's got Bill Twigg up to scratch at last."

Mary sat down abruptly now and, clasping her

hands, the bounced them on her lap as she leaned toward him and said, "No! What's brought it on?"

"Well, Harry Brown's wife died over Allendale way. He's got a bit of a farm, not much to brag about but enough to keep the wolf from the door. Well, he's been over three times in the last three months, an' each time stood chattin' and laughing with our Lily. It's made Bill think." He jerked his head as he ended, "An' so he should, he's been courtin' her for seven years. But it was his mother to blame there, at least up till three years ago when she died, 'cos she always used to tell him that it was unlucky to marry a woman older than himself. Two years, I ask you! Eeh! the things people say an' believe in. . . . This is a nice bit of fadge, Mary." He took another huge bite out of the buttered bread, then ended, "Folks in the main are ignorant, you know, ignorant. . . ."

In the sitting room Miss Brigmore was using the same words. "It is ignorance, my dear," she was saying, "just ignorance." Miss Brigmore did not speak as loudly as Mary Peel, but her voice was a pitch above normal, and she moved her lips in a slightly exaggerated fashion.

"She is horrible, and I hate her."

"You mustn't say that, Barbara. Sarah is only a little girl, she is but ten years old."

Miss Brigmore did not think that the girl standing before her at this moment was but twelve years old, for she considered Barbara older than her years. Knowledge, she thought, had made her so, the knowledge that she herself had imparted to her. The child, although having the terrible disadvantage of being almost completely deaf, nevertheless had the balancing advantage of being as well informed on a great many subjects as any young lady of twenty.

She gazed at the child, who was over-thin and over-tall for her age . . . and over-beautiful too. Her straight black hair was shining with the sheen of a wet seal. The skin that covered her long face was creamy and thick of texture and without tint. Her eyes were a dark brown and the look in them now, as at other

5

times, made Miss Brigmore uneasy, for it reminded her of the look in Donald Radlet's eyes, Donald Radlet who had been the husband of Barbara's aunt, Constance, but who was much closer to her than an uncle, did she but know it. This fact often kept Miss Brigmore awake at nights as she searched for a way to break to her beloved child the truth of her beginnings. She was fully aware that but for the girl's deafness her origin would have been made clear to her long before now, and, if by no one else, by one of the Waite family over at Wolfbur farm, for she had aroused the dislike not only of Harry and Daisy Waite, but also of Jim and Lily, their son and daughter, and all because she had taken a dislike to Harry Waite's niece, Sarah.

Harry Waite had brought Sarah to the farm when she was two years old, when her parents had both died of the fever. Sarah had grown into a pretty and lively little girl and she was popular not only with the Waite family, but with the mistress, Constance Radlet, and her mother-in-law Jane Radlet too.

All this would have been quite in order and accepted by Barbara had the attention to Sarah stopped there, but her cousin Michael had championed the little girl from the day she arrived on the farm, for Sarah, although so much younger than himself, was someone with whom he could play and at the same time protect. Previous to Sarah's coming the only time Michael had anyone of his own age to play with was when Barbara visited the farm. In the summer the visits could be frequent, but during the winter months the children were lucky if they saw each other twice.

The first time the rift between the children came into the open was one exceptionally mild Christmas. Miss Brigmore herself had driven Mary and the child over expecting to be able to return home within the week, but their stay on the farm had lengthened into almost three weeks, and although Michael, then eight years old, had played with Barbara and tolerated her domination, he had continued to take notice of young Sarah.

It happened during the evening of the yearly event

when Constance had the Waite family in for supper and, as Jane Radlet termed it, a bit of jollification. Little Sarah, after entertaining the company with a clog dance taught her by her cousin Jim, was receiving the loud applause of all those present when she found herself suddenly sitting on her bottom on the farm kitchen floor. Although the floor was covered with drugget it was made up of slabs of stone, and the impact caused the little girl to howl aloud. The only one who dared voice her disapproval was Constance, who said, "You're a naughty girl, Barbara," accompanying her words with slapping Barbara's hands.

Miss Brigmore was very annoyed and she expressed her annoyance to Constance. Didn't she understand the situation? she asked. Wasn't it natural that Barbara should be jealous when she saw Michael making a fuss of the Waite child? Didn't she understand that in her little mind she imagined Michael belonged to her, like a brother? It was merely a childish reaction and she would grow out of it.

Miss Brigmore remembered for a long time afterwards that Constance had made no reply whatever; she had just stood staring at her before turning about and walking out of the room.

Her prediction that Barbara would, with the years, change her attitude toward Michael had not, however, proved correct; if anything Barbara's possessiveness had increased, until now Miss Brigmore found herself longing for the winter so that their visits would be controlled by the weather. In the summer Barbara insisted on trailing her over the hills at least once a week. Lately, she had broached the subject of having a horse; if she had a horse she would not need to trouble anyone, was her argument now.

Among other fears also assailing Miss Brigmore was the fact that the childish infatuation Barbara had for her cousin Michael might not die away during her adolescence, but might mature into love, and such an outcome as this was definitely not in her plans for her child. As prosperous a farm as Wolfbur was, she did not see Thomas Mallen's daughter acting the farmer's

7

wife, No, the route she had mapped out for her lay in the opposite direction, just a mile or so down the road where stood the Hall, High Banks Hall in which Barbara's mother had spent her young days, and over which Miss Brigmore was determined her spiritual daughter should reign in the future. And everything would work out splendidly, she felt, for already John Bensham, at sixteen, was showing a marked interest in Barbara. If only the child would get over this obsession for Michael and also her equally strong hate for young Sarah Waite, for the two were linked together.

She would, at this moment, like to be able to reassure Barbara that she had nothing to fear from a girl like Sarah Waite, because after all what was she but a maid, and the niece of a farm laborer. True, she was not actually treated like a maid, and so therefore did not act like one, for Constance had made the mistake of teaching the girl to read and write. She would have been happy to reassure her that her Aunt Constance did not prefer a little working-class maid to herself. But she knew this was not true. Constance had no feeling for Barbara, and this was strange because she had loved Barbara's mother. The sisters had been inseparable. Yet Constance, she suspected, would prefer that her son stepped out of his class and took someone like the Waite child to wife rather than her own niece.

It was a most strange state of affairs. Miss Brigmore thought; yet it suited her book, because were it otherwise the second stage of her life's work would go for nought.

She now sat down on a chair and, drawing Barbara to her, she held the child's hands between her own, and, looking up at her, she said slowly, but in loud tones, "Don't you understand, my dear, that when you quarrel with Sarah you are bringing yourself down to her level?"

"Don't shout at me, I can hear you."

Miss Brigmore stared up into Barbara's eyes, which had now turned as black as her hair, and she dragged her lower lip slowly between her teeth before saying in a normal voice, "What did I say?"

"You said that when I quarrel with her I reduce myself to her level."

The answer was correct and the words were as precise as Miss Brigmore would have wished; she sometimes forgot that this child could read most of what she was saying by the movement of her lips, and so she said, "Well then, you understand what I mean, only inferior people quarrel openly. You mustn't forget that you are a young lady. . . ."

"And I mustn't forget that I am deaf. I'll soon be stone deaf, won't I?"

"No, no, my dear." Miss Brigmore's head was moving slowly, and her words were merely a whisper and full of compassion. "No, no," she repeated. "No, no; something will be done. Mr. Bensham promised to see a certain gentleman in Manchester; he's heard of a man who's very clever with ears. . . ."

"Yes, he'll give me a big horn to stick in it, like the caricatures in . . ."

"No! No! No!" Miss Brigmore's voice was loud again and with each word she shook Barbara's hands up and down. When she stopped they stared at each other, both in deep sadness. Then the girl, her thin body seeming to crumple, fell onto her knees and buried her face in Miss Brigmore's lap, and, her voice high and tear-broken now, she gasped, "Why am I deaf? Why? Why?" She lifted her face and appealed, "Brigie, why? why should I be deaf? Is it because Michael tipped me out of the barrow?"

Miss Brigmore did not answer immediately because this was always a question in her own mind. It had seemed that there had been no ear defect at all until the child was five years old; yet of late she had recalled having before this chastised her for disobedience, whenever she appeared to take no notice either of some question or of being called.

The accident appeared a minor one at the time. Michael had been wheeling her in the farm barrow when it capsized and she fell head over heels and suffered a slight concussion. Was it from that time that her deafness became noticeable? Or was it really from the time of her first nightmare?

As if the girl were picking up her thoughts she said, "I told Michael today that he was to blame for my deafness."

"You shouldn't have done that, my dear; it . . . it isn't true."

"It could be."

"Your hearing was slightly defective before that."

"Throwing me on my head didn't help."

"That was an accident."

"The doctor said it didn't help, didn't he?"

"Who told you that?"

"I saw you talking to Mrs. Bensham one day."

"Oh, my dear." Miss Brigmore closed her eyes; then slowly she said, "It may not have helped but . . . but you would have become deaf in any case, so I understand. Yet, as I have said, there are remedies; I refuse to believe there are not. And I want you to believe that too, you understand? Now dry your eyes." She dried them for her. Then taking the child's face gently between her two palms she looked down into it and said slowly, "It doesn't matter so much about your impediment, just remember you are very beautiful and highly intelligent."

A sad smile slowly spread over Barbara's face, but there was a glint of mischief in it now as she said, "I haven't got a bust, not a sign of one, and you can't be beautiful without a bust."

"Oh Barbara! Barbara!" Miss Brigmore was trying to suppress her laughter. "You shouldn't say things like that, one doesn't, they're not . . ."

"Ladylike?"

"Yes, if you put it that way."

"That doesn't alter the fact that I haven't one. And look at yours; you're old and you've got an enormous bust."

"Really! Barbara." Miss Brigmore rose to her feet and her voice lost a little of its controlled calmness as she retorted, "I'm not, I haven't."

10

Jumping up now, Barbara placed her hand over her mouth to stifle her laughter; then she fell against Miss Brigmore as she giggled, "Well, you have; and it's a lovely bust, a lovely bust."

When she went to put her hand on the tightly laced breasts Miss Brigmore slapped at it hard and, bringing her upright, said, "Barbara . . . Barbara, behave yourself." Her lips moved widely now. "One does not mention these things. I have told you before, there are certain parts of the anatomy to which one does not make reference. Nor does one refer to another's age. You're old enough to have learned these things, they are elementary."

"Oh, Brigie!" Barbara flounced away, only to be pulled sharply round to face Miss Brigmore again.

"Never mind taking that attitude. Come, sit down, I want to talk to you."

Seated once again, they looked at each other and Miss Brigmore's mind was distracted from her theme as her protesting thoughts said, Old, indeed! She felt younger now than she had when Thomas was alive. Her body was straight and firm; she had as yet no gray hairs, and but for some lines under her eyes her skin was smooth; as for her mind, it had never been more active than during these last few years. Old indeed! She swallowed deeply; then folding her hands on her lap, her head slightly tilted to the side, she said, "Tell me exactly what caused the rum . . ." She had almost said, rumpus—Mary's speech had a way of infiltrating. "What caused the altercation at the farm?"

"Need you ask? It was Sarah, as usual."

Miss Brigmore did not say, "Sarah is not always to blame"; instead she asked, "What did she do?"

"She said I was deaf."

"Did she say it spitefully?"

Barbara heaved a deep sigh, closed her eyes, and slumped back in her chair before saying, "Spitefully or not, she said it."

"Sit up straight; put your buttocks well back . . . straighter. Don't have to be told so often."

11

"Will sitting straight make me hear better?"

"Don't ask ridiculous questions, Barbara. You shall hear; I've told you, you shall hear; everything is being done. What you must understand is that you're not the only who has this impediment." She now tapped her ear; then dropped her hand away as if it had been stung, remembering too late that nothing angered the child more than sign language. Yet if only she'd admit to her deafness the sign language would be of untold help to her. She herself had been reading at great length recently about the different methods of sign language; it was amazing what one learned through tribulation. She would never have dreamed there had been methods of trying to make the deaf and dumb speak as far back as the seventeenth century. She had also learned that deafness could be brought about by shock. This new knowledge, gleaned only during the past week, had brought the nightmares into question again and opened up another possibility for the child's deafness. For she had received a shock; as she herself had the first night Barbara's screams had awakened her. When she had reached the child's bed it was to see her sitting stiffly upright, her arms stretched out, her finger pointing to the corner of the room, and screaming hysterically, "The man! The man! The big man! Send him away."

Even after she took Barbara into her own bed and soothed her by telling her that she had been dreaming, the child still insisted that there had been a big man in her room, a big man with a fat stomach and white hair all over his head and face, and blood coming out of his coat. The description had been like a pen picture of Thomas just before he died, and for nights afterwards she had hardly slept and she had talked to the unseen figure, begging him to go and rest in peace and not to frighten the child.

She had never before associated this, and further incidents of the same nature, with Barbara's deafness, being of the opinion that deafness was congenital and could slumber for years in a child, except in cases of malnutrition which supplied bad blood to the brain and resulted in bad eyesight, deafness, and rickets. Nor did she associate deafness such as Barbara had with that of the deaf and dumb. The latter she considered a malady quite apart, and associated with mental defects; at least she had done until she'd had cause to go more fully into the matter.

She said now, "Your deafness is different; it's a deafness that could go like that." She snapped her fingers.

"Or get worse like that!" Barbara imitated her.

"Barbara!" Miss Brigmore's voice was stern again. "You've got to believe what I say; and you've also got to help yourself."

"By talking on my hands?" She now made wild exaggerated gestures, then said, "I won't, I won't. It makes you look mad; people think you're mad, daft. That's what Mary said when I did it. 'Don't act daft,' she said."

Oh! Mary. Miss Brigmore said sharply, "Mary wasn't implying that you were . . ." She stopped, and now she closed her eyes in irritation and flicked her hand as if dismissing Mary before saying, "I have been reading about a Mr. Pestalozzi and a Mr. Froebel. Mr. Pestalozzi was from Switzerland; he had a school there. He was a great educationalist and advises . . ."

"That you should take your earwort medicine. Oh you! You! You're silly; with your Mr. Froebel and Mr. Pestalozzi, and all your ideas. Pestalozzi! Psst! Psst! . . ."

When Miss Brigmore's hand came out and struck Barbara's with two resounding blows the girl was really startled, for she couldn't ever remember Brigie striking her, not for insolence or anything else. Then her pale face went a shade paler as she read Miss Brigmore saying, "All right, all right, I'm silly, as is Mr. Pestalozzi, so we will have it the way you want it. I shall no longer pester you with my theories, I shall no longer continue to probe into ways and means of helping you. But one thing I shall do, I shall see that you are helped, I'll send you away to a school for the deaf. Yes, yes; that's what I'll do."

Miss Brigmore stood up. Her body was as straight as a ramrod, her neck was stretched and her head pushed back on her shoulders.

For the first time in her life Barbara now felt real fear. Brigie was wild; she . . . she could mean what she said. She was so determined that she should hear that she could really mean what she said and send her away. Oh no! She would die. . . . Like a young animal, she sprang on Miss Brigmore, clutching her, crying, pleading, "Brigie! Brigie! no. Please, don't be angry, don't be angry. I'm sorry, I'm sorry. I'll do what you say, I'll do all that you say, only don't, don't send me away to school. I'd die. Yes, I'd die, or do something. You know I would, because I get so angry inside, and I can't help it, and should you send me away I'll get worse. Please, please, Brigie, please. . . . Look, I'll go over, straight back tomorrow, to the farm and tell Sarah I'm sorry, because I know she didn't mean it, I know she didn't. It was Bill Twigg really. I couldn't make out what he was saying, he mumbles; and it was then that Sarah said to him, 'She's deaf. Don't you know she's deaf? Make your mouth go more.' It was that . . . when she said make your mouth go more. It was awful. It was as if they were talking to one of the animals; I felt like an animal I did, I did. Brigie, I felt like an animal and I went wild. I couldn't hit him so I hit her. I'll apologize, I will, next time, or tomorrow. I tell you I'll go over tomorrow." Her voice broke on a high sob.

"There, there." Miss Brigmore was breathing deeply. Her body slowly relaxing, she put her arms around the girl and drew her close and stroked her hair, murmuring now, "There, there; don't cry, don't cry."

After a moment Barbara raised her tear-stained face and said, "You'll never say that again will you, Brigie? Never say you'll send me away to one of those schools."

"Then you'll have to cooperate."

"I'll . . . I'll cooperate."

As Miss Brigmore stared into the beloved face and saw the fear still on it, she realized, perhaps for

14

the first time, the full extent of the child's agony of
mind caused by her affliction, but she also realized that
the very fear of being sent away had given herself a
handle, a handle that she meant to use.

TWO

The following day being Monday, they arrived at High Banks Hall at nine-thirty sharp. With the exception of holidays, this had been the daily procedure since Miss Brigmore had taken over the education of Mr. Bensham's daughter, Katie, ten years ago in 1865. Unless they were returning late in the evening or the weather was stormy Miss Brigmore insisted on them walking. The distance from the cottage to the Hall was well over a mile along the main road before they entered the gates, but unless she had been battling against the wind she always mounted the steps leading to the front door of the Hall without any show of exertion.

Brooks, the butler, invariably opened the door to her. He was no longer called 'Arry, for Miss Brigmore had pointed out, very tactfully, to the mistress of the house the fact that two 'Arrys in her household might cause some confusion, one being her husband, so 'Arry became Brooks to all except the master of the house. Miss Brigmore had found that there was very little she could do concerning certain matters when dealing with the master of the house. In some things he was quite pliable, in others most obdurate.

"Good morning, miss."

"Good morning, Brooks."

Miss Brigmore led the way across the hall, up the main staircase, turned to her right across a wide landing, and made her way toward the gallery. As she pushed open one of the double doors she almost knocked over a bucket of water from which Alice Dunn, the third housemaid, was wringing out a cloth.

"I'm sorry. Did I hurt you?"

"No, miss. No, miss." Alice Dunn smiled at she shook her head vigorously, then she sat back on her heels and watched the pair go down the long gallery before she dried up the soap from the mosaic tiles of the floor. It was as they said, she gave folks their place. Yet some resented her, saying they didn't know who was mistress of the Hall, her or Mrs. Bensham. Still, as everybody knew, Mrs. Bensham couldn't run a place like this, not really, not cut out for it. And The Brigadier, give her her due, had done a good job on the bairns, there was no doubt about that; they behaved themselves, at least when she was about. They could be devils, oh aye, but they weren't upstarts of devils like some she had seen in other houses; spit on you some of the young ones would, and did. Talking about spittin'; they were sayin' in the kitchen The Brigadier's next battle was to get the master to take the spittoon out of the bedroom. By! aye, that would be the day. She hoped she lived to see it.

Miss Brigmore continued through the gallery, through another set of double doors, across another landing at the end of which were two sets of stairs, one mounting to the second floor, the other descending to the corridor that led to the kitchen quarters.

The nursery floor, as it was called, had changed little over the years except that the room that had once been Miss Brigmore's bedroom was now a sitting room. When she had first taken up her duties she'd had her meal and Barbara's served in her sitting room; but this hadn't lasted for long. At the repeated requests of both the master and mistress she had joined them at their table, while Barbara had hers with the children. It is true to say that because of this arrangement Miss Brigmore's own education was advanced if not improved, for in the early days she learned the type of conversation that went on between two ordinary people, and she found it anything but edifying.

Having taken her outer clothes off in her room she

smoothed her hair from its center parting over her temples and her ears to where it was fastened in a knot at the nape of her neck. Then she looked Barbara over, puffed up the shoulder frills of her pinafore, and smiled at her before she said, "Come."

When they entered the schoolroom Katie Bensham, who had been reclining, not sitting, in the old leather chair near the fire, sprang to her feet, pulled her pinafore straight, smiled brightly and said, "Good morning, Miss Brigmore."

"Good morning, Katie."

The two girls now exchanged a glance that had a conspiratorial quality about it before they gave each other greeting.

"Good morning, Barbara."

"Good morning, Katie."

After which they both walked sedately down the long room and to a bookcase on the far wall, where from her own particular shelf each of them extracted a book, returned to the table, and stood behind her chair.

Miss Brigmore was already standing behind hers. She bowed her head, joined her hands together, and began to recite the Lord's Prayer.

"Amen."

"Amen—Amen."

They sat down. The girls, with their backs tight against the rails of the chairs, looked toward Miss Brigmore, waiting for her instructions, for they both knew it was no use their turning to the last lesson they'd had in English Literature, for she jumped about like a frog from one period to another; it was nothing for her to spring on you when you were in the middle of George III and demand to know where Boccaccio came in the Renaissance; if you hadn't linked him up with Dante and Petrarch you were lost; or she would throw Erasmus at you, and that was usually only the beginning. When she was in one of her memory moods she'd run the gamut of the Renaissance, finishing up with Marlowe and Shakespeare.

Katie Bensham had long ceased to wonder how

18

Miss Brigmore came by such knowledge. She didn't believe what John had said last holidays that she was like the masters at his boarding school, she read it up the night before. No one, she imagined, could read up Miss Brigmore's knowledge, it seemed as innate in her as if she had been born with it and never had to learn it. She admired Miss Brigmore, but she could laugh at her, and did, because she wasn't afraid of her. Funny that; everybody else seemed afraid of her in some degree, except perhaps her father. She prided herself that she was like her father, afraid of nothing or no one. But Brigie was speaking.

"We shall waive our lesson on the poets this morning and touch on the subject of educationalists. Of course, as you already know, Katie"—she cast her glance toward Katie while keeping her face in full view of Barbara—"in your home town of Manchester there was founded in 1515 a grammar school that has grown into a very large school. But who founded it? And *why* was it founded? That is a much more important question . . . why? Eton College was founded by Henry VI." She seemed to be speaking pointedly to Barbara now, her lips moving wider. "Why was it founded?" Although she paused they did not answer, for they knew from experience that she was far from finished. She now looked from one girl to the other as she went on: "The Sunday school movement was started by Robert Raikes; why? And only five years ago there was formed a compulsory system for education for all children; why? That is the question, *Why?* The answer is because of a need. . . . This morning we are going to deal with this question of need, and we're going to begin in France. Yes"—she nodded from one to the other —"in France, and with a priest, whose name was the Abbé de L'Épée, who lived in the eighteenth century. He began a particular kind of school; again why?" She divided her glance once more between them, and they stared back at her, their interest aroused, their faces holding a keen look, until she said slowly, while looking now straight at Barbara, "Because he felt compas-

19

sion for the numerous deaf children, deaf and dumb children . . . *really* deaf and dumb children, children without hope, children who were tied up like animals, hidden away in dark rooms, put into asylums because they could neither hear nor speak."

Barbara was staring back into Miss Brigmore's eyes. She seemed in this moment completely unmoved. But not so Katie; her face had gone red with indignation. Brigie was really playing The Brigadier with a vengeance, she was being cruel.

At this point there was a sharp knock on the door and Armstrong, the first footman, entered, and looking toward Miss Brigmore he said, "The master would like to see you, miss, if you can spare the time."

Miss Brigmore drew in a deep breath that clamped down on her impatience, then paused a moment before saying, "I shall be down," then repeating to herself, If you can spare the time! Mr. Harry Bensham would never have added those last words, not if she knew anything about him.

As she rose from the table Katie's glance caught hers. The child looked angry, and she understood why. Katie had a big heart and considered that she was being cruel to Barbara. In her ignorance, like that which pervaded her family, she, and by far the majority of the population, were in fact of the opinion that the inflictions of deafness, dumbness, and even blindness, should be ignored out of kindness; and as for any malformation of the body or defectiveness of the mind, that should be locked tightly behind barred doors.

She now picked up the book that had been to her hand on the table and said, "This book is in French; it tells of the struggle that the Abbé had to establish his system of teaching of the deaf, the teaching which, I may say, has been reviled and is questionable to this day. Nevertheless he was a good man, with good intentions; as also in a way was Monsieur Sicard. You will note"—she now again spoke pointedly to Barbara —"the Abbé advocates sign language. Bring your chairs together and read this book diligently until my return.

20

I shall expect to hear what you know of these men, and others you come across, all bent on the same purpose, that of assisting the deaf to hear and the dumb to speak in their own language."

When the door closed behind Miss Brigmore, Katie sat back in her chair and on a long, slow letting out of breath, she said, "We-ll! we-ll!" Then, putting her hand over Barbara's, she added, "She's cruel, she is. I can't understand her; she's supposed to love you and yet she's . . ."

"I understand her."

"You do?"

"Yes; and she's right. I should know about myself, about my disease."

"It's not a disease." Katie poked her face forward. "And don't start washing yourself in self-pity."

"I'm not." Barbara's denial was harsh. "And it is a disease. Do you know—" she stopped and her lips trembled slightly before she went on—"I . . . I can barely hear my own voice, even when I shout."

"You said you heard the bells ringing last week."

"Yes, but I was near them."

"And when I scraped the knife over the glass you heard that."

"They're unusual sounds. Just a short while ago I could hear the cry of a bird when it was startled. I can't now."

They looked at each other. Then Katie, her face sad, murmured softly, "Oh, Barbara. Mightn't it just be your imagination?"

"Now, now." Barbara leaned back in her chair and, her voice high and strident, said, "Who's talking of pity? Don't do it, because you know I can't stand it, it makes me feel like a cripple. And don't suggest, either, it's my imagination."

They stared at each other in silence for a time until Barbara asked flatly, "What happened this weekend, did the boys come? I looked for them downstairs but didn't see anyone."

Katie nodded. "Yes, they came; but they went

back last night. They missed you. They told me to tell you they missed you."

"Did they?" Barbara smiled slowly.

"Dan said it was awful having no one to fight with."

They both laughed; then leaning forward, Katie said, "Do you know who's here?"

"No."

"Willy."

Barbara screwed up her face and her lips formed the word slowly, *"Woolly."*

"Willy. Willy Brooks, you know. Of course you do."

"Oh, you mean Brooks's son?"

"Yes"—Katie drew back—"Brooks's son, Willy."

For the moment there was a look on Barbara's face very like one would expect to have seen on Miss Brigmore's had she been told that the daughter of the Hall was excited because the butler's son had arrived. Quick to notice this, Katie pushed Barbara none too gently with the flat of her hand, saying, "Don't be so priggish; Willy's nice, and Dad thinks a lot of him. He's promoted him, and he's got the idea of making him manager later on. . . . And don't you think he's good looking, handsome?"

"Not very."

"Not very! You must be . . ." She almost said blind, but that would have been awful; you had to be careful in a way what you said to Barbara; so she reverted to her mother's idiom and said, "You must be daft; he's the best-looking fellow I've ever seen; he's better looking than either our John or Dan."

"He's not; John's very good looking."

"Do you think so?"

"Yes, of course."

"But not so good looking as Michael Radlet." Now Katie's tongue was hanging well down over her lower lip, the teasing light was deep in her eyes, and it was Barbara's turn to push at her; then they both sat with their heads together for a moment as they laughed, before turning in a concerted movement to the book on the table.

Miss Brigmore heard the master of the house before she was halfway down the main staircase. His loud bellow was coming from the library, which room he also used for his office, not because he wanted the proximity of books, for she had never seen him read one, but because, he would have her understand, he liked the light from the tall windows. But her own opinion of why he preferred to work there when he was at home was because it was the one room in the house free from folderols, as he termed the over-ornate furnishings and decorations chosen by his wife. If a room had any dignity about it, Mrs. Bensham had the unfortunate knack of making it homely by adding bobbled and scalloped mantel-borders, antimacassars, and numerous "nice" pictures and hideous ornaments.

As she approached the library door Harry Bensham was yelling, "Why the hell didn't you bring this matter up afore, lad? On the point of leavin' and then you tell me this. 'Tisn't my business, 'tis the missus's by rights. . . . Come in. Come in." This was in answer to Miss Brigmore's knock on the door.

When she entered the room she saw that the lad in question was Willy Brooks, the butler's son, a tall young man, and she wondered what he was doing here at this time on a Monday morning. Her attention was brought from him, where he was standing at the side of the long table that served as a desk, to Harry Bensham, who was seated in a leather chair behind the table. His bullet head thrust forward, each of his short unruly gray hairs that never showed a parting seemed to be standing up in protest from his head; his face had a blotchy gray look, a sure sign that his temper was reaching its highest peak, for temper, in Harry Bensham's case, did not heighten his color but usually drained the natural redness from his face. In his hand he had a letter, and as she came to a stop before the

23

desk he thrust it out at her, saying, "Have a look at that; go on, have a look at that. Tell me what you think on't."

She took the letter from his hand and she read:

To Mabel Docherty: In reference to your application for the post of kitchen maid in High Banks Hall the mistress has consented to engage you. You will present yourself at twelve o'clock on Saturday, the fifteenth day of May, bringing with you two print dresses for weekday work, and one extra and of superior quality for Sunday, when you'll attend service; one pair of light boots, one pair of heavy boots; four pairs of black stockings, three changes of underclothing with two pairs of extra drawers, preferably woolen. Your duties will commence at six in the morning and will end at seven in the evening, except on Tuesdays when you will have a half day free starting at one o'clock and finishing at eight o'clock. You will have one Sunday off in three and you will receive three pounds eighteen shillings per year together with an allowance of extra tea or beer.

 Signed
 Hannah Fairweather (Mrs.), Housekeeper.

Miss Brigmore's mouth was slightly open when she looked back at Harry Bensham.

"Well?"

"What do you expect me to say?"

"What do I expect you to say!" He was on his feet now, his two hands flat on the desk, leaning toward her. "I expect you to say, the woman's a bloody fool. I expect you to say, how did she come to write that? I expect you to say, who gave her authority?"

Miss Brigmore's mouth was tightly closed. She could not stand to hear the man swear; not that she was unused to a man swearing. When Thomas Mallen had been master here he had done his share of it, but then Thomas had sworn in a different way altogether from Mr. Harry Bensham. When she opened her lips she said stiffly, "Shouldn't you be putting these questions to Mrs. Bensham?"

"No, I should not. Anyway"—he jerked his head to the side—"she's off color, she's bad this mornin'. But it was you who picked this one." He now grabbed the letter from her hand. "Housekeeper? Huh! bloody upstart. Fancy writing a letter like that to the Dochertys an' not a bloody one of them can read. They took it to Willy here." He thumbed it toward the young man. Then he turned his furious gaze on the letter again and read, "Two pairs of extra woolen drawers. God! I don't suppose the lass has had a pair of drawers on her in her life. As for two pairs of boots, the whole lot of them's run barefoot since they were born." He now banged the letter down on the desk, ending, "I'll break that buggerin' woman's neck, I will that. An' you're damn well to blame."

"I'll thank you, Mr. Bensham, not to swear at me, and also to get your facts right."

Harry Bensham now bowed his head, gnawed hard on his lower lip, banged his doubled fist once on the table before looking up at her and saying in a more moderate tone, "Aw, woman, I'm sorry. But I'm . . . I'm real narked, I am that." He put out his hand as if appealing to her now for understanding. "The Dochertys. All right, they're Irish an' they're feckless, like all their kin in Manchester, but Shane Docherty's worked for me for years, and Pat, his father, worked for mine. All right"—he now flapped his hand at her as if checking her protest—"they drank nearly all they earned and lived on tatties and oatmeal for the rest of the week, but what they did with their money was their business, what they did for me was another. They were good workers, an' still are, but Shane's worried about young Mabel, she has the cough. He wants her out of the mills an' the place altogether, an' I left word with Tilda last week to tell that Fairweather woman to write a note to the priest to tell him to what kind of place the child was comin'. Priests!" He again bit on his lip and banged his fist on the table. "It's fantastic; they rule the bloody lot of them. As I said at the merchants' meeting last week, if we had half the power of the priests we'd . . ." He stopped suddenly and looked toward the young man. "I'm sorry lad, I forgot."

"Oh, that's all right, Mr. Bensham, it's all right by me; you couldn't say nothin' that I haven't said meself about 'em."

"That so, lad?" Harry's face slowly relaxed, his eyes crinkled into a deep twinkle; then he said softly, "Well, I never! We've never got down to religion, have we? We'll have to think on't eh? 'Cos it's always riled me, the power they've got. Some of the poor buggers are frightened to breathe without the priests say so."

"Aye, Mr. Bensham, you're right there. By! you are; you're right there."

Miss Brigmore drew in an audible breath that brought their attention sharply back to her and she said stiffly, "Are you finished with me, Mr. Bensham?"

Harry Bensham looked at her, then he sat down slowly before he said, "No, I'm not."

"Then may I ask that our further business be discussed in private?"

Harry Bensham now stared at her under lowered brows. Then looking toward Willy Brooks, he said, "I'll give you a shout when I'm ready, Willy."

"Aye, Mr. Bensham."

As the young man moved from the table he turned his head and looked straight into Miss Brigmore's face; it was a bold look, the look of someone who had never known subservience.

Not until the door was closed did Miss Brigmore speak, and then coldly she said, "If you wish to reprimand me in the future, Mr. Bensham, I'll be obliged if you refrain from doing it before subordinates."

"Subordinates! Willy's no subordinate, not to nobody. And he's a good lad into the bargain, is Willy."

"I must take it then that you consider him my equal?"

Harry Bensham now screwed up his eyes and wagged his hand toward her, saying, "Aw, sit down, woman, and ease out of your starch; for God's sake let it crack for once."

26

It was some seconds before Miss Brigmore allowed herself to sit down, and when she did her back showed no indication of her starch having cracked.

"Now look—" His voice was quiet now, even placating, as, with his forearms on the table, he poked his head toward her and said, "We've got to get rid of her, Fairweather."

"You wanted a housekeeper. After Foster died you insisted on having a housekeeper. I told you another steward would be preferable."

"Aye, I know you did. You're always right, you're always"—he omitted the "bloody well" and ended lamely, "right. It was for the missus, you see; she thought a housekeeper would be better, more homely. She was a bit frightened of Foster, could never give him an order. You know how she is. It was different with you, you could manage him. Even me; I sometimes felt awkward when asking him for anything. It was like asking a grand duke to take your boots off."

"He was very competent; things ran very smoothly under his charge."

"Aye, they might have, but there's a difference between things being smooth and things being happy."

"You mean happy-go-lucky."

He leaned back in his chair now and let out a laugh. "Aye, that's it, happy-go-lucky. You can't change us, you know. You know that, don't you? You can't change us."

"I don't think I've tried."

He turned his head to the side while still keeping his eyes on her. "You've given us plenty of examples."

"My work was to inform the children."

"Aw, well"—he nodded his head now, slowly—"I'll grant you you've done a good job there; even the bits you did on the lads afore they went to school show. Why, when I listen to them talkin' I don't feel they're mine. But"—he screwed up his nose now—"I'm proud of them. An' Katie. Aw Katie." His expression changed. He leaned forward again but drooped his head, and, his voice deep in his throat, he said, "I love to hear her talkin' French. I don't understand a

27

word she says but I just love to hear the sound of it comin' from her mouth. Oh, an' by the way"—he lifted his head—"when we're on about talkin', which leads to hearin', I made some inquiries as I said I would. You know"—his eyes stretched wide now—"it's amazing what you learn 'bout different things. There I've been in Manchester, man and boy, all me life an' knew nothin' about the deaf school. An' started by a merchant man like meself, I understand. Phillips was his name. He got a committee together of bankers and manufacturers and such, chaired by Sir Oswald Mosley, an' they formed this school along Old Trafford. Amazing really when I come to think of it. I saw the place often enough, passed it for years, but took no interest. Well, when your own are all right you don't bother, do you? You should, but you don't. Anyway, they tell me they do a lot of good for deaf bairns there. Now I was just wondering this, how would you like to send her along? She could be boarded and I would see to it that . . ."

"No, Mr. Bensham, no . . ."

"What! You want her better, don't you? I mean you want all the assistance you can get for her?"

"Yes, yes, I do, but . . . but only yesterday when we were having a small altercation and I became annoyed with her, I told her I would do just that, what you have proposed, send her away to a school, and—" Now the starch appeared to crack, for her back sagged and she looked down at her hands folded in her lap and her head drooped before she said softly, "The anguish and fear on her face at such a proposal were as unbearable to me as the idea was to her. And, and I am not casting aspersions on the Manchester school, Mr. Bensham, but the conditions under which some of the children live in such schools are deplorable. I understand that some of these establishments demand long hours of religious instruction. To be made to sit in church for three hours at a time on a Sunday is not unusual for the children, and in winter time too."

"Aye, well," he sighed. "That's that, isn't it? Still"—he pulled his chin upwards—"never say die,

28

that's my motto, you know. What about tryin' some of the old cures? I'd lay me life some of them's a damn sight better than the new-fangled medicines. I mentioned it to Ted Spencer; you know Spencer, he's got the mill over other side, I told you afore, an' he said he'd heard of a dumb bairn whose tongue was loosened by big doses of cod liver oil. You could try it. If it could loosen the tongue it could loosen the eardrums."

Miss Brigmore looked across at him and her glance could not conceal a certain amount of pity for his ignorance. It was years ago, during the last century, that they had used cod liver oil for deafness, attacking the trouble as if it were one connected with the bowels, pouring the obnoxious unrefined oil down poor children's throats, ignoring their vomiting. all with the best intentions in the world, as those before them had used hot irons on the neck in order to create suppuration in the belief that pus could be drawn from the ears, being of the opinion that deafness was caused by a blockage. The agonies that some children had undergone, and to this very day were still undergoing, at the hands of those who wished them nothing but well was to her an agonizing thought in itself, as was the controversy that raged between the exponents of one method and those of another.

If she had spoken the truth to him she would have cast aspersions on the Manchester school for she abhorred the practice, started there in bygone times, of putting their children on exhibition in order to raise money. True, it was out of great necessity to keep the school going that the practice was first begun, but in her opinion it had put the children on a level with caged animals in a traveling zoo.

She had read exhaustively about the predicament of the deaf, and what she had hoped from Mr. Bensham's interest was that his influence, in such a place as Manchester, would have brought forth someone, some specialist whose methods were new, and that, if the treatment was expensive. he himself would act as patron. But what had he proffered? An ordinary school that dealt with children from all walks of life, and although she wanted all deaf children to receive the best of treatment she wanted her darling Barbara to receive specialized treatment; and now, now, before her ailment became worse. But could it become much worse than it was, for she was almost totally deaf, being able to hear only high and unusual sounds?

"You worry too much." The words were sharp and they startled her. "You're miles away. You're always thinkin' of that child; you want to think a bit more of yourself, for I'm gonna tell you something. She'll get by. I know people; she'll get what she wants out of life or die in the attempt; deaf or not, she'll have her way. She was a little monkey when she was young, she still is. Anyway, her looks'll get her where she wants to go, that's if she fills out a bit. Her deafness won't be all that much of a drawback. Any road, we can talk more on this later; the point now is, what are we going to do about Fairweather? You can't get over the fact she took it upon herself to tell the bairn she had to buy her own uniform. When did any of my lot buy their own uniform?"

"She was likely intending to start a new rule in order to economize. You do not hide the fact that you consider too much money is being spent on household expenses."

"Aw, well, that's just to keep them in mind that I know what's what. I'm away half me time, an' I don't want them to take advantage of Tilda. . . . So what's to be done?"

"What do you want to do?"

"Sack her."

"Then you must sack her."

"You picked her."

"I helped to choose her on her references. I recommended her because she was the best of the ten applicants, and I still think she's a good housekeeper. But perhaps . . ."

"Aye, perhaps what?"

"I will be as candid as you, Mr. Bensham. Perhaps not for this establishment."

"An' what do you mean by that?"

30

"Just what I said, not for this establishment. She has been used to managing a different kind of house and staff."

"What's the matter with me staff?"

"As regards work, nothing; as regards manners, some of them leave a lot to be desired."

"You mean the ones I brought from Manchester?"

"Yes, that is what I mean."

"Aye, well, it's my house and I want it run in my way. Everybody's got too much starch in this life."

When a silence fell between them he pursed his lips and stared at her fixedly, then said, "Go on, say somethin'. Why don't you say things aren't what they were in the old days? You've looked it for years, so you might as well say it, like the rest. They say, 'Common as muck, those Benshams are. Don't go huntin' or shootin'. Never have the hounds billeted on him,' they say. That's what they say, isn't it?"

"I don't know what they say, Mr. Bensham, my time is mostly taken up in the nursery."

Again there was silence between them, until he said grimly, "Aye, broken with trips across the hills to the lady farmer an' visits from Master an' Mistress Ferrier. They're glass people aren't they, the Ferriers, big pots in glass? An' they move among the top notchers, don't they? Hob-nob with the Percys and such, I'm told. You see I've got me Indian runners an' all; there's little goes on around here that I don't know. Not that I'm interested; but I can sit back and laugh."

"And do you?"

"What do you mean, do I?"

"Do you sit back and laugh?"

He did not answer her, he just sat staring at her; and then he said, "You know there's times I get so bloody annoyed with you that I could take me hand and skelp you across the mouth."

She was on her feet, her body rigid. He was on his feet too. Beads of sweat were showing on his forehead and he wiped them off with the side of his forefinger before he moved slowly around the table and stopped within a yard of her. Then, his voice thick, he

31

said, "I'm sorry, I really am; that was uncalled for. You've done nothin' but service to me and Tilda, an' then for me to go and say a thing like that. I don't know what got in me. Aye, yes I do, yes I do. Let's face it"—he put his hand to his brow again and pushed his fingers through his hair—"you never unbend, you're stiff, starchy, as I said. Admitted, you've learned Tilda a lot of things, you've carried her along through difficult times; and I'm not sayin' you haven't learned me something now and then; but you've never unbent. You should be one of the family by now, like a friend, but you're still Miss Brigmore. The bairns call you Brigie, but you know what the staff call you? The Brigadier. . . . Aw." He scratched his head in a number of places, then walked sharply away from her up the room to the fireplace, and standing with his hand outstretched gripping the mantelpiece, he said, "Here I am talkin' about trifles an' household bits and pieces when I should be on me way back to the mill. Why do you think Willy's here at this time?" He now turned and looked at her, but she was still facing the window, and he addressed her back as he said, "Strikes. He's found out that Pearson's bloody agitators are plannin' a strike. A strike, mind you, and in my factory! After what I've done for them; cut half an hour off their time these last two years, and an hour for those under twelve. There's not a bairn in my place works after six at night. An extra shilling in their Christmas packet; then bread and coal for those who are sick. An' then they'd harbor the thought of strikin' on me. But as Willy says, it's Pearson's lot; he's got a right rabble has Ted Pearson. Well, I'm going back there an' I'm going to remind them of what happened the last time the looms stopped spinning, an' by God I won't put a tooth in it." His voice suddenly changing, he asked softly, "Are you listening to me?"

She turned and walked slowly toward him, and when she stopped, he said, "No hard feelings?"

She did not answer for a moment, but when she did she was still Miss Brigmore. "I am what I am, Mr. Bensham. If I irritate you I would advise you to

32

dispense with my services." Even as she said this she knew it would be a major disaster for her if he were to take her at her word; but he wouldn't, and he didn't.

"Aw, dispense with your services? Don't be daft, woman!" He half turned from her. "How do you think we'll go on here without you? Why, if I even gave it a thought Tilda would have me skinned alive. She thinks very highly of you . . . Tilda. And that's another thing I wanted to ask you. Would you look in on her a bit more than usual these next few days, until I get back? She's got a pain. . . ."

"A pain?"

"Aye; here." He put his hand on his flat stomach. "I've told her she's got to see the doctor, but, you know, although she's so easygoin' in some ways she can be as tough and stubborn as dried hide in others, won't be pulled or pushed. She doesn't like doctors, frightened of 'em, so if you'd have a talk with her, ask her what it's like, the pain, I mean. That's all she says when I get at her, she's got a pain. And you know me, I've got no patience, I'm like a bull at a gap. Oh, aye! Oh, aye!"—his voice had a laughing note to it now—"I'm like you there, I am what I am, an' I know meself, nobody knows Harry Bensham like Harry Bensham, except perhaps"—his tone dropped to a lower key—"Tilda. I told you, didn't I, we were brought up next door to each other? Aye." He shook his head now. "That was in the early days when we were small; but when me dad got on we moved away and we lost touch for years. Until I saw her on the looms; but I was married then. Aye"—he turned and looked toward the fire and repeated, "I was married then, I'd married a factory." His head came round sharply and he stared at her.

"I knew what I wanted so I married a factory. Now you would have been interested in that kind of household." He nodded at her. "Aye, you would an' all. Upstarts. God Almighty! There's nothing makes me sick like an upstart; and embarrassed into the bargain. Now you wouldn't think that a fellow like me could be embarrassed, but upstarts embarrass me, get

33

me hot under the collar trying to be what they're not. . . . Anyway, that period passed and I married Tilda. Funny, but she'd been waitin' for me all those years; she had, she said she had. Women are queer cattle, queer cattle. . . . But here I go again, yammering like Bessie Bullock in the pea shop." His voice was rising again, and he turned from the fire, buttoned his coat briskly while looking at her, and said, "That's something I can't understand. Every time I'm along of you I start to yammer; I'm not a yammering man; and the funny thing about it is, you don't give a body any encouragement. Now do you?" A slow smile spread over his face and transformed it so that now Miss Brigmore, as she had at odd times before, saw someone other than the bigoted, ignorant, raw factory owner who took pride in keeping his image unchanged; she saw the man Tilda must have seen years ago, the man who, in spite of his shortcomings, was at the bottom just and kind.

He ended now, saying, "I can't even get a smile out of you, an' yet when you're with the bairns I often hear you laughin'. What makes you laugh? Aw"—he dismissed his own question—"I've got to get away. But you'll do what I ask, won't you? You'll look in on her?"

"Yes, I'll look in on her."

"Thanks. Ta-rah; ta-rah then; I'm off."

"Good-bye, Mr. Bensham."

After he had left the room Miss Brigmore sat down suddenly on the nearest chair. That man! She closed her eyes and said again to herself, That man! He was impossible, quite impossible. She had never encountered anyone like him. Daring to say to her he would skelp her across the mouth! She shouldn't be sitting here, she should be upstairs ordering Barbara to get her books and her belongings, for they were going to leave this house never to come back into it again. Skelp her across the mouth, really! Really!

She let out a long drawn breath, then sat perfectly still for a time, until she told herself, she must be fair.

34

Did her manner aggravate the man? It must do, for he had spoken to her in much the same manner as he spoke to his wife. In the early days here his manner of addressing his wife had shocked her, he used to go for her as if she were some kind of lower servant, rarely addressing her without using a swear word of some kind. Really! Really! He was the most amazing man. No, that wasn't the correct term for him. . . . Then what was?

She rose from the chair and made sure that the buttons on her bodice were intact, smoothed down the front of her dress, then went slowly from the room, across the hall and up the stairs and knocked on Mrs. Bensham's bedroom door.

When she entered the room she saw Matilda Bensham sitting propped up in bed. She was dressed in a bright pink flannelette nightdress which had a large collar trimmed with white lace; the sleeves, too, ended in large frills trimmed with white lace, and the whiteness was in sharp contrast to the grayness of her face and the mottled red-veined skin of her hands. "Hello there, dear," she said.

"Good morning, Mrs. Bensham. I hear that you are not feeling too well."

"It's me stomach." The words were hissed in a whisper and Matilda tapped the coverlet where it rested across her waist.

"Is it upset?"

"Well, not in the usual way, dear; but I've had a sort of constant nagging for some time now. . . . But mind, don't tell him. Now promise you won't tell him, 'cos he's got enough on his plate. By! he has that; I'd never have believed it. Willy came yesterday you know. Set off on Saturda' night he did; had the devil of a time gettin' here an' all. Those trains aren't what they're cracked up to be. Like the manager 'Arry's got in, they go when they're pushed. A strike's afoot and him not supposed to know! There's something fishy there, 'cos we don't have strikes, not us. 'Arry gives them the earth, even thinkin' of letting the women finish at three

35

on a Saturda' to save them having to do everything on a Sunday, you know like washing an' cleaning an' cooking, 'cos Sunday is the only day in the week they've got. And then a strike. So you understand, dear, I don't want him worried. So anything I tell you, you'll keep it to yourself now, won't you?"

"Yes, of course, Mrs. Bensham."

"Well, lass, it's like this. . . . Pull up your chair and sit down." She indicated a chair with a sweep of her arm. "I've had this pain on and off for over a year now; oh, more than that. Wind, I used to think it was, 'cos of the way I eat. You know I eat twice as much as our 'Arry. I don't know how he can resist some of the things that's put afore him, but he does. He takes pride in his stomach being all muscle an' not looking his age. He's vain, you know." She smiled widely now as she nodded toward Miss Brigmore. "And of course he's got every right to be, 'cos you'd never think he was fifty-six, would you? A man in his middle forties you could take him for any day in the week, and he knows it. Oh aye, he knows it. So you see, I thought it was what I was eatin'. But I've cut that down a lot and I've still got the pain, worse at times. It's gettin' so that I can't hide it."

"You must see a doctor, Mrs. Bensham."

"Do you think so, lass?"

"Oh yes, very definitely, if you've had the pain all this time. I think it was very unwise of you not to have it attended to before now. It might be some simple thing."

"Such as what, lass?"

The question was quiet, it even conveyed a hint of calm resignation.

"Well—" Miss Brigmore rubbed the tips of her fingers together and paused as if thinking, then said, "It could be colic, caused by the bowel twisting."

"The bowels can get twisted?"

"Oh yes, yes. If for instance there has been any undue strain owing to . . . to constipation."

"Oh. Oh, I see." Tilda looked over the foot of the bed and nodded, then said, "Well, you might be right,

36

lass, you might be at that. . . . Twisted bowel." She brought her eyes to Miss Brigmore again. "They could cure that?"

"Oh yes, yes. I'm sure they could cure that."

"Would that cause bleedin'?"

"Bleeding?"

"Aye, from inside like."

Miss Brigmore wetted her lips and said, "Well, yes; through . . . through inner hemorrhoids."

"Piles, you mean?"

"Yes."

"Inside?"

"Yes."

"Well, that puts a different complexion on it, doesn't it, as they say in upper circles?" She was laughing widely now, showing a mouthful of strong, short teeth, with two overlapping at each side of her mouth. "You've cheered me up, lass; it's true what our 'Arry always says, you're the only sensible bug . . . sensible one in the house. You always know the right answer, the right thing to do, you always have. Aye, I've often thought of how handicapped I'd have been right from the start in this place if it hadn't been for you. You were a godsend, a real godsend. You know something?" She leaned toward Miss Brigmore now, her voice low. " 'Arry's got plans for you." She nodded her head once. "Now mind, don't let on about this either, else he'll leave me black and blue from head to foot, but he's going to see that you're all right when you finish here, you'll be able to live better'n you've lived afore, apart from with us."

Miss Brigmore felt the color rising to her hairline. What could she say? She felt so ill at ease, yet she must not take this offer amiss; these people were kind, embarrassingly so. Reluctantly, she had to admit that they were far kinder than the previous owners of this establishment, far kinder.

It was in a surprisingly broken tone that she voiced her thanks. "You are very kind, Mrs. Bensham, very kind."

"Aw, lass, it's not me, it's him. He's always been

a kind man, always, not only just now. By! no. Oh, the things he's done for people; even the bloomin' Irish. Eeh! Mind they're a dirty lot, them Irish. Him and me were brought up next to each other. You know that, but did I tell you there were eleven of us in two rooms, while in 'Arry's house there was only five of them? They were lucky. But both our houses were clean as new pins. Me mam would be up at five o'clock in the mornin' gettin' us and herself off to the mill. In the beginnin' we were there until nine at night, but if it had been twelve o'clock she would have done her fireplace and shook her mats. The fireplace was black-leaded once a week until she died. . . . But the Irish! When 'Arry and his people left from next door we got a family in. Eeh! by, you never see anythin' like it. They brought a pig with them, they did." She made a deep obeisance with her head and began to laugh. "That's the Irishman's bank in Manchester, a pig; soon as they got a bit o' money in those days, if they didn't drink it, that is, they bought a pig. There were two families of them in those two rooms, seventeen there were; they didn't only sleep head to tail, they had to stand up against the walls." She was doubled forward with laughing now, and Miss Brigmore found herself laughing with her, while at the same time her mind was appalled at the conditions described.

"Eeh!"—Matilda dried her eyes—"me mother did work hard. Her only pleasure was her pipe. Twelve o'clock at night she would take it out and have a draw. You know, lass"—she lay back on her pillows—"I've been in bed since Friday. Just after you went I came up to bed, and it seemed a long weekend 'cos I've done nowt but think. I've gone back over all those early days, an' you know I just cannot believe I'm sittin' here in this house with umpteen servants to wait on me. I . . . just . . . cannot . . . believe . . . it. And how many years have I been here now? Nearly nine. Aye, well, they say a leopard cannot change its spots, an' I suppose they're right 'cos I'm still not at ease. You know that, lass, don't you? I'm still not at ease."

"Oh, Mrs. Bensham, you must feel at ease; this is

your home and . . . and every one of your staff respects you, and your family love you."

"Aye, aye, I suppose they do, I mean the family lovin' me, 'cos they haven't turned into upstarts yet. But still, there's plenty of time, they're still young. What'll they think though when they start courtin' and bringin' their lasses home, an' Katie her lad . . . or should I say finnances? Will they love me then, d'you think? Aw"—now she tossed her head—"why am I worryin', we could all be dead the morrow, couldn't we?" She stared at Miss Brigmore and Miss Brigmore, looking back at her, said, "That's very unlikely; you'll live to see your grandchildren, and very likely their offspring, too, running around the house."

There was a short silence before Matilda said softly, "No, lass; no, I won't."

As they continued to stare at each other Miss Brigmore swallowed deeply, then she whispered, "Oh, Mrs. Bensham."

"Don't you think you could call me Tilda just for once?"

"It . . . it would be very difficult." Miss Brigmore's voice was still soft. "And . . . and it would be out of place. But . . . but I want you to know that I regard you very highly and . . . and I will think of you as Matilda even if I don't allow myself to call you by your Christian name."

"You're a funny lass."

"Yes, I realize I am, in the way you infer. My manner must be very irritating to you at times, as it is to Mr. Bensham."

"WHAT! Oh, you don't irritate him. An' you don't irritate me. Now, don't get that into your head 'cos I've said you're a funny lass. What I should have said was you're a grand lass."

Miss Brigmore felt at this moment that she could not stand much more of the emotional stress being forced upon her this morning. Here she was at the age of fifty-four, nearing fifty-five, and being termed a lass, but in the most complimentary fashion, and from this woman, this dear woman, and she could think of her

39

as dear in spite of her ignorance and uncouth manner, for she was bravely facing the fact that she was carrying a disease inside her which was likely to terminate her life within a short period of time. As she went to rise to her feet Matilda said, "There's something you can do for me, lass."

"Anything."

"Willy was up, an' he told me about Mrs. Fairweather sending a letter off to the Dochertys. Do you know about it?"

"Yes."

"That's all right then. Well, I told him to show it to the boss and let him deal with it but not let on that I knew anything about it, for I knew that once 'Arry saw that letter he'd want to get rid of her, and I want to an' all but I've never had the pluck to tell her. Do, do you think you could see to it for me, lass?"

Miss Brigmore did not pause a moment to consider the unpleasantness of the task before she answered, "Yes, I'll deal with it. Don't worry yourself; I'll deal with it."

"Aw, ta, thanks. Did you see the letter? Did you ever see anything like it in your life? The Dochertys live in a warren. The men are good workers but the mother is hopeless. The last time I saw them the lice was carryin' them around, an' Mabel, the one that 'Arry wants to take on, she was just a bairn crawlin' in the filth of the gutter, and when I say filth I mean filth. Everything was thrown out of the door; it was piled up back and front. They died like flies around there. They tell me they've pulled Cods' Row down, an' not afore time I say, not afore time. Anyway, you tell her, lass, eh? You tell her."

"Yes, I'll tell her. Now rest quietly; don't attempt to get up; I'm going to send for the doctor."

"Aw . . ."

"No aw's." Miss Brigmore shook her head, and there was a reprimand in it; it was as if she were speaking to the girls. "You're going to see the doctor, and as soon as possible."

"It'll worry 'Arry if I have the doctor."

40

"It'll worry 'Ar . . . Mr. Bensham . . . if you don't have the doctor."

The room was filled with a great guffaw of laughter now as Matilda, holding her head, lay back among the pillows, saying, "Eeh! Eeh! you nearly said 'Arry. You did now, you did; you nearly said 'Arry."

Miss Brigmore tried to suppress a smile but she failed. She turned quickly about and went out of the room, but once on the landing she stopped and pressed her hand over her lips, for now she was on the point of weeping. Really, really, such courage. But she must not give way like this. She had two things to attend to immediately; first, she must send the coachman into the town for the doctor, then she must go into the library and from there she must send for the housekeeper and inform her that she had been given permission to dismiss her. What a morning!

THREE

"What are these Bensham fellows like, Mother?"

"Now you know as much about them as I do."
Constance Radlet turned out a great mold of brawn
onto a side dish before she went on, "I only know what
your Aunt Anna tells me. John is sixteen, Dan fifteen,
and the girl, Katie, is fourteen."

"And you've never seen any of them?"

"No, of course not." Constance turned and looked
at her son, where he was sitting at the end of the long
white scrubbed kitchen table, and as always when she
gazed on him a smile came to her lips, for as his grandmother, Jane Radlet, was fond of saying in her Biblical
way, he was good to look upon. His hair was a corn
yellow, his eyes were a clear gray, the lids inclining to
be overlong, giving him a slightly oriental look; his nose
was large and his mouth full, but it was a firm full-
ness; and the firmness was expressed in his chin which
had a squareness to it; yet his overall nature gave the
impression that he was an easygoing, indolent type of
boy; his movements were slow, his laughter came slow
and deep, but when it reached its full pitch it was an
infectious bellow. He was nearing thirteen years old and
was tall for his age, but he had bulk with it; he was
going to be a big man. Yes, he was good to look upon.

"Why do they want to come over, they've never
been before?"

"Likely that's the reason, because they've never
been before." Constance's smile widened.

"They go to a boarding school, so you say?"

"Yes, and so do you."

"But likely theirs is a very stylish affair; the father's rich, isn't he?"

"Yes, and common and ignorant from what I gather."

"They say he's good to his staff."

Constance turned to where her mother-in-law, Jane Radlet, was sitting peeling potatoes near the fire. She had her feet on a cracket and a large tin dish on her knees, and from it she kept dropping the peeled potatoes into a black kale pot on the floor at her side. She nodded at Constance as she smiled, and Constance returned her smile with cocked head now, saying, "Well, he's not the only one, so are we."

They both laughed and it was a harmonious sound as between friends.

Turning back to the table and pushing the plate of brawn away from her, Constance called across the room to a plump little girl standing over the sink washing pots. "Bring me a clean side dish, Sarah, please."

The girl came hurrying to the table, drying the dish on the way, and she placed it before Constance; then looking up at her, she said, "They don't hunt; they say they don't hunt, not even the hares, or partridge, not like the gentry."

"Who said they didn't hunt, Sarah?"

"Me . . . my dad." Sarah always called her uncle Dad.

"Well, that doesn't make them any better, or worse, than the next. Bring me the ham from the pantry."

The girl turned immediately to do Constance's bidding. But she did not, as would be expected, say, "Yes, ma'am." A stranger would have found the situation very curious that this orphan girl should be allowed to speak without first being spoken to unless she wished to convey something absolutely necessary, but in this instance she had casually joined in the conversation with her mistress and young master and the young man's grandmother.

And Sarah Waite's position was unusual in that the mistress of the house, besides teaching her to read and write, had shown her all the big towns in England on a map, and made her learn what they produced, and for a full year she had allowed her to sit by the young master's side when doing her lessons, until at seven years old he went away to the school in Hexham, only returning on the weekends, and during his absence she had continued to teach her head man's niece.

If anyone had dared to tell Constance that her philanthrophy had a selfish motive she would have denied it while admitting its truth to herself, for although most of her time was taken up with farm affairs, there were long hours in the evening, especially in the winter, when her mind craved for some other outlet besides those of making clothes, darning, and tapestry. She was slow to admit that she had imbibed some of Miss Brigmore's character while being taught by her, for she also had the desire to impart knowledge. When she reluctantly decided on the course of sending her son to a boarding school where he would come under influences other than those of the farm laborers, there was left in her a gap that could be filled only by the molding of another character. Then indeed, she knew that she had imbibed more than general knowledge from Miss Brigmore.

And there was also the necessity at that particular time of covering up her disappointment—she refused to acknowledge it as a dashing of her hopes. Although she had said more than once that she would never marry again, she had not rejected the advances of Bob Armstrong, the younger of the two farming brothers who lived but three miles away. From the night of that first harvest supper she had given in sixty-six he had openly shown his admiration for her. He had called in when passing, and when not passing he had made a point of visiting her, giving her advice, joking with her, letting his eyes tell her what was in his mind. And this silent courtship had gone on for three years.

It was when she had almost decided to give him

44

enough encouragement to speak that his visits ceased abruptly. He even avoided her on market day. It was from Peter, his honest but shambling brother, that she learned he was going to marry a Miss Fanny Winters, a farmer's daughter. The farmer had died, and his wife was oldish, and Miss Fanny Winters, a bit long in the tooth, as the forthright Peter had put it, had in a way offered. It was a big farm, and Bob had always hankered after a big farm. He would miss him, Peter said, 'cos he was good company was Bob. But twenty-five miles was twenty-five miles and you couldn't keep running back and forward all that way, now could you?

Constance hadn't cried at the news, she had been too angry, too humiliated; although she hadn't a doubt that he had desired her, nevertheless his need for a big farm had been greater. Wolfbur hadn't apparently been a large enough attraction.

So this was another reason why it was desirable for her to have a pastime, and Sarah Waite filled the need. It also deepened the gratitude of the entire Waite family toward her.

Sometimes when Constance looked in her mirror her reflection showed the inner panic that filled her, a panic created by the mounting years, for was she not thirty-two? And the question of age would engender in her the special terror that one day when Michael took a wife she might be brushed aside, discounted. That she was all-in-all to him now she was fully aware, but she knew that this emotional state couldn't last; another four, five years and he could marry.

When her mind touched on him marrying her nerves almost jangled into hysteria. What if he should choose Barbara? As things stood Barbara's father and Michael's grandfather were one and the same man, at least in the eyes of the world, and she would gladly have left the situation like this in order to prevent Michael bringing her niece into this house as his wife; but there were two others who knew the true situation, Anna and Jane, and Anna, she knew, would move hell and earth to make that girl happy; and Jane would

45

do the same for her grandson. She could, in times of such panic, see their combined efforts forcing her to reveal to her son the real truth of his beginnings.

And Michael, where did he stand in all this? The fact that Barbara was deaf would be no impediment to him taking her; rather the reverse, he would be drawn to her out of compassion. She was well aware that he had, since a small child, maintained a fondness for her. Although he teased her and called her Madam, and grumbled about her following him around, nevertheless she sensed that deep within him he had a strong emotional leaning toward his cousin. What she constantly hoped and prayed for was that with the years he would grow out of this feeling, for there was bad blood in Barbara, she being part Mallen.

"How will they get back if there's no moon?" Michael asked.

"What do you say?"

"I say how will they all get back if there's no moon?"

"Oh, there'll be a moon." It wasn't Constance who had answered but Sarah. She had turned from the sink and, her face bright and smiling, she nodded at them and repeated, "There'll be a moon tonight, sure there'll be a moon."

"Ah! The oracle has spoken." Michael raised his hand and his voice was solemn as he went on, "Listen . . . listen all ye present, listen to the voice of the sage . . . and onions."

As he and his grandmother laughed Constance asked, "How can you be sure, Sarah? There was mist last night."

"The sky this mornin', the way the sun came up while the moon was still showing."

"Is that a sign?" asked Constance.

It was Jane Radlet now who replied as she threw a potato into the pan with a plop. "Oh aye, it's a sign; she's right." She exchanged a smile with Sarah. "Of course, it's to do with the way the moon was lying at the beginning of the month, it had to be lying on its back if there were to be three full nights clear at the end."

Constance did not question the truth or otherwise of the forecast, for she had been proved wrong on similar points so many times before.

Michael rose from the table, saying, "Well, I'm off."

"Where?"

"I'm going with Jim to the top fields."

"Oh no, you're not!" Constance checked him with lifted hand. "They'll be here within half an hour."

"Well, I'll see them coming even before you do, and I'll scamper back."

"But you should be dressed . . . changed."

"Why? We're going to see the hill racing, aren't we? We'll all be up to our eyes in mud after the rain these last few days, if I know anything."

"That doesn't matter; you should be dressed to meet them, especially as you haven't met them before."

"Are you going to change?"

"Of course."

"And you, Grannie?" He lifted his head in Jane Radlet's direction, and Jane, laughing loudly, said, "Not me, lad, not me; they take me as they find me."

"And what about Sarah, has she got to change?" He looked toward the small girl, and she turned her head over her shoulder and laughed at him, while Constance answered for her, "Sarah's going with Jim to the games."

Michael gave an exaggerated sigh and was about to resume his seat when Constance said, "Now don't sit down again, there's no time to dawdle. Come, I'm going up too." She stretched out her hand and caught him by the ear, and he pretended to cringe and yelled, "Oh! . . . oh! . . . oh!" and they all laughed.

When Constance and Michael had left the room, Jane beckoned Sarah to her and in a conspiratorial whisper said, "Go on . . . over home, hinny, and make yourself tidy. Put your best hair ribbons on, and your clean pinny, and show the gentry what a bonny lass you are."

47

The bright smile left Sarah's face and she said quietly, "Dad says I've to keep out of the way once they come, and Uncle Jimmy's takin' me straight off to the games."

The old woman and the child looked at each other and knowledge of the situation was exchanged in their glance. "Aw well then," said Jane; "go on then and enjoy yourself."

"Yes, yes I will." Sarah turned away, her face still unsmiling, and made to go back to the sink, but Jane said, "Leave them be, I'll finish them; go on now," and the child went out.

The kitchen to herself, Jane stopped peeling the potatoes and through the window she watched the small girl dashing across the yard, and when she was gone from her sight she muttered, "All because that one's coming." And as if picking up Constance's thoughts, hers said, Everything old Mallen bred was tainted. Hadn't she herself proof of it? The result of Mallen's raping her when she was a girl had been her son Donald, and what had he turned out to be? A devil, yes a devil if ever there was one, and he had proved it when he wed the lass just gone upstairs there, for he had led her a hell of a life before he was . . . her mind shied away from the word murdered and substituted destroyed, which seemed less terrible to her.

And what of Mallen's last raping? That Barbara too had the devil in her, and a temper like a fiend, and she hated young Sarah because Michael made much of her. It was a great pity she hadn't been struck dumb as well as deaf.

It was at this point that her thinking proved Constance wrong, for she muttered aloud, "I'd sooner see him alone to the end of his days than take up with that one across the hills."

The trap driven by Miss Brigmore was first to come through the gateless gap in the stone wall. Seated opposite her was Mary Peel; they had the vehicle to themselves. Close behind came the wagonette; it was driven by Yates, the coachman, and seated behind him were John and Daniel Bensham, Katie Bensham, and Barbara.

As they alighted they were each greeted by Constance and Michael, who were standing outside the front door of the farmhouse.

"How nice to see you. How are you, dear?" Constance and Miss Brigmore exchanged kisses.

"And you, Barbara?" Constance and Barbara exchanged kisses, light touches on the cheek these. And then the introductions were made.

"Miss Katie Bensham . . . Mrs. Radlet."

"How-do-you-do, ma'am?"

"How-do-you-do?"

"Mr. John Bensham . . . Mrs. Radlet."

"How-do-you-do, ma'am?"

"How-do-you-do?"

"Mr. Dan Bensham . . . Mrs. Radlet."

"How-do-you-do, ma'am?"

"How-do-you-do?"

The same process was repeated but with Michael this time; then Constance led the way into the house, through the hall, not so dark now because of another window that had been added to it, and into the drawing room.

"Do please be seated." Constance spread her arm wide, and when they had taken chairs there fell on them an awkward silence, until it was broken by a high laugh from Barbara, which both startled and annoyed Miss Brigmore but which brought answering smiles from the younger folk when she said, "It's funny, we all look ridiculous, everybody sitting like waxworks."

Katie began to laugh and the boys to grin widely; then Michael, who had been standing near Barbara, leaned toward her and, mouthing his words, he said, "Trust you, Madam, to break eggs with a mallet," and as her hand went out to slap him Miss Brigmore said sharply, "Barbara!" But Barbara was not looking at

49

Miss Brigmore so didn't see her speak, and so she slapped Michael and went on, "We had a wonderful time coming across; we laughed all the way, didn't we, Dan?"

Daniel Bensham, fifteen years old, was of small stature but inclined to be thickset. His hair was sandy; his eyes, a deep blue, had a keenness to them; his nose was rather broad at the nostrils and his mouth was large. He had no claim whatever to good looks, yet there was something arresting about his face. He did not answer Barbara except by making a moue with his mouth, for his attention was taken up by the company, by the lady of the house in particular; the lady who had once lived in the Hall and who, he imagined, had expected to go on living there for ever. How had she felt when she was turfed out? Barbara said she was seven at the time; she must still remember. And then there was the son. This was the one that Barbara was always talking about, and he could see the reason, a mythological god here, a son of Olympus. Yet he didn't look as if he had much spunk; he had the look of Ripon about him. Ripon was in the Upper House; he looked in a daze most of the time and was always spouting poetry; he had been up before the Head this term for wearing fancy collars; he had copied Byron's dress from a picture hanging in his room. And yet for all his dreaminess they said he was a flogger, and because of him some of the boys were afraid to be sent up. He, himself, wasn't afraid; let him start any of his flogging antics on him and he'd kick him in the teeth. By God! yes; then he'd walk out. And his dad would support him. He already felt a deep animosity toward Ripon, and he could toward this fair fellow too.

"Dan, what are you staring at, you look all eyes and teeth?"

Dan turned his gaze from Michael onto Barbara, and he laughed with her as he said, "Well, I am all eyes and teeth." Then, turning, he smiled at his hostess; and she smiled back at him as she thought, What a nice boy! And such a nice voice. They appeared to be nice children, and all well-spoken. As usual, Anna had done a good job on the girl, and the public school had certainly left its stamp on the boys and erased the vernacular inheritance of their parents, which, from what she could gather from Anna, remained deplorable.

She looked from the sandy-haired boy to the taller red-headed one and said, "I see you have come suitably dressed for the walk. It's a good three miles across the moors and very rough terrain in parts. Have you been to the hill races before?"

"No, ma'am." John shook his head. "It may seem strange, but we've never been this side of the range before. It was lovely coming over, wonderful scenery. And you're in a beautiful valley here. The country appears much softer this side. Over home it's harsh . . ." he finished lamely, coloring a little as he too remembered that this woman had once lived "over home." It was all rather embarrassing. He was sorry that he had let Barbara persuade them to come; but then once Barbara got her teeth into anything you might as well give up. He looked now from this beautiful woman to Barbara. There wasn't a vestige of resemblance between them, yet there was a strong blood tie. He again concentrated his gaze on Constance. She'd kept her elegance and style even if she had been running a farm for years. This, he supposed, was what they meant by breeding.

Katie was also looking at Constance, and she was thinking, She keeps smiling all the time, but she looks sad.

"Excuse me a moment." Constance cast her glance over the visitors, adding, "You must have a little refreshment before you start on your . . . arduous journey, and I would also like you to meet my mother-in-law, Mrs. Radlet."

As she turned toward the door it opened and Jane entered. She glanced quickly at the assembled company; then putting her face close to Constance, she whispered, "There's a gentleman called. He wants to see you; he's in the yard on horseback."

Constance almost repeated aloud, "A gentleman on horseback?" Traps, carts, brakes, her visitors usually used one or the other of these vehicles, and if one came on horseback he was likely a farmer. She knew Jane well enough to know that she would not give this title to any of the farmers from hereabouts, she would have announced him with "It's Armstrong," or "Him over from Alston way," or "Bradley from Nenthead," but she had said, "A gentleman."

When she reached the kitchen door she stopped and stared at the man standing at the horse's head, and before she had time to prevent it her mouth dropped into a wide gape. Pat Ferrier—her heart lifted—Pat Ferrier who had at one time been a regular visitor to the cottage along with Will Headley, Will, who had courted her, then discarded her practically overnight for a young lady of wealth. It was on the day after she had learned of Will's desertion that Donald Radlet had proposed to her. How fate took advantage of the emotions.

And young Pat, he'd had an affection for her too, but she had laughed at him and treated him like a young boy. But here he was, and no longer young Pat, but a man, a handsome man.

"Pat! Pat!"

Pat Ferrier turned sharply toward her, then came forward with outstretched hands, and gripped hers. "Constance! Ah! Constance. How good to see you!"

"Come; come in." She was hanging on to his hand. "What are you doing here? I thought you had gone to live abroad permanently; the last I heard of you, you were in Austria."

"Oh, that was three years ago. I've been in London for the past year."

"You have? Oh! Come through." She led the way out of the kitchen, then stopped in the hallway. Her hand to her cheek now, she laughed as she said, "This is a day of surprises; I have three visitors from the Hall."

"The hall . . . you mean?"

She nodded quickly, "Yes, High Banks; the children of the present owner. Barbara brought them."

"Barbara? I thought . . ."

"Her daughter."

"Oh, her daughter. I see."

"You're not in a hurry, are you? Would you care to come and meet them? They'll be leaving shortly, they're going to see the games, and then we can talk. . . . Oh! Pat." She grabbed at his hands again. "It's lovely to see you; it just makes me happy to look at you."

"I should have said that."

"Yes, yes, of course." She lowered her eyes in a mock-modest fashion. "I forgot myself, sir."

At this they both laughed and as they walked toward the drawing room door, he said, "But I can endorse it a thousand-fold." Then after a pause he added, "You've changed, Connie."

"Yes, time doesn't stand still."

"You're more beautiful."

"If I remember rightly, Pat, you always did say the correct thing." She opened the door and ushered him in, and the whole company turned and looked toward him.

Miss Brigmore recognized him instantly, although he had been but a boy when she had last seen him. She remembered he had married quite young, but it had turned out to be a tragic affair, his bride having died within three months of the ceremony. This had driven him abroad, and there he had remained for years. They had heard of him now and again through Mr. Patrick Ferrier senior when on the rare occasions he called at the cottage. And now here he was. Had he married again? or was he still a widower? Why should he have sought out Constance? But why not? They were old friends. Dear, dear; her mind was in a whirl. Now wouldn't it be wonderful if . . .

She was shaking his outstretched hand, saying, "I recognized you immediately."

"And me you. You're like Constance, you haven't altered one iota."

"I've told him," Constance put in now, "that he always did say the right thing. You remember, Anna, you used to say, 'That young man is correct in every-

53

thing.' But isn't it lovely? And what a surprising day! Now let me introduce you."

As Miss Brigmore watched Constance, her face alight, making the introductions she thought, Indeed! Indeed, what a surprising day!

Everyone was in accord; it had been an exciting, happy, wonderful day. If anyone had enjoyed it more than another it was Barbara, for she'd had Michael to herself most of the time, at least while they were out. He had taken her hand and pulled her up gullies, he had caught her when she jumped from high banks, and she had felt so proud of him as he showed off his knowledge of country lore to the others: pointing out a badger's set, taking them to see an otter's slide, showing them the tracks of a weasel. She had noted that John got on very well with Michael, but that Dan had talked to him hardly at all. But then Dan had moods; and when he did talk he was inclined to be argumentative.

She herself had been charming to everyone; it was so easy when there was no one to irritate her. She hadn't set eyes on Sarah Waite since they had come into the farmyard. She didn't know where she was or what had happened to her and she didn't care; she only knew that life on the farm was wonderful when that girl wasn't there.

And the day wasn't quite over yet; but she knew it would end for her once she stepped up into the trap, or the wagonette; it would likely be the trap, but that didn't matter, she had no great longing to ride with the boys. But she had a longing, amounting to a craving, to dance with Michael once again, and alone, dance with him with no one else there, feeling him whirling her around in a polka. They'd all been dancing a Roger de Coverley in the drawing room. Katie had played the piano and her Aunt Constance had danced with Mr. Ferrier and she had looked quite gay, acting almost as though she were a girl again—skittish was

54

the term Brigie would use when describing someone old acting like someone young. Yet Brigie, too, had danced. At first she had thought she would die laughing when she saw Brigie dancing, yet she guided Dan through all the steps and was light on her feet.

But oh, she wanted to dance with Michael alone. Oh! she did, she did.

The room was full of chatter, noise, and laughter. Mrs. Radlet was handing round bowls of hot broth to support them on the journey, for it was already turning chilly and the full moon tonight would likely shine on an early frost. Her eyes strayed for a moment from Michael to where Katie was laughing with Mr. Ferrier. He was moving his hands and describing something to her; it looked as if he were showing her how he toppled from a horse. She thought she could hear the high note of Katie's laughter when she turned her eyes back to Michael, or to the spot where Michael had been; but now he was going into the hall.

Her thoughts galloped as she searched for an excuse to follow him. . . . Her handkerchief, there was mud on it, where she had wiped some spots from her face splashed up by a horse's hooves. She went hastily toward Constance where she was talking with John and said, "Do you think you could lend me a clean handkerchief, Aunt Constance? Look"—she drew the dirty handkerchief from her pocket and explained laughingly how it had come to be in such a soiled condition.

"Of course, of course, I'll get you one."

"No, no, let me."

Constance was about to affirm that she would go and get the handkerchief when Pat Ferrier came to her side, bringing Katie with him and saying, "This young lady tells me she doesn't ride, she hadn't a horse; now can you understand that?"

Constance looked at him and laughed; then turning fully to Barbara again, she said slowly, "You'll find some in the righthand top drawer of the dressing table in my room, the small drawer."

"Thank you, Aunt Constance." Before she finished speaking she turned and was about to rush away when Miss Brigmore's hand came out and stopped her. "Where are you going?"

"To get a handkerchief; Aunt Constance said I may go up to her room and get a handkerchief."

"Oh, very well. But don't be long because we're almost ready to go. And when you come down collect your cloak and bonnet from the other room."

"Yes, Brigie. Yes."

Once in the hall, she looked toward the stairs, then ran to the front door and down the steps along by the side of the house and into the farmyard. In the far corner of the yard she saw Michael talking to Mr. Waite; then she watched Mr. Waite turn and go into the stables, and when Michael was about to follow him she whispered loudly, "Michael! Michael!"

When he looked toward her it seemed almost as if he had no hair, a fading shaft of light had caught it as in a single beam. She gazed so entranced she wasn't aware that he had moved toward her.

"What is it?"

She looked into his face that was just above the level of her own and she said slowly, "It looked as if you hadn't any hair, your head had turned to gold."

"Don't be silly. Is that what you want to tell me?"

"No." She shook her head. "Michael"—she leaned further toward him and her voice dropped to a whisper now—"dance with me."

"What!"

"Dance with me."

"Out here? Are you *mad?* They'll lock us up."

She was laughing wildly now. "There's no one to see; he's gone, Waite has gone." She pointed toward the stable.

"Don't be stupid." He shook his head as he stepped back from her.

Her face now dropping into solemn lines and her mouth into a petulant droop, she muttered, "You danced with Katie."

"Yes, because"—he stopped himself only just in time from saying "because she can hear the music."

56

What he said was, "You danced in the de Coverley."

"That's not the same."

"But . . . but there's no music." He spread his arms wide.

"I don't need to hear music, I'll feel the motions through you."

"You're barmy." He accompanied the words with a soft smile; then said, "I'm no dancer anyway; Mother's found me hopeless. She said I glide as smoothly as Sandy, and I have six legs to his four."

"I saw you waltzing with her."

"She dragged me around; I tell you I'm clubfooted when it comes to dancing. Come on, come on in." He held out his hand and she took it; then she pulled him to a stop, saying quickly, "I'll take you, I can waltz. Katie and I often waltz together. Come round here." She now dragged him out of the yard and along past the kitchen to the corner of the house and then, stopping, she held her arms out to him. Clumsily he put one arm around her waist and took hold of her right hand; and now she commanded, "Sing! Go on, sing! I can follow you if you sing."

At this he threw his head backwards and forwards as if in despair; then sighing deeply, he began to hum a Viennese tune.

They danced in a small space at first, their bodies apart; then without being conscious of it, they moved round the corner and on to the drive fronting the house.

"Haven't you had enough?" He was panting with his effort to sing and dance at the same time.

"No! No!" She had lessened the space between them and consequently his arm had moved further around her waist. "I could go on like this all night; it's lovely, lovely. Do you think I'm beautiful?"

"WHAT!" When he went to stop she tugged him back into the step saying, "Don't bawl at me, I can read you. Brigie says I am."

"Well, if Brigie says you are, then you are; who dares dispute Brigie?" He was laughing down into her face now.

She went to shake him, and their bodies pressed close, and when like this she demanded, "But am I? Do you think I am?" he said haltingly, "Aw, Barbara. . . . Well, you're all right."

"Oh, Michael! Michael! Tell me, say it."

"Michael! Michael!"

The boy sprang around so quickly that he almost threw Barbara from him; but he still had hold of her hand as he looked toward his mother and Mr. Ferrier standing at the front door.

"Michael!" Constance went toward him. "What is this?"

He didn't speak, he just stared at her, his face scarlet.

"I thought you were seeing Mr. Yates about the carriage lights."

"I . . . I . . . w . . . was," he stammered in his confusion, "but . . . but Waite, he . . . he was talking w . . . with Mr. Yates."

"I should go and see if the traps are ready."

The boy hadn't been aware that he was still holding Barbara's hand; and now he dropped it like a hot coal and ran from them.

Constance stared at her niece, and Barbara stared back at her aunt, until the man in the doorway laughed and began to speak. He articulated well and Barbara read his lips. "She doesn't carry the Mallen streak, but she's a Mallen all right; I saw that instantly, deaf or not. You mustn't blame the boy, Constance. Anyway, what is a waltz? But it would have been better if they'd waited till the moon was up." He laughed softly.

Glancing at him for a moment, Constance repeated the words to herself, What is a waltz? Nothing, nothing in the ordinary way. But they were holding each other close, entwined. Really! That girl.

"You said that she couldn't hear at all, are you sure?" Pat Ferrier muttered as he turned toward Constance, now slightly concerned. "She looks as if she understood."

"She can read your lips."

"Oh Lord! I'm sorry. Still, she knows she's a

58

Mallen; and I suppose she knows all about the streak by now." His voice dropped even further, "I was always glad that you weren't one, Constance."

She wanted to say, "Were you, Pat?" She wanted to look at him, linger with him, because she had the feeling that this could be the beginning of a new lease on life for her. He had been in love with her one time; true it was a boyish love but it had nevertheless been ardent. But, but that must wait; there was this girl, this disturbing girl. She turned to Barbara where she was still standing staring at them and she said, "I thought you were going to get a handerchief?"

"Yes, I am." There was nothing subdued about the tone, no shame in it that she had been caught showing an utter lack of decorum, waltzing with a young boy in the farmyard like any common serving maid might do at a wedding or harvest supper.

She passed between them as they stood on the steps, glancing quickly first at one and then at the other, defiance showing in her back as she walked across the hall and up the stairs and into Constance's bedroom.

She had opened the door before she realized she could hardly see, for now the twilight had deepened and the room had but one small window, so she returned to the top of the landing and picked up the two-branched candelabrum that Jane had just lit and carried it into the room. She placed it on the dressing table and tugged open the drawer to the right of her; then she stared down into it, thinking as she looked at the sets of lace collars and cuffs and bodice frills. She said the drawer to the right. Well, this was the drawer to the right. She pulled it out a little further and thrust her hand to the back of it. She could feel no pile of neatly stacked handkerchiefs, nor yet a handkerchief satchel, but what she did feel was something hard beneath a bodice flounce.

Pulling the drawer open further still, she impatiently thrust the flounce to one side and saw that the hard thing it covered was a small framed picture. There was no immediate curiosity in her manner, she

59

did not even think, Why has Aunt Constance hidden this photograph under the flounce? Not until she drew it out and held it to the light and saw that she was looking down at a face like Michael's did excitement rise in her.

The face in the round frame was an exact replica of Michael's except that it looked older. The eyes, the nose, everything, especially the hair, were the same. There was only one difference, the face didn't show Michael's strength, it was a pale, sick face. She knew who this was; it was Matthew Radlet. She had seen another of him when he was a young boy. It had been taken with his elder brother, Michael's father. They were both wearing knickerbocker suits and caps. The picture was now hanging in Grandma Radlet's room, as was another picture of the brothers, taken when they were grown up. But this latter one was indistinct; it had been taken in the cattle market, and it merely showed a dark man and a fair one on each side of a cow.

The sound of laughter coming from below caused her to thrust the picture back into the drawer and close it. Then she stood biting on her little finger for a moment before shaking her head and murmuring, "Aye, Aunt Constance."

As if she had just experienced a revelation she turned and looked toward the door, and her gaze carried her beyond it down the stairs and onto the drive, and she saw her Aunt Constance standing there, as she had a moment ago, looking at her as if she had committed some crime.

Quickly she turned to the dressing table again and her darting gaze now alighted on a set of small drawers flanking the mirror. When she pulled the top one open she found it full of handkerchiefs, and she took one out and held it to her nose. It smelt strongly of lavender.

She stood now tucking the handkerchief into the cuff of her dress, her eyes were bright, her face alight as if it were going to burst into laughter. She looked about her. This was her Aunt Constance's room. She had never really seen it before although she had been in it many times; it was comfortable, colorful. It was almost as smart as the bedrooms in the Hall. Her Aunt Constance didn't like her; her Aunt Constance had never liked her; but now she had found something out about her Aunt Constance. She didn't really know the full extent of her discovery, but one thing was certain, she'd never be afraid of her Aunt Constance again.

She had always assumed an attitude to give the impression she was afraid of no one, but secretly she had stood in awe of her Aunt Constance; perhaps because she had such power over Michael, and it had been policy that she herself should remain in her aunt's good books. But now . . . Now.

She pressed her lips tightly together as if to prevent the excitement that was filling her from spilling over. . . . She knew about things, the forbidden things that happened between men and women. When they were alone Katie and she talked, and their talk hinted at these secret things. And now her Aunt Constance. Really! She could scarcely believe it, but it was true. Oh yes, the photograph was proof enough for her. She remembered her Aunt Constance saying, "Michael takes after his grandmother Radlet's side." And of course he did, but his father hadn't been Mr. Donald Radlet. Really! Really!

When she went out of the room there was a slight swagger to her walk.

Fifteen minutes later they were all ready for the road. Barbara had known that she would not be allowed to ride in the brake, not now it was coming on dark, even if the moon were to shine ever so brightly. But it didn't matter; it had been a wonderful day and she had danced alone with Michael. Her Aunt Constance could never take that from her. She could still feel him holding her close. She could still the pumping of his heart through her dress. If her Aunt Constance hadn't come on the scene at that moment he might have kissed her; he might, he just might. He had looked down on her and his eyes had been big and round and soft, and his hands had been hot with perspiration. Her Aunt Constance had made them lose something, but it would come again, that moment would come again. In the secret depths of her where her desires ranged wildly she felt old and full of knowledge, strange knowledge.

From her seat in the trap she looked toward where Mr. Ferrier was saying good-bye to Katie; and oh my! he was kissing her hand and Katie was dropping him a deep curtsy; everybody was laughing. . . . Now he was coming toward them.

"Good-bye, Miss Brigmore." Brigie and he were shaking hands.

Then he was talking to Mary. "Hello, Mary," he said. "I hope you are well. Do you remember me?"

"Indeed I do, sir. You haven't changed much." It was the first time on this occasion Mary had seen him, for she had been spending the day with her friend, Nancy Waite.

"That is very kind of you, Mary. If I remember rightly you were forever tactful; Miss Brigmore's influence, no doubt." He cast a glance toward Miss Brigmore. "Good-bye."

"Good-bye, sir. Good-bye."

Now he had hold of her own hand and, leaning forward, he put his lips to it; but his eyes were raised to hers, and they held a mischievous glint as if they shared a secret. "Good-bye, Miss Mallen." He stressed the Miss. "I trust you've had an enjoyable day."

She read only the latter end of his words because he had bowed his head, and she said, "Good-bye, sir, and thank you." It was a suitable retort covering all occasions.

When he stepped back, Yates cried "Gee-up!" and the brake went from the yard first; then Miss Brigmore shook the reins of the pony trap and the pony moved forward; and now those who had free hands began to wave. She waved to Michael where he was standing between his mother and his grandmother, with Mr. Ferrier behind him. He did not run beside the trap (as he usually did) and call a last farewell

from the road; but somehow it didn't matter for she
knew if it lay with him he would have done so. She
felt strong, powerful, important; her deafness didn't
matter. Was she only twelve, near thirteen? But she
felt so much older, and so full of knowledge. One
thing she was determined on; she wouldn't cease
pestering Brigie until she got her a pony, and then she
could ride over the hills whenever she liked, and no
one could stop her . . . no one.

They had gone about a quarter of a mile along
the road when two figures, one very tall and one very
small, jumped a ditch and mounted the high bank
that edged the road in order to let them pass; then
the two figures waved to them and they waved back.
Even when she saw it was Jim Waite and Sarah she
waved back, for as she looked at the small figure of
Sarah Waite, dressed in a common coat and heavy
boots and straw bonnet, she felt she had been silly to
be jealous of her, for what had she to fear from a
little thing like that. She knew that Jim Waite had
taken Sarah to the games, doubtless at the suggestion
of Aunt Constance and Brigie, because the Benshams
had been coming. If that hadn't been the case Sarah
Waite would have been allowed to tag along with them;
and as Brigie herself had said on other occasions, it
wasn't right to allow the girl such license. But it didn't
matter any more, nothing mattered any more; she had
danced with Michael alone and he had almost kissed
her.

The following morning at breakfast Barbara
caused Miss Brigmore to choke on her food and
drop her fork onto her plate when she was asked the
question, "What is the Mallen streak? Should I have
it? Oh, don't choke." Barbara rose hastily from her
chair and came round the table and patted Miss Brigmore between the shoulders as she asked, "Was it the
bacon, or what I said?"

"Don't, don't!" Miss Brigmore shrugged herself
away from Barbara's hand; then wiping her mouth

with her napkin, she muttered, "It was the bacon; Mary does it much too well. I've told her. What . . . what did you say about the Mallen streak?" She picked up her fork and proceeded with her breakfast, and as Barbara resumed her seat she said, "I asked you what it was, and should I have it."

"What makes you ask such a question? Where did you hear this?"

"Mr. Ferrier talking to Aunt Constance last night. He said I hadn't got it, nevertheless I was a Mallen all right, or words to that effect."

Dear, dear Lord! It was a silent exclamation but Miss Brigmore had closed her eyes and it took on the form of a prayer. She could not stand another tussle with the child and the truth would be disastrous at the present time for she was getting on so well with her sign language. She looked across the table and said, slowly now, "Most of the Mallen men who were born with black hair have a paler streak of hair running down from the crown"—she demonstrated—"usually on the left side."

"Did Mother's Uncle Thomas have it? His hair is white on his picture in the drawing room.

Miss Brigmore lowered her eyes before she said, "In his young days, yes, it was very prominent."

"Did my father have it?"

Again Miss Brigmore said silently, "Dear Lord! Oh dear Lord!" Now she must repeat the tale of Thomas Mallen's fictitious younger brother who had been drowned at sea before Barbara was born. She had invented the story when the child had first inquired about her father, and she had regretted it ever since, for it had further complicated an already very complicated situation.

When she spoke she mumbled her words and Barbara asked loudly, "What did you say?"

Miss Brigmore lifted her head sharply and her voice, too, was loud as she replied, "I said he had it slightly."

"Why haven't I got one then?" Barbara put her hand up to her hair.

"The women in the family don't carry the mark."

"Carry the mark?" The words were repeated slowly. "Why do you call it a mark?"

"Oh, child!" Miss Brigmore jerked her head to the side. "No reason. It, it was merely to describe the pigmentation of the hair."

"My uncle, Constance's husband, he was Uncle Thomas's son, wasn't he, the fat man?"

"Don't say, the fat man; your . . . your mother's Uncle Thomas was stout, stout, that's all."

"He was fat; in his picture he is fat."

"Barbara! You're being annoying, and acting like a small child."

"I'm sorry. But Brigie, listen to me, because I want to know. If Aunt Constance's husband Donald was Uncle Thomas's son why did he live on the farm? Why didn't he live at the Hall before it was sold, or here with you? Why? And why was he called Radlet and not Mallen?"

"Be . . . because, because, his, his mother married again."

"What!" Barbara screwed up her eyes. "But she couldn't marry again if Uncle Thomas was alive, and he'd only just died when I was born, you said so yourself, when he had his heart attack. And Uncle Donald's mother is Mrs. Radlet, isn't she, and she's still on the . . ."

Miss Brigmore sprang up from her seat and she did an unusual thing for Miss Brigmore, she doubled her fist and thumped the table, much in the fashion that Mr. Bensham would have done, and she shouted at Barbara even as she mouthed each word separately: "I am not going to go into the entire history of the family at this moment to please you or anyone else, do you hear? When I think the time is ripe I will give you the full story, I shall even write it down for you, but the time is not ripe, and I would thank you not to raise the subject again until I give you leave to. Is that understod?"

Barbara stared up at Miss Brigmore but she did not answer her; she could see that Brigie was furious and all because she was trying to keep something from her, and she imagined it concerned her Aunt Constance and the man called Donald Radlet who had been her husband, but who was Uncle Thomas Mallen's son.

She had the strong urge at this moment to say to Brigie, "Aunt Constance is a bad woman; she has a picture of her husband's brother secreted in her collar drawer, and his face looks exactly like Michael's." But no, this was her secret. Unlike this other business however she would not wait until she was given leave to speak about it. When she herself thought the time was ripe she would startle a number of people by asking questions, but most of all she would startle Aunt Constance, that's if Aunt Constance tried to thwart her.

"If you've finished your breakfast go and get ready for the Hall."

When Barbara reached her room she walked immediately to her dressing table and, sitting before it, she peered into the glass; and as she looked at her reflection she thought, I know a lot of things other people don't know; perhaps it's because of being deaf I notice more. When I am sixteen I shall be very knowledgeable in all ways, I shall know as much as . . . she was going to say Brigie, but she changed it to Aunt Constance, for she felt that her Aunt Constance knew much more of the world than Brigie did.

Of a sudden her mood altered. She leaned further toward the mirror and, the lines of her face drooping into sadness, she said to her reflection, "Parts of me are not nice and I want every bit of me to be nice so that Michael will love all of me. I want to be kind like Katie, and gentle like—" She actually started back from the mirror as she checked her mind forming the name Sarah; then, her body slumping, she asked herself, "Is that why I hate her? Not only because Michael makes a fuss of her but because she is so different from myself, being of a gentle nature?" Learning slightly forward again she peered at herself, then asked in a whisper, "Why am I not gentle and kind and loving? But . . . but I am loving. Oh, yes"—she shook her head as if in denial to a voice accusing her unjustly —"I am loving, I love Michael; I've always loved Michael, I don't know a time when I didn't love Michael; and Brigie; yes, I love Brigie, but in a different way; and I love Katie, because it would be hard not to love one so generous as Katie; and I like the boys, particularly John. I . . . I really like everyone, everybody except that Waite family and . . . and Aunt Constance."

Well—her spine straightened itself—if ever she hoped to have Michael she would have to learn to love Aunt Constance, wouldn't she, because when she and Michael married they'd all have to live in the same house, wouldn't they? Not necessarily. In her mind's eye she saw the picture of her Aunt Constance standing looking at Mr. Ferrier.

She was able to recognize love when she saw it.

So you see, she nodded at herself, she really did know a lot, much more than anyone else of her age. Perhaps it wasn't only because she was deaf, perhaps it was because she was a Mallen. Mallens seemed to be different, special because of that streak.

But Mr. Ferrier had recognized her as a Mallen without the streak.

Wouldn't it be strange if Mr. Ferrier proved to be the solution to her main problem.

BOOK II

MATILDA BENSHAM

ONE

"Now look here, lad; I'm going to put some straight questions to you and I want some straight answers; you've buggered me about enough over the last year or so. Why, in the name of God, can't you be like John there?"

"I can't be like him because I'm not him, I'm me." Dan Bensham leaned over the table toward his father and paused before he finished, "And it's like you to expect people to be of a pattern."

"Now look here, lad; I'll have none of that." Harry rose from his chair and came round the desk, his arm outstretched, his finger pointing toward his younger son. "You can act the man and the big fellow as much as you like among your fancy friends, but just you remember this is my house an' to me you're still a nipper, nowt more, just a nipper."

"Oh, I'm glad to hear that. Yesterday you said I was of an age to know my own mind."

"Well, so you are. An' that's what all this is about. I've slaved for years, an' me father afore me, to build up one of the best mills in Manchester, an' I've got two sons who should be damned glad they've got the chance to carry on after me. But here you are nineteen, an' not knowin' which bloody end of you's up. If you had stuck to the idea of goin' to one of those universities I'd've been with you; aye, I would, but now you come home and tell me you don't know what you want to do, except you want to travel about

71

until you find out. Well, I'm gonna tell you something, lad; you're not bloody well traveling about on my money."

"I can travel without money."

"Huh! Huh! Listen to him. I'd like to see you." Harry now stalked down the room, his arms spread wide; then he turned and came back and faced his son before he continued, "Just tell me this. What's wrong in you goin' into the mill for a year? It'll be half yours one day so you should know where your money's comin' from an' how it's got."

Dan didn't answer for a moment, but stood grinding one fist into the palm of his other hand, and he closed his eyes and his chin dug into his chest as he growled out, "That's just it, I've told you; if I've told you once, I've told you a dozen times I can't bear to see them from Monday morning till Saturday night working, working, never stopping. . . ."

"Now look you here, lad, let's get this straight; my . . . my people are better cared for than any others in town. Shaftesbury himself couldn't do more."

"NO?"

"NO! An' don't you insinuate otherwise with that tone of voice. God Almighty! you couldn't treat me worse if I was a John Bright and opposed nearly every damn reform along the line. Look what I've done over the last few years, aye, an' long afore that, long afore seventy-four I was ahead of me time for I never took a workhouse apprentice in if they were under ten, lass or lad, and then I raised it to twelve."

"Because it became law."

"Bugger you for an aggravating young snot. I could have kept it to ten an' been better thought of by other owners. I've been blacklisted by some of them, do you know that? Blacklisted, me! Now I'm tellin' you, lad, you'd better watch out else you'll find yourself lying on your back, as cocky as you are."

As father and son, similar in build and appearance, only different in age and not all that different in temperament, glared at each other, John's voice broke in on them quietly now, addressing Dan and saying, "If you're so troubled by the conditions why don't you do as Father suggests and give it a trial, find out where improvements are necessary and put them forward?"

Harry cast his enraged glance now toward his elder son as he cried, "Now there's sense, there's sense; see for yourself what goes on afore you start condemnin' wholesale out of hand." He looked at Dan again, then letting out a long slow breath that deflated his body he said in a slightly calmer tone, "And if you go off now what effect do you think it's goin' to have on your mother, and her bad as she is? And you know she's bad, don't you?" His voice sank lower still as he ended, "Real bad."

Dan's head was level now, and he asked tersely, "What do you mean, real bad?"

"Just what I say."

"But the operation, it was a success."

"For the time being, for the time being; but you might as well know, both of you"—he cast a glance toward John before lowering his head—"her days are numbered, they're fast runnin' out."

John rose hastily from where he had been sitting near the end window of the library, and he came and stood near Dan, and they both stared at their father, and he at them; and then he nodded slowly.

After a moment the two brothers glanced at each other, then Dan went to the fireplace and, putting his forearm on the mantelshelf, he leaned his head on it, and he did not lift it until he heard his father say, "That's why I've stayed back here more than usual of late, an' that's why I wanted the both of you at the mill; not just one, it takes more than one to run a place like that. I wanted you both to get the hang of it under Rington afore he retires, an' believe me that won't be soon enough to please my book. I've never relied on him, not fully, since he almost let that strike sweep our place. If it hadn't been for young Willy havin' his wits about him it would have an' all. Willy could take over the morrow 'cos he could buy and sell Rington in lots of ways, but then don't forget he was one of themsel's, and even the best of them'll take advantage if there's not a bit of class at the top; aye, class"—he nodded his head slowly before he went on—"like you would provide." He held their gaze, then said lamely, "It was different in my case an' that of me dad. We grew with it, we were part of the machinery you could say; but we made something. It mightn't be the biggest mill but it's always been my ambition to make it the best in the town, an' not only in turning out the cloth but for the conditions in which it's turned out, an' so it hurts me, lad, when I'm accused of neglecting me own folk." Harry now nodded sharply toward Dan, and on this emotional and strategic point he left the room.

After a moment the two brothers turned and looked squarely at each other; then John said quietly, "'Tisn't too bad, not too bad at all, you get used to it."

"I'll never get used to it. The place itself, the town, the muck. Oh God, the muck!"

"Well, you've got no need to go where the muck is, that's up to you. We live almost two miles away from the muck, as you call it."

"They live like . . . I was going to say cattle but cattle are clean. Have you seen how they live?"

"Yes, of course I have."

"And didn't it affect you?"

"It's awful, but what can you do? I mean you can't reform the whole town, not at one go. They've pulled a lot of places down and are rebuilding."

"Yes, and what? I saw some of the rebuildings, streets and streets of houses no bigger than huts."

"They're clean, new, and some of them have water laid on in the backyards."

The scathing expression on Dan's face caused John to wet his lips and flush slightly, and when Dan repeated, "Some of them have water laid on in the backyards," then added, "and some of them haven't; and some of them still throw their filth into the street," he cried angrily, "They're not all like that, you've only

74

seen half the picture. There's lots of our folks whose places are as clean as it's possible for them to be."

"You've said it"—Dan's voice had risen too—"as it is possible for them to be. And look, you're blaming me as much as he is, but I ask you this, why did he move us here in the first place, miles away from grime of any kind, right into the heart of the country, this wild country, fresh air, hills and rivers all about us, and then expect us to go back into Manchester? All right, all right, we've got a house on the outskirts— like all the rest of the wise merchants—but even there you can't get away from the filth, their fancy buildings, their churches, their assembly rooms, the lot; to me they still reek of the filth, for they were built out of filth."

John stared at this brother whom he cared for dearly. Dan was almost a head shorter than himself in height but thicker in stature, and he had a spark, a vitality that he himself lacked; he also had the power to express himself on all subjects whether taboo or not. Yet in a way he was indolent, and of course too he was idealistic. This last trait created the Manchester conflict. He said quietly, "It's because of Blake's 'Dark Satanic Mills' that we've been able to enjoy the fresh air, and the hills and the streams; you mustn't forget that."

A slow smile now spread over Dan's face for, as usual, he had regained his temper quickly, and he said on a laugh, "Trust you to bring everything down to earth and plain facts."

"Well, isn't it better so?"

It was a moment before Dan asked flatly, "What am I going to do?"

"Well, if you'll take my advice you'll do as he says and give it a chance, and . . . and also, if as he says Mother's so ill, well you couldn't possibly go away now even if he gave you the money."

Dan turned and looked into the fire again, and then he muttered, "What'll we do if Mother goes?"

"I don't know; we'll have to wait and see."

For a time they were both silent, then John

glanced at his watch and said, "I'll have to be going."

"Where to?" Dan looked to where John was walking slowly toward the door.

"I promised to ride over to the farm with Barbara."

"Since when have you taken to accompanying Madam when she goes a-visiting the lord of the hills?"

"It appears that Brigie won't let her go over on her own since she was lost in the mist that time. . . ."

"And so she's making use of you?"

"And so she's making use of me."

"How do you feel playing second fiddle to the farmer?"

"I didn't know I was playing the fiddle at all."

Dan went toward John now and he did not put the question until he was level with him. "You serious about Barbara?" he asked quietly.

"No."

The answer was firm and definite, and caused Dan's face to stretch as he repeated, "No? Then Brigie's going to have a surprise, isn't she?"

"Brigie's not such a fool."

"Brigie is a fool where Madam is concerned. Brigie's determined you'll marry her long lovely child and you'll all live here happy ever after." He waved his hand above his head.

"Don't talk rubbish. Brigie hasn't been with Barbara all these years not to know there's one person and one person only on her horizon, and that's the farmer."

"Oh, Brigie knows that, and Barbara knows that, and I know that, and you know that; there's only one person who doesn't know it and that's the fair farmer himself."

"What do you mean? He . . . he's devoted to her."

"Yes, in a brotherly fashion, like we all are, but I'll lay a hundred to one now that he doesn't marry her, and you do. I'd bet my last penny on Brigie."

At this John put his head back and laughed quietly as he said, "Make it two hundred."

"Done! What about a time limit?"

"A year today."

"A year today it is."

They were smiling as they walked out into the hall; then they both looked slightly embarrassed when their eyes alighted on the objects of their discussion. Barbara had just come in from the front porch and Armstrong was already helping Miss Brigmore off with her coat.

After greetings had been exchanged Miss Brigmore looked at John and said, "It's a beautiful day, I'm sure you'll enjoy your ride; but bring her back early mind, well before dusk sets in."

"Never fear; I'm too careful of my own skin to come across those hills in the dark."

"What did you say?" It was Barbara looking at John now, but it was Dan who answered for him. Rapidly on his fingers he repeated what John had said, and Barbara answered with her fingers. Then speaking verbally to John in a throaty muffled voice, she said, "Don't worry, I'll look after you."

John laughed as he turned away, saying to Miss Brigmore, "Excuse me a moment, I'll just say good-bye to Mother."

Now looking Barbara straight in the face, Miss Brigmore said, "Give your Aunt Constance my warm regards, won't you?"

"Yes, Brigie."

"And tell her I shall try to get across next week, weather permitting of course." She turned to Dan with a smile, saying, "It's always weather permitting here. Isn't it strange how our lives are ruled by the weather? How's your mother this morning?"

"She seemed a little better, quite lively." And he had thought she was. But he felt slightly sick now with the weight of his present knowledge.

"Oh, I'm glad." Miss Brigmore nodded and smiled. She had no doubt but at the moment of death Matilda would appear quite lively. Of late years she had come to admire Matilda Bensham more and more, and there had grown in her a deep affection for the woman who was, after all, her mistress.

She spoke to Barbara again, saying, "Now take care, won't you?" then turned and went toward the stairs.

Dan, left alone with Barbara, looked at her quizzically for a moment before saying on his fingers, "Come and wait in the drawing room."

"He won't be a minute," she answered verbally.

"You never know with John. Anyway, you can come and sit down."

When they entered the room Barbara sat down on an occasional chair not far from the door, which caused Dan, still speaking to her on his fingers, to say, "That's it, don't come right in, you'll have farther to run."

Before answering him she tossed her head to one side; then said, "Don't be silly," and made to rise, but he checked her with an exaggerated movement, saying, "Oh, don't get up; you make me less embarrassed when you're sitting; we're of a height then." He surveyed her teasingly, his head on one side; then stretching out his arm, he spaced his thumb and finger as he said, "I suppose you are about two inches taller than me now, and if you keep on growing until you're twenty-one, just imagine what you'll be like then, a beanstalk!"

"And if you don't grow any more just imagine what you'll be like then."

This brisk sparring was always the tone of the conversation between them, whether with gesture or lips, and seemed at times to border on open hostility.

"You going to see the farmer?"

"Who else?"

"You're making a convenience of John."

"I'm making a convenience of no one. John proposed coming with me."

"You wouldn't have been allowed over if he hadn't."

She pressed her lips tightly together as she stared at him, and then she said verbally, "Your advanced education was intended to give you the cloak of a gentleman. . . ."

When his head went back and he burst out laughing she jumped to her feet, and he now looked straight into her face and answered her, also verbally, saying, "You sounded just like Brigie; and you know, you are like Brigie; under the skin you're just like her."

"I'm like no one but myself."

The light in his eyes changed, his face took on a stiff look for a moment as he stared at her: that is just what he had said a short while ago to his father. The mischievous glint returned, and now he nodded at her as he said, "You're right, you're like no one but yourself, you're very leggy." He looked down her length, over her slight bust and narrow waist, to the long flow of her riding skirt, and he said, "You'll soon have to have a bigger mount than the cob, else your feet will be trailing on the ground, like the picture of Christ in the nursery where He's riding the donkey. . . ."

Now she was shocked, he had really roused her. "You're being blasphemous, and it isn't amusing. You never succeed in being amusing, only aggravating, and now you have to resort to blasphemy."

His whole attitude changing, he said contritely, "I'm sorry; I am, I'm really sorry." But when he put out his hand to touch her arm she slapped it away, saying, "One of these days you'll be sorrier still"; and on this she turned and marched out of the room.

He stood staring at the closed door. One of these days he'd be sorrier still. He couldn't be sorrier than he was at this moment, and about a number of things: Manchester, the mill, his mother, the frustrated desire to roam, and then this other thing, this other hopeless thing, this thing he had mismanaged for years, this thing without hope. This thing that was perhaps the main reason for him wanting to get away.

Once again he went to the fireplace and put his arm on the mantelshelf and rested his head on it.

Miss Brigmore automatically smoothed down each side of her hair and straightened the skirt of her gray cotton dress before tapping on the bedroom door and entering. It was many years now since she had waited to be bidden to enter.

"Aw, hello there." Matilda's voice greeted her from the window. "You see I'm up; she's got me up afore me clothes are on." She jerked her head toward where the nurse was making the bed; then added, "Come and sit down. Come and sit down."

As Miss Brigmore took a seat opposite her she asked, "And how do you feel this morning?"

"Oh fine, fine; can't you see? I was just sayin' to 'Arry there, that if this weather keeps up he's going to drive me into Newcastle and I'm goin' to buy a complete rig-out, maybe two, and stay in one of them big hotels. Didn't I? Didn't I, 'Arry?"

"Aye, you did, lass; and just you say the word and we'll be off any minute now."

"There, what did I tell you? And how are you yourself?"

"Oh, I'm very well, thank you."

"Well, you couldn't help be otherwise, could you, on a mornin' like this. Just look out there, isn't it grand? Look at those hills. Eeh! You know, the times I've promised meself I'd climb those hills. Just one of them, I've said to meself, go on, just climb one, just to say you've done it; but the most climbing I've done is to get into the carriage. Laziness it is; that's what it is, nothing but laziness. Isn't it, 'Arry?"

"Aye, you're right there, Tilda. As lazy as you're long, you are. Never done a hand's turn in your life as far back as I can remember."

As their laughter joined, Miss Brigmore looked from one to the other. They could laugh about it. Never done a hand's turn in her life, this woman who started to work when she was six years old, walking the dark muddy streets, her eyes gummed with sleep, the only guide her mother's skirt. Six o'clock in the morning till seven or eight at night. As lazy as she was long! This woman had told her tales that had actually brought the tears to her eyes, of how her sister had lost her hand when she was nine years old. Running between the machines, she had been so overcome with sleep that she had fallen forward and put her hand out to save herself, and, as Tilda had said, it was God's blessing she hadn't put both out. It hadn't come off right away, she said, it was just mangled at first, but when they got her to the infirmary they had chopped it off.

Over the years Miss Brigmore had come to realize that her wisdom gained from the reading of books had not increased half as much as had her knowledge of human nature which she had gained from listening to Matilda Bensham.

"John's just been in to tell me he's ridin' over to the farm with Barbara. If we keep our weather eye open we'll see them passin' the end of the drive there. By! she looks a picture on a horse, does Barbara. Not like our Katie; a real bundle of duds our Katie looks on a horse. Did he tell you about the visitor we had yesterday?" She nodded again toward Harry, and he replied, "No, I didn't. What time have I had; she's just come in, hasn't she? And anyway, I've spent the mornin' talking to those two numskulls of yours, tryin' to knock some sense into them, at least into that Dan."

"Oh, Dan's all right, he'll get by." A warm smile spread over Matilda's pale bloated face. "But about our Katie and the visitor"—she nodded to Miss Brigmore—"that Mr. Ferrier called yesterday."

"Really! I didn't know he was home."

"Oh, he's home all right. He took her for a short dander, as he calls it, on the horses, and he's callin' for her the day again. He's bringing the coach this time an' takin' her into Hexham. Now what do you make of that? I ask you, what do you make of it? I thought nothin' of it last year when he went to the school in Hexham and picked her up, but now he comes a callin', and this is the second year runnin' you know. Oh, what am I talkin' about? More than that; he's called

81

every year since he's come back from abroad, since the first time he met her on the farm. Now what do you make of it?"

What did she make of it? And what would Constance make of it when her secret hopes—that weren't so secret—were dashed yet again?

When Pat Ferrier first returned to England from abroad he stayed only a matter of weeks, but during that time he was very attentive to Constance, and she regained her youth, hope acting like an elixir on her, but when he told her of his departure through a letter, as Will Headley had once done, the elixir lost its effect and she reverted to the farmer's wife, and the loving mother, and the very, very irritable aunt. When the following year he reappeared on the scene he again paid attention to her, if not court, and so it had gone on for nearly five years, until now she felt that the hope that lingered in Constance was but a dim spark, yet nevertheless was lying waiting to be kindled. But if she were to hear that he was visiting the Hall with the precise intention of seeking the company of Katie, then the spark would be finally quenched, and what would the dead embers do to her character? A marriage such as she had made, and then to be spurned by two would-be suitors, because spurned was the correct word. Oh! It wasn't to be thought of.

"He's all of fifteen years older than her, but it would be a good match, grand. Don't you think it would be a good match? Imagine our Katie with a house in London, and one in Paris, France, and a manor in Westmoreland. My! My!"

"That means nowt."

They both turned and looked toward Harry. "We've got a house here in Northumberland, we've got one in Manchester. I could take one in London the morrow and another in Paris and it wouldn't make a dent in what we've got. It isn't the property a body wants to consider, it's the man."

"But you like him?"

"He's all right, aye, I like him; he hasn't acted like the rest of them, too big for his boots. But still

82

who's to know whether we would've seen hilt or hair
of him if he hadn't been after something, and that
something Katie? Aye, let's face up to it; he wouldn't
have come knockin' at our front door if it hadn't been
for our Katie."

"Well, that's the way of things with any lad, isn't
it? Anyroad, he seems set on her."

"Now don't get ideas, Tilda. Two visits an' you
say he's set on her. Why, I know some folks who've
courted ten years and then it's fallen through. Set on
her!" The sound he made was a definite pig snort.

"Look, there they go, Barbara and John. And
look, they've stopped; our Katie's runnin' up to them,
likely giving Barbara her news. Oh, they're a pair,
those two; been like sisters, haven't they?" She turned
to Miss Brigmore, and Miss Brigmore nodded and
said, "Yes, indeed, like sisters."

"An' they're very fond of each other; different
as chalk from cheese but very fond of each other, you
can see it."

"Yes, they're very fond of each other."

"By! as I said, she looks well on a horse, does
Barbara. An' so does our John; he's well set up is our
John. Don't you think he's well set up, Brigie?"

"Yes, indeed, he's a very smart young man."

"They make a nice looking pair."

"Yes, they do." Oh yes, indeed, they made a nice
looking pair, and they were suited. Miss Brigmore endorsed this firmly to herself. John was kind, gentle,
and thoughtful, and he could handle Barbara. He had
the knack of talking her out of her tantrums; but
such exhibitions had been replaced of late by moods. In
the beginning, she had called them thoughtful periods,
moods, but now she thought of them as black spasms,
for when Barbara was in them she would neither speak
verbally nor communicate on her fingers but would
go out and walk the hills, very like her mother had
done when she was carrying her. Sometimes Miss
Brigmore would find her staring fixedly at her, a
question deep in her eyes, many questions deep in her
eyes, but as yet she hadn't asked them with her lips,

nor with her fingers; but increasingly Miss Brigmore
felt that the day was not far off when she would be
confronted by a young woman who would want to
know the whole truth.

She started slightly when Matilda shouted across
the room, "Would you go and get us a glass of wine,
nurse?" That was one thing she had never been able
to do, instill into Matilda the fitness of things, the
manner in which to address a servant. The nurse was
a new addition to the household and was looking
slightly indignant when Harry said, "Don't worry her,
I'll ring for Brooks."

"No, 'Arry; she'll go and get it, won't you, dear?"

The nurse looked from Matilda to Miss Brigmore
and when Miss Brigmore made an almost imperceptible
movement with her head she turned away and went
out of the room.

"That's it. I just want to get rid of her for a
minute, we can't talk in front of her. It's not policy
to let everybody know your business, now is it? Sit
down, 'Arry, and stop gallopin' about, you're actin'
like a dray horse that's been let loose in the cellars.
Tell her what we were talkin' about last night, go on."
She looked at her husband but pointed at Miss Brigmore, and Harry, seating himself with unusual obedi-
ence, said, "Oh, there's plenty of time for that, Tilda."

"There's no time like the present, that's what
you're always sayin'; you said that to me years ago,
remember? There's no time like the present, you said;
get your hat and coat on and we'll go an' get married."
She threw her head back and her sagging cheeks
wobbled with her laughter, and Harry smiled as he
looked down and nodded his head, then said, "Aye,
aye, I remember, there's no time like the present.
Although mind"—he nodded and glanced toward Miss
Brigmore—"it wasn't done nearly as quick as that, it
took us almost a week."

Again Tilda's laughter filled the room; and then
ceasing abruptly, she put out her hand toward Miss
Brigmore and, gripping her wrist, she said, "We want
to do that something for you, lass, we talked about ages

ago. Something permanent like, something that'll put you over in the meantime until the next lot's ready for you to have a go on."

Looking her bewilderment, Miss Brigmore turned her face toward Harry and as her eyes questioned him he said with a grin, "She's meaning when they get married an' their bairns start comin' up and you take them on."

"Oh Oh!" The syllables came out on a shaky laugh. "Oh, I doubt if I shall ever take on any more children, not in my lifetime."

"Why not? Why not? you could have another thirty years afore you, twenty of them workable ones." It was Harry speaking directly to her now. "You don't look anything near your age, not by a long chalk, does she, Tilda?"

"No, not by a long chalk; an' I've always said it, haven't I? I have, I have."

"Well, let's get down to brass tacks." Harry's manner was brisk now. "It's like this; let's put our side of it first. We want you to come along here every day, as usual, but not any settled hours, just please yourself, but just pop in and give Tilda a hand here and there with the running, as you've always done. But if there's days when you don't feel up to it an' don't want to bother, well, that'll be all right with us. And so's you can feel independent like we thought about settling a sum on you."

"Oh no! No!" The movement Miss Brigmore made caused the chair leg to slip over the edge of the carpet and to scrape against the polished boards. "I have been well paid, very well paid, you have been over-generous. Look what you have done for Barbara, and the horse and trap; and caring for the horse too. I could never repay your generosity. Oh no! No! I couldn't accept anything more."

"It isn't what you could accept or what you couldn't accept." Harry Bensham was on his feet again, his usual manner to the fore. "A hundred and fifty pounds a year you've got to live on, oh I know, I know; an' the three of you were cheeseparing out of

that afore you came here." He swept his hand in a
wide motion toward her as if wiping away her denial
and went on. "And if Barbara gets married, who knows
but that she'll want that hundred of hers; it all depends on who she takes. Aye"—he nodded—"it all
depends on who she takes." He was not so cruel as
to add "or who takes her," but instead said, "There's
many a slip, an' then where will you be? You'd have
a house over your head and a pound a week for two
of you to live on."

As she looked at him she thought, The incongruity; he was pitying her for living on an income of a
pound a week, yet that was almost three times as much
as he paid some of his hands. He was an odd man, an
intractable man, but a generous one, and she knew in
her heart that no matter what protestations she made,
as courtesy demanded, she should be glad to accept
his offer, for even now finance was a constant problem
to her because Barbara had tastes that went far beyond
their income.

But when she heard him say, "Three thousand,
that's what we thought, Tilda and me, three thousand;
and I'll invest it for you. That'll bring you in nearly
as much as you're getting now, if not more," she did
protest. But he silenced her with, "Now don't start,"
pointing his finger at her as she rose hastily to her feet,
and he went on, "I'm not going to hear one word from
you for, knowin' you, if you open your mouth you'll
come out with something that'll floor me. So it's
settled. I'll be away downstairs. And you sit still." He
nodded toward his wife, and she nodded back at him,
a quiet smile on her face as she said, "Aye, 'Arry,
aye, I'll sit still." "As for you"—he was again looking
at Miss Brigmore, but now as if she were a culprit—
"if you can spare me a minute in a while or so, I'd
like to have a word with you about something."

"Yes, very well." Her voice was small.

"Well then"—he nodded from one to the other—
"that's that."

"Won't . . . won't you stay for a glass of wine?"

He turned from the door and looked toward Miss

86

Brigmore. "Aw, there's plenty of time for that; wine never troubles me. Nobody's going to accuse me of having a belly." He patted the front of his trousers, jerked his head, then went out.

Uncouthness, kindness, love: this house was a mixture of those.

Sitting down again, she now put out her hands and gently took hold of those of Matilda and murmured softly, "What can I say?"

"Nowt, lass, nowt; about that anyway. About other things, do as you always do, give it straight from the shoulder an' in your proper English, an' without fear or favor. That's what 'Arry says about you, you speak without fear or favor. He thinks you're a lady, 'Arry does, and he's right. By aye! he's right, and I'm glad to have known you. So, talkin' of getting things straight, tell me, lass . . . how much longer do you think I've got?"

"Oh, Matilda."

"Now, now, don't you give way. You see I know me time's short, but I don't know if it's a week or a month, an' there's things I want to do, set right."

Miss Brigmore bit deeply down into her lower lip and for once words failed her.

"Do you think he knows?"

"No, no," she lied firmly.

"He's been quiet lately, an' soft like, you know. I thought he might have a glimmer."

"No, no; he's kind because he's concerned for you. He thinks of you very, very dearly."

"Aye, aye, he does. But an outsider wouldn't think it 'cos of the way he used to go for me. But it was like water off a duck's back, 'cos that was his way. And I aggravated him for I was always a bit of a numskull where learnin' was concerned. He wanted me to learn 'cos his first wife was learned but as I said to him once"—she was smiling faintly again— "'She didn't do much bloody good for you with her learnin', did she?' Eeh! There. I go; I shouldn't swear afore you, but that's what I said to him, an' he laughed and slapped me on the backside, and he said, 'No,

87

you're right there'; and that's the last time he tried to learn me. And you know, lass, I've thought to meself over these past years, if you couldn't learn me nobody could 'cos you're marvelous at learnin' people. . . . I . . . I don't want to die, Brigie."

Miss Brigmore looked helplessly at the woman gazing at her now with tears in her eyes and found it impossible to make a reply. Her throat was full, her heart was full. People who followed no rules with regards to the course that conversation, even of the most personal kind, should take, disturbed you; flummoxed you, Mary would have said. She gulped audibly as Matilda went on, her voice thick now with emotion, "It's not because I want to leave all this, 'cos this hasn't meant more than a pennorth of drippin' to me; I'd have been just as happy in a two-up, two-down, an' I've missed Manchester, I have, I have, but I wouldn't let on to him. No, no. But why I don't want to go is 'cos of him. You see, I don't know what he'll do, lass; I only hope to God Florrie Talbot doesn't get her hooks into him. I would hate to see her in me place here. By God! I don't think I could stand it, just the thought. . . ."

Miss Brigmore again swallowed audibly, then asked on a cough, "Flor-Florrie Talbot? I haven't heard of her."

"No, we don't speak of her very much, it's his cousin. When his first wife died she made a dead set at him, an' she was younger than me by over six years. She's just in her late forties now, but she's a blowzy bitch. An' she's no better than she should be; when she was young her father had to go an' bring her from the yards more than once."

Miss Brigmore's eyes narrowed questioningly and Matilda said, "You know, I told you about them, where the whores hung out; daylight, starlight, midnight, made no difference to that lot. Eeh! they were brazen; an' she was among them. Her father hammered her black and blue from head to foot an' kept her for three days in a room without a stitch on to cure her. But I doubt if she was ever cured. Still, she married respectable after that, a gaffer on the Liverpool docks. When he died she came back to Manchester. She's there still, an' the minute I'm gone she'll be on my 'Arry like a bloodthirsty leech."

"Oh no! no! Don't worry, Matilda. Mr. Bensham would never dream of putting anyone in your place."

"No, not for a while he wouldn't. An' I'll always have a corner of his heart, I'm sure of that, but human nature's human nature all the world over as you an' I know, lass, an' when needs must the devil drives. It was that I wanted to ask you about. If she should turn up here—and I wouldn't put it past her, I'd hardly have time to settle in me grave afore she'll be comin' up that drive, I bet what you like. Well, if she should, you have a talk with him, will you, and tell him to wait; wait for a year, say, eh? He'll listen to you. He's got great respect for you, you've no idea."

"I'll do what I can, don't worry about anything. Oh"—she turned toward the door with relief—"here's the wine. A glass of wine will make you feel better."

"Aye, lass, aye; there's nothin' like a glass of wine for puttin' new life into you." Matilda now blew her nose while managing to wipe her eyes at the same time, and she smiled at the stiff-faced nurse as she placed the tray on the bedside table.

TWO

"You knew I was coming."

"I didn't."

"You got my letter?"

"Yes, but only yesterday, and it was too late, the arrangements were already made." Michael spoke quietly and slowly.

"The arrangements!" Barbara tossed her head scornfully. "To go into the town with the Waites! Arrangements! Who are the Waites anyway? You'd think they were royalty. They're servants."

"Now stop it, Barbara." He mouthed the words widely.

"What do you mean, stop it? I said they're servants and they are servants; you know they're servants."

"We're all servants."

"Don't start on that philosophical tack, you know what I mean."

"I know what you mean and it can't be done; Jim and I have business to do."

"And Sarah makes three."

"Yes, and Sarah makes three, as you say."

As she stood looking at him, her eyes wide and glistening with unshed tears, his tone, as always, immediately softened and he took her hand and said slowly, "Oh Barbara, Barbara, don't be silly, there'll be other times. And look; you've brought John over with you."

90

"Simply because Brigie wouldn't let me come alone."

"All right then, I'll come over next Saturday and fetch you."

"You will?" Her face brightened.

"Yes; that's a promise."

The prospect of spending hours alone with him caused her face to shine with uninhibited pleasure and love, until she thought that that was a week ahead and if Brigie could stop her being alone with Michael she would, even going as far as to accompany them herself. She was back with today's problem.

"Michael."

"Yes, what is it?"

"Do something for me."

"Anything, anything, Madam." It was strange that he should use the title for her as Dan Bensham did. He didn't know if he had copied Dan or Dan him.

"Don't, don't take Sarah with you."

"Now, now." He turned half from her, then slowly back toward her again. "You're being ridiculous. Sarah goes into town with us every week. Why should I stop her today?"

"Every week! Always?"

"Yes, every week, always."

"I . . . I didn't know."

"Well, you know now. Look, Barbara, this is all nonsense. You've got to get over this."

"Get over what?"

The question nonplused him. He did not say, "Your jealousy of Sarah," but neither did he say, "There is no reason for you to feel like this." Perhaps last year or the year before he might have said that, but as he had grown older his feelings had changed; not entirely, oh no, he still had a deep affection for her, and sometimes he thought it was more than affection, for she fascinated him, and she was beautiful. Her handicap did not mar her in any way. She was full of life, vital, and she was so attractive and pleasing, when she was in a good mood. But she had this obses-

91

sion about Sarah that marred her, and it had grown so strong of late that it raised some disquiet in him; he would not term it fear.

"I hate that girl."

"You mustn't say that, Barbara; she's never done anything to you to deserve it."

"She inveigled herself into the household and into Aunt Constance's good books."

"She's done nothing of the sort; she's worked hard and made herself pleasant, she's naturally pleasant."

"Oh, is she? I'm glad you find her so. And you intend to take her with you?"

"Yes, I intend to take her with me. . . . Oh no I don't, I mean I'm not, I'm not taking her with me, she's coming along with Jim as she always does. And look" —his face became stiff—"when you're acting like this I could get on my high horse about him." He pointed toward the dining room door and in the direction of the sitting room where John was talking to Constance.

"Why don't you then?"

"Because . . ." Could he say, "It doesn't bother me who you ride with," because in an odd way it did? He was concerned for her, concerned about her; it could not be otherwise with the association they'd had since they were children. And it wasn't only that, his feelings went further. Oh, he just didn't know what he felt. But he knew how his mother felt; she didn't like Barbara—would it have made any difference to his feelings if she had liked her? He ended lamely, "Because I don't like rows. We don't row, except when . . ."

"Except when I visit. I suppose Aunt Constance says that, and I suppose she hasn't objected to you associating with a maid?"

His tone matching her own now, he answered, "No, she hasn't voiced any objection because I'm sure she doesn't feel any. She's got no feeling about class. Anyway, who are we to be uppish, we're simply farmers. You're the only one who's got ideas about class."

"And rightly so"—she drew herself up as she ended childishly—"as I'm from class on both sides."

This was too much; he'd have to get away from her before he said something that would set her thinking. He was aware of his father's parentage—his mother had told him last year that his father had been the natural son of Thomas Mallen. She had not told him this until after his grandmother had died so that he would not think less of his grandmother. He thought it was from this time too that his feelings toward Barbara had changed; he just had had to change them when he realized that he must be just once removed from being her half-brother. He also knew that she was not aware of her real parentage but had been given some fairy-tale version by Brigie.

"Where are you? Michael! Michael!" It was with relief he heard his mother's voice, and going to the door, he called, "Here we are."

Constance came and stood within the threshold and looked to where Barbara was standing, her face stiff and white and as always appealingly beautiful, and as always she thought, Oh that girl! Then turning to Michael she said, "They're waiting."

"Oh! Well, I'm ready." He glanced back at Barbara. "I'll be over next Saturday," he said, then hurried away.

Constance now went toward John, saying, "They're off to the market, usual routine." Together they walked across the hall and through the kitchen; and it wasn't until they had been in the yard for a few minutes that Barbara joined them.

Standing apart, she looked to where Michael was sitting at the front of the wagon with the reins in his hand, and from the ground Jim Waite with one sweep and heave was lifting Sarah onto the seat beside him. Then he himself mounted the cart.

When Constance waved Sarah waved back. Then John raised his hand while he said quietly, "I hardly recognized her; she's grown so tall in the past year, and pretty with it. She still seemed a child last year at the harvest supper. Does she still dance?"

"Like a linty; she's so light on her feet."

Constance had turned in Barbara's direction and so she caught the last words: light on her feet, like a linty!

Constance was still facing her but, addressing John, she said, "I don't know what I would have done without her over the years. I have played Brigie to her; you know what I mean?"

"Yes, yes, indeed." He nodded as he laughed.

"Did you know Mr. Ferrier was home?" Barbara's voice was low, her speech blurred.

The question obviously startled Constance, and caught her off her guard; she looked straight at Barbara and it was some seconds before she made a slight movement with her head and said, "No."

"Oh, I thought he would have called; he's been home for some days. He went riding with Katie yesterday and he's bringing the coach for her today to drive her into Hexham. . . . It is Hexham, isn't it, they're going to?" She appealed to John, but he made no answer; he just stared fixedly at her.

"Shall I give him your regards if I see him?"

Again there was a moment's pause before Constance said, "Yes, do that. Please do that."

"Well, we must be off." She moved a step forward, then stopped. "Oh, I did tell you that Brigie sent her warm regards and says she'll be over some time next week?"

"You did tell me." Constance's face was expressionless.

"Michael's coming over for me next Saturday; we're going for a run."

Constance made no reply.

"Well, we really must be off." She went toward where the horses were tethered to a standing post, calling over her shoulder, "Help me up, John."

Unsmiling, John performed the task of putting her in the saddle; then he mounted his own horse, and they were about to move off when Barbara reined her horse sharply in again, and now looking back down on Constance, she said, "Oh, I knew there was something I meant to tell you. It was odd, but I saw a man in

Hexham when I was last there. He was dark but had a fair streak down the side of his hair." She demonstrated by running her finger down her riding hat. "Brigie says it's called the Mallen streak; Michael's father had one, hadn't he? Mary tells me his hair was as black as mine except for this white piece; she tells me it's always passed on to the male offspring; isn't it odd that Michael should be so fair?"

The young face looked down into the older one; their eyes poured their animosity each into the other. The years of polite courtesy were swept away and what was revealed was hatred.

It was John who urged the horses forward, saying hastily, "Good-bye. Good-bye, Mrs. Radlet." He knew that he had just witnessed an asp using its barbed fang. What poison was in the venom he could only guess at, but from the look on Mrs. Radlet's face it might mean death. She was a young devil, Barbara, she was vicious. . . . And they imagined he might marry her. Not him! . . .

Constance, back in the house and alone in it, felt so overcome by her emotions that she thought for a moment she would collapse. Going into the dining room, she went to the sideboard and took up a bottle of brandy from which she poured out a good measure and sipped at it as she left the room and hurried up the stairs and into her bedroom. Dropping into a chair, she took a longer drink from the glass, then leaned back and closed her eyes.

That girl! That vixen, for she was a vixen. There was something in her that was bad, equally as bad as that which had been in Donald. Both sired by the same father, they may not have inherited their wickedness from him for, as she remembered, he was not a bad man, but somewhere in his lineage there was evil. How did she know about Michael? How had she found out? Not through Anna. No. No. Anna would never have told her. Oh God! If Michael should ever find out, how would he then act toward her? He loved her. You could say he adored her; and more, he reverenced her as an ideal woman. She put down the glass, then turned and buried her face in the wing of the chair.

Sometime later, after dabbing her face with cold water, she stood before her mirror and her mind touched on the other humiliation. Pat in England; to be near and not to call, but to visit the Hall two days running and to see that young girl. But then she was no young girl, she was a woman; she was older than she herself had been when she had married. Katie Bensham was nineteen, or almost, old enough to marry and to consider a man fifteen years her senior quite suitable. . . . Will Headley, and Bob Armstrong, and now Pat. Why, why was she treated so? She seemed fated to be spurned by the men who attracted her, and desired by those she couldn't stand. But she must not forget Matthew Radlet. She had loved Matthew, and he her. But the need in her, the loneliness in her, was nothing compared to the new threat hanging over her. That girl! That girl! How had she come by the knowledge of Michael's real parentage? No one had ever questioned it before, either by hint or look: Michael took after his grandmother's side of the family, and his grandmother's side was fair. That had been all there was about it until now. She felt almost physically sick as she realized the girl's knowledge had wiped away the last defense she had against her and Michael coming together. If the worst had come to the worst and Michael had declared his love for her then she would have felt forced to beg Anna to explain to the girl the close relationship between them, even knowing she was asking her to countenance a lie. But as it stood now Barbara was aware that there was no blood tie between her and Michael. That scene in the yard had in a way been a declaration of war.

There swept over her the feeling that had been constantly with her while Donald was alive, the feeling that he had her trapped and that she could never escape him. Yet she had escaped him. But in the present case there was no one willing enough to free her from Barbara as to do murder. It wouldn't be the case of Donald and Matthew over again.

THREE

"You are late in getting back."

"Am I?"

"Barbara, please don't answer me in that manner." Miss Brigmore's mouth went into a tight line; and when Barbara remained silent she asked, "Did you have an enjoyable ride?"

"No."

"Then I assume the fault was yours?"

"Yes, you would assume that, wouldn't you? You're lining up on the other side."

"Barbara, don't talk in that fashion to me; I've told you. Come, tell me, what has happened?"

"Nothing has happened, what could happen?"

"Don't raise your voice, Barbara." Miss Brigmore now spoke rapidly on her fingers, and looked to where Brooks was mounting the main staircase. Then she turned about and walked quickly toward the gallery, through it and up the flight of stairs that led to the nursery floor, and she did not look around until she'd actually entered her sitting room. Here she stood stiffly in the midde of the room awaiting Barbara's approach.

Barbara entered the room slowly, and when she did not turn and close the door behind her, Miss Brigmore, forming her words with extra precision, which was a definite sign of her annoyance, said, "Be good enough to close the door behind you. . . . Now then." She looked at the tall, thin figure clothed in the green cord riding habit, her jet hair lifted high from her pale face, a brown velvet stiff-brimmed hat perched on top of her hair, and even in her annoyance and irritation she could not help but be aware of the girl's beauty. Her tone a little gentler now, she asked, "What is all this about? What has put you in a temper? Have you quarreled with John?"

"Quarreled with John?" Barbara's eyes widened in mock surprise. "Whoever quarrels with John? I left him at the cottage and galloped across the fells; gave him a run for his money, as Mary would say; and when he caught up with me all he could pant was, 'Barbara! Barbara! You! You!'"

"It's to his credit that he kept his temper. Remember what happened the last time you decided to take a run over the fells?"

"I knew he would follow me. Anyway, the sun was shining." She pulled off her hat and threw it aside.

If it were someone other than her beloved child who was talking and acting in this manner Miss Brigmore knew that she would dislike her intensely, but because it was her beloved Barbara she laid the blame for her attitude against the affliction; that one so beautifully endowed should be so cursed could create nothing but conflict inside. She took a step toward her now, saying gently, "John is very fond of you, you know that."

"I don't want John to be very fond of me, and you know that."

"Barbara! Come." Miss Brigmore now caught hold of her hand and pulled her toward the couch, and when they were both seated she looked straight into her face for a moment before she said, "You're no longer a child, not even a young girl, you are on the threshold of womanhood. . . ."

"Oh, Brigie, Brigie, please!" The words were drawn out, and now Barbara covered her face with her hands and she kept them there for a moment before slowly dragging them downwards to her neck and gripping it while her eyes remained closed. When she opened her eyes and looked into Miss Brigmore's startled face she said flatly, "I'm not going to marry

John, so get that plan out of your mind. Anyway, he doesn't want me."

Miss Brigmore's tightly bound bust stretched. She swallowed twice before saying, "Of course he wants you."

"What makes you think so? Because he's kind to me? John's kind to everybody, polite and kind . . . and wary. Nobody really knows what John's thinking. But I know what he isn't thinking; he isn't thinking of asking me to marry him. At the present moment he doesn't even like me. And he's like all the rest, always has been, he's sorry for me. Anyway, can you imagine me in Manchester mouthing my way among his friends? How . . . are . . . you . . . Mrs. . . . Moneybags. . . . ? How's-ta-mill?"

"Stop it! Stop it this moment." Miss Brigmore, reverting to nursery days, slapped out at Barbara's hands; and as if she had been struck a blow on the face, Barbara sprang to her feet and her voice was muffled now as she said, "Don't do that, Brigie! You said I was no longer a child, so don't treat me as one. And let us put this matter straight once and for all. There's only one person I want to marry and you know who that is. You've always known, as I have; and if I can't have him I'll have no one."

Miss Brigmore's lips were trembling, and her fingers could do nothing to still their trembling. She kept patting them as if trying to stop herself from speaking, but the words came out slowly and sadly as she said, "You can't marry Michael."

"Why not?"

"Because . . . well, there are so many things against it."

"You mean Aunt Constance?"

"Perhaps."

"She hates me. Do you know that? Aunt Constance hates me. You know something else? I hate her."

"Barbara! Barbara!" Miss Brigmore bowed her head now and held her brow in her hand; then her head was jerked up as if someone had given her a blow under the chin and she was staring at Barbara as the girl said

99

rapidly, "But she'd better be careful and not try me too far else I'll explode her nice comfortable little world. I know something about her, I've known it for years but I've kept it to myself. But if she stops me having Michael I'll see she won't have him either."

Miss Brigmore felt very sick. When she spoke her lips were widely articulating but her voice was a mere whisper. "What do you mean? What can you possibly do to separate Constance and Michael?" But even as she asked the question she was already aware of the answer that Barbara was going to give her.

"I could tell him that Mama whom he idolizes and imagines is a queen among women is nothing more than a slut, and he nothing more than a bastard."

Miss Brigmore felt she was going to faint. She put out her hand and gripped the head of the couch, all the while staring into Barbara's passion-swept face; and when Barbara, now bending toward her, her voice low and heavy with excitement, said, "I am right? I am right then?" Miss Brigmore closed her eyes and shook her head while Barbara went on, "I knew I was, I knew I was, for I found proof of it. Why else would she have his picture hidden in her collar drawer? I found it years ago when she sent me up to her room for a handkerchief. Why should she keep her brother-in-law's picture hidden away in her drawer and not her husband's, I ask you? And they weren't real brothers either, only half-brothers, for her husband was the son of Uncle Thomas. He was a bastard too because Mrs. Radlet was never married to Uncle Thomas. You were his housekeeper, you should have known she was a . . ."

Miss Brigmore was on her feet now and was crying, "Don't you dare use that word again in my presence! What has come over you, girl? You're acting like a fiend. All these years of training and this is the result; you are talking like some low kitchen slut."

"I am merely speaking the truth."

"Truth!" Miss Brigmore barked the word. Then her head moved slowly from side to side before she said, "Girl, you know nothing about the truth," and a voice inside her added, "I hope to God you never do," while at the same time she knew that this was the opportune moment in which to tell her all the truth, the complicated, bitter truth of her own beginnings. But she warned herself against taking such action for the result might be disastrous, coming as it would on top of this distressing scene.

As Barbara glared back into Miss Brigmore's face that for once was showing neither understanding, nor love, nor compassion, there was in her the craving to probe into something that she felt was being withheld from her. But there was also that in her, the fear that made her shy away from the knowledge; the fear was like a mist that was pursuing her and would one day catch up with her and envelop her, and she'd become lost in it.

They were staring at each other in as near enmity as they had ever been when Katie's voice came from the landing, calling, "Are you there, Barbara? Barbara!" There was a sound of a door opening and closing, then another, and a tap came on Miss Brigmore's door. Before she could speak it opened and Katie bounced in. Her round face was alight, her eyes shining; she was swinging her bonnet widely by the strings, but as she looked from one to the other she brought the swinging bonnet to a stop and, taking in the tense situation, she said, "I'm sorry; I didn't know you were . . ." She paused for a word to substitute for arguing, because she knew from experience that when Barbara got on her high horse a discussion could quickly turn into an argument, and an argument into open battle, and so, lamely, she substituted, "busy."

"No, no, we're not busy, Katie. Do come in." It looked to Katie as if Miss Brigmore were openly welcoming the intrusion, and when adopting her usually polite manner she asked, "Have you had an enjoyable day?" Katie answered on a high laugh, "Oh wonderful! It's been fun. He's great fun is Mr. Ferrier, so very entertaining. You wouldn't have approved a bit, Brigie, because he made me laugh out loud in public in the tea room."

"You had tea?"

"Yes. In a sort of club, a gentlemen's club. The seats were plush, and there were waiters. It was all so very grand." She ended her words in mock solemnity, then burst out laughing. Now, turning fully to Barbara, she asked. "Did you have a good day?"

"Very good."

"So we've all had a good day."

There was a slight pause in the conversation as she and Barbara looked at each other; then swinging the bonnet once more, Katie addressed herself in mocking tones to Miss Brigmore but in such a way that Barbara could read her. "I have to inform you, Brigie, that I am going to dinner at Burndale Manor. Evening dinner, not a three o'clock do, with entertainment to follow. I'm going to get an evening dress cut low, right down to—" She was pointing to the middle of her breasts when Miss Brigmore said stiffly, "And you accepted without consulting your parents?"

"Oh, Brigie!" Katie swung the bonnet in Miss Brigmore's direction. "Mother's tickled to death; I've just told her, and she said—" Now she adopted an attitude very like that of her mother. Holding out her arms and wagging her head, her voice took on the unmistakable Manchester accent: "Well lass, what d'you think of that! You're going up in the world, eh?"

"Don't make mock of your mother, Katie." Miss Brigmore's voice was stern, and Katie, now standing still, her bonnet held between her hands, looked straight at Miss Brigmore. "I am not making mock of my mother, not in the way you imply; and if I may mimic her face to face and she doesn't object I cannot see why. . ."

Miss Brigmore, her voice still stern, now checked her with, "If you cannot see why there is a difference in what you do in the privacy of your family and with its members, and what you do outside it, I'm afraid all my years of teaching have been for nought."

Katie continued to look into Miss Brigmore's face before she said slowly and in the diction of which Miss Brigmore would have approved, "I have been laboring under a false impression then; in fact, I think I may be correct in saying our entire family have been laboring under a false impression; and that impression has been created by you, because we, for our part, considered you were of our family. But I know now that we have presumed, and you are still Miss Brigmore and we are still the Benshams and that the gulf between us is very wide."

Miss Brigmore again had her fingers across her lips and was about to speak when Katie swung round and made for the door. But when she pulled it open with a jerk she was brought to stop; confronting her was the upper housemaid, Jenny Dring. Her hand raised as if about to knock, she gabbled, "Oh! Miss, miss; the master wants you in the bedroom. It's the mistress; she's, she's . . ."

"But . . . but I was . . . I've just left her."

"It's happened suddenly."

As Katie ran from the girl Miss Brigmore hurried to the door. "What has happened?" she asked softly.

"I don't know, miss, only that everybody's in a panic down there all of a sudden. The mistress was asking for them, and Mr. Brooks sent Armstrong post haste to the stables to get Mr. John and find Mr. Dan."

With Barbara behind her, Miss Brigmore now hurried down the stairs and through the gallery, and when they reached the main landing she turned to Barbara and said, "Go downstairs and wait." When Barbara hesitated, she added firmly, "Please." Then she went toward the door, knocked gently, and entered the bedroom.

Matilda was lying deep in her pillows; her face was drawn and gray, even her lips looked colorless. They were moving slowly as if mouthing words but making no sound, and Harry Bensham's voice, gentle and his tone unlike any Miss Brigmore had heard, was saying, "Yes, lass; it's all right, everything'll be done as you want." Then, his words dropping into muttered thickness, he said, "Here's Katie." He moved slightly aside but still retained hold of the fat pudgy hand.

The door behind Miss Brigmore opened and John and Dan entered, and when they went hastily to the bed she could no longer see Matilda's face, not only because she was surrounded by her family, but because she was allowing herself to cry audibly in public for the first time in her life. She knew in this moment that she was losing a friend, a friend who had considered her one of the family. Yet Katie's accusation was true, because on her part she had been in the family but not of it. The feeling of superiority that was a natural part of her nature and which had been engendered still further by the association with Thomas Mallen had created a gulf too wide for her to step across and embrace the Benshams, but she had been willing that they should cross it and benefit from the standards she set. She wasn't, however, entirely to blame for this situation because from the beginning they themselves had set her apart by deferring to her for advice on problems appertaining to the correct procedure to be taken, not only in the running of the household, but in personal matters also.

She looked toward the wash-hand stand by the side of which the day nurse was standing, her hands idly folded one on top of the other at her waist; and the fact that she was making no move toward the bed seemed to add a touch of absolute finality to Matilda Bensham's life. Blindly Miss Brigmore turned and went silently from the room.

Three maids were standing close together at the top of the stairs. They looked at Miss Brigmore's face and they bowed their heads and began to cry.

She went on down the stairs and was met at the bottom by Brooks. Brooks had never been the imperturbable butler; he had remained very much a working man; he had not acquired the subservience necessary for a good servant. There was an aggression, not only in his way of addressing one, but even in his stance, that would have made him absolutely unem-

104

ployable in the capacity of butler in any household other than this.

Now she looked at him through a tear-misted gaze and saw his chin going into a hard knobbled flatness as his lips pressed tightly against one another, and when he said, "It won't be the same; nothing will be the same," she moved her head once as she replied, "As you say, Brooks, nothing will be the same." She passed him and Armstrong, the first footman, and Alice Conway, the stillroom maid, where they were standing with their heads slightly bent, and she went into the drawing room.

Barbara, sitting on the couch, was not aware of her presence until she stepped in front of her, and when she looked into her face she stammered, saying, "Sh . . . she's not, she's not?"

"She soon will be."

"Oh. Oh." Barbara's face now crumpled; and then she whispered, "I'm sorry; I am sorry; you know that, don't you?"

"Yes, I know that, because you, like me, are losing a very good friend." She now lowered herself slowly down onto the couch. Her head bowed and, aloud but to herself, she said, "Things will never be the same again. He's right, so right."

It was strange, she thought, that a woman as common as Matilda Bensham had maintained the love of her family through their years of transition from the level on which she herself stood, to the present one, where they could class themselves as equals, at least in manner and speech, with any family in the country.

On looking back she remembered seeing herself in the position of buffer between Katie, the young lady who would emerge from her teaching and example, and the young lady's parents, for she had imagined the newly made young lady would undoubtedly look down upon them. How wrong she had been; Matilda Bensham had evoked a love in her family that could not be marred by education and the trappings of society.

If only Barbara showed half the love for her that

105

Katie showed toward her mother, then she would have had no need of late to stamp down on the comparisons she was frequently making between them, because these comparisons were creating a deep hollow within her, a hollow wherein she felt she would be forced to spend the remainder of her life.

FOUR

Matilda would have been proud of her funeral, for she had twelve coaches following her coffin, and all the horses wore bouncing black plumes. The drivers of the coaches were encased in deep black with tall shiny hats and bows of black ribbons on their long whips.

In the first coach sat Harry, John, Dan, and Katie; the next three coaches were taken up with Matilda's closest relatives. The fifth, sixth, seventh and eighth coaches held those nearest in relationship to Harry, and in the ninth coach sat Miss Brigmore, Barbara, and Mr. Pat Ferrier.

Three neighboring families were also represented. The Eldens had come, father and son, both having taken a day's leave from their chain of haberdashery businesses in Newcastle and district; the Fairbairns, too, he being of much more note than the Eldens in that he was a mine owner, at least in partnership with Jonathan Pearce; and Mr. Pearce was also represented by his son and his son-in-law. That these six gentlemen had been regular visitors at Burndale Manor for many years, being friends of Mr. Patrick Ferrier senior until his death, and afterwards continued to visit whenever young Mr. Pat was in residence, may have had some bearing on their showing their last respects to a woman at whom they had scoffed, and to whom their wives, after meeting her but once, had resolutely refused to proffer further invitations.

Following the last carriage came the male servants of the household, then the gardeners; lastly, the farm manager and his men. There were no female servants at the funeral; in fact, it had been a debated question whether any of the female relatives should attend, for it wasn't really etiquette; but as Harry's cousin Florrie Talbot had pointed out, who was there to notice or talk in this empty neck of the woods; now, if it had been in Manchester then things would have been different; you had to keep up a certain style there if you didn't want to get talked about.

And for once the female members of the family had agreed with Mrs. Talbot.

The sun was shining brightly; the birds were singing; they seemed to have assembled from the whole countryside in the trees bordering the small cemetery, and their song seemed to mute the sound of the first shovelful of earth being dropped onto the coffin, making it seem as if there were nothing in the highly polished, ornately decorated box. But there was something in it, and Katie, standing between her father and Dan, whimpered, "Oh! Mam. Mam." Her mother had liked to be called Mam, and so she had often used the term when Brigie wasn't about. She wondered why she wasn't crying. Dan was crying silently; she could feel the shudders that were passing through his body. It was odd, she thought, that Dan should be the one to cry. Dan, of course, had had a special love for their mother; it was undemonstrative but deep; but she, too, had borne a special love toward her. So why wasn't she crying? She had hardly shed a tear since her mother had died; she had felt over the past days that because she couldn't cry she'd never smile again, never love again. All the heart-lifting joy that had been part of her nature had, as it were, sought another course, and was flowing in another direction, a direction that was going to change her life.

It was just five days ago that she was in Hexham with Pat. He had said she must call him Pat, and before the carriage had reached the Hall he had taken her hand and told her he would like her to see his home, and would she come to dinner? Up till that moment she had looked upon it all as a game; as her

108

mother might have put it, she was tickled to death that a man like Mr. Ferrier should be seeking her out, while at the same time she kept her eyes shut to the consequences of his attention. But looking into his face that night, she had been unable any longer to close her eyes and her ears to the question he would be putting to her sooner or later; and also in that moment she was human enough to think, He is next in line to a title. . . . Sir Patrick and Lady Ferrier! She had almost giggled at the picture in her mind. She had giggled, too, a short while later as she bent over her mother and asked in a whisper, "How would you like your daughter to have a title?"

Her mother had smiled and touched her cheek and said slowly, and now she remembered how slowly her words had come, "All I would like for you, lass, is to know that you'll marry somebody who can keep you happy always . . . always."

Why hadn't she stayed with her then instead of dancing out of the room? Why hadn't she known that she was fading away before her eyes? And now she was down there and the sun was shining and the birds were singing and Dan's body was shuddering with his weeping, and her father was crying; all the family were crying now, everybody except her.

When she turned from the grave she took hold of Dan's arm; it looked as if he were supporting her and not she him.

There was a gigantic meal set in the dining room but only relatives were seated round the table. The seven gentlemen, including Mr. Ferrier, had taken wine in the breakfast room; then, after offering their condolences to Harry, they had departed in their carriages.

Katie did not take a seat at the table but slipped quietly away upstairs to the nursery. She hoped to find Dan there, for she hadn't seen him since their return. Instead, she found Barbara.

Barbara was standing looking out of the window,

and she had to touch her arm to attract her attention, and when they looked at each other Katie saw that Barbara too was crying.

Barbara now put out her hands and caught hers and said, "I'm . . . I'm sorry, Katie, so sorry. I . . . I was very fond of her."

For a moment Katie stared into the beautiful face, the face that at times she envied, the face that had often aroused her keen jealousy, which she would sublimate into compassion because of the affliction behind it, and she was surprised at herself as she said, "Were you?" for this wasn't a statement but a question, a question asked flatly, even accusingly.

"Yes, yes." Barbara had interpreted the tone of the words from the look on Katie's face and she added, "You know I was."

"You thought she was common."

"Oh! Katie. How . . . how could you say such a thing! And on a day like this too."

"Because it's true. You did, didn't you? You thought she was common, so common, not a bit like Brigie. You laughed at her at times."

"I never did."

"No, not to me you didn't, but with Brigie years ago when you first came, I heard you."

Such memories don't die and the color rushed over Barbara's pale skin. She said now in her own defense and quietly, "You . . . you must admit it is not a week since you were mimicking her yourself."

"I explained all that. It's a family license; you're allowed to mimic those you love."

"I . . . I loved her. You . . . you can't understand; I can't explain myself, but deep inside I . . . I did love your mother because . . . and not only because she was kind to me, more than kind, getting your father to give me the horse and clothes and so many other things, but oh"—she put her hand to her head now and screwed up her eyes—"how can I explain? I . . . I am not a nice person, I know I'm not, I say awful things, and I do awful things, and I put it down to my deafness, but it stems from something more than that.

110

But I want you to believe I was more than fond of your mother, because I . . . I envied you having her. When she used to put her arms around you and call you love or lass, I lost something; every time she did it I lost something. Oh, I can't explain, I can only tell you that many and many a time I wished she was my mother."

"What about Brigie?" Katie's voice was soft now, the stiffness had gone from her face. She sat down on the wooden nursery chair near the table and her body slumped but she still looked up at Barbara waiting for her answer.

Not until Barbara was seated opposite her, her hands joined, her forearms on the table, did she say, "It's different, Brigie is not my mother, she's . . . she's not even a relation. I love her, but in a different way; it's . . . it's gratitude, I think, yes, out of gratitude."

They stared at each other. Then Katie said quietly, "It seems to be a moment of truth, doesn't it?"

"Yes, yes, you could say something like that."

"Life's never going to be the same again."

"I know that."

"What are you going to do?"

"Marry Michael."

"What if you can't?"

"I will. If I can't have Michael there is no meaning to anything, nothing to life."

"Brigie's against it."

"I know."

"She wants you to have John."

"John doesn't want me."

"I wouldn't be too sure. I used to think he did. Yet at the same time you never know what John's thinking, not really."

"Anyway, I wouldn't have John; I want no one but Michael. And you? What are you going to do?"

"I don't know, I can't think. It's very odd; it's just as if I have changed to someone else over these past few days."

"Do you think Mr. Ferrier might ask you to marry him?"

111

"Perhaps, or perhaps not. He may just be amusing himself, as I was."

"Do you like him?"

"Yes, I like him, but liking isn't loving. The last time I spoke to Mother I said to her, 'How would you like me to marry a title?' and she said to me, 'All I would like for you, lass, is to know that you'll marry somebody who can keep you happy always . . . always.' And I think that is what one has got to find out. But how can you know if a man is going to care for you always? I think the best thing to do is to ask yourself if you can put up with him when he's not his charming self, when he's not laughing and joking and paying you attention. Dad used to yell at Mam"—Katie gave a cynical smile here. "You see how quickly one reverts, not Father and Mother as Brigie would have it, but Dad and Mam. At times they fought like cat and dog; he used to call her such awful names. When I was young I thought her second name was numskull." She smiled again, but the smile was tender now. "But all through it she loved him, and she knew that he loved her. She may have been a numskull—she was in lots of ways, she wasn't intelligent—but she was wise in her own way and she was full of heart, and I wouldn't have changed her for anyone. Do you hear that, Barbara? I wouldn't have changed her for anyone, not for all your Brigies, or your Aunt Constances, or any of the big-pots you're so proud of being connected with, because at bottom they weren't fit to wipe her boots! Do you hear me?"

She was shouting. The blocked reservoir inside her was spilling over. The tears were flooding up through her chest and blocking her throat; with an explosive sound they gushed out of her eyes, down her nose and out of her mouth, and she jumped up from the table and ran from the room.

Barbara made no effort to follow her, but she rose from the chair and tried to steady the trembling of her body by going to the window and gripping the high sill. She gazed out over the gardens and into the far distance where the moorland joined the hills, and she thought that they had indeed experienced a moment of truth, a moment of truth in which she had been made to face what she had always known deep within her, that you could love only one person, really love that is, and you could really like only a few people. She liked Katie, but she thought that Katie would never really like her again, and it wasn't only because she imagined she had looked down on her mother, it was something that went deeper, some change that had taken place in Katie.

And then there was John. She liked John, because John had always been kind to her.

And Dan? No, she didn't really like Dan; Dan annoyed her; Dan had never treated her with sympathy, but had acted toward her as if she were of no account. . . . And Brigie?

She had said that she had wished at times Mrs. Bensham had been her mother, yet hadn't Brigie played mother to her since she was born, and she should be grateful for that alone. She was, she was; then when had she stopped loving her? Gradually, she supposed, as she realized that she did not want her to have Michael; and also when she realized that she was withholding something from her, something that she should know, that it was her right to know; something that even Mary knew, because whenever she tried to get Mary to talk about the Mallen family she would become too busy, or would have a sudden toothache, or her leg would hurt her, always something to put one off.

Because of her deafness she had acquired a subtle sense that probed people's attitudes toward her even when she could not read their lips; but this did not overcome the handicap of being unable to hear snatches of conversation that might have helped her to piece things together.

There was no means of finding out what she should know other than through another moment of truth, and she was aware that that moment would only come when she herself forced it; and this she knew she was afraid of doing, for truth was cruel, it changed

113

the pattern of one's life. But didn't she want the pattern of her life changed? Didn't she want to fly from the cottage to the farm across the hills and spend her life by Michael's side? In his arms? In his bed? She bowed her head and bit tightly on her lip. Oh yes, in his bed. Nights were becoming nightmarish because she could think of nothing now but being beside Michael in his bed. Her thoughts on this subject, she imagined, would have shocked Brigie to the core of her being, for in that no-man's land before sleep finally takes over she saw herself standing naked before Michael; and not only that, Michael standing naked before her.

In the light of day she realized she was wicked, not so much because of what she imagined about herself and Michael, but because of the thoughts that always accompanied this image, the realization of which could alone turn her desires of the night into reality, and when, as today, the thoughts had dared to creep into the light as she watched the coffin being borne to the hearse, she had become physically sick with the force of the wish that it were bearing her Aunt Constance to the grave and not Mrs. Bensham.

Harry Bensham rarely called Miss Brigmore to his presence; if he wanted to talk to her he went up to the nursery floor where she was usually to be found; but this morning he sent for her.

Brooks informed Armstrong that the master wanted to see Miss Brigmore. Armstrong gave the message to Emerson, the second footman, who carried the message to the first floor, where he met Jenny Dring, the upper housemaid, and he passed it on to her.

Miss Brigmore was in her sitting room. She had just taken off her cloak and bonnet and sat down to review, calmly if possible, the situation.

It was a week since the funeral, and not during all the years she had spent in this house had she ex-

114

perienced such irritation. Matilda's prophecy had certainly come true. Mrs. Talbot was indeed attaching herself to Mr. Bensham like a blood-starved leech. The woman was an impossible creature, common—in such a way that Miss Brigmore regretted ever having applied the appellation to Matilda—while at the same time adopting a pseudo-veneer of refinement. Her accent and her idea of correctness both in manner and conversation would have been laughable if they hadn't aroused her disdain for the woman. To use Matilda's expression, Mrs. Talbot was scavenger material, and what was more distressing still, he, Mr. Bensham, did not seem to be adversely affected by her, in fact, at times appearing to be grateful for her solicitude.

One thing was certain, she herself could not remain in this house in any capacity were that woman to become its mistress. Although she had promised Matilda she would try to influence her husband against a close association with her she knew that this would be impossible; Harry Bensham was a headstrong opinionated man, and even softened as he was now by his bereavement, she couldn't see him accepting any advice from her with regard to his personal behavior.

Having received the message, she obeyed it. The expression on her face matched the stiffness of her back as she went down the main staircase, across the hall, and into the library. She opened the door and Florrie Talbot's shrill voice greeted her: "Oh, there you are! Thought you were never comin', dear. I was just saying to 'Arry here, he should close it up, for the winter like, like they do, 'cos he's got his house in the town. Haven't you, 'Arry?" She turned her big, fresh-colored face toward Harry, where he stood before the fire, one elbow resting on the mantelshelf. He did not reply, and she went on, "I just said to him, as good as you are, it's too much to manage on your own; 'tisn't fair, 'tisn't fair now, dear, is it? 'Tisn't like as if you were young any more, and sprightly. What's more . . ."

"Florrie!" Harry's voice was quiet, but although

the tone conveyed a command for her to be quiet it held no impatience; he might have been addressing Matilda when in one of his good moods.

"Well, I was just sayin'. I've been working it out, 'Arry. You've got enough on your plate with the mill and all that lot without having to bother about 'ouses, big, little or middling."

Again Harry said, "Florrie!" this time, adding "Go and see if Katie's near ready."

When, however, Mrs. Talbot showed no sign of rising from her chair and when the oily smile slid from her puffed features and her round blue eyes took on a steely glint, Harry's tone altered. There was a touch of the old harshness in it now as he said bluntly, "I want a word alone with Brigie. Now get on your way, Florrie; no more of it."

Mrs. Talbot lifted her heavy body from the chair; she did it slowly as if to add to her show of indignation, and she paused to adjust the bows of black ribbons on the six-inch wired platform of material that circled her already ample waist, and her departure from the room matched her dress, for she flounced out.

When the door closed behind her none too quietly, Harry looked at Miss Brigmore and, shaking his head, said, "She means well; and you know, I've been thinking these last few days she might be right. What do I want two houses for now? But as I've asked meself, if I had to give one up which would be the easiest for me to part with? And I've got to admit, the Manchester one." His lips bared from his teeth but not into a smile, it was more of a self-derisive gesture.

He stood now with his back to the big well of the empty fireplace and he rubbed his hands down the seat of his trousers, as he often did when the fire was blazing. He lowered his head for a moment before slowly turning his gaze round the room and saying, "It's funny how a place like this grows on you. You don't belong, you're an intruder, an outsider, yet you've got the upper hand, 'cos you've got the money, and you think you can buy yourself in . . . but you can't, 'cos money isn't what it wants, not a house like this." He brought his gaze onto Miss Brigmore now and said, "It was only me that wanted to stay put here. Matilda would have gone back to the town years ago if I'd said the word. But what I said was, it's the best place to bring up the bairns. And I was right, at least I think I was. What do you say?"

"Yes, I think you were right."

"Aye, you would say that, of course you would, and I think I was. But then again, it might've proved that we were both wrong, for in the first place there's our Danny. He can't bear to look on muck or poverty, it upsets him; he's got the make-up of a reformer or, worse still, an agitator; perhaps it was a damn good job he wasn't in the mill from a lad. Still, he's promised to give it a try for the next year; and he'll be along of John, and John's steady. Aye, I've got one rock at least."

He moved from the fireplace and, pointing to a chair, said, "You might as well get off your feet."

When she was seated he walked from her toward the desk at the end of the room, and stood to the side of it idly pushing papers here and there until she said, "Katie; she is going with you to Manchester?"

"Aye." He turned his head in her direction. "She made up her mind at the last minute; that's what I wanted to see you about really." He came slowly toward her again and, stopping within an arm's length of her, he asked, "Has she said anything to you on the side about this fellow Ferrier?"

A moment passed before she answered, "No, she hasn't given me her confidence."

"So you don't know if anything happened atween them?"

"No."

"He came late on yesterday and she wouldn't see him, said she had a headache; that's one thing she's learned, the ladies' excuse, a headache; meaning no offense to you." He gave her a sharp nod. "Well, he came in here, and from what he said, not right out like, but as they put it he implied his intentions were honorable, and I told her as much when I went up to see her.

117

It was after that she decided to come along of me the day. Her mother going has hit her hard; she hasn't taken it like the rest, no crying that I've seen. But with regard to the Ferrier chap, I can't understand it. She seemed all for him up to a week or so ago, and I don't mind telling you on the quiet I thought it would have been a damn good match. What is more, I like the fellow. He's almost twice her age, admitted, but that's not a bad thing. What do you say?"

"No, it isn't a bad thing."

"I don't mean about age, I mean about the man himself and the match."

"It would be very good on both sides; she'd make him an excellent wife."

"Aye, but you're thinking along the lines that she could pass herself, and there's all credit due to you for fittin' her for that kind of life. Aw well"—he pulled from his waistcoat pocket a heavy gold watch and, clicking the case open, looked at the bold-lettered face and said, "Time's running on, we want to make the town afore dark, I'd better be putting a move on. I just wanted to say one thing further; will you keep an eye on the place while I'm away? It may be a fortnight or more afore I'm back; I've already told Brooks to refer to you for anything he might want. And I think you could give an eye to the household accounts if you've a minute, they're getting staggerin'. The amount of tea that's used in the kitchen, they must be washin' in it. I've an idea there's quite a bit of stuff going out on the side. They get their perks and I'm generous with them at that, but I won't stand being done; I can't bear to be made a monkey out of; so will you look into it?"

She had risen from the chair, and she said quietly, "I'll attend to the accounts, but you'll understand that I cannot go over Brooks's head and investigate unless I have your authority. If you remember, I warned you that this situation might arise when you decided not to engage another housekeeper or steward after Mrs. Fairweather left."

"Aye, you did, I know you did." He was walking

away from her now. "And you needn't rub it in. Yes, you have my authority to investigate all you like, and I'll tell him that afore I go. And if you think it will help matters"—he half turned toward her now—"you can see about engaging a housekeeper because I can't expect to keep putting the load on you. But for how long she'll be here God knows, with the state me mind's in."

He turned more fully toward her now and finished quietly, "What I meant to say straightaway was, thanks for all you've done this past week, seeing to the crowd of them and everything. You impressed them, you did that, although I think they were a bit frightened of you." Again his lips moved from his teeth. "You know something?" His voice dropped low in his throat as he ended, "They're my folks but I was glad to see the back of them. Funny how your ideas change. But a little of them goes a long way now. And yet I'm ashamed of meself, thinking along those lines. Money's a curse, you know. You know that? It is"—he nodded slowly at her—"it's a curse, it makes you so that you're neither flesh, fish, nor fowl. . . . So long for the present, I'll be seeing you."

Flesh, fish, nor fowl. She turned and moved slowly back up the room toward the desk and, seating herself in a leather chair, she drew the scattered accounts toward her.

He had left her with the unenviable job of curbing extravagance and putting a stop to pilfering, and of choosing a suitable housekeeper, one capable of keeping Brooks in his place. And why would she be doing this? Merely to set the house in order for a new mistress after a suitable lapse of time. And most likely it would be that obnoxious creature who, because of their common ancestry and her past experience of men, would, as Matilda had prophesied, hook him on the rebound.

Well, there was one thing certain, the day that woman came permanently into the Hall would be the last time she herself would set foot in it.

BOOK III

DANIEL

ONE

It was now over three months since Matilda had died and during that time Harry had spent only four weekends at the Hall, on two of which he was accompanied by Mrs. Talbot; John's visits, too, had been fewer; only Dan had come every other weekend.

As for Katie, she had stayed five weeks in Manchester before paying a visit to the Hall, and after only one week she had returned to Manchester because, she gave Miss Brigmore to understand, she had taken up various interests there, one of which she was sure would gain her approval in that it had to do with education. She was, she said, teaching girls and women to write their names and addresses, as she considered it demeaning that any human being should be identified by an unidentifiable cross.

Of all the people and things affected by Matilda's death, and many were, Katie and her reaction were to Miss Brigmore the most mystifying. More mystifying still was the very fact that a person of such lowly birth, and one so utterly devoid of education or culture of any kind as Matilda had been, should now be influencing a number of people in such a way as to alter their lives.

That she herself had come under this influence was more than she cared to admit, but it added to the unexplainable situation when she posed herself the question, Was education so necessary after all for human happiness?

One thing Miss Brigmore was extremely grateful for during these trying weeks of being in sole charge of the Hall was that Barbara seemed to be making an effort to cooperate, in that her temper was more even and that they had on several occasions talked like two amicable companions.

On one special occasion when Barbara had reopened the delicate subject surrounding Michael's birth, she had thought it wise to tell her the truth so that she might view Constance in a more friendly and understanding light. It was true, she said, as Barbara had discovered, that Michael was not the son of Donald Radlet but of his brother Matthew. Constance and Matthew had discovered that they loved each other when they were forced to take shelter from a storm in the old ruined house on the fell. Barbara had sat enraptured during the telling, only breaking in to ask that things might be explained more fully on her fingers. One such point she had to make clear to her was that Michael had not been born in the ruined house up in the hills; Barbara had misunderstood her on this. She had not gone on to explain that he was merely conceived there. She had ended by saying, "You must never, never voice this. Promise me, now promise me, Barbara, that under no circumstances will you ever speak of this again. You discovered the truth by accident, and it is a secret you must keep to yourself."

Barbara had not promised immediately, but said, "Michael's no relation to the Mallens at all then? If Aunt Constance's husband was not Michael's father then Thomas Mallen was not his grandfather, then we are not even distantly related through my father being Thomas's brother—we're just cousins on our mother's side?"

Miss Brigmore had taken some time to answer, stooping first to attend to her shoelace before she had said slowly, "No, he is no relation." She had surrendered her last defense, at least in this sector of her private war, and she sighed deeply before she said again, "But now I ask you once more to promise me, Barbara."

Barbara had promised, and life had run very smoothly in the cottage since that night.

But Michael's own attitude toward Barbara puzzled Miss Brigmore at times for although he always appeared pleased to see her wherever they met, whether at the farm or the cottage, it seemed that he was merely humoring her and that his show of affection was drawn from him because of her affliction. Yet at other times when she watched them walking together and she could not overhear what they were saying, she imagined she could detect an affinity between them expressed merely by their proximity to each other. But what gave her hope that his affection was nothing more than brotherly was that he was in his twentieth year and if he were going to speak surely he would have done it before now.

And John? She was disappointed in John; she had pinned her hopes on John, for his manner toward Barbara had always been very affectionate. But he had scarcely been home since his mother died. Yet, perhaps it was the pressure of business that was keeping him away at the moment, rather than his recent bereavement. In any case, under the circumstances it would not have been correct to make a fuss over Barbara, and he always made a fuss over her when they met. But let her ask herself a straight question: Did he pay her more attention than he did others? She couldn't answer this because everyone was considerate for her; her looks plus her affliction seemed to draw men to her, all except Dan.

But there, she herself had never understood Dan; he had been one apart even as a child. Dan had been an obstinate, rebellious boy and had grown into an obstinate, rebellious young man, as his father only too well knew. She was finding his presence, when he visited home, more and more annoying, for he had developed the habit of drawing her into arguments with regard to class and social conditions. . . . Why should there be three classes of travel on the railway, he demanded to know. Some of the compartments weren't fit for pigs to travel in, and he knew because he had traveled by

125

all three. Eight hours from Manchester on wooden seats in a freezing box, would she like it? And why should one human being have to raise his hat and address another as "sir" just because the "sir" was driving in the carriage and the man was pulling down the steps for him to alight, or holding his horse's head? Things weren't right, wealth was badly distributed.

She had the idea that if Master Dan did not curb his tongue he would find himself in trouble before many years had passed over his head. Yet looking back, she recalled the time when she had found him interesting because of his lively mind. But minds needed to be kept under control, especially when they tended to be influenced by radical ideas.

There were times since Matilda's death when Miss Brigmore thought that she would gladly sever her connections with the family and retire to the cottage and live out her life quietly. Yet this thought would always be attacked by another; to do so would be dire ingratitude. Anyway, it would not be possible as the arrangement stood now, for Harry Bensham, in his generosity to her, had in a way elicited from her an unwritten agreement that she would help in the administration of the house for as long as she were needed.

It was not unusual for any member of the family to turn up unexpectedly, so on this particular Sunday morning in late September when Miss Brigmore entered the Hall she was not altogether surprised to see Katie descending the stairs, and she greeted her warmly, even forgetting to thank Armstrong when he relieved her of her cloak. Hurrying forward, she said, "When did you arrive, you must have got in very late? I did not leave until about seven last evening."

"Oh, we arrived about nine. How are you?" They were walking toward the breakfast room now.

"I'm very well. And you?"

"Oh, I'm fine."

Miss Brigmore looked at Katie and confirmed in

126

her mind that she did look fine. Her cheeks were red, her complexion clear, her eyes bright, her abundant hair glossy. She looked as she used to look; it was only her manner that had changed. There was a covert defiance in it, as if they were at loggerheads but being polite about it. But this was not so, for she was very fond of Katie.

"Is your father with you?"

"No."

They had entered the breakfast room where Brooks was placing a large covered dish on the sideboard. He turned toward them and said, "Good mornin', Miss Katie. . . . Good mornin', miss." The last was addressed to Miss Brigmore and she answered, politely, "Good morning, Brooks."

Katie hadn't answered the butler's greeting, which Miss Brigmore thought was very remiss of her but was in keeping with her new attitude.

"Would you like some breakfast an' all, miss?"

"No, thank you, Brooks." Miss Brigmore sat in the big chair at the head of the table and Katie sat to the right of her.

"Are the boys with you?"

"No, no they're not with me; you know, Saturday's a working day." Katie made the latter statement as if she were pointing out the fact that most people had to work on a Saturday and Miss Brigmore should be old enough to understand this.

"You didn't travel alone?" Miss Brigmore left her lips apart as she waited for the answer. But it did not come immediately, for Brooks was now placing before Katie a plate on which reposed two slices of crisp bacon, an egg, and a kidney, and when he said, "Will that do, Miss Katie?" she answered, "Yes, thanks, Brooks; just what I want."

As the man returned to the sideboard and lifted the covered dish Miss Brigmore asked again, "But you didn't, you didn't travel alone?"

"No, I didn't travel alone, Brigie; I came down with Willy."

The butler was walking down the room now and

Miss Brigmore, glancing at his back, waited until the door had closed behind him; then she said one word, "Really!"

"Yes, really, Brigie, I really traveled down with Willy." Katie swallowed a mouthful of bacon, then glanced sideways at Miss Brigmore. "Terrible, isn't it? I spent eight hours with the butler's son; no, nearer ten by the time we got here."

Miss Brigmore swallowed, then swallowed again before she said stiffly, "I don't know what you're trying to prove, Katie, but I can only tell you that if you're not embarrassing yourself, you are embarrassing others, and not least of all Brooks."

"Brooks?" Katie brought out the word on a high laugh. "Me embarrass Brooks because I traveled with his son? You don't know Brooks, Brigie; you never have."

Miss Brigmore eased herself back into the chair and sat stiffly upright, and she allowed a period of time to pass before she said, "And I'm beginning to think that I don't know you and never have."

"That could be." The words were flat, ordinary sounding. Then the tone changed as if a sharp gust of wind had blown open a door, and Katie's voice now was harsh, Miss Brigmore would have said commonly strident, as she said rapidly, "You've lived in a cocoon all your life, Brigie, and like all the people who've lived in this house before us you're half dead, you don't know what is going on in the world. I was saved, we were all saved, all our family, because we were born in Manchester, and our threads—and that's a big pun—the cotton threads drew us back there. It seems impossible to believe that you're shocked because I traveled in a train with a man whose father is a butler; you wouldn't have minded in the least if it had been Mr. Pat Ferrier, would you? Before Mother died I spent a full day with him and that didn't turn anyone's hair white, but because it's Willy, whom I've known all my life, it comes under the heading of lack of decorum. . . ."

As suddenly as her tirade had begun so it stopped,

128

and her whole manner changing, she put out her hand and grasped Miss Brigmore's arm and, her voice soft now, she said, "Oh, I'm sorry; I'm sorry, Brigie. Don't look like that, please. I . . . I owe you so much, I know I do, we all do. It's just that, well"—she shook her head from side to side—"they're two different worlds, this and . . . and the house in Manchester. There's only four servants there altogether and it's more like home. I can't explain."

The room became quiet. Miss Brigmore stared straight before her while Katie rested her head on her hand.

After a while Katie began to speak. Her voice low, her words hesitant, she said, "Before Mother died I used to have bouts when I thought I wasn't happy, and . . . and then I would tell myself I was, because I had everything to make me happy, and I'd laugh at everything and work up an excitement about clothes and horses; and finally when Mr. Pat Ferrier started paying me attention, and not just this year but last, I told myself that this was what I wanted. Then from Mother dying it all changed; it was just as if a curtain had come down on a play and I had to step back from the stage into real life. I . . . I know I've been horrible to you lately. You see. . . . How can I explain?"

"I shouldn't try, Katie." There was a deep hurt in Miss Brigmore's voice as she rose from the table, and Katie, grabbing at her hand, said, "But I must. I must. You see, you represent the, the other side of me, the refined side, and there is a refined side, and a taste for gracious living, and good books, and art, and all the things a young lady is supposed to want, all the things a young lady is supposed to need. But, Brigie, you were dealing with very raw material. We were already formed before you had us, and even when you had us there was still Mam and Dad on the side pointing out to us from where we had sprung. Don't you understand, Brigie? You know, as Danny said the other night, John's the only one you've succeeded with. John acts the gentleman, and he feels a gentleman, he's the same in whatever company he finds himself. I'm

129

not; neither is Danny. But . . . but we don't blame you, we love you none the less; it's just that you don't know the outer world, the rough and tumble of living. You ignore it as something not quite nice, you do, Brigie, you do."

Miss Brigmore slowly withdrew her hands from those of Katie, and she flicked imaginary specks from each side of her bodice below her breasts before she joined her hands together at her waist and said quietly, "You are under the mistaken impression, as many another, that only the poor suffer, that you've got to be cold, or hungry, or ill-housed before your heart breaks. Well, let me tell you that the poor have a great advantage over their superiors, for they can cry out loud when hurt, they can afford the relief of tears, they can wail in unison over bereavement, and when they are scorned they can, as they often do, stick their tongues out. Some male members of the upper class allow themselves certain relief to their feelings, but the female members rarely, and"—she paused long here before finishing, "governesses never," and on this she walked out of the room.

Turning to the table, Katie pushed her breakfast to one side and, covering her face with her hands, ground out, "Oh, Brigie, damn you! Damn you!"

Miss Brigmore was greatly disturbed, but she showed no sign of it as she took the morning's report from the new housekeeper.

Mrs. Kenley was an efficient, sensible woman, who was slowly winning the war against Brooks. Mrs. Kenley had been in good service and, as Mary would have said, she knew how many beans made five. Privately, Mrs. Kenley considered Miss Brigmore to be the only person in the household superior to herself, and this included members of the family, and so, therefore, she gave her the respect that was due to her. The term the other members of the staff gave to her loyalty toward The Brigadier was, sucking up; even so the majority were glad that she had quickly put a stop to old Brooks feathering his nest, the privilege which he had, over the years, claimed to be his, and his alone.

At this particular meeting Miss Brigmore informed Mrs. Kenley that she would not be staying to either lunch or dinner, nor would she be in tomorrow, but she could be expected on Monday morning. She trusted that Mrs. Kenley would see to the comfort of Miss Bensham.

Mrs. Kenley said she would indeed, and she assured her she would find everything to her satisfaction when she returned on Monday and that she hoped she would enjoy her rest.

Miss Brigmore thanked Mrs. Kenley, and Mrs. Kenley thanked Miss Brigmore, then departed, accompanied by the rustle of her black alpaca skirt.

The library to herself, Miss Brigmore sat for a moment stiffly upright in her chair; then rising, she went up to the nursery, where she stayed for an hour before going downstairs again, collecting her hat and cloak and leaving the Hall.

Her departure looked unhurried, as she intended it should.

She knew that Katie, when she discovered that she had gone to the cottage without leaving any verbal message, would go up to the nursery expecting to find a letter; and she would not be disappointed. The letter was merely a note saying that under the circumstances she felt that Katie was quite capable of looking after herself and in no way required a chaperon over the weekend.

Miss Brigmore defended her attitude as she walked briskly along the road to the cottage, for the brief, one-sided conversation in the breakfast room had put to nought almost fifteen years' work. Granted she had been well paid—when she counted their kindness and indulgence toward Barbara, she would concede, more than well paid—but money did not pay for everything; there were such things as loyalty and respect, and both had been denied her.

Why was it, she asked herself, that her life had

131

been made up of frustrated endeavor? Putting aside personal desire, she had gained little or no satisfaction from those on whom she had spent her life's work.

When she entered the cottage Mary's first words to her were, "By! you look off color." Then she added, "You're back early."

"I have a headache," said Miss Brigmore. "I excused myself. Do you think I could have a cup of strong tea?"

"Why yes, certainly, this minute. But if you ask me, you want more than a strong cup of tea. And I've said it for weeks, you want a break, a holiday, a long one."

Ignoring this comment, Miss Brigmore said, "Did they get away all right?"

"Oh aye; but not without an argument."

"An argument, what about? "

"Oh, Michael said he couldn't stay all that long, he had promised to be back by two o'clock or something like that. And you know she'd expected him to take her into Allendale! Still, don't you worry about her, go and sit down and I'll bring you that tea."

Miss Brigmore went upstairs and took off her outdoor clothes; then she sat down on the cradle stool in front of the dressing table and quietly and thoughtfully looked into the mirror. It was right what Mary said, she needed a change, she needed a rest; she wasn't as young as she was, almost in her sixtieth year. Of course no one would guess it to look at her. The few gray hairs that appeared she treated successfully with cold tea, and now they were hardly distinguishable from the natural brown. Her skin was still clear and although her cheeks had lost a little of their roundness there were few lines on her face except those at the corners of her eyes, and two vertical ones on her upper lip. Moreover, her figure was still very trim and firm. No; no one would ever guess that she was almost sixty. She could pass for fifty or less. . . . That was outwardly, but inwardly at this moment she felt every day of her age—and, moreover, she felt so alone, so very much alone. . . . She hadn't experienced this feeling so acutely

132

since the day the shot had rung out in Thomas's study and she had rushed in to find him slumped over the desk. Then she had known what it was to be alone, for no one had understood her like Thomas, no one but he had known Anna Brigmore. It was only at night in his arms that she had become Anna Brigmore; in the daytime she had remained Miss Brigmore even with him, and it had been a joke between them. But now she was Miss Brigmore to everyone; Miss Brigmore, Brigie, The Brigadier—and a person who lived in a cocoon. Such sweeping statements were forgivable because they came from youth, yet they nevertheless pierced you and thrust you deeper into isolation.

She had her cup of tea but did not follow Mary's advice of putting her feet up; instead, years of discipline coming to her aid, she decided to read; but something light, diverting. Yet when she went to the bookcase her fingers hesitated on picking up *Vanity Fair,* which she had read at least six times before, and hesitated over Mrs. Gaskell's *Mary Barton;* then returned to *Vanity Fair* and almost snatched it from the shelf. The last thing she wanted to read this morning was the problems of life facing Manchester mills and factory hands.

Yet it was at the precise moment when her mind rejected delving into this social problem that a "factory hand" knocked on the cottage door.

Mary entered the room almost on tiptoe and made her announcement in an undertone as if the visitor were a personage of high importance. "It's young Brooks, Willy, Brooks's son; he says he wants to see you."

Miss Brigmore put her head to the side as if thinking before she said, "Show him in, Mary."

Young Brooks was twenty-four years old, but the appellation young did not apply to him, he looked a man, a stiff-faced, arrogant man. He was above average build for a mill worker, for malnutrition and excessively long hours of labor when the bones were still soft did not usually tend toward natural growth. He was over five foot ten in height and broadly built with

133

it. His eyes were deep set and did not show their color at first glance, appearing to be black instead of blue. His mouth was full-lipped and wide, but his face was thin and would tend later to be lantern-jawed. His hair was brown and had a deep ridge in it like a wave running over the top of his head. He held his hard hat in one hand that hung down by his side, not as was usual with a man in his position, in both hands and in front of his chest. But what was his position? She was soon to know.

"Good morning, Miss Brigmore," he said.

"Good morning, Willy." The tone was the polite one she kept for the family servants, not stiff but without any touch of familiarity. She did not ask him to be seated but added, "What can I do for you?"

"Give me the key to the safe."

His request and the manner in which he made it nonpulsed her for a moment; then, her back stiffening, she definitely became Miss Brigmore. "By whose authority are you asking for the keys?"

"Mr. Bensham's."

They stared at each other before she said, "I have received no letter from Mr. Bensham to the effect that I must hand you the keys to the safe."

"Look"—he gnawed on his lip for a moment, then looked toward the carpet as if something had attracted his attention before returning his gaze to her and continuing, "Mr. Bensham wants a certain paper out of the safe and as I was comin' down to see me father he said it would save him a trip, he said you would give me the key."

"Mr. Bensham usually informs me by letter if there is anything out of the usual that he requires to be done."

"Well, apparently this time he didn't; he's a busy man. And anyway he likely saw no need for it when I was comin' down."

"What is so important about the paper that it cannot wait until he comes down himself?"

She watched the rough tweed of his waistcoat swell, then deflate again, before he said, "It's a deed."

134

"Mr. Bensham has a bank; I understand he keeps his deeds there."

He stared at her for what must have been a full minute, during which the point of his tongue came out between his teeth and traced his bottom lip several times. Then he said, "Well, apparently you don't know everything, Miss Brigmore. The boss—Mr. Bensham—told me there's a deed in the safe with the name of Pollard and Bensham on the envelope in the left-hand corner. He must have forgotten to mention it to you."

"I want none of your sarcasm, Mr. Brooks."

"Fair enough, Miss Brigmore. And I want none of your suspicion, or condescension."

Really! Really! What were things coming to! She was, to put it mildly, flabbergasted.

"And I don't happen to be one of the servants at the Hall, Miss Brigmore, I'll have you bear that in mind. I'm under-manager in the firm of Bensham & Sons; I have a standin', whether you like to recognize it or not; and what's more I've worked for that standin' from I was six years old. I'll shortly be made the manager of the factory under Mr. John. I bend me knee to nobody, miss, nobody."

Dreadful man, awful person, and yet she felt she could be listening to his master, Harry Bensham, when he would have been the same age, for this undoubtedly would have been his attitude. Then at his next words she found herself gripping the front of her bodice.

"While I'm on, I'll take advantage of the opportunity to tell you that although I might travel in a train with Katie, it doesn't mean I'm going to take her down, or that 'cos she sits next to me she'll get the smit. I might as well make it plain to you now, I've got a great concern for Katie, always have had, 'cos one day I'm going to marry her."

She did not feel faint as might have been expected on hearing the fate of a young lady whom she had trained to take her place as mistress of at least an upper-middle-class establishment, but she felt anger rising in her at the thought of all her efforts, all her work wasted on a man such as this.

Her words were cold and pointed like icicles as she said, "Have you made Miss Bensham aware of your intentions?"

"Not in so many words but she knows which way the wind's blowin', she's no fool; which she proved lately when she turned down the moneyed geyser you'd set up for her."

"You are being offensive, Mr. Brooks."

"Perhaps I am, but it's the only way to get through to you and your like; you live your lives on the side as it were, cosily shut off from the rest, and you never call a spade a spade." His tone softened, and again he looked down at the carpet before saying, "I suppose it's not your fault, you are how you are, no more than it's mine that I was born with nowt; the thing is, as I said, it isn't our faults, but it's up to us to change things if we don't like them. Apparently you've got nothin' to grumble about in your way of life, so you remain what you are; me, I don't change much in meself, but I'm determined, and always have been, to change the place and conditions in which this self has got to live, if you follow me."

She followed him all right, and she asked herself a question: Were all the men in Manchester like this, uncouth, raw, brash individuals? Was he really the cause of the change in Katie? No; as hard as it was to accept, she recognized that Katie was in essence made up of the same material as this man, he represented the other side she had spoken of.

The ice still in her tone, she asked, "Is Mr. Bensham aware of your intentions?"

"Not so far; I didn't want to say anythin' so soon after Mrs. Bensham going, but I mean to tell him as soon as I get back. It'll save you breaking the news to him."

"And you're already sure in your mind that he will approve."

"Well, almost you could say, 'cos he values me, not only because he knows that I could run the mill blindfold, but because he likes me for what I am! I'm a pusher just the same as he was."

136

What could one say to a man who openly exposed his less creditable traits in such a fashion, almost as if he were proud of them, as undoubtedly he was? Oh, she was tired of it all, worn out by the futility of trying to shape people who were already set in strong molds.

Again they were staring at each other; then turning stiffly from him, she said, "If you will kindly wait I will get my cloak."

"There's no need for that, just give me the key and I'll bring it back to you, or leave it on the desk."

Facing him fully, she said slowly, "Mr. Bensham left the keys in my charge; I will open the safe and allow you to take out the paper he requires."

She walked from him, her back like a ramrod, and while passing from the sitting room into the hall, she only just prevented herself from turning around and showing her indignation when his words, delivered on a deep laugh, came at her back, saying, "How did they stick it all them years!"

The weekend was over. Katie and that individual, as she now thought of Brooks's son, had left the house that morning together to return to Manchester.

During the farewells Katie had returned to her old self for a moment, saying softly, "Aw, Brigie, try to understand. I wouldn't have you hurt for the world, I wouldn't really. I'll never shame you, because there's part of me cannot forget that I am *Miss Bensham.*"

The farewell had done little to soothe Miss Brigmore's feelings. During the remainder of the morning she went about her duties, most of them self-imposed. Everything seemed to be as usual except there was that in Brooks's expression that annoyed her. He did not actually wear a half smile on his face, nor were his eyes laughing, but when he happened to address her she imagined she could hear him thinking in Mary's vernacular, You've had one in the eye this weekend, miss, haven't you?

Brooks, to say the least, irritated her and always

137

had done. However, in his case one avenue of relief was in sight; he was past sixty-six and he was no longer over-steady on his feet, there could be a possibility of him retiring shortly. But then, it wasn't her concern. If that dreadful woman became mistress of the house, which seemed more than likely, then there would be two of a kind controlling affairs, and it would be no longer any of her business, and so she need not trouble herself about it; but until such time she intended to keep Brooks in his place and also to make him aware of the fact.

So it was after lunch she provided herself with the opportunity by sending for Mrs. Kenley and informing her that the stewed carp had not been sufficiently cooked, nor yet had enough salt to flavor it; moreover, the last time she had ordered it, she had precisely asked that there should be quin's sauce served with the carp, not parsley. Would she inform the cook of this and she herself ensure that the error did not occur again?

Under ordinary circumstances she would have shown no such finickiness, but she wished for a confrontation with Brooks, and for it to be sought by him; he would undoubtedly mount his high horse when he found that she had ignored his superior position and made her complaints to the housekeeper concerning things appertaining to the table, for he considered the dining room and all therein his special domain.

She waited all afternoon for him to approach her; when he at last did, it was to announce in his most polite tone, "Mr. Patrick Ferrier, miss."

She was slightly startled by this announcement and she had to collect her wits from trifling mundane things to meet the questions she knew Pat Ferrier had come to ask.

"How nice to see you!" She extended her hand toward him, and he took it and bowed over it saying, "And to see you. And I hope I find you well?"

"Yes, I'm very well, thank you; one could hardly be otherwise, the weather has been so good."

138

"Yes, indeed; most unusual for England, and especially for this part of it."

"Do sit down."

When they were both seated she bent her head toward him and smiled as she said, "I had the idea that you had returned to France." She'd had no such idea, and she wondered herself why she'd said it.

"Oh, someone has been precipitate in forecasting my future plans. . . . Is everyone well in the family?"

"Yes, as far as I know they are all well."

Mr. Ferrier now gently stroked each side of his small moustache, which was immaculately cut leaving about an eighth of an inch of bare lip below its even line, and each hair looked as if it had been individually set into place. His clothes were also immaculately cut, the tails of his long cord riding coat hanging down each side of the chair like panniers, their color matching to perfection the soft shining brown leather of his high boots.

There was a certain asceticism about his thin face, yet his eyes had a merry glint to them, which was prominent now as he looked at her and said, "I'm happy to hear that Katie has returned home."

"Oh, I'm afraid her visit was very short; she left for Manchester this morning."

His chin moved to the side; his glance now shaded by his eyelids was cast toward the long windows as if he had just noticed someone passing, and when he looked at her again the merry gleam was no longer to be seen. As Willy Brooks had done, so he now stared at her for almost a minute without speaking; but unlike the reaction that other period of silence had had on her, she now felt a deep sympathy going out toward this man. She did not know what kind of life he had led when abroad, she only knew that he had loved his first wife and lost her so early in their marriage, and he must have seen in Katie a chance of reviving that brief happiness. She did not, at the moment, think of Constance in connection with him.

"Brigie—I may call you that, may I not?"

139

"Yes, Pat, of course you may."

"May I also ask you a very straightforward question?"

Unblinking, she stared at him before answering, "Yes, yes, of course."

"And expect a straightforward answer?" His voice was very low now.

Again she paused before saying, "Yes, if . . . if I consider it expedient."

"Only that?"

"Please ask me the question."

The leather reinforcing the inside legs of his riding breeches squeaked slightly as it moved against the silk tapestry of the chair before he said, "Is Katie purposely avoiding me?"

Expediency. There were many ways this word could be adapted; using expediency she could hedge, she could lie tactfully, or she could lie outright saying she knew nothing of Katie's intentions. What she did say was, "I think so."

He moved his head twice in small nods before he said, "Can you give me the reason for it?"

"No, not really; except that after her mother died her attitude to life seemed to change; she considered this"—she spread out her hands to indicate the drawing room—"and what the house stood for as too great a contrast to the lives that some people are forced to live. I . . . I think with her mother's passing she may have recalled much too vividly her early beginnings."

"She hasn't gone back to live under those conditions?" His face was stretched in inquiry now, and she shook her head and said, "Oh no, no; but she is busying herself with what is usually"—she gave a slight shrug of her shoulders now—"termed good works."

"Well, she must not be criticized for that. But I cannot see her changed opinions in that direction as an entire reason for avoiding me. Do you not know of any other, a new interest perhaps?"

She picked up the inference in his voice and replied, "Yes, a new interest perhaps."

"Oh." Again his finger went to his moustache, but

140

now he stroked it thoughtfully from the middle of his lip to the end, first one side and then the other, before he said, "Don't you think she might have told me? We had become rather good friends, you know."

"As far as I can gather the new interest has only been recently acquired. The first reason I gave you I think was the main one. She is very young and sees everything at present in black and white; there is only good and bad."

"Well"—he smoothed down the front of his coat, his fingers pausing as they came to each button, and when he came to the last one he rose to his feet, saying, "I mustn't detain you; I have a great deal to attend to before I leave."

"You are going away again then?"

"Yes, yes; your precipitate guess was correct."

As she looked at him she knew that her guess had been just that, merely a guess, and that his intention of leaving suddenly had been kept in abeyance, a reserve defense to counter what might be disappointment. As she walked into the hall with him she asked, "Have you seen Constance lately?"

"Yes, we met about a fortnight ago in Hexham; she was on a shopping spree, we had tea together."

On the terrace they stood for a moment in the late-afternoon sunshine looking over the garden, and as he raised his hand toward the groom on the drive below, which was an order for his horse to be brought round, Miss Brigmore said gently, "Constance is very fond of you, Pat; I believe you know that."

She hadn't looked at him as she spoke and she heard him sigh before replying, "Constance and I understand each other, Brigie; we always have done. I had a very youthful passion for her at one time; when she married it died. It would have died in any case, I think, because first loves are based on pure idealism and idealism is never strong enough to hold up life, married life. Yes, Constance and I understand each other."

She was looking at him now and she thought sadly, very sadly, how blind some men were, especially if they happened to be moral men. Thomas had never been blind to a woman's needs; but then Thomas had never been a moral man.

He was bowing over her hand again and saying, "When you next see Constance give her my warmest regards, won't you? Good-bye, Brigie. And . . . and thank you for your candor; you have been very helpful."

She said nothing. She watched him running down the steps on to the drive; he was still a young man, his step was light, his bearing and everything about him was what any sensible girl would admire. But were girls ever sensible?

A few minutes later, after he had mounted, he raised his hand to her in farewell, then urged his horse forward into a trot, and as she watched him disappearing down the avenue of trees she thought, Constance and I understand each other. Poor Constance. She did not think, Poor Pat, deprived of love for the second time, because a man such as he could find consolation if he so desired; nor did she think, Poor Katie, for although it went against the grain to admit it, Katie as she had become would be much happier with Brooks's son than ever she would have been as Mrs. Ferrier, perhaps someday Lady Ferrier. There remained Constance, and again she thought, Poor Constance.

TWO

Dan arrived at the Hall unexpectedly in the middle of the week, but it was not unusual for him to arrive at odd times for apparently his absence from the mill in no way affected the workings of that establishment. Since the staff had been given no notice of his arrival the carriage wasn't at the station to meet him, so he had taken a lift on the carrier's cart, he informed Brooks, then asked, "Miss Brigmore about?"

"No, she's not in today, Mr. Dan; Miss Barbara came along a while back to say she'd caught a bit of a chill an' was staying indoors."

"Oh." He walked across the hall to the foot of the stairs, and there he turned and said, "I'm going to have a wash. Have a drink sent up to my room, will you? Whiskey."

Not being an imperturbable butler, Brooks showed his surprise on his face. He hadn't known Mr. Dan to drink whiskey; a glass of wine with his dinner perhaps, and then he didn't seem overfond of that either.

When, a few minutes later, he handed the tray to Armstrong he said confidentially, "I've made it a double, he needs it by the look of him. Peaked, he is; hard work doesn't seem to agree with him."

When Dan came downstairs again he ordered a meal. "Something light," he said; "I'll have it on a tray by the fire, and I'll have it now."

The young master's attitude huffed Brooks. He considered that the six months Mr. Dan had spent in

143

the factory had not only taken some of the flesh off his bones and the color from his cheeks, but also it had altered his manner; there was a grittiness about it that hadn't been there before. He would have said he had turned from a boy into a man, even more so than Mr. John had, and Mr. John was older by more than a year. He didn't approve of the change; once upon a time Mr. Dan's manner had been almost chummy; now, the name he would put to it was bossy.

Brooks would have been very surprised indeed had he been able to read Dan's mind as he placed the tray on a small table before him.

It was hardly believable to Dan now that at one time all his sympathy had lain with the staff, when he had seen them as the poor underdogs; but, after having spent six months in Manchester he had become not only appalled with the conditions in his father's mill, which were considered good by the standards of the time, but also more incensed with conditions in mills known to be behinds the times. The whole scene horrified him and aroused in him an anger that he knew to be fruitless, for he could do nothing to alleviate the conditions he saw, or, more to the point, he was going to do nothing to alleviate the conditions, for once his year of probation was up he was getting out, and as far away as possible from the grime, poverty, and sordidness that hurt him. Time and again over the past months he had asked himself why he didn't do something, but he was honest in that he knew his efforts would be futile, for he wasn't the crusading type. There was in him, he knew, a soft core; how it had come to be there he didn't know, being the offspring of Harry and Matilda Bensham. He only knew that the sight of barefoot women, their bodies stripped of all but garments that looked like shifts, working like clockwork bees in an overheated hive caused in him a pain for which there was no salve but beauty.

Yet when he talked to the clockwork bees the majority of them would laugh and joke with him, especially the spinners whose ambitions or dreams he understood from them were simply of becoming weavers.

But there were those who didn't laugh and joke at their lot, for they were too old, too worn, too pain-racked, yet had to continue to work in order to die slowly.

Like Engels before him, he, too, drove through the streets of the poor on his way from his home on the outskirts of the town to the mill in an earnest endeavor to enable him to realize the real position of the workers. Idealistically, at first he had scorned the carriage, but a week of plodding through narrow alleys, battling his way through the stench that surrounded everything like a curtain of gas, of finding his boots covered with excrement, and more than once missing by inches an indescribable deluge from a bucket heaved out of an upper window, locked out for good and all his feeble ardor in that direction.

When he tackled his father about the conditions, suggesting that many of their own workers had to suffer them, Harry's caustic answer to his son's tirade had been short and telling: "Put a paddy in a palace and he'll fetch in a pig."

As time went on he had to admit that his father was right. They were a feckless crew, the Irish; yet strangely, these were the ones who, besides the stench, gave off the aroma of cheerfulness. They were also, he soon found out, no respecters of class, for they didn't recognize the barriers. Within a couple of days of his being in the factory they were addressing him as if they had known him all their lives. "Begod! You're looking well this morning, Mr. Dan. Now isn't that a fine piece of cloth you've got on you, as good as they'd make in any cottage in the old country. Tweed that is, isn't it? And every thread crossed with love. And you're the man to carry it, Mr. Dan. Christ Jesus! But you're an attractive looking fellow, you are that."

What could you say? What could you do?

What he could do and now, was to tell Brooks that he was having it soft, that the whole lot of them here were having it soft. But then Brooks had not always had it soft; wouldn't this be the life he, too, would like to give all of them, every man Jack of them back

145

there in the mill? There were seven of the indoor staff here from Manchester, his father had done that at least.

Oh. . . . He lay back in the chair, his meal untouched. This was Wednesday; he had up till next Monday to fill his body with fresh air and feast his eyes on the endless hills—and to see Barbara.

"Why hello, Mr. Dan," said Mary, "you dropped out of the sky?"

"Yes, Mary, just this very minute." Dan laughed down into her round, rosy face. "I'm the second fallen angel; I was on my way to join Lucifer, but I thought I'd just pop in."

"Aw you! Mr. Dan." Mary pushed him in the back as she had done since he was a small boy, then added, "Miss is in bed. She's got a cold on her chest an' I wouldn't let her up. You go in the sitting room there and I'll tell Miss Barbara you're here."

As he crossed the hall he cast a glance toward the stairs which Mary was now mounting stiffly, for her leg was troubling her. Then he saw her stop, and he too stopped and looked upwards to where Barbara was standing at the head of the stairs, one minute looking down at him, the next running down toward him, her face alight as if she were glad to see him. He stared at her as she came forward, her hand outstretched, and when he grasped it he did not speak but just continued to look at her.

"Why have you come? Anything wrong? It's only Wednesday." Her voice was high, her words clipped.

"Is it? I wouldn't know, I never count days." Automatically he mouthed the words.

"Oh." She shook her head at him the while she continued to smile. "Well, how did you get here? Did they know you were coming? Brigie didn't say."

"I arrived on the carrier cart; no one knew I was coming, not even Brigie."

They were in the sitting room now and as they

146

seated themselves at opposite ends of the small couch, he said rapidly on his fingers, "Are you very bored?"

"Bored?" She spoke the word.

"Yes, bored." He, too, now spoke the word.

"No. Why? Why do you ask that?"

"Oh"—he shrugged his shoulders—"I imagined you must be because you were so pleased to see me. The women have a saying in the mill, Better the divil for company than be alone with your mind."

The smile slid from her face, her chin went up, and her lips fell tightly together for a moment before she said, "The same old Dan."

"Yes"—he was smiling now—"the same old Dan, irritating, annoying, always saying the wrong thing. Anyway, how is Brigie, not really ill I hope?"

"No." She shook her head. "It's just a cold and . . . and she's tired. I've been worried of late; she seems listless, not her brisk self, you know?" She shook her body, stretched up her neck, and put her head to one side in a good imitation of Brigie, and he laughed and said, "Yes, I know."

"But what's brought you here, I mean in the middle of the week? How is the mill managing without you?"

"Oh, the mill." He pursed his lips. "It's closed down until I go back; everybody's out of work, but"—his lips pouted further—"what do I care? Let them starve." He waved his hand airily, and she, joining in his mood, waved hers too and repeated, "Yes, let them starve." Then they both laughed together.

"Are you getting used to it there?" she now asked.

"No."

"Why?"

"That would take a long time to answer. Come and see the mill and then you'll know. Yes, that's what you should do"—he was nodding deeply at her as he spoke on his fingers—"you should come and see the mill, it would do you good."

"It doesn't seem to have done you much good, you look thinner, much thinner."

147

"Yes." His face took on a mock sad expression. "I know, I've shrunk still further; I should say I'm almost three inches shorter than you now."

"Yes." She too assumed a mock attitude and her manner became matronly as she said, "I should say you are. Yet when I saw you standing at the bottom of the stairs I imagined you had grown taller. It was a mistake."

"Undoubtedly."

They were sparring but sparring amicably, which was a change.

"But tell me," she insisted, "what's brought you in the middle of the week?"

"Oh"—he made a dramatic gesture—"Dad thought it advisable to get rid of me for a time. You see"—he leaned toward her—"I'd fallen in love with one of the mill girls, handsome"—he spread his two arms in an embracing curve—"jet black hair"—he waved his hand around his head—"flashing black eyes." He now took his eyebrows between his middle finger and thumb and pushed them up and down. "Really, really attractive. He had the idea I was going to run off with her, so he separated us."

She gave him a scornful look before closing her eyes and turning her head to the side, and when she looked at him again he said solemnly, "It's a fact."

And in a way it was a fact; his father had separated him from young Mary McBride, for twice in two days she had made him sick. The first time she affected his stomach was when he was crossing the yard from the mill to the office. It was bait time. He saw her running to a bench in order to be first to get a seat when she slipped in a thick puddle near the closets. She had managed to save herself from falling but her bait had burst from the hanky, the slices of bread spattering into the filth. He had paused for a moment, thinking to go to her aid if she fell, and he still paused as he watched her pick up the bread and rub it on her skirt, then bite into it as she sat down.

His breakfast had been well digested when he witnessed this, and so the nausea had no result; but the

148

following day when by his father's side he saw her running between looms, then stop for a moment to scratch her head vigorously, take something from it, examine it for another second as she held it between her finger and thumb, then squash it under her nail against the side of the machine, he had put his hand over his mouth. Only fifteen minutes before he had returned from the club after eating a very heavy meal, and the sight of the girl ridding herself of head lice had the effect upon his stomach as a storm at sea might.

Looking at him in some alarm, Harry had shouted, "What in Christ's name! lad, you're not going to bilk, are you? My God! Because you saw her killing a dicky? Don't you know all their heads are walkin'?"

No, he hadn't known all their heads were walking. He knew that the body smell of some of them was nauseating, he knew that their lives were crude and their language cruder still, but what he remembered at that moment was what this girl had eaten yesterday, and the combination of the two was too much.

When his father joined him in the office a short while later he had looked at him somewhat sadly and said, "Look lad, I've been noticing, you've been peaked for days now. I was going to write to Brigie and tell her about the weekend, but you can take the message down instead. Get yersel' off first thing in the mornin'."

He had made no protest, it was like a reprieve; as he had told himself, the only antidote against it was beauty.

Now he was feasting his eyes on it. She grew more beautiful every time he saw her. Some day when some man told her she was beautiful she wouldn't be able to appreciate it, for soundless words and fingers, no matter how expressive, had unfortunately no inflexion.

When he saw that she was not going to meet his bantering mood much longer he said, "What I really came down for was to tell Brigie that the family will be arriving en masse on Friday afternoon, together with one extra guest."

"Katie too?"

"Yes, Katie too."

149

"And who is the guest?"

"Ah! Ah! That's a secret, I haven't to let on." He dropped into the vernacular.

"Don't be silly."

"I'm not being silly. I was told I hadn't to say anything about the extra guest until they arrived."

She looked intrigued now. "Is it someone that's been before?"

"Ah! You're trying to catch me. I cannot tell you."

She again assumed Miss Brigmore's attitude but quite unconsciously now as she said, "You are reverting to your irritating self. Why did you mention the extra guest if you weren't going to tell me who it is?"

"Because my orders were to ask Brigie to tell Mrs. Kenley to prepare an extra room."

"Male or female?"

"It doesn't matter as long as the room is habitable, the roof doesn't leak, the bed has sheets on it, and there's a fire in the grate."

She looked at him in annoyance for a moment; then, her manner changing, she asked, "Is . . . is the guest someone important, I mean is there something connected with him or her, some event?"

"Yes; yes, you could say that, there's something connected with him or her, some event."

"Oh, Danny!" She moved her head in two wide sweeps before going on, "No one in this world has been able to irritate me like you have. I . . . I was really pleased to see you, I haven't seen anyone for nearly a fortnight, and . . ."

"What's happened to the blond farmer?"

"The blond farmer as you call him has been very busy, it's the end of the harvest; they're preparing for the winter."

"Did they have a harvest supper this year?"

"No, no, they didn't have one." Her face was straight; her expression told him nothing.

"But they always have a harvest supper."

"Not always. Apparently Aunt Constance didn't feel up to it."

"Oh."

150

"Satisfied?"

"No. Do you still go over there a lot?"

"Yes, frequently."

"How frequently?"

"What a silly question! Whenever I can."

He was staring into her face as he told himself not to ask the question, but he did. "When are you going to be married?" he said.

"Married? Who said I was going to be married?"

"Well . . . well, aren't you? You're getting on, you know. You're nineteen this month and as Mary would put it"—he nodded toward the door—"you've been courtin' for years."

She was on her feet now, her expression almost ferocious and her voice high and shrill as she cried, "You're . . . you're impossible, Danny Bensham! You always have been. You are tactless, uncouth. . . ."

"Look, look." He rose slowly to his feet, but his hands came out quickly and grabbed her by the shoulders as she went to turn away, and he held her in a grip that hurt her as he mouthed, "It's no insult to ask if you are going to be married when you've been stark staring mad over the fellow for years. Hasn't he asked you?"

She went to wrench herself away but he still held her as he repeated, "Hasn't he?"

When her lips showed a slight tremble his own voice dropped and the mouthing of his words became less exaggerated as he said, "Well, if he hasn't it's about time he did, don't you think so?"

He watched her throat swell, he watched her gulping before she could get out the words, "Why don't you mind your own business!"

"Yes; why don't I. . . . Tell me, does Brigie still not allow you to go over alone?"

Her lids drooped and she made a small movement with her head. Taking his hands from her shoulders but bringing them together, he spoke on them, placing them so that she could read them from her lowered gaze: "I'd like to take a ride; shall we go out tomorrow?"

She kept the eagerness from her voice but was unable to do anything with the light in her eyes as she said, in mock politeness now, "Thank you, Mr. Bensham, I will accept your company, but as yet I cannot say if I shall enjoy it. Now would you like to come upstairs and see Brigie for a moment?"

He did not immediately follow her but remained until he heard her running up the stairs.

When he entered the bedroom, guided by her voice because it was the first time he had been upstairs in the cottage, she was saying to Miss Brigmore, "And they're bringing a guest and he's very mysterious, he won't tell me who it is."

"Good afternoon, Brigie."

"Good afternoon, Dan."

"I'm sorry to see you unwell."

"Oh, I'm not unwell, not really; this is Mary's doing, she is coddling me. Do sit down. Barbara tells me that the family will be down at the weekend and . . . and you have a guest, a surprise guest."

"Yes, you could say that, a surprise guest."

"It sounds very mysterious. Why haven't you to say who it is we may expect?"

"Because he wants to tell you himself. . . . Dash, now I've indicated that the guest in question is female."

Miss Brigmore continued to keep the thin smile on her face as she looked at Dan; it hadn't been hard for her to identify the mysterious guest as female. She asked now, "Is it to be an occasion?"

"Yes; as I said to Barbara it's to be an occasion, but not a very elaborate one under the circumstances."

Why couldn't he have told her himself? He must have known what was in his mind a fortnight ago when he was here, but likely he was ashamed of the fact that he had chosen someone so soon to take Matilda's place. She had promised Matilda she would try to do something to prevent this very happening, but what could she do? Mrs. Talbot was a woman who would bulldoze her way through a stone wall. From something John had let slip on his last visit she had gathered that the woman had almost taken over the housekeeping of the

Manchester house. Never off the doorstep was the term he had used, and he had added, as his father had done, "She means well, does Auntie Florrie." And now the mysterious guest was to be Mrs. Talbot and the occasion, the announcement of their forthcoming marriage. Really! When she came to think of it it was disgraceful, disrespectful; it would never happen in organized society. Matilda had said she'd hardly be cold in her grave before that woman got to work on him, and her words had come true, for it was now just over six months since she had died. Well, two things were certain: first, the announcement would put the seal on the plans for her own future; secondly, as much as she owed Mr. Harry Bensham no amount of gratitude on her part and no persuasive talk on his would coerce her into attempting to make a silk purse out of that big gormless numskull.

Part of her mind chastised her for resorting to Mary's verbal level for words to describe the woman; pretentious, ignoramus, would have been more appropriate.

"Shall I pass the order on to Brooks with regard to what you would like doing, it will save you having to bother?"

"Not at all, not at all." She shook her head sharply. "I shall be down tomorrow, and I shall make the preparations, as usual, with Mrs. Kenley. I shall work out some menus tonight."

"You shouldn't get up for a day or two."

Miss Brigmore looked at Barbara and replied, "I am perfectly all right; it's nonsense that I should be in bed at all." She turned to Dan now. "Will you be at home for dinner tomorrow?"

"Well, I thought about going out riding, and I've asked Barbara if she'd like to come along, that's, of course, if you can spare her."

"Oh, yes, of course." Miss Brigmore looked at Barbara now as she answered Dan. "That'll be nice. You can go into Hexham and get some shopping; I need some wool and tapestry threads."

Barbara's expression did not alter but her voice

was flat as she said, "Danny said he would like to go over to the farm."

"Oh." Miss Brigmore blinked now; then again she said, "Oh," and turned her head slightly toward Dan while keeping her face in full view of Barbara's as she said, "I'm afraid that would be inconvenient because of the wedding."

"What! What did you say?"

"The wedding, dear." She spoke directly to Barbara now. "Lily Waite is marrying Bill Twigg."

Barbara could not prevent her body from slumping visibly, and her hands gripping the bed rail relaxed. She smiled faintly as she said, "Oh, Lily Waite. I didn't know."

"Nor did I until Mary told me just a short while ago. Apparently Jim Waite called in and he mentioned they were all very busy. Constance is giving the couple a wedding breakfast in the barn."

Barbara was staring at Miss Brigmore, repeating in her mind, a wedding breakfast in the barn. She had seen Michael a week gone Sunday. He must have known about the wedding then yet he hadn't mentioned it. A wedding breakfast in the barn . . . there'd be dancing. Sarah Waite would dance; she'd do the clog dance and then she would waltz, she'd waltz with Michael. She felt the old fury rising in her again, then checked it. She must stop thinking this way. Michael had been wonderful to her the last time they had met; they hadn't ridden into town but had raced all over the moors; they had sat on the stone bridge over the burn, then he had guided her over the stepping stones and had caught her when she slipped, holding her close for a moment, and they had laughed into each other's face. It had been a wonderful day. She had never been so happy for a long time, and the happiness had stayed with her up till now. But a moment ago she had received a shock when Brigie mentioned the word wedding at the farm. This, coming on top of Dan asking her when she was going to be married, revived the question she was continually asking herself: When was she going to be married? It was time he spoke; if he didn't speak soon, she would, because she couldn't bear the uncertainty much longer. He wanted her as much as she did him, she knew this, she was positive of it. Deep within she knew that he desired her, and there was only one thing, one person, stopping him from declaring his love for her, and that was his mother.

He could not help but be aware that his mother didn't like her, and so he was torn between two loyalties; but he was young and had his needs, needs which a mother couldn't fulfill; yet her Aunt Constance had done her level best to supply them all, with the exception of the most vital one. And it was here that she herself held the winning card; for this need, sooner or later, would bring Michael to her, and a thousand mothers, a thousand Aunt Constances couldn't prevent it.

She was unaware that Mary had entered the room until she passed her and put a tray on the bedside table to Miss Brigmore's hand and, turning to her, said, "I've set yours downstairs, don't let it get cold."

"You should have asked me, I would have brought it up." Barbara's manner was now conciliatory as she looked down at Mary's swollen foot, and Mary said, "Stop blatherin' and go and get your tea. You an' all, Mr. Dan." And she now shooed them both out of the room as if they were children; then coming back to the bed, she poured out a cup of tea for Miss Brigmore and as she handed it to her she asked, "What's brought him then?"

"Just to say that the family are expected home for the weekend and they're bringing a guest."

"A guest? Who's it likely to be?"

"I don't know, Mary." Miss Brigmore and Mary exchanged straight looks. "But it's my guess it's the future Mrs. Bensham."

"Well, well." Mary shook her head. "If he had galloped from the grave he couldn't have done it much quicker, could he? Disrespectful I'd say, wouldn't you? Is it that woman, that Mrs. Talbot who got on your wick?"

"Yes, Mary, Mrs. Talbot; at least, I assume it is."

Well, there's one thing certain, an' I suppose you can be glad of that, being the age she is there'll be no bairns to bring up. Not that you would want to, for you've had enough. Anyway, at your time of life you're past it, and about time too, I'd say. . . . There now, drink your tea; I'll go down and see to the pair of them."

Miss Brigmore did not seem to draw in another breath until the door had closed on Mary. Past it! She was past nothing, nothing at all, nothing that went to make up life. Inside, her emotions were still flourishing, every single one of them, and painfully. That was why she was so incensed about this woman, this Talbot woman. Thomas would surely turn in his grave at the thought of such a creature being mistress of the Hall. . . . Yet she hadn't thought of him turning in his grave when Matilda became mistress of it. Oh, Matilda was different. . . . But what had Thomas to do with it anyway; it was Mr. Harry Bensham's business, his choice. The man had no taste. Of course this was no news to her. In taking the Talbot woman he was but keeping to his own standards. And could she really blame him? Yes.

THREE

The big black iron-studded doors were wide open. Miss Brigmore stood some way back within the lobby while Brooks and Armstrong went down the steps to where the carriage was drawing up on the drive below.

When the carriage door was opened and the steps were pulled down Harry Bensham was the first to alight. He did not turn to assist anyone out of the carriage but spread his arms wide, took in one gulp of air, then came up onto the terrace and into the house.

"Well! Here we are again. By! It's grand to smell the air. I think I'll bottle some and take it back with us. How are you? Let me look at you." To her embarrassment he put one hand on her shoulder and pulled her round toward the light so that her eyes were taken from the carriage for a moment.

"You're lookin' washy; aren't you eating? With air like this and good food you should be as round and as comfortable as a tub."

When she could get a word in she said, "My health is quite all right, thank you. And yours?"

"Oh me?" He was letting Emerson divest him of his coat. "No need to ask about me; I'll never die from disease, they'll have to shoot me. You know the best cure against disease?" He poked his face toward her. "Go amongst it, that's what I say, live amongst it. . . . Well, it's nice to be back again." He cast a quick glance around the hall, then turned toward the door where Katie was entering with a strange young woman by her side.

Where was Mrs. Talbot, she certainly wouldn't be coming up in the rear? Mrs. Talbot was always to the fore. And who was this person?

As Katie came up and kissed her on the cheek, saying, "Hello, Brigie," and she was about to give her a greeting, Harry Bensham shouted to John, who was entering the hall, "Come on then, lad, come on, do the honors, it's your business."

"Hello there, Brigie." John was bending down to her. He also kissed her cheek; then putting his hand out toward the stranger, he drew her nearer, saying, "May I present Miss Jenny Pearson. Miss Brigmore, Jenny."

The young lady extended her hand and Miss Brigmore took it. This then was the surprise, not Mr. Bensham going to marry the Talbot woman, but John presenting his future wife. The hopes that had become slender of late, yet which she stubbornly insisted on preserving, snapped and sank into the well among her other unfulfilled desires, taking with them the picture of Barbara ever becoming mistress of this house.

It was unfair. He had over the years shown an open affection for Barbara, at the same time giving evidence of having no interest in any other woman . . . yet what proof had she of this when for the past six months nearly all his time had been spent in Manchester? The name Pearson had a familiar ring. Yes, yes, of course; this was likely the daughter of the rival mill owner. She remembered first hearing the name years ago when there was talk of a strike. She could even recall the exact time; she pinpointed it by remembering it was the first time she had seen Willy Brooks in the library.

But this girl; she was plain, tastefully and well dressed admitted, but very plain; and he had chosen her rather than Barbara. Yet the reason, she felt, wasn't far to seek. Like his father before him he was marrying a mill, in this case another mill; very likely a bigger

and wealthier mill . . . women always had values set
on them.

"How-do-you-do?"

"How-d'you-do? I've heard so much about you,
Miss Brigmore; I am very pleased that I'm able to make
your acquaintance at last."

Well, she had been educated, that was something;
and her voice was pleasing, musical she could say;
and now she was smiling she did not look so plain.
She could imagine that she could be of a kindly nature.

"Come on, come on, what are we standing here
for?" Harry was shouting across the hall now. "You
take Jenny up to her room, Katie. By the way"—he
turned around and looked toward Miss Brigmore—
"where's our Dan? And for that matter, where's Barbara?"

"They're . . . they're both up in the nursery. . . ."

"What! At their age?" He put his head back and
let out a great bellow of a laugh. Then noticing the
expression on Miss Brigmore's face, he flapped his hand
at her and said, "All right, all right, bad joke, but what
they doin' up there?"

Miss Brigmore hesitated before giving him the
answer. "Dan is doing a sketch of Barbara in an endeavor to paint her portrait."

"Paint her portrait! Well! Well! And by, you've
said it, endeavor's the right word, for if he's as successful at that as he is at learnin' a business. . . . Aw! What's
the good of keeping on. Come in here a minute"—he
jerked his head in her direction—"I want a word with
you afore I go upstairs. And as for you, Katie"—he
now called toward his daughter where she was mounting the stairs with Miss Pearson—"when you've got the
dust off you you'd better take Jenny up to the nursery
an' introduce her to Barbara; better get it over."

On this he turned and walked toward the library,
and after a moment Miss Brigmore followed him. Having to pass John on the way, she stopped and, looking
straight at him, she said, "On short acquaintance I approve your choice, John."

A flush spread over his face, and she could not say whether it was caused through embarrassment or pride; but he answered warmly, "Thanks, Brigie, thanks."

She went into the library, and after closing the door quietly she walked down the room to where Harry was already standing in his usual position with his back to the fire, his hands on his buttocks. As she moved toward him she felt she had been doing this at intervals all her life, walking down the room toward this man while her body stiffened and she bristled inwardly in preparation for the attack he would undoubtedly make on her senses. And today, as on other occasions, she did not find the preparation had been unnecessary, for the first thing he said to her was, "I've just told Katie to break it to Barbara. But she'll take it all right, that one, 'cos she's got her sights set elsewhere; it's you it should have been broken to, isn't it, 'cos you thought John had his sights on her? In fact, in a way, I could say you've been working at it."

"Really, Mr. Bensham!" Her indignation was evident, in her voice, her face, her back. "You are insulting. You . . ."

"Aw now, Brigie, you know me; a spade's a spade. And be honest. Come on, woman, be honest, you hoped to make a match of them. And you know, I'm going to tell you something, I did an' all. I was a bit put off by her deafness at first, but then I thought, He likes her, he understands her, he's got sympathy for her; and her drawback's more than made up for by how she looks, because she looks a spanker, like a thoroughbred. But over the past year or so I've realized it was just sympathy, that's all, 'cos she draws it from you, you know; she draws it from everybody."

He stared at her now in silence and when she made no effort to speak he slapped at his buttocks and the sound was like that on a horse's flank. Then, half apologetically, he said, "I'm not saying, mind, I wasn't pleased about him wanting Jenny, and for more reasons than one, because I'm human. She's an only child, she'll come into the mill. Yet with him, it was

160

meself over again as I once told you, but in a different way, 'cos he's taken Jenny because he loves her, and that's the right reason. And you know, when he first let on to me about this I thought of you. Aye, you were my first thought. She's going to be disappointed, I thought."

She closed her eyes, then opened them sharply to find him standing in front of her, his hand coming out to take her arm.

"Come on, come on, sit down. Get out of your stays."

Really! Really! Why did she submit to it?

She submitted to being led to the couch and plonked down as if she were a willful child; and there he was standing in front of her grinning; then turning abruptly away he said, "Let's have a drink, I'm parched."

He pulled the tasseled cord to the side of the fireplace and a moment later, when Brooks entered, he said, "Get us a drink, Brooks. Bring the decanter."

"No spirits for me, thank you." Her voice was merely a stiff whisper, and he said, "Oh aye." Then turning to Brooks again, he added, "Put some wine on the tray, a port."

"Aye, sir."

"How you gettin' on with him now?" Harry jerked his head toward the door, and Miss Brigmore jerked her chin upwards as she asked, "Getting on with whom?"

"Brooks, of course; you know who I mean, don't play dumb, Brooks. You've never hit it off, now have you? No. Anyway, I was thinkin' about him recently. He's gettin' past it; I'll pension him off soon. And while I'm on about him I'd better tell you something else. It won't come as such a shock to you as it might have done because, as I understand it, he baited you in your den."

"Baited me in my . . . what do you mean?"

"I mean Willy. You know I do, don't you? Now mind. . . ." He now came and sat on the couch, not beside her but in the further corner away from her, and

161

he leaned his head against the back of it before he said, "I can't say I was over the moon at his proposal, not that I've got anything against him, he's a good lad is Willy, but at the same time I'd somehow set me sights high for our Katie. I thought she had an' all, and I'm positive that she would have made a go of it with Ferrier if Matilda hadn't gone when she did. But it was something in her going that changed our Katie. She's tried to explain it to me, but I'm not one for delving into the cobwebs of the mind. She says now she wants to live out her mother's life, do the things she knew her mother wanted to do deep within her, make things better for people like her mother used to be when she was young. Well, that was all very well, and worthy, but I put my side of it to her and told her what's being done in the town. I pointed out to her there was an Education Act gone through these last few years, and a lot of my younger lasses could read. I won't say they favor the *Saturday Review,* but I've caught them pushing *Ella the Outcast* into their busts, and *Gentleman Jack* an' all. I've had a laugh about that one many's the time." He put his head back and laughed now while she continued to stare at him, then he went on, "Well, like I told her, Manchester hasn't just been dug up, there's dozens of bookshops all over the place if folks want to read, but like all reformers she's got the idea that they've been sitting in the mud just waitin' for her to come and clean them up, mentally like—I won't say that some of them don't want cleanin' up otherwise—but that'll come in time. But being Katie she's not content to wait, nothing's being done in the way she thinks it should be. . . . You know, her and our Danny are a pair, but with this difference, she goes in head first and does something about it, while our Danny turns and runs. It's funny, isn't it, them both thinking alike, having the same things at heart, and yet it's the woman, the female, doin' the pushing. That's something that's hard for me to stomach, you know. . . . Oh"—he leaned toward her now and wagged his finger at her—"you're not the one with worries, I've had me share these past few

162

months. Anyroad, I found Willy's intentions more honorable that those of some of the gentlemen I could name, for he said he'd say nothing to her until a year had passed from Matilda going. By that time, too, he hoped for a rise in position."

He laughed now, a deep rumbling laugh coming from his belly as he said, "He told me as much. Aye, you know, he's very like meself at his age; the things he says and the things he does was just me at that age. And so I cannot help but like the lad. You understand that?"

The question had been put to her softly and she answered, "Yes, yes, I can understand that."

He was looking into the fire as he said, "Their concerns have kept me mind off meself these past months. You know, it's funny, but sometimes I didn't see Matilda for two to three weeks at a time, but I knew she was here waitin', and the minute I came in at the door she would say, 'Oh, there you are, lad. Well, how is it?' and with that I would know I was home, because it's a woman that makes a place a home, not furniture and folderols." He allowed his gaze to travel slowly from one side to the other of the fireplace, then said, "I've told you, I think, that I like this place better than me house in Manchester, aye, much better; yet that's become more like home recently because they're all there, you see, Katie, John, Dan. And then there's Florrie. Huh!" He jerked his chin. "Florrie . . . Florrie's always there, she's so big and bouncin', she's there when she's not there, if you know what I mean."

He turned his head and looked at her, and she at him, and she replied stiffly, "Yes, I know what you mean."

Now he was leaning toward her again, his voice a humorous murmur now. "She's another one you didn't cotton on to, isn't she?"

"I suppose you could say so; I didn't find her company compatible."

"Eeh!" He shook his head at her while laughing loudly again. "That's putting it mildly. By! You have a nice way of expressing yourself. But then you always had. That's your business, isn't it, to express yourself nicely? Aw"—he turned round—"here's the drink."

After Brooks had placed the tray on a side table and Harry had poured out a glass of port and for himself a good measure of whiskey, he handed her the wine, then held his glass toward her as he said, "Here's to a better understanding, eh, all round?"

She did not reply to the toast but inclined her head slightly toward him; then when he was seated again he almost catapulted her from the couch with his next remark.

"You know, Brigie, it's hard to believe, in fact it's almost impossible to believe you've been married in a way—being a man's mistress for over ten years is just the same as . . . oh God! don't choke yourself." He took the glass from her hand. "I . . . I haven't said anything out of place. What I mean is, I meant no offense, I was just leading up to something I was meanin' to tell you. . . . Oh blast!" The exclamation was muttered as the door opened and John entered.

Miss Brigmore had risen from the couch. She did not look at Harry but walked behind it, her hand over her mouth as she tried to restrain her coughing.

As she passed John he looked toward his father, and Harry said, "The wine, it went down the wrong way. Aw, I'm off to change." Yet he didn't move but brought a look of surprise to John's face and caused Miss Brigmore's chin to jerk upwards and her coughing to increase with his remark, "There's a lot to be said for the Florrie Talbots of this world. You take my word for it, lad."

When Miss Brigmore reached the nursery floor she did not pause on her way to her room, nor cast a glance toward the schoolroom from where were coming very unladylike peals of laughter, among which she recognized Barbara's; but the sound bore out Mr. Harry Bensham's remark that Barbara would be unaffected by John's news.

Reaching her own room, she stood leaning with her back against the door, her hands joined tightly together at the nape of her neck. He had dared to say

164

that to her. It was impossible to believe. . . . Married in a way, a man's mistress! She had never been Thomas's mistress, she had been his wife in all but a marriage ceremony, she had been his wife, a true wife. Laws! What did laws know about relationships? With a swift movement she turned and buried her face in the crook of her arm against the door and she cried as she hadn't done in years.

When the door was thrust open she stumbled backwards gasping; then, her eyes blinded with tears, she looked into Barbara's startled face.

"What . . . what is it, Brigie? Oh! Brigie." Barbara's arms were around her, leading her to a chair, sitting her down; then she was on her knees, her arms still about her waist, still saying, "Oh! Brigie, Brigie; what is it?" And all of a sudden she was sitting back on her heels and, her fingers moving rapidly, saying, "Oh! Brigie, don't take it like that; John wasn't meant for me, nor I for John. You must have known it for a long time. Brigie, Brigie darling." She brought herself upwards and took Miss Brigmore's wet face between her palms and, her own eyes soft and pleading now, she gazed into the face of the woman who had been mother to her all her life, and she said, "It's no good, Brigie, you've got to face up to it; there's only one for me, ever, and that's Michael. If I don't have Michael I don't want anyone. I'll end my life like you, an old ma—" Her fingers stopped tapping, her head drooped quickly and she said, verbally, "I'm sorry, I didn't mean that; you . . . you could never be an old maid. And if I end my days like you, it . . . it will be an honor. But I could never really be like you, I know that, I'm too selfish, too headstrong. But I also know that I will be a different person altogether once . . . once I marry Michael. He'll make me different, he'll make me good. I don't expect you to understand my . . . my need for him, but . . . but I need him so much. You . . . you wouldn't know how I feel, not having experienced . . ."

"Be quiet! Be quiet!"

"But Brigie."

"Be quiet, girl! Say no more."

165

It was too much, it was too much. Within the last few days she had been told that she was too old to experience emotions, she had been reminded only a few minutes ago that she had played mistress to a man for a great number of years, which in the ordinary way had stamped her as a whore, and now here was Barbara trying to explain to her that because she had never been married she was unable to understand the needs of the body.

But when all was said and done she was still Miss Brigmore.

Drying her face she turned to Barbara now and said, "Leave me for a while; I'm going to wash and change. I'll see you downstairs in a short while."

"Don't be vexed with me, Brigie."

"I'm not vexed, dear."

"But you're very disappointed."

"Disappointed, yes, but not very." She did not add that this was not the reason for her distress; but it was just as well to let her think it was.

"She's . . . she's quite a nice girl and I think very suited to John."

"Yes . . . yes, I'm sure what you say is quite true."

"You know I wouldn't hurt you willfully, don't you, Brigie?"

"Yes, yes, dear, I do."

In this moment Barbara meant what she said for all the old feeling of affection had rushed back into her as she had witnessed Brigie crying so passionately. She had never thought to see old Brigie give way like this, and all because John hadn't chosen her. For her part, she was relieved that the obstacle of John had been taken from her path. Of course he had never been much of an obstacle for she had always known he had paid her attention because he was kind at heart, and it hadn't been hard for him to be nice to her because she was pretty, beautiful.

She was glad she was aware of her beauty; it was some small compensation for the silent mountain inside her, the mountain she yelled at, screamed at, hated,

166

and which answered her by buzzing in her ears, and tapping with a hammer on the inside of her skull.

It was a happy weekend, at least for some members of the household. As John explained to Miss Brigmore, they couldn't have a formal engagement party until his mother had been dead a year and Jenny understood that, but when they should have it her father insisted that it be a big affair. John also said that he thought they could be married a year from now; that would leave eighteen months for respect, as his father put it. What did she think of that?

She thought it met the demands of decency.

She'd had little or no private conversation with Katie during their stay, for Katie seemed to avoid being left alone with her.

Nor did Mr. Bensham show any sign of attempting to continue the conversation so mercifully terminated by John; but she felt he was talking at her when, just before their departure on the Sunday, he complained irritably about the long and tedious journey ahead of them and, in his inimitable fashion, said, "We want our heads lookin' at, traveling all this way for little more than a day in between. I'll get rid of the place, that's what I'll do, I'll get rid of it."

There were only Dan and herself within earshot when he made this remark, and she could hear him saying at some future date, "Well, I did warn you, didn't I? Anyway, Florrie would never be comfortable here, she's more at home in forty-seven."

Different members of the family had over the weekend talked of forty-seven, referring to it as home; it was as if they had been brought up there, and not in this house.

No, it wouldn't come as any surprise to her when he told her he was getting rid of the place, and she told herself she wouldn't mind if he made his final decision tomorrow because she was tired of it all, tired of them

167

all. One way and another they had drained her dry; what was left of her she would take to the cottage and quietly let it shrivel into old age. Mary had been right after all.

FOUR

Sarah Waite covered the round mold of freshly made butter on the wooden platter with a muslin cloth, which she then carried out of the dairy, across the yard into the farm kitchen.

As she entered the door Constance turned from the long narrow delph rack fronting the wall opposite the fireplace and said, "We simply must get rid of some of this stuff or it'll go bad on us. Daisy has just taken as much as she can carry over home, and I said I know who wouldn't turn their noses up at a ham shank or the remainder of the veal pie."

"Lily and Bill."

"You've named them." Constance smiled over her shoulder. "Lily and Bill; cooking was never one of Lily's assets, was it?"

"No, it wasn't, although Ma's shown her enough times. But as she said to her on the very morning of the wedding: 'You're on your own now, and I can tell you one thing that men don't like and that's burnt water.'"

As they laughed together Constance brought from the pantry a ham bone, still with a large quantity of meat on it, and half of an enormous veal pie, the last of a dozen that had graced Lily Waite's wedding table the previous Saturday, and she said, "I'll put one of the rice loaves in too; you can tell Lily to tell him she's baked it."

Again they laughed together.

Sarah now sat down on a wooden chair and placed her elbows on the corner of the table and, cupping her chin in her hands, she said dreamily, "Twas a lovely wedding though, wasn't it? Do you know, Mam, I'm still dancing."

Neither she nor Constance could have told you now whether her "mam" was meant to convey the title ma'am or was taking familiar license and using the word in a parental way; true it was that she addressed as Da and Ma Harry and Daisy Waite, who were actually her uncle and aunt, so perhaps if Constance had been asked she might have pointed out that the term after all was one that a maid naturally used to a mistress; yet the relationship between the two was not that of mistress and maid but rather one of mother and daughter, and Constance was well aware of this. She smiled down on the girl now as she said, "I wonder you had any legs left, you were never off the floor for one minute."

"No, I wasn't, was I?" Sarah's round face shone with the memory, her eyes sparkled and her lips fell apart and, her voice still with a faraway quality to it, she said, "And I could have gone on and on. Fancy dancing till five o'clock in the morning and then not going to bed until it was light. Oh, it was a wonderful wedding. As me da said, she had waited long enough to bring Bill up to scratch, but even he must have thought it was worth it with the do you gave them. Da said they were talking about it in the market in Hexham; Mr. Randall met him and said, 'I hear you had some do up at Wolfbur, danced over the hills with the bride and bridegroom in the small hours.' Isn't it funny how people add things on, because we set them off in the cart themselves from the yard afore twelve, didn't we?"

"Oh yes, well before twelve; but that's people, especially in the market."

"Did you like dancing when you were young, Mam?"

Did she like dancing when she was young? To Sarah at seventeen, she must appear old. And had she

170

liked dancing? She'd never had much opportunity to dance. The first time she had really danced was on this very farm in the barn at the harvest supper when Bob Armstrong had whirled her round the rough floor and laughed into her face and told her with his eyes that she was desirable. She was a young widow then and intoxicated with her freedom; if she hadn't been so she would have married him straightaway. Yes, yes, she would have married him straightaway. And another man she had danced with had looked into her face and told her that she was still desirable. His grip hadn't been so close as Bob Armstrong's, he had held her more as a gentleman should, and it had pleased her more, because by this time she was weary of her widowhood and her freedom and craved to belong to someone again before it was too late; but already it was too late. She should have known that men when they are reaching middle age clutch backwards to youth in order to revitalize their masculinity and that women who have reached her age are already considered old and should expect to be spurned. Yet in this case the cavalier attitude had been dealt with justly, for he, in his turn, had been spurned. Why otherwise should he have left the country once again?

Constance knew that she'd never again see Pat Ferrier, and she also knew that she would carry bitterness against him in her heart until she died.

Last Saturday she had danced again, but mostly with Michael, that was when he wasn't dancing with Sarah. But even dancing with Michael had afforded her no pleasure for her heart had ached while she smiled, and as the night wore on and she watched the schottisches, the polkas, the de Coverleys and the clog dances, she wondered if the next time the festivities were held in the barn it would be for Michael's wedding, and when she asked herself who would then be his bride she could not put an actual face or name to her.

The fear in her that Barbara might become her daughter-in-law had lessened slightly during the past year for Michael had seen less of her; whereas he still welcomed her warmly when she came here, his visits

171

to the cottage had become shorter and with longer intervals between them. Sometimes she thought he was more than a little attracted to Sarah; but then again, they had been brought up almost as brother and sister and his attitude toward her was much the same as that which he showed toward Barbara.

That he may have acquired female interests in Hexham had not escaped her, for he had twice of late called at the McCullen's home. Mr. McCullen had been his English master at school and he had first gone to his house when, as a pupil, he had been invited to dinner. Mr. McCullen had three daughters and a son. James was Michael's age, but she did not think it was James that Michael went to see, for he had recently received a letter from Hexham, and when she had handed it to him she had smiled and was about to remark on the scent of perfume that emanated from the envelope, but the blank look that appeared on his face had checked any flippancy on her part.

Then there was Miss Ann Hunnetson; yet she could not see him becoming attached to Miss Hunnetson because Miss Hunnetson was very scholastic. Even in her ordinary conversation she impressed you with her scholarship, as, she supposed, was necessary in order to run a bookshop. She herself frequented Miss Hunnetson's bookshop whenever she visited Hexham, and on these occasions Michael had shown a desire to accompany her. But she dismissed Miss Hunnetson, for even in her early twenties, as she surely was, she was already too much like Brigie.

And there was no way of finding out what was in Michael's mind for during the past year he had become, what was the word she could use? Reticent? Well, at least not so open where his thoughts were concerned. He was no longer spontaneous in his opinions of this one or that one, and he no longer discussed Barbara with her. At one time, after Barbara's visits he would have said, "Madam's on her high horse today" or perhaps "Madam has behaved herself today," but not any more. She realized that very often now after visits from Brigie and Barbara he would take himself off for a long walk, or visit the fields, or check on the sheep, anything that would take him from the house—and herself.

There was a barrier rising between them and she couldn't break it down because she didn't really know what was creating it, except that her son had left youth behind and now in his twentieth year had become a man.

Sarah said, "While I'm that way shall I take a can of tea to Michael and Uncle Jim, it'll be nippy up there?"

"No, I shouldn't bother; they won't be long. It isn't foot rot, so they won't be bringing any of them down."

"What is it then?"

"Oh, one of them had got a piece of wire round its foot and another had a festered pad; they have no sense, sheep. Still I shouldn't say that, they have sense enough to keep warm in weather that would freeze us to death."

"Yes, Da says they save themselves by all going to bed together." She laughed gaily. "I remember the six last year that were buried in the snow lying head to tail as if they'd been put to bed, and the lambs we brought up in the stable. Oh, poor things." She put her head on one side. "They didn't know what had hit them when they were pushed out onto the fells. I thought about them for days after, especially at night when the frost was still thick, because like always the ewes give them a rough time. I can never understand that part of it, pushing their own out, it's funny, isn't it?"

"You mustn't get sentimental about sheep, or any other animals on the farm except the dogs and horses; the rest are just part of a business."

Constance was no longer surprised that she could talk this way. It had been hard at first to clamp down on sentimentality but she had achieved it, as she had achieved supremacy over other weak facets of her personality.

"Well, there's the bits and pieces; put them in a

173

basket. But first run and get your cloak, for as you say it'll be cold up there."

A few minutes later Sarah left the farmyard carrying the basket of eatables. She wore a green cloth cloak with a hood to it which she had made during last winter, the material having been a Christmas present from Constance. She swung the basket as she walked and every now and again she hitched a step or two as a child might do.

After keeping to the cart track for some distance from the farm she mounted a bank, went through a small copse, and when she emerged kept to a footpath that ran along a ridge. The ground to her left dropped sharply for a distance of about twenty feet to a long strip of land that didn't deserve the name of valley, for it was more like a narrow passage bordering the foothills where they mounted gradually to their larger companions.

The slope and the strip of land were known as Rotten Bottom, a name it had earned because most of it was scree-covered, and here and there large boulders stuck out of the earth. Also at one point it had become a dump for old and useless farm machinery. Like most farms Wolfbur at one time had, scattered around its corners, old plows, rusty scythes, broken blades, wagon wheels and often old wagons themselves, and the rubbish and litter strangely did not, in any way, detract from the farm being considered successful. No farmer was thought to be a bad manager because he did not get rid of useless tools. Who knew but that the very thing they might throw away today they might want tomorrow. So Wolfbur for years had had its assortment of useless implements, until Constance had taken over and found that the litter in the yard and surrounding buildings offended her eye, and so she'd had it all gathered up and thrown down into Rotten Bottom.

The path was a short cut to the cottage now occupied by Lily and Bill Twigg, and it ended abruptly at a roughly made gate that hung in two stone sockets between the dry-stone walls that bordered a field.

Sarah climbed the gate—nobody went to the trouble of lifting it out of the sockets, not even the men—and she crossed the field that now went sharply uphill. When she reached its summit she stopped for a moment and looked first to the right in the direction of Alston and then to the far left where Allenheads lay. The sky was high, the light was white and clear. She felt she was looking to each end of the earth; then a movement attracted her attention and she brought her gaze down to the track that she had left earlier, and there, making their way back toward the farm, she saw the small figure of her da leading Chester and Nellie, the two Clydesdales, and even from this distance she could see that they were all walking in unison. She could even see their fetlock hair bouncing with each step they made; even if she couldn't see their color, she knew which was which because her da always walked next to Chester who was black while Nellie was bay-colored. Her da was bringing them back from the blacksmith's where they had been shod. It was funny but Nellie didn't like being shod; Chester would stand without murmur but Nellie would do quite a bit of stamping before she could be induced to lift her foot. Nellie was all woman, her da said.

Oh, it was a beautiful day, frosty, sharp; she wanted to run, fly. She often wondered what a bird felt like. There was an old buzzard hereabouts; she always stood and watched him whenever he came in sight.

Suddenly she sprang from the top of the hill and took the steep slope to the field below at a run that gained momentum as she neared the bottom. When she reached the level ground she kept on running like a spring unwinding until she came up against a wall, and she leaned on it gasping, then looked down into the basket. The cloth had come off the ham bone, the crust had fallen away from the pie. Eeh! what was the matter with her? She could have joggled the lot out of the basket running like that. She placed the basket on the ground and, putting her forearms on the top of the wall, she rested her chin on them and gazed into the

175

distance where the smoke from Lily's chimney spiraled straight upwards. She felt so happy, so light inside; she felt she was still dancing, that she had never stopped dancing since Sunday morning. Why was she feeling like this? The answer she gave herself caused her to bring her head down; and now her brow was resting on her forearms. And thus she stayed for some minutes; then, straightening, she picked up the basket, went along by the wall until she found a gap, and went through it and over the narrow footpath that led to the cottage.

On a distant slope Jim Waite turned to Michael and said, "Did you see that? That was our Sarah coming down the hill. What was she doing, trying to fly? She could have broken her neck."

"Not her"—Michael jerked his head upwards— "she's as sure-footed as a mountain goat."

"Well, I'll believe that after seeing her doing that stunt. That was Head's Hill she came down; I mean to say, you take that carefully at any time; an' with its face to the north as it is, the frost'll still be thick on it."

"Well, she reached the bottom all right. And there she goes across to Lily's."

They stood looking at the distant figure for a moment before Jim said, "Aye . . . well, I think that's about the lot. Are we for making our way back?"

"Yes, Jim, but I think I'll go the top road just to make sure there's none over there. If they get over the burn they could make for the lead workings; we've had it before."

"Aye; but I don't think you'll find any of them over there. Still you never know; best put your mind at rest. I'll go down the bottom track. See you."

Michael did not move away immediately from the hillside. He thought he could still see Sarah as she made her way round the side of the cottage and his mind stayed on her. Only last night he had asked himself what his true feelings were concerning her. He always liked to be with her; he missed her when she wasn't there, even the kitchen seemed bare when she left it. He felt at peace when in her company; her face was always bright, her laughter gay. Was it just sisterly affection he had for her? Was it just sisterly affection he had for Barbara? God! he didn't know. . . . Well, he should know; he had reached the age when he should know. Barbara had the opposite effect on him altogether from Sarah; Barbara disturbed him, Sarah soothed. He didn't seem to worry when he was with Sarah; there were no problems to life when he was with Sarah; perhaps because Sarah's thoughts never went beyond the farm, and cooking, but life became one big problem when he was with Barbara.

He had tried the association of others. There was Beatrice McCullen; Beatrice was pretty and entertaining but she didn't affect his senses in any way. He must stop seeing her for he wasn't really being fair to her. And then Miss Hunnetson. Oh, Miss Hunnetson; now Miss Hunnetson had an effect on him, but mostly on his mind. He liked talking to Miss Hunnetson. She had stretched his view of the world, had Miss Hunnetson, by suggesting that he should read more books. The names of the authors she gave him he had never heard of, nor yet, he was sure, had his mother. Miss Hunnetson was what you would call one of the new women. The newspapers ridiculed them and made funny sketches of them, put them into trousers and, taking the ridicule to extremes, made the men half their size. Miss Hunnetson also believed in unions for women as well as for men, and votes too. He had to laugh at that. Why, it was only a matter of thirteen years ago that they allowed the working man a vote. She was a very odd person, was Miss Hunnetson, yet informative. Oh yes. She had been the means of clarifying his thinking which had made him reassess his values. He happened to say to her one day as he was looking at a book how he envied any man who could write at such length, even without taking the quality of the substance into account; it was an achievement, he considered, to write words to fill six hundred and

177

seventy pages. Whereupon she had asked him if he had read any of the essays by a man called Addison. He had blushed when he admitted he had never heard of Addison.

The next time he went into the shop she said she would loan him an old book; it was called *Selections From The Spectator,* and in it she had penciled an essay by this man. It had impressed him so much that he had rewritten part of it out, and had read it so many times since that he knew most of it by heart. It ran like a piece of poetry in his mind:

> *When I look upon the tombs of the great*
> *Every emotion of envy dies in me;*
> *When I read the epitaphs of the beautiful,*
> *Every inordinate desire goes out;*
> *When I meet the grief of parents upon a tombstone,*
> *My heart melts with compassion;*
> *When I see the tomb of the parents themselves,*
> *I consider the vanity of grieving*
> *For those whom we must quickly follow;*
> *When I see kings lying by those who deposed them,*
> *When I consider rival wits placed side by side,*
> *Or the holy men that divided the world with their*
> *   conquests and disputes,*
> *I reflect with sorrow and astonishment on the little*
> *   competitions, factions and debates of mankind.*
> *When I read the several dates on the tombs of those*
> *   that died yesterday,*
> *And some six hundred years ago,*
> *I consider that great day when we shall all of us be*
> *   contemporaries,*
> *And make our appearance together.*

The more he recited these words to himself the more often he knew that here was fundamental truth, here was the clarification of all the jumbled thoughts and probings of his late school days, and the past few years, especially of the year just past, for during this time his mind and emotions had been taxed so much he knew that it was imperative he should soon find a solution to the things that were troubling him.

He was a farmer and he'd always be a farmer, but he had no intention of being a gormless one. As he sowed the crops, so he intended to sow knowledge. He sometimes thought it had been a mistake on his mother's part to send him away to school because there the main part of his education had been to make him think, and when this process was once begun there was no stopping it. It would have been better if, together with Jim and boys from surrounding farms, he had attended the day school, for here no depths of his mind would have been stirred, and his main thought in life would have been the concern of the farm and the people on it.

Yet wasn't that still so? Weren't the farm and the people on it his main concern? He turned abruptly now and went in the direction of the ridge, thinking, why trouble one's mind, for as Addison said, we would all one day be contemporaries; yet his mind countered with the statement, That's all very well, but until that day you have to go on living, and he was brought back to the beginning, Barbara, Sarah . . . and his mother.

As he walked briskly along the side of the hill his feet kept slipping from under him and each time he only just saved himself from falling. When he reached the brow he went along by the wall until he came to the gate where Sarah had crossed earlier and as he looked over it and upwards he saw her coming away from the cottage, and he stopped and waited.

She was some way down the sloping field before she saw him. As soon as she caught sight of him however she began to run, and he laughed as she approached and shouted and made pretense of lifting the gate off its hinges to let her through.

When she flung herself against the gate she was hardly out of breath, her uplifted heart-shaped face was rosy, the green hood had fallen back from her cloak, and her brown hair looked tousled as if the wind had been blowing through it, or hands had teased it.

He laughed down into her face before he said, "You'll break your neck one of these days; can't you walk?"

"No."

"I don't suppose it has occurred to you, Miss Waite"—he now assumed a mock fatherly manner—"that young ladies bordering on seventeen years of age do not run, they have reached a stage of decorum, or should have."

"Yes, sir."

"Don't you want to be a young lady?"

"No, sir." Taking her cue from him, she had assumed the attitude of a child now.

"Why?"

"'Cos . . . 'cos I ain't cut out for it."

"Monkey! Come on, get yourself over."

As she climbed up the bars he put his hands under her oxters, and when he was about to lift her over the top, he stopped and set her down on the bar with a plop, saying now, as he looked up into her face, "I'm serious though, really I am. If you had lost your footing on Head's Hill you could have broken your neck; I'm not laughing."

"No, Mis . . . ter Mi . . . chael."

He shook her and she laughed, her face hanging over his.

Slowly now he lifted her to the ground but still held her; then, as if testing her weight, he lifted her slight form lightly upwards, saying, "By! you're going to be a fat old woman in no time. You must be all of twelve stone now."

"Thirteen."

His face was close to hers, and in the silence that held them it moved closer still until the silence was shattered and the moment torn from them by Jim Waite's voice shouting, "Mr. Michael! Mr. Michael! Here a minute."

When Michael turned round, Jim, in the field behind them, was stubbing his finger toward the ground.

"What is it?"

"Come and have a look; this one's bad."

"Oh Lord!" He looked back at Sarah and, putting his hand out, he gently pushed her away in the direction of the path along which she had come, saying, "You go on home. I don't know what it is he's found, but I don't want you to be sick all over me. You know what you are."

"I'll not, I'll . . ."

"Go on with you." He made to chase her, and once again she was running and laughing as she ran; and she continued to laugh until she came to the beginning of Rotten Bottom and saw a figure emerge from the copse and come swiftly toward her. . . .

Miss Brigmore and Barbara had arrived about twenty minutes previously. Barbara had remained patient long enough to drink a cup of tea in the sitting room before inquiring where Michael was, and, having been told by Constance that he was attending to some sick sheep up on the high lands, she had said quietly, "Oh, I'll take a walk in that direction because we can't stay long; Brigie wants to get back before dark."

The fact that she had said that the visit was going to be short checked the protest the Constance would otherwise have made.

Like Sarah, Barbara, too, took the short cut through the copse, and it was as she emerged that she saw the figures by the gate. She saw the girl sitting on the top bar and Michael with his arms up and about her. She saw that they were talking, their faces close. She saw him lift her to the ground, then bounce her. She saw them become still while staring at each other, and although she couldn't hear the call nor see who had made it, she knew the lover-like trance had been broken by a voice.

The feeling the picture of them evoked in her mind was unbearable; she was being consumed by a flame of jealous hatred that had been smoldering for years and now was enveloping her in a white heat that blotted out sanity. There was in her a desire to rend,

181

to tear, to grind her heel into the face of the girl approaching her. So powerful were the emotions controlling her that Sarah's features were blotted from her sight for a moment as they came face to face.

Then words erupted from her throat. She was aware of shouting but not of how loud, or of how terrible her voice was. "You! You! you're trying to steal him, you horrible, low dirty creature you!"

"I'm not. I'm not."

She read the whispered frightened words coming from between Sarah's trembling lips.

"You are! You are!" As she advanced on her, Sarah retreated. "You common low creature you!" With the last words her hands came out like talons and would have gripped Sarah's throat only that in the last moment Sarah strained away. But as the hands clutched at the front of her cloak and flung her from side to side, the terrified girl screamed, *"Michael! Michael!"* Then the scream ended in a long drawn out *"O O O Oh!"* as the hands sent her flying and she felt herself falling backwards.

Like an animal deprived of its prey, Barbara stood on the brink of the slope and watched the green-enfolded figure tumbling downwards toward the bottom, and she did not hear the long bloodcurdling cry that Sarah uttered as her body fell in among the rusty machinery. Nor did she see the two men racing toward her. Not until they paused at the top of the bank beside her and looked downwards was she aware of their presence. Then the look they both turned on her took the blood mist from her eyes and she staggered back as they jumped downwards and disappeared from her sight.

The sweat was running down her face and her garments were wet with it. She went back to the copse, leaned against the bole of a tree and waited; she waited for an eternity that covered five minutes, and then they came into sight struggling upwards over the top of the bank, carrying the limp form between them.

They didn't look toward her, they didn't know she was there. She didn't move from the tree but she

182

turned her head and followed them with her eyes. Their arms entwined, they walked crabwise, Sarah's head hanging down between their shoulders and her legs dangling over their clasped hands. One end of her green cloak trailed on the ground, but it was green no longer, for its color was marred with dark brown patches, as was the color of her white apron, but here the color was scarlet, bright scarlet.

She began to moan inside herself like a child calling for its mother. She repeated over and over again, "Brigie. Oh! Brigie." What had she done? Had she killed her? Well . . . well, if she had she wasn't sorry. . . . Yes she was; oh, yes she was. But he had been about to kiss her; and she had enticed him, she had held her face up to him. She hoped she would die. No! No! She didn't. Oh dear Lord! Dear God! What was the matter with her? Brigie. Oh! Brigie.

She moved from the tree and began to walk round the copse, circling the small area again and again as if she were in a dark forest trying to find a way out.

Why didn't Brigie come? Why? She wanted to feel her arms about her, to see her say she understood; she wanted someone to understand. She stumbled toward the end of the copse facing the road, and there on the sunken track coming from the farm she saw Jim Waite urging his horse forward.

He had almost passed her when some movement she made brought his head round toward her, and he reared the horse in sharply, and he stared at her for a moment before alighting from the saddle and coming up the bank, even in his climb not taking his eyes from her.

As he came slowly toward her the look she saw on his face interpreted in some strange fashion the feeling she herself had experienced so short a while ago. He looked fierce, mad, no relation whatsoever to the Jim Waite she had known from childhood and had never really liked.

"*You . . . murdering . . . bitch . . . you!*" His big mouth looked cave-like as he stretched his lips in slow enunciation. "*I've . . . a . . . good . . . mind . . . to . . .*"

kill . . . you . . . meself." His great arm swung up in front of her eyes and when the flat of his hand crashed against the side of her head the world exploded. As she fell against a tree all the sounds on earth reverberated through her. She heard a voice, something that she hadn't heard in years, but this was a screaming terrible voice, like the voice of God, a fearsome God. She heard the birds screeching, the branches groaning; she heard the very air breathing in on itself. The silent mountain within her was being filled with noise, indescribable hell-exploding noise. She wanted to flee from it, rush back into the silence, away from this sense she had longed for but which was now beating on her with physical force.

She pressed tight against the tree, her head thrust back on her neck, while staring into Jim Waite's mouth. Hearing and seeing his words at the same time had a double impact on her. "You're a cruel bugger, you always have been; you're like all your breed, you've got the streak of the Mallens in you. By God! you have. White and wide it is on the men and there to see, but black in you and hidden. You're a chip off the old block, you are that. One of old Tom Mallen's bastards to a tee, an' the worst of the bunch if you ask me. You were bred of a rape. Do you hear me? You were bred of a rape!" His mouth opened so wide it seemed to envelop his face. "They say you don't know about it; well, I'm tellin' you. Do you hear? You were bred of a rape. He raped your mother who he had brought up as his daughter. Rotten he was, fat, dirty old bastard. An' the one that brought you up wasn't much better than a whore, for she was his kept woman for years, and she stole from the house to keep him, aye she did, silver, jewelry, the lot. She should have been nabbed an' all. Oh, you've come from good stock you have and don't my family know it. Your uncle. . . . No. No, he wasn't your uncle, he was your brother, the one that ran away after he nearly murdered one of the bailiffs they put in at High Banks when old Mallen went bust. An' he tried to do for me

184

dad an' all. And now you, true to your breed, have done for our Sarah."

His arm was lifted once again, and again he struck her. Her head bounced with a resounding crack against the trunk of the tree and for a moment she could see nothing. The current of noise made by the trees, the air, and the birds was still tearing through her. He mouthed at her, "Did you take it in, you dirty bastard? Did you take it in? And now listen an' take this in an' all. If she pegs out I'll come and do for you, I will. That's a promise. With these very hands I'll come and do for you."

Gripping her by the shoulders now, he shook her like a rat, and when he released her she slowly slid down to the ground. Her eyes were wide, her mouth was wide, her face in front had the pallor of death on it, but at each side it was red. She saw him go toward the bank, then he disappeared from her view, to appear again by the side of the horse. Then as he was about to swing himself up into the saddle she heard a voice shout, "Hie! there, Jim. Wait! Wait a minute." It was a man's voice, one she hadn't heard before, but she knew it to be Michael's.

Unblinking she stared before her until his head and shoulders came into view. She saw him speak rapidly to Jim Waite but she could not hear what he said, nor Jim Waite's answer, but a moment later they both looked in her direction. Then Jim Waite mounted the horse and put it into a gallop. She knew it was galloping because she could hear the dull thud of the hooves.

When Michael disappeared from her view too she thought he had returned up the road; but just as she pulled herself drunkenly to her feet in order to call to him he came over the top of the bank.

Her hands thrust backwards gripping the trunk for support, her breath coming in great gasps that caused her head to wobble, she watched him cover the distance between them. He stopped when about two yards from her and she saw instantly that he, like

Jim Waite, had also changed. There seemed to be no recognizable feature in the face before her for it was suffused with an anger that had given the fair skin a purple hue and made it look old in contrast to the disheveled mop of straw-colored hair.

She watched his teeth grind against each other before his lips too moved into wide articulating movements. "You've done it at last, haven't you? You've always meant to; you always meant to hurt her. YOU!" He drew the word out and shook his head slowly as the echo of it died away.

Michael was talking to her, she was hearing his voice and she didn't like it for it matched the man before her; it wasn't the voice she put to her Michael, her beloved Michael; it wasn't the voice that whispered to her in the night telling her that she was beautiful, beloved, adored, desired.

"You're cruel. Mother's always said there was a cruel streak in you, and she's right; she's been right about everything. I must have been mad to think that I could care for you. Well now, listen to me and listen well. Read my lips because what I'm going to say I would have likely said to you in any case. I'm going to marry Sarah, do you hear? I'm going to marry Sarah; that's . . . that's if she lives. If she doesn't I'll hate you, I'll curse you till the day I die. I'll curse you anyway because it's ten to one you've left her crippled. That would please you, wouldn't it, if you knew she was a cripple? You used to hate to see her dance. You! I . . . I wonder how I came up from the same branch?"

"M . . . M . . . Michael."

"Don't Michael me."

"Please, please, Michael, listen to me."

"I never want to see you again, to speak to you again, do you hear, never!" His body was half bent toward her.

When he flung round from her the pain in her head, the noises beating on her brain were for the moment blotted out by a rebirth of her anger. Like lightning it flared through her and she yelled at him

186

now, "Who are you to feel so proud of your beginnings! And you needn't wonder any more about coming from the same branch because you didn't. He wasn't your father; Mallen's son wasn't your father."

He had stopped at the top of the rise, his face half turned over his shoulder staring at her. She was still supporting herself against the tree trunk, but her upper body was straining forward; and now she screamed at him, "You're like me, there's a pair of us did you but know it. We're both bastards. And your mother's no better than a whore, for no one but a whore would go with her husband's brother in the filthy derelict house on the high fell, and that's where you were begat. Now, now, how do you like the truth, Mr. Michael Radlet?"

He did not move for some seconds and their eyes held like joined firebrands across the distance; then he turned slowly from her and went down the slope.

Once again she slid to the ground, weighed down by the renewed rage still burning within her. It was churning all the strange sounds about in her head. She wished they would stop; she wanted silence, silence. Suddenly her body doubled up, she buried her face in her hands, and rocked from side to side. The great cacophony of sound was terrifying and she had no way of modifying it.

Her silent world had disintegrated when Jim Waite struck her across the ears. Brigie had said it could happen, that one day she might hear again, but it had come too late. Her life was finished, she had nothing more to live for. . . .

The sound of the trap wheels as they came over the rough road screeched through her eardrums.

When Miss Brigmore came into view sitting erect in the front seat she did not rise and go toward her but watched her lift her hand and imperiously beckon to her.

It was a full minute before she dragged herself to her feet; then slowly, as if slightly intoxicated, she walked toward the top of the bank, stumbled down it onto the road and around the back of the trap. When

187

she pulled herself up into the seat she did not look at Miss Brigmore, nor Miss Brigmore at her; and so they began the journey.

Not a word was exchanged throughout the journey because Miss Brigmore did not turn her head toward her once, but when she murmured in an agonized fashion to herself, "Oh girl, you have not only almost severed that child's leg off, you have, did you but know it, severed a number of lives this day. What is in you? What is in you? Where have I failed? It must be me for there was no real harm in Thomas, and none whatever in your mother," the words resounded like a bell tolling out doom in Barbara's ears.

Thomas, the big, pot-bellied man whose picture dominated the fireplace in the cottage; that man was her father. The truth had indeed been spilled today. That horrible fat man had raped her mother, and this after having brought her up as his own child. Yet here was Brigie saying there was no real harm in him. And she had been his mistress, this prim, even sanctimonious woman had been her father's mistress, not his housekeeper as she had understood, but had slept in his bed, in the bed of that man with the big fat stomach and the fleshy jowls. . . . And he was her father! No wonder Brigie had been afraid of her knowing. *She was sick. She was sick,* she would vomit.

Was it surprising there was wickedness in her? Was it surprising there was violence in her? Was she to blame for what she did? And Jim Waite had said that her brother—she had a brother then, or a half-brother, and he had almost murdered two men. The Mallen streak. . . . This is what they meant by the Mallen streak. Badness. Badness of all kinds. And she was a Mallen! But was she to blame for that?

The question was as loud now in her head as was the noise and creaking of the cart, the clop-clopping of the horses' hooves, the sound of the wind, the cutting wind that was chilling her through. The wind was made up of voices; they were coming over the valley, shouting at her in Jim Waite's voice, in Michael's voice: "You're a bastard, that's what you

188

are, a murdering bastard! I'm going to marry her. I never want to see you again. I'll hate you all my life."

They were passing the house where he was begot, the filthy house with the holes in the roof. Michael himself had taken her there. They had ridden their horses up to the doorless gap and it was he who had pointed out where the tramps slept. Ha! ha! ha! Ha! ha! she was laughing loudly inside. It was funny, funny. He had come into being on that filthy floor; his mother and father were no better than the tramps. Her Aunt Constance was a tramp, a road woman; and he, who was he to spurn her? He had left her with the weight of the world on her; he had burnt out her heart so that she could feel no more, but he would go on feeling, on and on, and every time he looked on his mother he would hate her. Oh, she hoped that he would hate her; she hoped that her Aunt Constance would live in misery for the rest of her life.

The wind's voice became louder as they went downwards toward the valley, and it was screaming in her ears when Brigie stopped the trap outside the cottage gate. But even before the horse had put its last foot down she had jumped from the seat and was running. She heard the voice calling, "Barbara! Barbara! Come back. Don't be silly, come back. Please! Please! Barbara. Do you hear?" Brigie must have forgotten that she couldn't hear. Her mind was still sufficiently rational for her to realize the incongruity of this reaction.

The twilight was falling and she ran into it, on and on toward the time when she would feel no more.

FIVE

"Now look here, lad, what you've got to understand is that a mill has a six-day working week and that you can't go jaunting off every weekend. I've been very lenient; you can't say but I haven't. I meself would like to go down every weekend. . . ."

"Then why don't you? There's nothing really stopping you."

"Nothing stopping me!" Harry's brows gathered over the top of his nose and he flung his arm outwards indicating that beyond the office walls lay the mill that couldn't manage without him.

"Well, what's Rington there for? . . . and Willy? Willy's just waiting for the chance to run the whole concern on his own."

"Oh, is that what you think about Willy?"

"Yes, it is. He's not satisfied with a ten-hour day, he goes to extremes and works twelve, and would make everybody else do the same if he got the chance. Oh, I've got Willy's measure; there's two distinct sides to Willy, and that you'll find out."

"Well, that's interesting to hear; it's as much as tellin' me I've been blind all these years, and don't know men."

"You don't know Willy. Anyway, there's our John. What do you think he's doing, if not seeing to the mill . . . and all its works?"

"John's got to spend most of his time in the office, like meself. Anyway, that's not the point; the point is you're here to learn the ropes, and if you let hands see you going jauntin' off on a Friday night, week after week, they'll go slack."

"Oh, Dad, who'll go slack under you? Anyway, no one pays much attention to me. As McClurk said only yesterday, 'You, Mr. Dan, are only here to make the number up.'"

"McClurk wants his big mouth stopped. If he's not careful he'll get his pay stopped an' all; that'll keep him dry for a time. I would have done it long since if it hadn't been for the thirteen he's got in his squad. Aw, go on." He flapped his hand now toward Dan. "Get yourself away."

"No, I won't bother."

"Get yourself off, I tell you. God Almighty! I don't want to spend three nights and all day Sunday lookin' at your face."

"Is Aunt Florrie coming on Sunday?"

"Aye, I suppose so. Why d'you ask?"

"Well, you won't have to bother looking at my face."

"Now look here, lad, your Aunt Florrie means . . ."

"Yes, I know; I've heard it all before, my Aunt Florrie means well. But she gets on my nerves. And why do you encourage her?"

"Encourage her! What do you mean, encourage her?"

"Just that. Tell me something. Have . . . have you ideas in her direction?"

"Hell's flames! Who do you think you are, lad, questioning me along those lines? Look, it doesn't matter what ideas I've got in that direction, it's got nowt to do with you."

"You wouldn't, would you?" Dan's voice was quiet and serious now.

"Wouldn't what? What the hell are you on about?"

"You know."

"All right I know, an' I think I'm old enough to please meself, that is when the time comes, when it's

191

decent to talk about such things. Now get out of me sight, and if you're going over you'd better get a move on 'cos as it is you won't land there till late the night. And by the way"—Harry checked Dan as he made for the door—"you and The Brigadier can get talkin' and comfort each other over the same subject, your Aunt Florrie, because she sniffs every time she looks at her. Aye, that's it, you get talking to her and tell her how worried you are about me having ideas in that direction, eh. And give her my regards when you're at it. And listen a minute." He again checked Dan. "Bring some butter and cheese back with you from the farm; the stuff I've had the last few days has never seen a cow. An' that's an idea. Tell Brigie that if there's none of us there at the weekend to send on some farm stuff. I don't see why they should all stuff their kites with the fat of my land and us livin' here on shop ket. I must have been barmy all these years. And by! Lad"—he now nodded his head sharply—"I'm positive I'm still barmy, 'cos why do I keep the bloody place on anyway? You tell me that."

"So as I can go down at weekends."

Harry didn't answer this, but leaned back in his chair and said quietly, "You know, I think I'd be savin' money if I let you go your own way now, but I said a year, and you said a year, and we'll stick to it. Go on, get yourself out afore I change me mind." His voice trailed away; then he grabbed some papers toward him and looked to where Dan was still standing near the door, and now he bellowed, "Go on with you! Else I will, mind."

"Why don't you come down? I'll wait till tomorrow morning if you'll come down. There's no need for you to stay. . . ."

"Look, lad, I see no fun in scurrying to a train, spending eight solid hours traveling, only to get a whiff of fresh air, have a meal, go to bed, and then do it all backwards again."

"You enjoyed last weekend."

"You think so? Well, for your information I'll tell you this, I didn't. I had a bloody miserable weekend. Once in three weeks or a month is enough for me. And there's nothing hurting down there. As long as The Brigadier's in charge things will be run accordin' to the book." He pressed his lips together and jerked his head and ended, "I picked a good 'un there. I've often thought that if she was at this end there wouldn't be need for half the staff. By the way, lad—I suppose I should have thought of this afore to ask you —what's your attraction down there? What makes you want to take such a journey for so little?"

"Let's say it's the air, Dad." Dan nodded at his father, grinned, then went out, and Harry, tapping the desk, said, "The air? Now who is there down there that would qualify for air?"

Long before Dan reached his destination he was thinking his father was right. Why make this long tedious journey by train, and a further bone-rattling one by cart or carriage from the station, twice in forty-eight hours, and for what? Yes, for what?

His only guide in the black dark as he went down the road from the little station to the cluster of cottages was the distant dim lights in the windows.

He had to knock three times on Ben Taggert's door, and the third time he banged on it to make himself heard above the din of voices coming from within. The door was opened by a boy of about ten who peered up at him and said, "Aye, what's it?"

"Is your father in?"

"No." The boy now turned his head on his shoulder and yelled, "Ma! a man wants me da."

The woman who came to the door was surrounded by a group of children that looked a series of steps and stairs, and by the roundness of her middle she was about to add to their number.

"Ben's not in, mister," she said.

"When is he due back?"

"Don't know; couldn't say the night."

"But is he coming back tonight?"

"Couldn't say, mister, not with the carry-on. Finished his journey around five, then went off again to help in the search."

She turned to one of the children, crying now, "Bring the lamp!" and when the child brought the lamp she held it up high and exclaimed on a laugh, "Ho! it's you, mister, one from High Banks. Aw well, 'tis to your part he's gone an' workin' round there this minute."

He paused for a moment before he asked her, "Has he taken visitors?"

"No, no, not visitors; looking for the girl he is; lost yesterday on the hills. All Hall an' farm out, an' lots of others all night. Perhaps you know her, it's the Mallen girl. Ben's known her from she was a mite, an' her mother afore her, took 'em over the hills many's the time. . . ."

Incredulously he repeated the name, then added, "Lost last night? How?"

"No tellin'; just know she went out on the hills an' the folk from your place went a-lookin for her, and when Ben went that way this mornin' the place was an uproar. They asked him to keep on the lookout an' he did, but t'wer no sign of her he says, and as soon as he got back the night off he went again. Knew her he did, and her mother afore her, like I said. But there's more in it than meets the eye, he said. Picked up something at Wolfbur Farm, he did. She'd been over, the Mallen girl. In an uproar there an' all. I couldn't get the bottom of it. He just gulped his tea an' off he went. Usually tells me the tale he does but just said, 'More in it than meets the eye,' he said. Big trouble over at Wolfbur. You can come in and wait if you like."

No, no. He shook his head and tried to control his thinking. Barbara gone and trouble at Wolfbur. What trouble? Had she in desperation done something to Michael? And where had she gotten to since last night?

"Do you know where I could get a horse?"

"A horse?" The woman spoke as if she had never

194

heard of a horse before; then she repeated, "A horse, this time a night?"

"Big Ned's got one in the smithy, not being collected till the day after the morrow." It was the boy who had opened the door speaking. "Might lend it to you, mister. It's not his, but still he might lend it to you."

"Whereabouts is the smithy?"

There was a chortle from the children at the ignorance of the man, and some of them chorused together, "Why! yon end, round the corner."

"Light a lantern and take the gentleman to Big Ned's." The mother was commanding the tallest boy now, and the boy went back into the room and appeared within a minute with a candle lantern.

Dan thanked the woman, and the children chorused after him, "So long, mister! So long, mister!" And he looked back at them where they stood huddled round the woman like a group of little demons in the dim light and he answered them in kind, saying, "So long. So long."

The blacksmith was on the point of retiring. "A horse at this time of night!" he said. "I don't know, I don't know; it isn't mine."

"Whose . . . whose is it?"

"Jim Shallbrank's."

"Oh, the farmer on the Allendale road. I know him slightly, I'm sure he wouldn't mind. I'll recompense him well for it. Anyway, you'll have it back tomorrow."

"You from the Hall you say?"

"Yes."

"They don't bring their shoeing here, do they?"

"No, no, I don't suppose they do."

"No, they don't."

"I suppose it's because there's a smithy much nearer."

"Not so much as all that."

Dan took a half-sovereign from his purse. It shone like a small new moon as he held it out between his finger and thumb and the man, looking at it, said,

"Aw, well, well. You'll have to wait till I get me things on, coat and the like; it's bitter the night an' . . . an' it'll be worse afore mornin'. Black frost this is."

Fifteen minutes later the horse was saddled and Dan was mounted and the boy walking by his side from the smithy yard on to the rough road and there Dan, again putting his hand into his pocket, drew forth a coin which he handed down to the boy, and the boy, his mouth agape, took it, then stared at it as he said, "But . . . but 'tis a full golden sovereign, an' . . . an' I've done nowt."

"You got me a horse. And now you can do me another favor; you can loan me that lantern, it'll be returned to you tomorrow."

"Aye, sir, aye, with pleasure." The boy handed the lantern up to him and Dan, gathering the reins in one hand, took it from him and held it against the pommel. Then nodding down at the boy and saying to the horse, "Get up there," he moved off; while the boy's voice came through the darkness, shouting, "I'm your man, mister. Any time, any job, I'm your man."

"Good enough," he called back, then held the lantern up over the horse's head until they were clear of the pot-holed lane and had reached the carriage road.

That he did the journey without mishap he knew was more by good luck than management, for the lantern proved of dubious benefit to both the horse and himself. Not being stabilized, the candle several times threatened to extinguish itself, and it was only by the horse's instinct and good sense that he had been saved from going over its head more than once.

When he slipped from the saddle onto the empty drive there was no one to be seen, not even in the stable yard, nothing to suggest any anxiety being present. He looped the reins over a post, then ran up the steps, but when he turned the handle of the front door and found it open he knew that this was unusual, for his parents, being town bred, never went to bed without bolting the doors and had insisted on the same habit being carried out since they had come to the Hall.

There was no one to be seen when he entered the house but making a guess where Brooks would be at this time if still up, he made for the staff room, and as he thrust open the door three startled faces turned from the table toward him, those of Mrs. Kenley, Brooks, and Armstrong.

Without preamble he demanded, "What's happened, what's this they're saying? Is there any truth in it?"

"Why! Mr. Dan, we didn't expect you." Mrs. Kenley was the first to rise; and Brooks, following, said, "No, Mr. Dan, we didn't expect you, we didn't think you'd get the letter till the morrow mornin'."

"Letter! We've had no letter. But . . . but tell me, what has happened?"

They now looked from one to the other. Then Brooks, assuming the debatable position as head of the house in the absence of his master and The Brigadier, said, "If you'll just come this way, Mr. Dan, I'll give you the details as far as is known."

As they reached the door Mrs. Kenley said, "Would you like something to eat, sir?"

"Yes, please, Mrs. Kenley, but just a snack. It's a hot drink I need most."

After standing aside to let Dan enter the drawing room, Brooks closed the door, then stood just within the room because Dan too had stopped.

Showing impatience and his voice bearing this out, Dan demanded, "What is it? What is all this about, Brooks? They say Miss Barbara's missing."

"Yes, sir, she's missing. Been gone since yesterday afternoon. Coming on dark when she ran from the trap and onto the fells. So . . . so Miss Brigmore says."

After a moment, during which Dan gulped in his throat and his hands, which had been stiff with cold, became suddenly clammy, he muttered, "And there's been no sign of her since?"

"Neither hilt nor hair. The staff's taken it in turns all day to scour the hillsides an' the countryside, to

197

Hexham one way, Haltwhistle t'other. But, as I said I couldn't see her gettin' that far; she'd be dead beat long afore she reached there, it being eight to ten miles' distance. . . ."

"Did . . . did they search the river?" He asked this question quietly.

"She didn't go that way, so Miss Brigmore said. She's convinced she went into the hills. As for meself I'm convinced that if she did, an' didn't get into shelter, there's not much use searching for her. A night up on there and her without a pick on her bones she wouldn't . . ."

"All right, all right." He walked slowly toward the fire, then turned to where Brooks was still standing and asked, "Where's Miss Brigmore now?"

"The last I saw of her was around five o'clock. Mrs. Kenley tried to get her to lie down 'cos she was droppin' on her feet but she wouldn't stay; she went along home; like a mad woman she is. It's been a time, I can tell you. . . ."

The door was pushed open and Armstrong entered with a tray and when he placed it on a table to the side of the fireplace and began to arrange the things on it, Dan said sharply, "Don't fuss with that. Tell me, is there anyone in the stables?"

"Yes, Master Dan; Howard's there, but the rest are still out lookin', but they should be back anytime 'cos it's not much use. . . ."

"Tell Howard to get me the trap ready." Dan cut him off. "No, on second thought, just a horse. And have him fix me a lantern. Oh, and by the way, I've left a horse on the drive, I forgot." He shook his head. "Tell him to see to the animal; it's got to be returned to Shallbrank's farm tomorrow. I'll send a note along with it. Tell him to remind me."

After the two men had left the room he stood, his head bowed, gripping the mantelpiece while his teeth dug deep into his lower lip.

After a moment he turned and poured out a cup of black coffee, which he drank almost at one go, then picking up a piece of cold pie he chewed on it as he hurried out, then ran across the hall and up the stairs to his room to change into clothes suitable for a night ride.

It was Mary who opened the door to him. Her face weary for want of sleep and tear-stained, she peered at him, then said, "Oh! Mr. Dan, Mr. Dan. Oh, am I pleased to see you! Oh am I! Am I! Come in, come in. She's in the sittin' room. Do something with her, will you? Get her to rest. Oh! Mr. Dan, for such a thing to happen to her. Is it never going to end?"

She kept talking to him as he crossed the hall and opened the sitting room door, and when he saw Brigie sitting before the fire, her body lost in the big leather-backed chair, he groaned inwardly, for her whole appearance spoke of despair.

"Dan." She brought herself wearily upright. "Dan. You've heard?"

"Yes, yes, a little."

"My Barbara's dead, Dan."

He forced the saliva down his dry throat before asking, "They . . . they've found her?"

"No, no; but if she were alive she would have come back."

"She could have tripped and fallen, and be . . . be lying in some ditch, or deep gully."

She was looking into his eyes now and she repeated, "Or deep gully, Dan; and all night in the freezing cold. What she did was terrible, but . . . but she didn't deserve that. Poor, poor Barbara, she didn't deserve that."

"What did she do?" he asked quietly.

"She . . . she pushed Sarah down a hill, the place where they throw the old machinery. She wasn't to know what would happen. Sarah's leg was badly hurt." Her head moved again in small slow movements, and as if she were making a confession she said, "More than badly hurt, broken, and the flesh torn and gashed

199

to the bone." She closed her eyes as if shutting out the picture, then ended, "And . . . and then she was attacked by Jim."

"Attacked? Barbara?" He screwed up his face at her.

"By his own words he struck her and . . . and if she understood one quarter of what he said he had told her, part of her must have died then; and the rest Michael killed, for his fury was as great as her own must have been as he looked into my face and repeated what Jim Waite had said to her, and then he added, 'Never come back here again, do you hear?' Those were Michael's words to me, Dan, 'Never come back here again. Moreover,' he went on, 'I've told her I never want to see her as long as she lives, and if anything happens to Sarah I'll hate her until my dying day. I've told her I'm going to marry Sarah. And that's for you too, do you hear? I'm going to marry Sarah. It's finished, the plotting, the scheming, it's finished.' And it was finished, Dan. When she mounted the trap on the road I knew it was finished. She was already dead inside, the only thing that was left to her then was to kill her body and . . ."

"Stop it, Brigie." His voice held the same note as it had done when he checked Brooks's ramblings. "If you haven't found her there's still hope. Look, tell me, tell me exactly which way she went."

"She mounted the bank just along the road that would take her on to the fells, and from there she could go either straight ahead toward Allendale, or to the left toward Catton.

"She would never get that far. And anyway she'd have to cross the river."

"There are stepping stones and bridges."

"She would never find them; it was near dark they tell me."

"Then she's in the river."

"If she were in the river at this end they would have found her by now. In the South Tyne it might be different, there's pools there she could be lost in, but not this end."

200

"Yes, this end too, Dan, there are . . ."

"Stop it! For God's sake, stop it, Brigie! I'm amazed at you giving in like this." He held his hand to his head for a moment. "Did they look in the pits . . . I mean the lead mines?"

"I don't know. They would most surely do so. But she wouldn't go that way, she would never go that way again, not in that direction, no, she would never go in that direction. He said he never wanted to see her as . . ."

"Brigie"—his voice was gentle now—"you must rest, you must go to bed for at least a few hours. Look, I'm . . . I'm going out. I can't do much until daylight but nevertheless I'm going out, but only if you'll promise me you'll go to bed."

She lay back in the chair again and stared up at him and said quietly, "It's strange how the Waites have been Jonahs of the Mallens. It was Jim's father, Harry Waite, who was the means of Thomas's downfall. If he hadn't been overheard slating the young master, Thomas wouldn't have been made bankrupt, he wouldn't have had to spend his last days in this house and . . . and Barbara would never have been born. Now Jim Waite has killed Barbara."

"Don't talk like that, Brigie." He turned round and shouted, "Mary! Mary!" and when Mary came scurrying into the room, he said, "Brigie's going to bed for a few hours."

Miss Brigmore shook her head. "I'll . . . I'll rest here; I'll sleep here."

"Then if you do, I'll stay here too, I won't go out."

They stared at each other. "Very well," she said, "I'll go presently."

"You'll go now. Go up with her, Mary."

"Yes, yes, I will, I will that. There'll be another one on our hands if she doesn't."

"And I'll stay here until you come back and tell me she's in bed."

Miss Brigmore got slowly to her feet. She looked at Dan but did not speak further, nor did she sway as she walked down the room, but her step was like that of a mechanical figure.

It was almost ten minutes later when Mary came into the sitting room again, and she said, "Well, she's in bed, but I can't promise she'll sleep."

"She'll sleep once she's lying down."

"Aw, Mr. Dan, isn't it awful? Did you ever hear of anything like it? You know there's something in old wives' tales, by! there is, an' it's been proved again. They've always said the Mallens are fated to bring death an' disaster an' this last business is proving it, for what Miss doesn't know is that that poor lass, Sarah, is handicapped for life."

"What do you mean?"

"Ben Taggert told me on his way back the night; he dropped in for a minute to see if they'd found her, and as he said, it'd be God's blessing if she's stiff when they do, for if not she'll have to answer for her last act. He said they'd taken young Sarah's leg off; when they got her to the hospital they couldn't do anything, broken and splintered all over it was, and the flesh torn from the bone as if a wild animal had ravished her. 'It's a black day for them over there,' he said, 'for she was a bonny lass.' And she was, she was the star that shone in Waite's house she was. Harry Waite's niece she was, but they looked on her as a daughter, and Jim Waite worshiped her, he did. He was more like a father to her than a cousin. Ben said you'd have thought a plague had hit the farm and it's understandable, isn't it, a lass like that, bonny, to be left with one leg. . . . Aw! Miss Barbara. But I'm not at all surprised, Mr. Dan, not at all surprised; she was a willful child and a willful young woman. It's all to do with Mr. Michael, you know. Unnatural her feelings for him because between you and me"—she stooped toward him—"it could never have come to anything, being just once removed from half-brother and sister, 'twasn't natural, was it? Her whole life's been twisted. Aye, the things I've seen in my time, and in this very house. It was me who found her mother after the master had done his work on her, and it was me who laid him out when he

202

shot himself. Aye, aye, I tell you. And then some folks say it's the back of beyond here and nothin' happens. . . . Where you going, Mr. Dan?"

"I'm going to see if I can find her, Mary."

"But you might go and get yourself lost, Mr. Dan; and it's a bitter night, there's a frost formin', it's not safe for the horse. We don't want any more trouble."

"I don't think you need worry about me, or the horse, Mary."

She followed him to the door and as he opened it she said quietly, " 'Twould be better, Mr. Dan, if you made up your mind, like her, that she's gone. Tonight's bad, but last night was worse. It would have finished a bear off if it had to lie out in it."

"We can but see, Mary."

There was no more said and he went around by the side of the house, across the yard to the old stable where he had left the horse in shelter, and, mounting it, he rode out into the blackness.

Yet he had only gone a few yards from the cottage when he stopped and asked himself which way should he go? Before him was the road over the hills, but to the left of him was a narrow bridle path that eventually came to an old tollgate. There were two paths beyond the gate, and both led into the foothills. There were caves up there and an isolated stripped lead mine which he remembered exploring years ago; he also recalled to mind an old house of some kind.

He turned the horse onto the overgrown bridle path and as he went on he had at times to bring his feet forward to prevent himself being whipped out of the saddle by the entangling branches. Twice the animal stopped and refused to go on, until he used his heels on its haunches. When it stopped for a third time he saw in the faint gleam from the lantern that they had reached the turnpike gate.

Dismounting stiffly, for he was already cold, he thought of Mary's words: "It would finish a bear off if he had to lie out in it." And he knew it would for there would be little chance of her surviving a night on the open hills in cold such as this.

Pushing the broken gate to one side, he led the horse through; then mounting again, he took the path to the right. Half a mile on he came on the remnants of the house, shrunken now compared with his memories of it. Dismounting once more, he led the horse into the questionable shelter of the ruined barn, and after tying it to a stanchion and covering it with the blanket from the back of the saddle he took the lantern and went to move away from it when the animal neighed loudly as if in fear. He went back and patted it and said, "It's all right, it's all right; I won't be long."

He could see nothing beyond the radius of the lantern light, but he knew that there were a number of small hills clustered closely together around this part.

When he attempted to climb up the side of the first slope he came to he slipped and fell onto his knees and only just saved the lantern from being extinguished.

When he pulled himself to his feet he stood muttering aloud. This was stupid, bloody stupid! What did he expect to find here? But within a minute he was climbing again and, still slipping and sliding, he reached the top of the slope. And now he did what later he considered an odd thing, for, putting the lantern down, he cupped his hands over his mouth and called into the night, "Barbara! Barbara!"

There was a scurrying to the right of him as if an animal had been startled; then a small, thin scream from somewhere down below which indicated that an animal not startled enough was meeting its end.

He now looked at the lantern; it was running out, he must get down or he, too, would be lost in a very short time. Without the light he'd never find his way back.

The horse neighed again as he went toward it, but it was the sound of welcome now, and as soon as he untied the reins from the post it made an effort to be off before he could mount.

When he came out onto the road near the cottage he saw that the house itself was in darkness, which he took to mean that Brigie was asleep, so he rode on to the Hall.

There was no sign of life in the house except faint gleams coming from side windows. He went into the stable yard, and here too everything was quiet. He had the desire to bawl and wake them up, but instead he unsaddled the horse, gave it a brief rubdown, put it into its stall and saw it had food, then returned to the house.

The front door was unlocked and the lobby was lit with only one candelabrum, as was the hall; all the other lights had been extinguished. Again he had the desire to bawl until his reason told him that they were the sensible ones, they had gone to bed in order to meet the day, and he must do the same.

He did not undress, except to take off his two outer coats and his boots; then, lying on top of the bed with just the eiderdown over him, he lay staring at the ceiling.

The wind had come up and was buffeting the gable, but so stout were the walls and so strong the frames that supported the windows that the flame of the single candle burned straight and steady, its edge unruffled.

Perhaps she wasn't out there; perhaps she had found shelter somewhere; perhaps she had gotten as far as the town. . . . What! In the dark, and in her state of mind? All things taken into consideration, it was more likely to be as Brigie said. NO. NO. He turned over in the bed and buried his face in the pillows. If that were so, his own life would have been senseless. For her to be dead and him never to have told her that he loved her. Risking her laughing in his face, he should have told her. There would have been some point, some meaning to all the years of make-believe if he had given them a climax and come out in the open and said, "Barbara, I've been in love with you all my life, well, at least from the first time I saw you standing in the nursery with Brigie, so cocky, so sure of yourself, the little Madam. You spoke and acted like no one I'd ever seen before, and because I was

205

small, hardly any bigger than you then, you treated me as so much dirt on your shoes, and you became for me then an aim in life, something to conquer; and all I conquered were my feelings and the power to hide them from you by covering them with quips and sarcasm and teasing."

He screwed his face into the pillow and muttered brokenly now, "Oh, Barbara, Barbara, don't die, don't be dead. If you had married Michael I would have gone away. In any case I would have gone away, but I would have still had you there in my mind, beautiful, yet maimed by your affliction; tortured by it; but if you had been blind too it would not have mattered to me. Oh, how many times have I wanted to say that to you, to take your hands and look into your eyes and say, "Blind and deaf I would still love you. But not dumb. I would have to hear your voice, cracking and breaking on the words, pitching them to unnatural heights. Yes, I'd always have to hear your voice. Don't be dead, Barbara, don't be dead. For God's sake! Don't be dead."

"Oh, I'm sorry, sir; I . . . I didn't know you'd got back. They said you were out so I brought the warming pan up for the bed."

The girl stood at the bottom of the bed holding out the pan toward him, and he pulled himself up and muttered, "What time is it?"

"About half six, sir."

"Six, six o'clock?" He threw the cover back and swung his feet onto the floor, saying to the girl as he did so, "Bring me some hot water, will you, and a pot of coffee? Bring the water first; leave the coffee downstairs."

"Yes, sir. Yes, sir. Will . . . will I put the pan in the bed?"

"No, no, take it away. Oh, by the way." He checked her as she was going out of the door. "Send word to the stables to have The Colonel saddled for me right away. . . ."

206

The clock above the stables struck seven as he crossed the yard. Knowles, the stable boy, sleep still in his eyes, met him almost at the stable door leading the horse. "Mornin', sir," he said. "Snifter, ain't it! I've put the blanket on the back like you like it."

"Thanks, Knowles. By the way, have . . . have you heard anything more?"

"No, sir. I was out meself with Mr. Steele till right late on; the Morgans' men had coupled up with them from over Catton; they had the dogs out an' all but they couldn't make much headway in the dark, though we all had lights. The constables from Hexham are goin' to start again soon's it's daylight; they said they would give it another day but it's a poor look-out."

Shut up, buy! Shut up, boy! his mind yelled at the boy while he said, "I'm going in the direction of Studdon and over to Sinderhope; I'll make my way to Blanchland Moor. Should any of the men come, tell them that I've gone in that direction. It's no use us all going over the same ground. And bring me Bess."

"Aye, sir. Aye, sir, I'll tell them. . . . But Bess, sir, she ain't got no nose, never had, an' she's gettin' on."

"You may be right, Knowles, but nevertheless I'll take her."

"As you say, sir."

The morning light was lifting rapidly and it appeared at first sight that there had been a light fall of snow, so white was the ground with frost. In the fields the grass was banded together in stiff contorted tufts and where the cattle hadn't trod each blade stood up individually encased in white rime.

The air cut a way down his throat and seared his gullet until he coughed it out again in steam. He put the horse into a trot, and before he reached the cottage he mounted the bank to the fells and went over the burn and crossed a sloping field and eventually came to the tollgate by this shorter route.

He did not immediately dismount from his horse but sat looking around him as he asked himself why he had come back here. If she had intended to run away she would have run away much further than this. He was wasting his time. And what did he expect Bess to do here with the ground like iron? He looked down at her. It was right what young Knowles had said, she hadn't a good nose on her and she was getting on. She looked up at him and wagged her tail and he nodded as if they were exchanging words; then he went through the broken gate and took the path that led to the ruined farmhouse.

Having tethered the horse, he left the clearing and immediately scrambled upwards, wondering as he did so how he had avoided breaking his neck in the dark last night. Stopping at one point he called the dog to him, and then looked about him. The light was playing tricks with the valley bottoms; the green and brown of the land were molded into gigantic waves that flowed to the foot of the far hills, whose peaks were now being teased and rolled about by low clouds; not one yard of this land remained the same for an hour at a time. He remembered vaguely standing on this spot before; it was a natural plateau. He turned his eyes away from the valley and up toward the next hill. Somewhere around here there was the old lead mine; you had to round a butte to come to it. He remembered once likening it to a huge scab on delicate skin. Yet who would call any part of the earth hereabouts delicate?

It was years since he had been here; and then he hadn't been alone. He had been young, they'd all been young, and had scampered over these hills shouting to one another, John, Katie, Constance, Barbara, and he. His legs were short and so he was last, and they had laughed at him because he slid down a slope and the rough scree had torn at the back of his legs and made them bleed; the girls had been full of contrition.

How many years ago was that? He couldn't remember. But would she have remembered and come up here and gone into the dark hole? He could see them now, all of them, standing within the bricked arch of the mine, pushing each other, urging each other to go forward; then John bringing their play to an abrupt end, saying, "We must get back, Brigie will be wondering," and he had thought, John's afraid; he's just said that because he's afraid to go inside.

"Come, Bess. Come." He now hurried forward, urging the dog with him, over another hill and another, slipping and sliding, until there was the butte facing him. It stood alone, cut off from its rock fellows, as if isolated by its ugliness.

His feet giving way with every other step he went crabwise down the hill; then with labored breathing he climbed halfway up the steep side of the butte until he reached a narrow rough path no wider than a goat track. Following this, he came round to the other side, and right opposite him was the entrance to the lead mine.

The hillside, like the butte, was scarred but softened here and there with patches of brush and greenery and bracken singed to winter brown.

Not more than a matter of minutes later he was standing in front of the opening, but it looked so much smaller than he remembered it, in fact he wondered if it was the right one, for he guessed there were other such mines and he had but to search the hills to find them. But now as he stood in front of this one he was experiencing a strange feeling, it was as if it were yesterday when he had been here with the others; seeing that he'd only ever been here that once why should he choose to come here rather than any other place?

In his waking hours last night his mind had led him round and round these hills; yet when he rose this morning he had thought of taking the opposite direction, that was until he was out on the road; then it had seemed that his horse, not he, had taken the initiative.

Now, as all those years ago, like John, he was afraid to enter, afraid to go into the darkness. Bess was sniffing at the ground. He saw her nose go down to a small pool of water some way inside, and when her paw rippled the surface he was surprised that it was not frozen; the minute waves were crested with dull streaks of color as on oil.

When Bess disappeared from view he called her

sharply, saying, "Here! Here, Bess! Bess!" He could see some way ahead, perhaps for a distance of four or five yards, but Bess had gone beyond the light. He heard her snuffling and called again, "Bess! Bess!" He did not know how far the workings went into the hillside, and there could be passages or drops. He yelled again, "Here! Bess! Here!" and she came scrambling back into view. Then coming to his feet, she sat on her haunches, looked up at him and barked twice, and he bent down to her and asked, "What is it?" and she turned from him and ran into the darkness again, and once again he heard her snuffling.

Slowly he moved forward; then stopped abruptly, for there on the floor against the wall of rock something was lying. He could just dimly make out the shape in the diminishing light. Bess was sniffing at it, and as he sprang forward his foot caught a jutting piece of rock and he almost fell alongside the form on the ground.

He was on his knees, his hands moving over the prone figure. He gave a great gasp before he cried, "Barbara! Barbara!"

She was lying with her face to the rock wall, her arms crossed on her breast and her hands doubled under her chin; her knees were drawn up and almost touching her elbows. He turned her over, muttering all the while, Barbara! Oh Barbara! Thank God!" Then when he tried to straighten her body he wondered why he was thanking God, for it was stiff and unyielding. Rapidly now he got to his feet and attempted to lift her, but found it impossible, so he put his hands under her armpits and drew her slowly over the rough floor toward the opening.

In the light of day he looked down at her. Those parts of her face that were not covered with dirt had the waxen color of death on them. The upper garments felt dry but her skirt and the lower parts were heavy with water, and the bottom of her coat and dress and her boots were caked with wet mud, pointing to her having gone through some part of the river, for the roads were dry and hard.

Hastily now he forced her arms apart, undid the front of her coat and her dress, then put his hand inside her bodice. He could feel no movement, no beat. Frantically he undid some buttons that were evident, then thrust his hand between a lawn garment and her bare flesh. Still he could feel nothing. Now his ear was pressed against her breast bone; perhaps it was imagination but he thought that he could hear a faint beat. Plunging his hand into his overcoat pocket he brought out his flask. He unscrewed the silver top that could be used as a cup and filled it to the brim; then cradling her shoulders and upper body against his knees he brought her head upwards and gently poured the liquid between her slightly open lips.

When the cup was half empty the brandy was running out from the side of her mouth. And now he began frantically to stroke her neck with his fingers, talking all the while, pleading: "Barbara; come on, come on; let it go down. Barbara, for God's sake, come on!" It couldn't be too late, it couldn't. Why had he to come up here if it was too late? No, no. "Come on." Oh God! Christ! Make her swallow it.

As if his prayer had been instantly answered she gulped and he almost laughed aloud.

She gulped again, and after the third gulp she began to cough. It was a small faint sound, reluctant; following it she drew in a deep breath and her body shuddered; her knees began to tremble, then her trunk, then her arms until the whole of her was shaking violently.

Holding her tightly to him for a moment he rocked her; then laying her back on the ground he tore off his overcoat and put it around her, then again he held her, talking quietly to her now, knowing that she could not hear. "It's all right, my love, it's all right, it's all over, you'll soon be home and warm. Oh my dear, my dear; that you should have been driven to this. I don't care what you've done, or who you've done it to, it'll make no matter to me. Oh, Barbara. Barbara."

When her eyes slowly opened he looked down into them and said, "You're all right, there is nothing to worry about, you'll soon be home. Do . . . do you think you can get to your feet?"

She showed no sign of understanding him; her face was expressionless and still held the deathly pallor.

He now put one arm right around her shoulders and tried to raise her upwards, but her weight remained a dead weight; the stiffness had gone from her body only to leave a shivering limpness that was equally heavy. He urged her now, mouthing his words slowly, "Try, Barbara, try to stand. Come on, come on." But there was no movement from her body, no flicker from her eyes.

He laid her back and stood up and looked down over the hills to the valley; then he brought his gaze to Bess and shook his head. He should have paid heed to Knowles; all Bess was good for was wagging her tail, or licking your face. If he had brought Rory he could have given him his hat and he would have gone down there in a flash and led someone back. This is what came of being sentimental and impractical because of boyhood associations.

But it was no use ranting at the dog, he must get her down. But how? He couldn't carry her. In a moment of bitterness he thought that if he had been made like the blond farmer he could have done so; and to drag her down to the clearing was out of the question. It was either going for help himself or attracting it.

He looked down toward her and he kept his gaze on her for a moment before turning away and running swiftly to the butte. After climbing to its highest point he stood and, placing his hands around his mouth, bellowed over the hills, *"He . . . lp! He . . . lp!* then added, *"Any . . . body . . . there? He . . . lp!"*

He waited some seconds before calling again. And again he waited. Then just when he had made up his mind to dash down to the clearing and ride to the cottage he saw two moving figures far away down in the valley. They came into view from behind a stone wall and stopped and looked upwards. And now he was bellowing again and waving them toward him.

212

After some minutes of watching them moving along the valley bottom a voice came up to him, calling, *"Hello there! . . . What is it?"*

Again he waved and shouted *"Help!"* then pointed away to his right.

He thought for a moment that they were going back the way they had come, and they did for some distance, for they disappeared from view, but reappeared again much nearer, mounting the hills. They did not approach him by the way he had come but cut knowledgeably across the foot of the hills until they came out almost below the butte on a path screened by bracken. One man he recognized as one of their farm hands, the other man, a big broad-shouldered tousle-headed youth, he did not know.

The farm hand shouted up, "You found her, sir?"

"Yes, over here; quick!"

Before they reached the path he was already going ahead, and by the time they had caught up with him he was kneeling by Barbara and had raised her head once again from the ground.

Looking down at her, the farm hand said, "Aye, God! but she's in a state. She alive, master?"

"Yes, yes; but . . . but she's ill, and very cold; we must get her down as quickly as possible. I'll . . . I'll carry her shoulders if you'll support her legs."

"Lumbersome way that."

Dan turned and looked up at the big face hanging over him, and the young man said, " 'Twould be all right if she were on a door, but going like that she'd be joggled. Best let me carry her alone."

" 'Twould be best thing, master." It was the farm hand speaking now. "Barney's very strong, he's champion wrestler round these parts, she'd be nothin' to him to carry."

Dan rose to his feet, saying, "Of course. Doesn't matter how we get her down so long as we get her down, and quick."

Not without envy, he watched the young fellow stoop, place one arm under the inert figure's legs, the

213

other under her shoulders, and lift her up as if she were a child; then, sure-footed as a goat, he went before them, but again not by the way he had come up. Now he followed the path round the butte and down toward the clearing, while Bess ran to and fro in front of him yapping and barking as if it were all a game.

When they reached the clearing the young fellow stopped and, hitching his burden higher up against his chest, he asked, "Where am I for?"

"The cottage, Miss Brigmore's cottage. You know it?"

"Aye, I know it."

"I'll . . . I'll get my horse."

Neither the young fellow nor the farm hand waited for him and so, once mounted, he had to put the horse into a trot to catch up with them.

As they neared the cottage he galloped ahead; then jumping from the horse he ran across the yard and burst unceremoniously into the kitchen, startling Mary so that she cried out, "God's sake! What is it now?"

"I've . . . I've found her!" He was gasping as if he had run all the way.

"Oh! No, no. Oh! Dan; you haven't have you, you haven't?"

"Yes, yes. Where's Brigie?"

"She's asleep; she didn't go off until nearly dawn, nor me neither. I . . . I just got up meself. But oh, thanks be to God! Thanks be to God! I'll tell her, I'll tell her." She ran from the kitchen, shouting, "Miss! Miss! Come. She's here! She's here!"

He ran into the yard again where the two men were entering, and he beckoned them toward him, and the young redheaded fellow walked sideways into the kitchen while Dan, backing from him saying, "Through here, through here," opened the door into the little hall, then the door into the sitting room; he then pointed to the couch and the young fellow went to it and laid the now utterly limp form down on it.

When he straightened up he stood for a moment looking down at the girl; then turning away, he said,

"Well, that's done," and marched out of the room, just as Miss Brigmore came running down the stairs. Her eyes wide, she stared at the strange man for a moment before darting into the sitting room and to the couch, where, cradling her child in her arms, she moaned over her while Mary stood to her side wringing her hands.

Dan stood just within the doorway looking at them. He could do nothing for the moment and, remembering the men, at least the stranger whom he would have to compensate, he hurried back into the kitchen. As he went in one door they were going out of the other and the young redheaded fellow was grinning as he said, "Aggie, she'll laugh her head off when she knows 'twas me who carried the Mallen girl down from the hills. 'Barney Moorhead,' she'll say, ''twould have to be you.' Oh, Aggie'll get a laugh over this, right sure she will."

"A moment, a moment, please." He was standing in front of the young redheaded fellow, having to look up to him. "Thank you, thank you very much indeed for what you've done this morning. If . . . if you will come to the Hall later I'll . . . I'll see you."

"Oh, no need for that, sir, 'twas a pleasure, an' I don't want payin' for pleasures. Ain't every morning I get the chance to carry a young lady over the mountains, or the hills, or over a hummock for that matter. It's me should be payin' gate fee. Mornin' to you, sir." At this he turned about and stalked slowly away.

The farm hand, looking apprehensively from the straight back toward the young master, said as if pleading the other man's cause, "He's very strong is Barney, sir; but he holds to be no man's man; 'tis with the wrestlin' like, master. He meant no offense."

"And there was none taken. What is your name again?"

"Cousins, sir; I'm . . . I'm on your farm."

"Yes, yes, I've seen you. Yes, yes, I know you. Thank you, Cousins, thank you. Perhaps . . . perhaps you'll be able to pass on something to . . . to . . . what did he say his name was?"

"Moorhead, sir, Barney Moorhead. And no, sir"
—he gave a short sharp laugh now as he ended—"not
me, sir; 'twouldn't be me, sir, that would pass anythin' on to Barney. No, as he said, sir, he don't want
nothin', not Barney. I'm glad she's found, sir. I'll skip
back to the Hall and tell 'em, they'll bring the men in,
for some of them have been out since early on. I was
out lookin' meself when I came across Barney. 'Twas
fortunate-like that I did."

"Yes, indeed it was. Thank you, Cousins."

"Very welcome, sir. Good mornin' to you."

"Good morning." He went back into the kitchen,
stood a moment by the table, drew in a long breath,
then went slowly, walking like a sick man himself,
toward the sitting room.

He hadn't entered the doorway before Miss Brigmore came swiftly to him, saying, "Oh! Dan, Dan,
thank God. But she's ill, very ill. We must get a doctor
quickly."

"I know, I'll see to it right away."

"How can I thank you?" She was gripping his
hands.

"By getting her better."

"Oh yes, yes; with God's help we'll get her better.
But she . . . she's so cold, her body's like a piece of
ice. Where did you find her?"

"Not so far away, up in an old lead working, just
. . . just inside. But I couldn't get her down myself.
That . . . that young fellow carried her. We have him
to thank really. If she had been left any longer out
there she might have died."

"Who . . . who was he? I've never seen him before."

"He said his name was Moorhead, Barney Moorhead."

"Moorhead . . . Moorhead." She repeated the word
to herself. There was only one Moorhead hereabouts
and she lived over near Studdon. She was that dreadful, dreadful woman, Aggie Moorhead, the woman
who had helped to clean the Hall before the Benshams
took it, the woman Thomas used to meet on the road,

the woman whom he chose to satisfy his need and then thought he was doing so, but in the confusion of the storm and the blackness of the barn he had raped Barbara's mother instead with the result that she lost the will to live, and upon the birth of her daughter she had voluntarily released her hold on life.

In some strange way she too had lost her life, for from the moment she had taken the baby Barbara into her arms, every motion, every thought and action became centered around the child, then the young girl, and more so, if that were possible, around the young woman.

Life was strange, very strange in that it should fall to one of Aggie Moorhead's illegitimate offspring to carry Barbara to safety. She had the odd fancy that someone somewhere was laughing at the word illegitimate. Perhaps it was herself and she was going insane, and she would not be at all surprised at that. But enough of herself for the present; her child was back. Oh! her child was back.

She almost pushed Dan toward the door, saying, "Ride, ride yourself and bring the doctor will you, will you please?"

"Yes, yes, I'll do that, Brigie, right away." As he reached the door she actually ran to him and gripped his hands again and said, "Oh! Dan, I'll never be able to thank you enough for finding her; and it's because you didn't give up hope, you believed. But you look so tired, are you all right, are you fit to ride?"

"Yes, yes, I'm all right, Brigie."

He left her without any further words and she watched him for a moment as she thought, And I have never really liked him.

SIX

"You mean to leave then?" John looked at Dan with a sadness in his face.

"Yes."

"What about if she doesn't have you?"

"Well"—Dan paused—"I'll . . . I'll go in any case, I'll have to. But I suppose I'll come back sooner than I would have done."

"Does she know how you feel?"

"No. No, I shouldn't think so. She only sees me as someone kind and attentive; I'm the only one besides Brigie and Mary she's seen in weeks: When I asked if she'd like to see Katie she became agitated."

"How did you make that out, when she doesn't speak?"

"Oh, just something in her face."

"She doesn't attempt to talk on her fingers?"

"No, she just lies there."

"But she knows what's going on?"

"I don't really know, but there's a keenness in her look as if she were talking with her eyes."

"Does Dad know how you feel about her?"

"Not from me he doesn't but . . . but from his reactions, letting me stay down there those first two weeks, and sending me off early on a Friday, he might have guessed. On the other hand, he just might want me out of the way, my absence is less of a handicap than my presence, I think."

"Nonsense! You're getting on splendidly; and

you're handling number-two shop very well. They like you, all of them, and there's more than a few hard cases among that lot."

Dan laughed gently now as he said, "You might change your tune if I were to stay on, because then I'd likely join Katie, and you'd have a pair of agitators to contend with. It'll be funny, you know, if she ever marries Willy, because he's moving away from workers into management, he's aping the boss's outlook—you can hear it in the new tone he's adopted, and see it in the cock of his head—while she's going the other way, defending the downtrodden: higher wages, shorter hours, water in the houses, and closets; full-time school for all children. By! I can see the sparks flying if those two ever make a match of it."

"Oh, I don't know." John shook his head. "I think they'll be well suited that way. But I might as well tell you, as much as I like Willy, I wish she had set her sights on someone else, it's going to be awkward. Jenny would accept the situation but old Pearson's bristles'll rise when he hears of it, and there'll be a large family conference, no doubt of it."

Dan laughed and repeated, "No doubt of it." Then as he made his way through the overcrowded furniture in the sitting room toward the door, John said, "If I don't see you in the morning give Brigie my regards, and . . . and convey to Barbara I'm thinking of her."

Dan paused at the open door and looked over his shoulder, saying, "Yes, yes, I will, John." Then his head jerked round as his father's voice came from across the hall, saying, "Here a minute, lad."

Harry was beckoning him from outside the room that was termed the office, and when he reached him he said, "I've just been thinkin', I've a mind to go down with you the morrow."

"Oh! Good, good."

"Aye, aye. Come in a minute." He went into the room.

Dan followed him and he stood by the side of a long littered ornate ugly desk as Harry dropped heavily into the leather chair behind it, and when his father didn't immediately speak, Dan asked, "Is anything wrong?"

"No, no." Harry began to sort some papers in front of him; then leaning back he said, "Well, nothing that can't be put right. It's the house, the Hall; I'm in two minds about keepin' it on. Brooks and Mrs. Kenley appear to be waging their own private war down there, an' there's no arbitrator sort of to keep things on an even keel since Brigie's been so occupied, and the way things are shapin' it looks as if she could be occupied forevermore. I want to ask you"—he nodded his head slowly now—"and I want your honest opinion, do you think Barbara will ever really get her senses back?"

"She hasn't lost her senses, Dad."

"Well, she's lost something, lad; if she won't open her mouth or talk with her hands as she used to I can see Brigie having to nurse her for the rest of her life."

"No, no."

"You say no, no, as if you know something different. Does she talk to you?"

"No."

They were staring at each other very hard when Harry said quietly, "It surprised me, you know, when I discovered you had ideas in that direction. Gave me a gliff, to say the least. I used to think you liked going down there for the air and change 'cos your nose couldn't bear the rotten stink round these quarters, and then, well quite candidly, lad, I thought you were a bit gone in the nut, even to think of her, because as far as I could see she had firmly made up her mind in another direction. And another thing, if I remember rightly, you two never did hit it off, sparring was your occupation when you met. Now, well, I've got to thinking otherwise. Am I right?"

"Yes, yes, you're right, Dad."

"Well, what are you going to do about it?"

"Try to get her to marry me."

"Aw, lad! lad!" Harry pulled himself forward to the edge of the chair, leaned his forearms on the desk and bowed his head over them before he went on, "You're lashing a dead horse, aren't you, from all sides as I see it. In the first place, if she was so mad over the young farmer that she almost killed the lass because he looked at her, then she's not goin' to forget him lightly. Have you thought of that?"

"I've thought of that."

Harry lifted his head back on his hunched shoulders and stared at his son, and his voice had a kindly note to it as he continued, "And then apart from her being in this trancelike state, and from what I can gather from Doctor Carr, aye"—he nodded sharply now—"I had a talk with him about it. He explained it like, to use his words, it's sort of like a safety guard on a loom, as I see it, put there so's you can't probe too far, and as he said it could go on for years. Then there's this other thing she's got to live with, her deafness. Lad, have you thought well about it 'cos you'll be taking something on your plate whichever way you look at it?"

"I'll be glad to take it on my plate, that's if I get the chance."

"Oh, well, you know your own business best. Does it mean then you're going to settle down and stick it out here?"

"No." The answer came sharp and definite, and Harry showed his surprise on his stretched face and he repeated, "No? Then what do you intend to do, 'cos in any case she'll have to be kept in the style, as they say in that class, to which she has been accustomed? Brigie has given her the manners and education, and it's meself that has supplied most of the trimmings, so to speak. Not that I minded doing it, 'cos I was very grateful for what Brigie did for you all, especially Katie. But now"—he gave a short laugh—"it looks to me that Brigie's efforts in that quarter have been wasted an' all 'cos something'll have to be done with our Katie. Talk about a rebel in the camp, my God! I never thought to live to see the day. But that's another story and it'll have to be dealt with later. At present we're talking about you and . . . and Barbara. You say you're not staying on here, so would you mind telling me what you intend to do?"

Dan moved a step away from the end of the desk. He turned his head and looked at a glass-fronted bookcase that held few books but stacks of ledgers and papers; then he rubbed his hand hard over the lower part of his face before looking at his father again and saying, "We . . . ll, it's something I was going to bring up with you but . . . but later. I was going to ask you if you'd be kind enough to give me my share that would be due. . . ." He closed his eyes and gave his head a quick jerk to the side, then added rapidly, "I didn't mean that, there's nothing due to me, you've given me everything so far and generously, but . . . but you would in the end, I suppose, be sharing things out between the three of us, and . . . and I wondered if you'd give me what you consider, well, the amount that . . . that I might get later on, or at least some of it, enough to enable me to travel for a while with. . . ." He stopped.

Harry was glaring at him now but his voice was quiet as he said, "Aye, go on."

"Well, with Barbara; if she'll have me."

"And . . . and how much do you think your share will be?"

"I've . . . I've no idea."

"But you've got a sum in mind?"

"Well, I thought three or four thousand."

"Three or four thousand." Harry pressed his lips tightly together and sucked them inward for a moment, then he said, still quietly, "Three or four thousand, just like that; three or four thousand. And if you get it, how long do you think it's going to last you travelin' the world?"

"Quite some time the way I would spend it; I'm . . . I'm not looking for the high life. I . . . I just want to see places, learn, think. Oh"—again he shook his head, closed his eyes, then jerked his chin upwards— "I . . . I can't explain it properly, I'm not putting it over as I should. I . . . I only know that I've got this urge in me to move. And whether she comes with me or not, I've got to get away."

Harry now dropped his chin forward and, his voice very low, he said, "That makes me sad, lad, to hear you say that you've got to get away; it's as if we had the mange."

"Aw! no, no, Dad. You've got me wrong, quite wrong. I . . . well, how can I put it? I . . . I care deeply for you and John and Katie. We're a family, we've always been happy together. How can I make you understand my need?"

"Don't try, lad, don't try; but if gettin' away's so important to you there's nothing more to be said. You know me, I keep nobody against their will. But let me put this to you, have you thought about if she'll marry you and not want to move? An' then there's the woman who's been mother and father to her, who she's clung to all these years, will Barbara want to leave her? And there's still another side to it. You take Barbara away from that cottage and what has Brigie got left? Nowt as I can see. She's built her world around that lass, she's eaten, breathed, and slept her. I can look back to when she was a little bairn, Barbara, and Brigie holding her in her arms and the mother look on her face. Have you thought about that side of it?"

"No, but now that you mention it I . . . I would be very concerned for Brigie's feelings; but it wouldn't stop me taking Barbara if she'd come."

"Well then, that's settled." Harry now clapped his two hands flat down on the desk. "As I see it all you've got to do is to persuade the lass to come back to life, then woo her as the saying goes, marry her, and go off. . . . How long do you think it's going to take you?"

"I don't know."

"And if she doesn't have you, you say you'll still go off?"

"Yes, I'll still go off."

"Aye, well"—Harry pulled himself to his feet—"now we know where we stand, at least you do, but I'm still left with that bloody house and all its bloody problems." His voice was getting louder now. "And I've

223

nobody to go to but meself to ask for advice, so I ask you, do you see any reason for me keeping it on? John doesn't. As soon as he's settled he'll go over to Pearson's semi-mansion 'cos Jenny doesn't want to leave old Walter. Funny that, John gone, you gone; I wonder if Katie will insist on bringing Willy here 'cos she'll think I'll be lonely. Well, if she does, I'll say this to her, no bloody fear. I like Willy, I've got nothin' against him, but when I leave the mill, I leave the mill, I don't bring it home to bed. The mill's becoming a mania with Willy. . . . You said something along those lines a while ago, if I remember, not that it's a bad thing mind, as long as it's kept in its place. Well, what I'm saying is, I just couldn't stand the two of them in the house: trade unions, politics, slum conditions, an' the poor for breakfast, dinner, and tea. No, no, I'd rather finish the race on me own. But I can't see meself finishing it sitting in that Hall alone, nor yet here."

There was a faint smile on Dan's face as he said, "Aunt Florrie's doing her best."

Harry turned his head slightly to the side while keeping his eyes fixed on Dan, and he said, "Aye-aye. Don't think I haven't noticed. But I thought you didn't fancy her as a stepmother."

"I don't."

"Oh, well, whether you do or don't makes little odds, your future's yours, though of the two, mine seems more plain-sailing. Anyway, lad, let's get to bed if we want to get up in the mornin' with the lark."

Dan did not move for a moment, but stood looking toward Harry before he said quietly, "Thank you, Dad, thank you for everything. And . . . and I'd like you to know that I've always appreciated what you've done for me."

Harry, his head nodding up and down now and a twisted smile on his face, said, "Well, that's something to know; 'tisn't every son that thanks his father for bringing him up. But if the truth were told I've only been the provider, standin' in the margin so to speak, letting the others get on with it, while your mother and, of course, not forgetting Brigie, did the work. . . . Aw,

Brigie"—he put his hand onto Dan's shoulder and led him toward the door and out into the hall, saying now, "Funny how that woman's been the pivot we've swung round on for years, isn't it? Brigie this, Brigie that; would Brigie like it? Would Brigie approve? And if ever there was a bloody stiff starchy bitch, she's been it; never bend an inch, would she? An' still won't."

As they looked at each other and laughed, Harry said, "You know, I've only seen her off her guard once, an' then it was 'cos she thought I'd insulted her, but . . . but I was just leading up to something, something I was going to say to her when our John came in and that was that. I admitted to meself later on that I might have been a bit tactless in the way I put it, saying to her that nobody would think she'd been mistress to a man for ten years, but in my way I meant it as a compliment and . . ."

Dan stopped at the bottom of the stairs and his mouth remained open for a moment before he whispered, "You . . . you didn't, Dad! You didn't say that to her?"

"Aye. Well"—Harry looked to the side—"I suppose saying it ice-cold like that it does sound a bit much, but, as I said, I was leadin' up to something else and I thought it was common knowledge anyway, and she knew that. And it is, it is. She was an old man's mistress, wasn't she? Talk of the countryside. I'd heard all of it afore I ever clapped eyes on her, and when I did meet her I couldn't believe it. She was so blasted ladylike, I couldn't imagine her ever taking her shift off to go to bed."

"Oh! Dad." Dan was laughing deep in his stomach now and as the laughter rose he again said, "Oh! Dad." And Harry's laugh now joined his and he gasped, "By! it is funny, isn't it, when you come to think on't? I'm still a bloody ignorant bugger at bottom. It's true what they say about silk purses and sows' ears."

They went upstairs together, step in step, their heads back, their mouths wide, and when they parted on the landing and went to their respective rooms they were still laughing.

SEVEN

Dan sat by the side of the bed and looked at Barbara lying propped up on her pillows. Her cheeks were hollow, her face was colorless, she could have been thirty years old from the look of her. Her hands lay on top of the coverlet, separate, the fingers straight out.

"Would you like to see Dad, he's downstairs with Brigie?"

Her eyelids closed, which meant no, and when her mouth opened and her lips trembled slightly he said quickly, "All right, all right." Then after the pause that followed he said, "It was an awful journey down, freezing, but I was better off than Dad, I was squashed between two fat women." He demonstrated with his hands the size of the women. "It was so desperately cold that I nearly cuddled up to one, the one with the foot warmer."

There was no flicker of amusement on Barbara's face, but her gaze held his and he went on, "But I'd pass through Ireland to get out of Manchester and away from the mill and"—he smiled wryly now— "number forty-seven. I can look back to the times when the meals used to be jolly affairs, but not since Katie took over. Oh my! Our Katie!" He shook his head. "You wouldn't believe the change in her, you wouldn't, Barbara." He nodded at her. "The only thing I can say in her favor is that she's taught me a lot of social history just from listening to her. How she must have read this last year! And you know, she's made me read too, just to be able to argue with her. I got a bit tired of hearing the unions glorified. And there's so many of them: the Amalgamated Society of Engineers, the Amalgamated Society of Carpenters and Joiners, societies of bricklayers, iron founders, iron workers, cotton spinners, weavers' unions, and I forgot to mention black pudding, pease pudding, and rice pudding associations."

He laughed down into her face as she stared back at him; then his smile slowly fading, he asked softly, "Do you feel any better, Barbara?"

Was there a slight movement of her head or did he just imagine it? There was another pause while he looked into her eyes, then he sat back and, assuming his jocular tone, went on, "To hear our Katie talking about the unions you would think their members had been bred in monasteries, all the men are so good, honest, upright individuals, all fighting their wicked masters. Mind, I'm not saying that some of the masters don't deserve that title and they need to be fought, but hearing it from Katie meal after meal got to be too much, so"—he now nodded his head at her—"you can understand when I came across a certain piece of information concerning a little gunpowder plot, and nothing to do with Guy Fawkes but with a union and its members, I lapped it up, so the next time she started I said to her, in my most aggravating and superior way, you know what that's like"—he pulled a face at her— "I said to her, 'Did you ever hear of a tin of gunpowder that was placed in the house of a Sheffield non-unionist in an attempt to blow him up?' Oh, you should have heard her. Yes, she had heard of it. But that was in sixty-six and the men had been provoked beyond endurance, she said. And then I asked if she had heard of the Sheffield unionists and those members of the Manchester brickmakers' clubs who had done murders in the name of the unions—they had actually killed one employer whom they considered was unfair. Of course, they'd hired someone to do their dirty work and paid him twenty pounds for the job." He laughed again as he ended, "Believe me, Barbara, I nearly laid myself out for assassination, she became so angry. She was red in the face and bawling. This was an isolated case, she said; the unions were fighting for their lives, which meant the lives of their wives and children. . . . Do you know, it's a good job they don't allow women in Parliament else she'd be there tomorrow. If the men of the towns hadn't got the vote in sixty-seven, believe me she would have got it for them this year. She talks of a junta, of Comte's theories, you know positivism. Or perhaps you don't. I didn't. Anyway, he was some French philosopher who died over twenty years ago. He started a religion of humanity, as he called it, and this is what our Katie keeps on about, among other things of course. You wouldn't recognize her, Barbara. I tell you you wouldn't. She quotes from some fellow called Harney, who ran a newspaper, The Red Republican. Every proletarian who does not see and feel that he belongs to an enslaved and degraded class is a *FOOL,* was what he said, and she believes it. She talks about the death of the Chartists' Movement as if it were a family affair. There was a prominent member of it called O'Connor and the other night during the whole of dinner she gave us his life. I went to blow her up but Dad just laughed. Fifty thousand people followed his hearse, she said. The poor fellow had died in the asylum, I think, and I told her that that's where she'd end up if she didn't stop all this ranting."

He stopped suddenly; and now, his voice very soft again and his lips moving widely, he said, "You're tired; you don't want to hear all this rubbish." And when her eyes blinked rapidly he said, "Oh well, then, our Katie's doing some good with her life after all."

But he found he couldn't continue yapping about Katie and her socialistic ideas; for at this moment he had the painful, awful, gnawing desire to drop his head forward and rest it on her shoulder, on her breast, to put his arms about her, to put his lips on that still mouth, gently at first, then hard, fiercely, to bring it into life. He took up her hand and held it between his own, stroking the thin, bony fingers, and he looked into her face again, saying, "It's beginning to snow again. Remember when we used to take the sledge over to the hills? Remember the time when I went head first into a drift and there were just my legs sticking out and nobody bothered to pull me out right away because you were all laughing your heads off? I might have died." He shook his head slowly. "I might at that, and you would still have gone on laughing. Do you remember?"

There was no movement from her lids and he bent forward and said softly, still mouthing the words, "Oh! Barbara."

He was brought upright by the door being pushed open and Mary entering carrying a tea tray. When he turned toward her she cried at him, "Sitting on the bed again, Mr. Dan! I've told you it spoils the mattress, it does."

"I'll buy you a new one, Mary."

"Likely have to by the time you're finished."

"I thought you were out."

"Well, I'm not, am I? I got back fifteen minutes or more ago. By! It's cold. It would freeze the nose of a brass monkey, and sittin' on that cart I told him, I told Ben, I did. You should have a cover over this, I said, an' supply blankets. By the time I got off I didn't know whether me feet finished at me knees or not. And then in the town you couldn't get moved."

She kept up her chattering as she poured out the tea; then taking a cup to the bed she put it to Barbara's lips, saying, "There, dear, there; just as you like it," and as Barbara sipped at the tea, she added, "That's a good girl. That's a good girl," as if she were speaking to a small child. Then turning to Dan, she added, "If you want to go downstairs, Mr. Dan, I'll stay put here for a time."

"No, thank you, Mary, I can stay put too. You brought an extra cup, I see."

"Oh, aye. Knowin' you never say no to tea I came prepared."

After she had poured out two more cups of tea she took hers and sat in a basket chair at the head of the bed, almost on a level with Barbara herself, and Dan resumed his seat on the edge of the bed and spoke to Barbara, saying jocularly, "She makes a good cup of tea, I'll say that for her, if she can do nothing else." Mary, talking between gulping from her cup, said, "Good cup of tea indeed! And I say what I've said afore, 'tisn't seemly you sittin' on the bed, Mr. Dan, 'tisn't right, 'tisn't right or proper. Yet"—she took another gulp of tea—"what does it matter. As I said to meself earlier on, what does it matter, what does anything matter. Aye, I felt awful in the town the day, Mr. Dan. I've said nothin' to Miss about it, but eeh! I felt awful."

Dan cast a look in Mary's direction, and he knew from the tone of her voice that what she had to say wasn't for Barbara's eyes, and as if it even might reach Barbara's ears her voice was low as she continued, "Saw young Sarah I did, went slap into her. There she was, crutch an' all. Eeh! it was a shock seein' her like that. I knew she had lost her leg, but it was different, different seein' her with just one leg and a crutch, and he was with her, Michael, an' they looked happy enough. But . . . but I was cut to the bone, 'cos you know what, Mr. Dan? They passed me as if they didn't know me. I could have touched them by just puttin' me hand out, but they both passed me as if they had never seen me afore in their life. Eeh! I was cut up. I did a bit of a cry when I got on the cart. Ben Taggert said they were married last Saturday and . . ."

It was almost as if an explosion had thrown him off the side of the bed. The cup went spinning from his hand and Barbara's tea came onto his face and neck; then the scream that she emitted almost brought his hands from his scalded flesh to block out the sound from his ears. The next minute he was struggling with her, trying to hold her down while her screams, mixed with Mary's cries, seemed to shatter the walls of the room.

It seemed only seconds before Miss Brigmore's hands were entangled with his own, and also those of his father.

As quickly as Barbara's screaming had begun so it ended and brought them all into a huddle in the middle of the bed, and from their several contorted positions they gazed in alarm at the limp figure, thinking that now she really had died.

It was Harry at this point who took command of things, saying, "Come on then; come on then; get her up onto her pillows. It's all right; she's just passed out; her heart's still going. What was it all about?" He turned an accusing gaze on Dan, who from the other side of the bed and still gasping said, "You . . . you know as much about it as me."

Having settled Barbara more comfortably against the pillows, and covered her discreetly once more with the bedclothes, Miss Brigmore looked from Dan to Mary and asked in a murmur, "What . . . what upset her?"

Again Dan answered, "I don't know. No one, nobody."

"You . . . you weren't talking to her about anything in . . . in particular?"

"No, I was just sitting on the bed like this"—he demonstrated—"facing her and . . . Mary, Mary was sitting there. She . . . she was telling me . . ." He stopped, and now Mary and he stared at each other. Then he moved his head, saying, "But she couldn't! She couldn't have heard you from there."

"Heard what?" Miss Brigmore's voice had the old ring to it as she confronted Mary, and Mary, with a defiant movement of her head, now said, "She couldn't have heard; I was dead level with her, or behind her, like this." She now demonstrated how she had been sitting when she was talking.

Miss Brigmore, still with her gaze intently bent on Mary, asked slowly, "What were you talking about?"

Mary turned her head to the side. There was a look of defiance on her face now and she did not answer until Miss Brigmore said again, "Well, I'm waiting."

"I . . . I just said I'd seen them, Sarah and him, in the town and . . . and she was using her crutch and"—her voice sank low—"I said Ben Taggert had told me they had been married a week gone." She faced

231

Miss Brigmore again. "She couldn't have read me mouth 'cos she couldn't see me, an' I talked low, right low. I . . . I had to tell somebody; I couldn't tell you, so I told Mr. Dan there 'cos I was upset like, 'cos they cut me dead as if they'd never seen me afore. It was natural I was upset."

Miss Brigmore stood perfectly still as she stared back at Mary. After a moment she turned slowly about and looked at the white mask-like face sunk in the pillows; then she brought her gaze to Dan and asked quietly, "Do you think she could have read Mary's lips?"

"No, definitely no, not from the way she was lying. And . . . and she was looking at me. The only way she could have taken in what was being said was if she could hear. . . ."

Now Miss Brigmore looked at Harry, who a moment ago had turned from the bed, and she asked, "What do you think?"

"Well"—he rubbed his hand hard over his mouth before saying—"from what I gather she threw that fit because of what she heard Mary say, an' she could have only heard what Mary said if she had got her hearin' back. It looks as though when she lost one sense she gained the other. It seems far-fetched but that's the way I see it at the moment. We'll have to see what line she takes when she comes round. Look, she's moving now. . . ."

Barbara was moving. She was fighting her way up through layers of blackness. There was no substance to the blackness. As she grabbed at it, it melted through her fingers like mist, and as she breathed it, it blocked her throat as if she were trying to swallow wool, and it weighed on her as if blanket after blanket were piled on her body. It was when she was feeling she could struggle no more that she saw a glimmer of light. It became stronger, like the dawn seeping through the curtains, and the nearer she got toward it the brighter it became, and the nearer she got toward it the more fearful she became, for now she had a desperate urge to fall back into the blackness out of which she was

232

emerging, for a voice was screaming through her head, "We'll have to see what line she takes when she comes around. We will have to see what line she takes when she comes round. *We will have to see what line she takes when she comes round.*"

She had heard every word that had been spoken in the room since she had regained consciousness that long, long time ago. When at first she had tried to tell them that she could hear and there was no longer any necessity for them to mouth their words at her, or contort their fingers into language, she had found she was unable to do so. But what did it matter anyway? She was dead.

When she had jumped down from the trap she had run wildly through the dusk to meet death. Reaching the river she had determined to lie in it and bring her dying to quick finality. But when she fell forward it was onto rock, and the water just flowed gently over her. It wasn't until she dragged herself up and went toward the middle and found the mud sucking her down that, in spite of what her mind was telling her, her body automatically struggled until she freed herself.

She ran no more after that, she just walked and stumbled and fell, and rose again, and repeated this as she mounted the hills. The twilight had almost gone when she came across the workings and, falling into its shelter, she lay down and began the process of dying. But it was long in coming, as sleep was, and she lay shivering well into the night.

When she awoke the daylight was streaming through the entrance and her body felt hot and she wanted a drink, above all things she wanted a drink. She slept fitfully all day and the last time her eyes opened it was into terrifying blackness and to the sound of someone calling her name. The voice came from a great distance, "Bar . . . bara! Bar . . . bara!" it said, and she answered, "I'm coming," and as she closed her eyes she knew it was for the last time.

The memories after that were dim and confused. A man was holding her in his arms as a lover would hold her, but it wasn't Michael. Then she seemed to

233

sleep for an eternity, and when at last she awoke she knew that in a way she had gotten her wish and she had died, for there was no desire in her either to move or to speak. So she didn't move or speak but lay through aeons of time listening, and as she listened she knew that everybody was different. None of them were as they had been before, not Brigie or Mary or Dan, particularly Dan, Dan was quite different; Dan had turned into a lover. If she hadn't died she would have laughed at the absurdity of this, but there was no mirth in her for the dead cannot laugh.

Yet as the eternities passed she found that she could listen to Dan without irritation. His voice was not stiff like Brigie's, nor chattering like Mary's, and it wasn't the voice of the irritating youth, it was the voice of a man, it was deep and warm and kind. It was a large voice, much larger than his body, yet it lay gently on her eardrums. She had been listening to it telling of Katie's doings in the social field. . . . And then . . . then came Mary's prattle saying that Sarah had only one leg and was walking on a crutch. She was already screaming in her head when she heard the words "Ben Taggert said they were married last Saturday." At that moment the fact that Michael had married Sarah did not seem to matter so much, because she knew that, in a way, he would be forced to do so to compensate for her own act, her vile act of ripping Sarah's leg off. And through the screaming in her head she heard Jim Waite's voice screaming at her again, "You're a devil! You're a bastard! You've hated her all your life."

She knew she was a devil, and a bastard, and she had hated Sarah all her life. Yet at the present moment there was no hate left in her, not even for her Aunt Constance. The void that the deafness had created was lost in a greater void, for now she could not feel emotion of any kind. She did not hate, she did not love, they were emotions that belonged to another life, and in her present life, this still life on the bed, she felt she was being born again; she was emerging from a dark world. And her thoughts were new, different; but they did not help her to want to live for they were constantly stressing the fact that she was bad; because she was a Mallen she was bad and she would do less harm if she stayed forever in this half world.

Faces wove in and out of her vision now, hands touched her and she pushed them away. She didn't like hands touching her. Her body was burning, she was parched, she was back in the hole on the hillside. She gasped, "Water. Water."

"Yes, dear. Oh yes, dear; here it is."

Miss Brigmore supported her head as she gulped at the water.

"Are you feeling better now?"

"Yes."

Miss Brigmore turned her head away as she now asked, "Would you like another drink?"

"No."

"Barbara, Barbara my darling, you can hear?"

Barbara stared up into Miss Brigmore's drawn face, but she did not answer her.

"You heard, you heard me speak. Tell me that you can hear. Barbara, Barbara, tell me that you can hear."

"I can hear." The words were flat, unemotional.

Miss Brigmore turned round quickly, looking for somewhere to sit, and it was Dan who pushed a chair forward, and it seemed only just in time for Miss Brigmore was evidently overcome. Her tightly buttoned bodice swelled and the buttons strained from their moorings. Her whole face was alive with love and wonder as she looked at her beloved child. When she turned her gaze on Harry he smiled at her and nodded reassuringly; then turning to Dan, he said, "Come along, lad."

Dan stood for a moment looking toward the bed, then turned and followed his father; Mary, the tears raining from her eyes, her apron held to her face, went with them; and Miss Brigmore was left alone with her child, her daughter, her beloved Barbara.

She leaned forward and with the tips of her fingers gently stroked the hands now joined tightly together on the coverlet, but when they flinched from her touch

235

she also flinched as if she had been stung, and the joy drained from her face as she looked into the eyes now holding hers, and she murmured, "Oh! Barbara. Barbara, my dear, what is it? What is it now?"

What was it now? It was to stop the words which were tumbling about in her mind, leaping bridges of time and yelling, "You're to blame, you're to blame for all that's happened. You lived in sin with that man all those years, that fat man whose flesh I am. And . . . and since I can remember you have made me think I was different, something special, rare; when what you should have done was tell me the truth and let me start life with my feet on the earth instead of my head in the clouds. I see now that the only reason you ever went to the Hall to teach was because you wanted to install me there; you've used me as a salve on your frustrated life, you've turned me into an expensive doll, not fit to cope with ordinary living. If I had any hate left in me I would hate you, Brigie. What I want to say to you now is, don't touch me. Don't come near me, for if I am to live then I must learn to live."

On a long intake of breath she checked the leaping words and said slowly, "I'm going to get up."

"Yes, yes, dear; come then." Miss Brigmore rose hastily from the chair and went to turn the coverlet back, but Barbara held onto it, and, still slowly, she said, "No, I do not want help any more; I . . . I am going to get up on my . . ."

"You can't get up on your own, dear." Miss Brigmore's voice was quivering now. "You're too weak, you have been in bed for months, you'll fall."

"I am going to get up myself, Brigie. I . . . I will sit in a chair for a while. Would . . . would you mind leaving me alone?"

The rusty scythe that had lacerated Sarah's leg could not have caused her half the pain that Barbara's words were causing Miss Brigmore. Like poisoned spears they penetrated the stiff correct façade and thrust deep into the desolate creature that lived hidden within her. Nothing that had happened in her life before had had the power to wound her as Barbara's attitude toward her now. Not the devastation of her comfortable family home brought about by her father's bankrupty and imprisonment, which had also caused her mother's death; no humiliating trials in those first situations as governess; not the fact that Thomas would never give her his name although she had given him everything she had in life; not the shock of his raping Barbara's mother or the shock of his death by his own hand; not the latest blow that she was to be cut off forever from Constance; none of these things had made her feel as she was feeling at this moment.

For nineteen years she had devoted her life to this girl, she was the child she had never had. She had been mother, nurse, and governess to her. In the early days she had worn herself out trying to find a cure for her deafness. She had taken on the post of educating the children at the Hall merely in order that Barbara should have advantages that the cottage could not afford. She had allowed her everything, except one thing, the love of Michael, and that she had striven to deny her whenever possible, as Constance had done. But it was she alone who was now to bear the blame for it.

Blindly, she turned about and went out of the room; in her own room she dropped onto her knees by the side of the bed and asked God, Why? *Why?*

EIGHT

Christmas had come and gone. The Benshams had spent it at the Hall, accompanied by two guests, Miss Pearson and Mrs. Florrie Talbot. Harry had hoped that Miss Brigmore and Barbara would join them. When his invitation was politely refused, he went to the cottage and tried coaxing, but to no avail. Losing his temper, he had stormed out saying that living in bloody isolation was going to do nobody any good, and that was the last they would see of him.

When the rest of the family called en masse to deliver their presents and to wish them all a happy Christmas, Barbara absented herself; the only one of them Barbara still continued to talk to was Dan. . . .

January was a bitter month. The roads became impassable and there were drifts of snow twelve feet deep. Sheep were frozen to death, and when there was a sudden thaw toward the end of the month, Ben Taggert's horse and cart got bogged down in a ditch. It took ten men to lever them out and after such an experience, the horse was no further good and Ben reluctantly let it go to the knacker's yard; nor was he himself the same afterwards.

When it froze again the roads became more treacherous than when covered with the thick snow, and no human nor animal could be sure of a footing on them. The navvies kept the railway lines clear, and the trains still ran, if not on time, but the carriage could not get from the Hall to the station, and no one but a madman would have attempted to walk the distance.

So when a madman, so rimed with frost that he appeared like a ghost, thrust open the studded door and walked through the vestibule into the lamp-lighted hall, two maids coming slowly down the stairs checked their laughter and gave a high concerted scream before running back up again.

There was no sight of any manservant, and Dan slowly made his way across the hall toward the drawing room. He did not attempt to unbutton his coat because he could not feel his fingers inside his gloves. When he thrust open the drawing room door he was met with similar reactions, but without the squeals, as Brooks, Armstrong, and Emerson drew their outstretched legs and stockinged feet sharply upwards and scrambled from where they had been reclining on the couch in front of the fire.

"Why . . . why, Mr. Dan! Where you sprung from?"

"Manchester." Dan's voice was as cold as his body. He stared from one to the other of the men, then deliberately lowered his gaze to the table at the side of the couch on which stood two decanters and three glasses, not wine glasses, but ale glasses which were more than half full of whiskey, and he now added grimly, "It's evident when the cat's away the staff can play. And how they can play! You don't do things by half, do you?" He looked at the glasses again. "I understood you have a sitting room of your own."

"Aye, sir." Armstrong was sidling around the head of the couch now. "We . . . we had just sat, dropped for a minute." Emerson followed him silently, his eyes blinking, his face red with heat and whiskey, and he jumped when Dan barked, "Don't lie to me!"

Dan was now tugging at the buttons of his coat and when Armstrong attempted to come to his assistance he thrust him aside with a jab of his arm, saying, "Keep out of my way!" then he ended, "No wonder my father's thinking about closing this rest home up.

239

And not before time. Where's Mrs. Kenley in all this?"
He was now addressing Brooks, but he, showing none
of the trepidation of the other men, replied surlily, "In
bed, where she's been for the past week; says she's
got a cold."

"Well, if she says she's got a cold I'd be inclined
to believe her. Get going."

Brooks now made to walk away; then he turned
and looked at Dan and muttered, "Your dad would
have made no fuss about . . ."

"There you are mistaken; he's been making a fuss
for a long time now about a number of things, not
least the wine bill." He pointed toward the decanter.
"And let me tell you he doesn't blame Mrs. Kenley.
He did you a good turn once by bringing you here, and
he's done your son more than a good turn, and how
have you repaid him? You've taken advantage of him
for years. You're the worst of your breed, Brooks. Go
on, get out! And first thing in the morning see that
the outside steps are cleared of snow, and the drive
also."

The door had scarcely closed behind the butler
when he bawled at it, "Brooks!"

It was some seconds before the door was reopened, and when Brooks appeared he said to him,
"Bring me a clean glass."

While waiting for the glass he bent forward and
crouched over the fire, and the steam rose from his
hair and face and life flowed painfully back into his
limbs again.

He was sitting on the couch pulling his boots off
when Armstrong placed a glass to the side of the decanter, then slowly picked up the three glasses that
still held the good measures of whiskey, put them on
the tray, and went out.

Dan took a long drink and when, like a thin
stream of fire, it rushed into his body, he lay back and
held his bare feet out to the blaze.

The second glass of whiskey not only thawed the
cold out of him but also softened his thinking. Perhaps
he had come down on them a little too hard; and yet

240

they had no right in here, they had a comfortable room of their own. And then again, it wasn't a case of having no right, it was a case of discipline and loyalty on Brooks's part. He didn't blame Armstrong, or Emerson, for taking advantage, for they had received no such kindnesses from his father as Brooks and Willy had. He'd never liked Brooks. He might have been a good mill worker in his day but only because, he suspected, he wanted to ingratiate himself into his father's good books. But for years now he had also suspected him of being on the make. He was the kind of working man that got his own class a bad name, the you've-got-it-why-shouldn't-I-have-it? type. There were a number of them in the mill and, unfortunately, these were among those who ran the unions because most of them had the gift of the gab and, like Brooks, they gloried in the fact that the bosses didn't frighten them.

With his third glass he wished he were miles away. He soon would be, he told himself; yes, he soon would be, and not only from Manchester but from here, this raving mad stretch of country that hemmed you in with its hills and mountains, that drowned you in its swelling rivers, that froze you with its everlasting snow and ice, that brought your spirit low, that made you long for warmth and sunshine with an ardor the equal of the desire for a woman.

It was the desire for a woman that had made him risk his life covering those miles from the station to here. He had met not one soul on the road, nor seen one live beast, nor bird. He could have slipped and fallen and stayed where he lay, and tomorrow they would have found him stiff. He was mad; and what for? All these weeks, all the months of talking hadn't, he knew, brought them one inch closer together; the only difference in her attitude toward him was that she argued with him no longer and did not seek to quarrel with everything he said. In fact now she listened intently to all he had to say; but it was as if she were listening to a disembodied voice. And the voice now hadn't the courage to say, "Barbara, will you marry me?" for he knew what the answer would

241

be. The truth was, he told himself, Barbara would never marry for she had still not come alive.

Well, he had made up his mind. Or had he? Wasn't it his father who had made it up for him? "Get yourself away, lad," he said, "you're wearing yourself out. The money's there for you when you want it. I'm going to give you five thousand, not all at once, and it isn't all your share. There'll be a bit over when things come to be divided; but I can tell you, lad, that's not going to be for some time, I'm not ready for me box yet. I'll see that there's two thousand in the bank for you; when you want any more you can send to me for it, it'll give me some idea of where you're at."

Looking back now, he realized that it had been a very emotional moment. He'd had the almost womanish desire to lay his head on his father's shoulder, to put his arms about him, and to express by such action the feelings that were in his heart, but all he had been able to say was, "It's more than generous of you; you can be sure I won't squander it."

And now all that remained was to go along there tomorrow and tell them, tell her, and then he would pack. But he would have little to pack, for he was going to travel light. This time next week he'd be in France, or beyond. Just think of it, France or beyond.

He thought of it, and it brought him no joy.

After kicking the snow off his boots against the wall and having to lift his foot high up to do so, for the foot scraper was hidden under the snow, and knocking on the door, he entered the kitchen, as he was used to doing. Mary turned from the fire and Miss Brigmore from the delph rack, and they both exclaimed aloud much as the maids had done: "Oh! you've never made it in this weather, Mr. Dan!" Mary cried, and Miss Brigmore echoed, "Why! Dan, Dan, we didn't expect you. How on earth have you managed to travel?"

Dan laughed from one to the other as he drew off his gloves, then took off his outer coat, and when

Mary took them from him and, looking up into his face, said, "Eeh! Mr. Dan," he bent toward her and whispered with a jocularity he didn't feel, "There isn't the weather manufactured, Mary, that could stop me coming to see you."

"Aw! You, Mr. Dan." She flapped his hat at him, then hurried out of the kitchen, saying, "You must have smelled the broth, that's it."

"Is . . . is anything wrong, Dan?" Miss Brigmore came toward him now, to where he was standing holding his hands over the open fire that flared brightly between the black-leaded ovens, and he turned his head and looked at her for a moment before answering, "No, there's nothing wrong. I . . . I only thought I'd come to see you before, well, before I leave. I couldn't go without saying good-bye to you."

"Before you leave, where?"

"Home . . . here . . . Manchester, the mill . . . England. . . ."

"You're leaving England, Dan?"

As he was about to answer, he turned and looked toward the door; Mary had left it ajar and he thought someone was about to enter; but no one did and he went on, "Well, you know I've . . . I've always meant to go; it was only a year's probation at the mill in the hope I might settle. But I knew I couldn't. I . . . I did it to please Dad. He's . . . he's been very, very good, generous."

"Oh, Dan." Miss Brigmore turned to the table and, with her back to him, she said, "We'll . . . we'll miss you. Barbara, Barbara will miss you; you're . . . you're the only one she sees, in fact you're the only one she seems to want to see."

He made a small deprecating sound in his throat. "It's because she's house-bound," he said. "Once the fine weather comes she'll get out and about."

Miss Brigmore was facing him again, and now she said slowly, "I doubt it, Dan. Barbara has changed. You know it's in my heart to wish that her . . . her deafness had never left her because she's taken her hearing as a new affliction."

243

"No, no; you must imagine that. It's wonderful that she can hear again. Come on, cheer up." He went toward her. "You're looking very peaky yourself, aren't you well?"

"Yes, yes, I am quite well, Dan." She moved her head in small jerks and blinked her eyes, and there was a slight tremor in her voice as she added, "I was about to pour the soup out; we generally have it mid-morning, it warms one better than tea. Go along into the sitting room."

As Dan moved away from her she stopped him, saying, "On second thought, I won't bring it in for a while, I think you'd better tell her first."

"Very well. Yes, yes, I will."

He went out and crossed the hall and paused for a moment before he tapped on the sitting room door and entered the room.

Barbara was standing near the window. She turned immediately and faced him, and as always he was aware of her height. Since her illness she had seemed to grow taller; perhaps it was because she had become thinner. He walked slowly toward the middle of the room and when she did not come toward him, he said, "Aren't you surprised to see me, everybody else seems to be? Two of the maids nearly fell downstairs last night when I walked in, or rather, fell in. I told them not to try to bend me or I would snap like an icicle. And now Mary nearly falls into the fire and Brigie spills the soup; but you, you look as if you expected me."

"I did. I . . . I heard you in the kitchen."

"Oh! Oh!" He made a deep obeisance with his head. "That's it, is it? Still I didn't expect to surprise you; you know me so well that nothing I would ever do or say would surprise . . ."

"Don't joke, Dan." She came slowly toward him now and she repeated, "Don't joke."

"Why? Why must I not joke? Joking's part of my stock in trade."

"Because . . . because you've . . . you've come to tell me you're going away. I heard you talking to Brigie."

244

"Oh well, that's over then, isn't it?"

"Dan." She came near to him.

"What is it?"

"Dan." She was actually gripping his arm now, and he said, "Now, now; don't get so agitated. Sit down. What is it?" When he had placed her gently on the couch she gripped her hands together and pressed them between her bent head and her breast bone as if she were trying to push them into herself, and then she whispered something.

He bent his head toward her. "What did you say?"

She repeated the words and suddenly he jerked her chin from her hands and brought her face to front him, and now he whispered, "Do you know what you've just said?"

She moved her head once.

" 'Take me with you,' you said. You want to come with me? Barbara. Barbara!" His voice had risen from the whisper and was getting louder, and he glanced back toward the door, then lowered his tone again as he said, "You . . . you can't mean it?"

"I do, I do, Dan. Please, please take me with me, away from here. I . . . I mean to go in any case, I mean to leave, but . . . but I'm frightened on my own."

The light faded from his face now as he said, "There's only one way you could come with me, Barbara, you know that?"

Her eyes were steady as she looked into his and said, "I know."

"You would marry me?"

Her gaze still remained steady. "Yes, Dan."

"Oh! Barbara." He drew her hands toward his chest; then bending his head over them he kissed the white knuckles twice, three times before looking at her again and saying thickly, "You know I love you?"

She nodded once before answering in a low murmur, "Yes, yes, I know."

"How long have you known?"

"Since . . . since you began to visit me."

He smiled now, a sad smile, as he said, "You didn't know before?"

"How . . . how could I? We always seemed to quarrel."

"I've loved you all my life; can you believe that? Right from the first time I saw you in the nursery. I can remember the picture you made as clear as I'm seeing you now. Katie came rushing out of the nursery, crying, 'The Mallen girl's hit me!' then I saw you standing straight like a young willow tree. . . . What's the matter? Don't bow your head."

"I . . . I hate that name, my name is Farrington."

"All right, all right, darling," he said soothingly; "but it won't be Farrington much longer. I . . . I can't believe it; I can't believe that you want to marry me. But"—he shook his head sadly now—"you don't really, do you, it's only a means of escape? But . . . but don't worry"—he almost gabbled now—"doesn't matter why you want to as long as you want to. You don't love me, I know that, I don't expect you to, not yet anyway. . . ."

When she lifted her head and looked into his eyes he added jocularly, "I'm the kind that never gives up hope." Then his voice changing, he asked seriously, "But you like me a little, don't you?"

"I've . . . I've grown to like you a lot, Dan."

"Thank you, thank you, Barbara. That'll do for the present."

"When . . . when can we leave?"

He looked slightly surprised at her haste, then said, "As soon as ever you're ready. But . . . but have you thought about Brigie, how she'll take it, how she's going to feel about it?"

"Yes, yes I have; I've thought about it a lot; but I must say this, and I can only say it to you, it's Brigie I must get away from."

"Brigie?"

"Yes, Brigie. I can't explain it. I know it's wrong, I know in my mind I am wrong to blame her for all that's happened, yet I do. I can't help it but it's her I blame."

"Oh! Barbara, you mustn't think like that, not about Brigie; she's . . . she's given you her life."

246

"That's it, that's just it, Dan." She turned away from him now. "She's given me her life, and the weight of it is lying on me, and . . . and I can see it getting heavier with the years as she protects me and turns me into a replica of herself, Miss Mallen; the spinster lady, Miss Mallen."

"Oh! Barbara dear, darling." Impulsively he put his arms around her, but when he drew her close there was no response from her body, and his own became still. She was looking straight into his eyes as she said softly, "Give me time, Dan, give me time," and as softly he answered, "All the time in the world, dear."

He was not to know that another man, her half-brother, had said those exact words to her Aunt Constance in this very room over twenty years ago.

"Will . . . will you tell her first?"

"You wish me to?"

"Please."

"Very well." His arms dropped from around her; he turned abruptly and went out.

She stood looking toward the door for a moment; then swiftly she went to the window and, one fist tightly closed, she bit hard on the knuckles as she gazed out onto the never-ending whiteness that covered the garden, the fells, and the hills beyond, and the bleak iciness of the land was reflected deep within her. Yet she strove to melt it, crying at it, "I will love him! I will learn to love him! It can be done."

She swung round as the door opened and Miss Brigmore entered, but neither of them moved toward the other, and when Miss Brigmore spoke her voice was so low, so distant, that Barbara imagined for a moment she had lost her hearing again. "You can't, you can't do this," she said.

"I can, I can, Brigie, and I'm going to."

"You mean to say you would willingly go away to . . . to a foreign country?"

"Yes, that is what I mean to say."

Both their voices were muted now as if they were afraid of hearing not only what the other had to say, but also what they were saying themselves.

247

"You mean you would leave me, leave me here on my own?"

"I . . . I would have left you in any case had I married before now."

"That would have been different; you would have been in the neighborhood."

"*Yes.*"

Miss Brigmore started as the monosyllable rang out like a cry, and then was repeated, "*Yes,* in the Hall, or over the hills. You wouldn't even have minded that, would you, in the end, if I'd gone over the hills, as long as you had me at hand? And then you would have had more children to mold into your ladylike pattern, the pattern that has no association with life. It's been proved, it's been proved by everyone you've touched: Aunt Constance; as much as I hated her, I realized that her life had gone awry in the first place through ignorance; and then my mother, the other Barbara, what happened to her? What happened to her, eh? And at the hands of the man you played mistress to." She thrust out her arm now and pointed to the picture above the mantelpiece. "I want to smash that, him that you cosseted in all ways. If you hadn't allowed his woman to come to the barn my mother wouldn't have been raped and I wouldn't have been here. You brought your pupils up in a house of sin, and you were surprised and shocked when things went wrong. You still retain the power to be surprised and shocked after all that's happened. Katie, even Katie, rebelled. . . ." Her voice was almost a scream now.

As Miss Brigmore leaned back against the door it was thrust open and Dan entered. He stared hard for a moment at Barbara; then turned his attention quickly to Brigie where the opening door had thrust her against the wall, and as she was about to slide down it he caught her and, supporting her, led her to the couch. Then turning to Mary, who was now in the room, he ordered, "Bring a little brandy."

As Mary scampered away Dan glanced up at Barbara. His face was stiff, his eyes hard, even accusing; and now, her voice a whimper, she said, "I'm . . . I'm sorry, I . . . I didn't mean all I said, it just . . ."

"Then you shouldn't have said it."

"I . . . I know that." Her long body slumped and she sat down abruptly on a chair.

Miss Brigmore now put her hand to her head and murmured, "It's all right, it's all right." But when she attempted to sit upright Dan pressed her gently back, saying, "Sit quiet."

"I . . . I would rather go to my room." Her voice was weak, and Dan said, "You will in a moment; Mary's bringing you a drink. Ah, here she is." He took the glass from Mary's hand, but when he went to hold it to Miss Brigmore's lips she waved his aid aside and, taking the glass from him, sipped at the brandy.

"I'm . . . I'm sorry, Brigie." Barbara had not moved from her chair, and Miss Brigmore looked toward her and answered simply, "It's all right, dear."

There was a sudden rush and Barbara was kneeling by the couch, her head buried in Miss Brigmore's lap, her arms about her waist, and, the sobs now shaking her body, she cried, "It isn't all right. It isn't all right. I'm wicked, bad, and you have been so good to me all my life. I didn't mean any of those things, I didn't, but . . . but I can't stay, Brigie, I can't, I'd die. And it isn't because of you, it's because"—she now lifted her head and looked up appealingly into Miss Brigmore's white face and, her words slow and her voice more quiet, she added, "It's everybody all around; I'd . . . I'd never be able to go into a town, Allendale, Hexham, anywhere, not even walk the country roads but I'd be pointed at, the Mallen girl who caused Sarah Waite to lose her leg. And . . . and I know if Jim Waite had his way I'd be publicly hounded, taken to court. I . . . I couldn't bear it, Brigie."

Neither Brigie nor Dan, nor even Mary, contradicted her in any way for they all knew that what she was saying was true, although it was something they hadn't openly faced.

249

As Miss Brigmore put her hand on the black shining hair and gently stroked it she turned her eyes to where Dan was sitting to her side and said, "When will you be going?"

"There's . . . there's no real hurry now."

"You must not alter your plans; the sooner it's done the better."

"No; as I said, there's no real hurry. What does a week or two matter? And . . . and we'll be married from here, Brigie." He now brought his eyes down and looked into those of Barbara. She was still kneeling, holding Brigie, but her head was back on her shoulders now and her mouth was open to protest, but she didn't. Something in his face cut off any protest she was about to make, and some detached corner of her mind was pointing out to her that this man who was so much shorter than herself, and so much in love with her, and always had been, to use his own words, would not be as pliable as she had imagined, and as she stared at him she thought for a moment she was gazing into the face of his father.

When her head drooped he said, "Well, that's settled. Now Brigie, try not to worry any more; things will work out."

"Yes, yes, Dan, things will work out. Would you excuse me now? . . . would you mind, dear?" She gently extricated herself from Barbara's arms and, her usual dignity hardly impaired, she rose from the couch and walked slowly out of the room and up the stairs and into her bedroom. Again she stood with her back to the door but now she covered her face with her hands and murmured through her fingers. "Oh! God. Oh! God, help me to bear this."

After a moment she walked to her bed and sat down on the chair at the head of it, and clasping her hands in her lap she sat staring straight ahead, looking, as it were, down the years that were to come when she and Mary would be alone in this house, cut off from the house over the hills, and cut off from the Hall, for she knew, from what Harry Bensham had said over the past weeks, that he was really seriously considering selling the place, and if this were so she would never set foot in it again. So here she would be, alone with Mary, who, although a dear soul, was intellectually as companionable as an arid desert. But it would be on Mary she'd have to rely for companionship until one or the other of them died. The prospect caused her to close her eyes tightly.

And now she asked of God what she had done that such justice was meted out to her; was this payment for the pleasure she had derived from comforting Thomas? If it were, it was a high price to pay. Life, she thought, was a sort of madhouse. There was no reason or logic in it. You were brought into it and molded in a certain way; the mold was termed environment, and its early years shaped your thoughts, and your thoughts dictated your actions and set your principles, and you lived up to them, except when, as she had done, you violated the laws of society and gave yourself to a man outside the sanctity of marriage.

But reviewing her life through the ideals of justice, she considered that she had paid for the liberty she had taken because she had lost her good name and become publicly known as Mallen's mistress. One time in the market she had been laughingly referred to as one of Mallen's night workers; she had actually overheard this with her own ears; and so, speaking of justice, hadn't she made payment enough for her one misdeed, and she admitted to it being a misdeed?

What she didn't admit to was the accusation that Barbara had just leveled at her, that she was responsible through her teaching for what had happened to Constance and the other Barbara, and even to Katie with her radical thinking. But most of all she denied the responsibility for what had happened to Barbara herself, for from the very day she was born she had thought of nothing but guiding her aright.

She recalled the agony of the day she rode across the hills to beg Donald Radlet not to take the child from her, the child who was his half-sister. The hollowness inside of her that day when she watched him prepare to go and fetch the child himself was in her

251

now. His death on the fell—his murder on the fell—
had saved Barbara from his diabolical rule, and herself
from dire loneliness. Now, almost twenty years later,
it was Barbara who was inflicting on her a future of
loneliness, and she didn't know if she'd be able to bear
it. Yet she must appear to bear, if only until she was
gone—married.

Dan was a kind man, and although he appeared
of small stature he was in a way not unlike his father
in that there was a determination in him, perhaps not
so strong as was in his father, nevertheless it was there,
but she wondered if he realized what he was taking on
in marrying Barbara, in marrying a girl who had not a
vestige of love left in her. No one who had been ob-
sessed with a love such as hers for Michael, and who
had gone through the sufferings of the past months,
could scrape from the dregs of her feelings anything
approaching love for another.

An overwhelming feeling of sorrow swept over
her, and not only for herself, it enveloped Dan and
Barbara, and Constance, and Michael, and Sarah; oh
yes, Sarah. What was it about the Mallens that they
should at one point in their lives do something evil?
There were strange stories still current of the evil
doings of the Mallens over the last hundred years or so.

During her own stay at the Hall Thomas's legiti-
mate son, Dick, had almost killed a bailiff in the kitchen
and he would have certainly killed Waite had the same
bailiff not prevented him. And it was she herself who
had provided the money for his bail by secreting valu-
ables out of the house with the cooperation of Mary
Peel and the children. And what had he done when
he had been bailed? Run away to France, and she had
heard of him no more until he had died, strangely
enough within a short time of Thomas; and the solicitor
had come to the house to say he had left two thousand
pounds, but not to her, no, because she wasn't Thomas's
wife. The money had gone to Thomas's daughter Bessie
who had married an Italian count. She thought, in an
aside, should I tell Barbara about Bessie before she

252

leaves; it may make her feel better knowing she had a relative among the foreign aristocracy.

They said the Mallen wickedness was depicted by the white streak in the black hair. Dick Mallen had carried the streak, as also had Thomas's natural son, Donald Radlet, and the cruelty in Donald had been deep and wide. Yet Thomas himself had carried the streak, and Thomas had not been evil, unless you would place his desires under that heading, and these were no worse than those of many another man of his time and position.

Barbara had no visible streak to identify her as a Mallen; yet the streak was there, deep inside. She had always known it, and feared it and what it might lead her to. And her fears had not been unfounded.

But there were two types of cruelty; there were physical cruelty and mental cruelty, and Barbara was capable of using both. She had read somewhere that you hurt those you loved most. She did not believe this maxim; no one, unless his mind was deranged in some way, stabbed himself to death, and that is what you did when you hurt those you loved, stabbed yourself to death.

She looked across the room to where she could see the reflection of herself in the long mirror, and what she saw was a middle-aged—no, she must be truthful —an old, staid, primly dressed governess, the latter expressed by every detail of her.

She had the greatest desire, the strongest desire of her life, to die at this moment, to die before her child walked out of her life, to die before the loneliness of the house and of her mind drove her mad.

NINE

"Dearly beloved, we are gathered together here in the sight of God and in the face of the Congregation. . . ."

There was no congregation except the four people standing below the altar steps. The church was cold and dark, it was almost like a preview of the tomb to come.

Barbara's thin body, shivering within a beautiful fur cape, which was part of Harry's wedding present to her, did not stand dazedly as one in a dream but was alert to everything about her. The old minister's voice, thin and piercing, sent each word like a steel wire through her brain.

". . . and therefore is not by any to be enterprised, nor taken in hand, unadvisedly, lightly, or wantonly, to satisfy men's carnal lusts and appetites, like brute beasts that have no understanding: but reverently, discreetly, advisedly, soberly, and in the fear of God. . . ."

In the fear of God. Did she fear God? She should fear God; Brigie had brought her up to fear God; but she feared herself more.

"It was ordained for a remedy against sin, and to avoid fornication. . . ."

Was she sinning more now than she would have sinned if she had made Michael love her, love her without marrying her? And she could have done it, she could have, *she could have.* The voice in her mind was drowning that of the minister.

"I require and charge you both, as ye will answer

*at the dreadful day of judgment, when the secrets of all
hearts shall be disclosed, that if either of you know any
impediment why ye should not be lawfully joined together in Matrimony . . ."*

Yes, yes, she knew of an impediment. There was
no love in her for the man at her side. And he knew
that; but he would comply with what the minister was
saying to him now.

*"Wilt thou love her, comfort her, honor, and keep
her, in sickness and in health; and, forsaking all others,
keep thee only unto her, as long as ye both shall live?"*

"I will."

*"Wilt thou have this man to thy wedded husband,
to live together after God's ordinance in the holy estate
of Matrimony? Wilt thou obey him, and serve him, love,
honor, and keep him, in sickness and in health; and,
forsaking all others, keep thee only unto him, so long
as ye both shall live?"*

". . . I will."

*"Who giveth this woman to be married to this
man?"*

Harry took a short step toward Barbara, touched
her arm, and mumbled something.

Dan had hold of her hand. He was repeating
words after the minister; their voices see-sawed through
her head. To love and cherish till death us do part.

*"I Barbara take thee Daniel to my wedded hus-
band, to have and to hold from this day forward. . . ."*

He was putting the ring on her finger.

*"With this ring I thee wed, with my body I thee
worship, and with all my worldly goods I thee en-
dow. . . ."*

It was done. They were kneeling side by side,
but she was in the black hole again, her body shivering
as she waited to die.

They were walking over the rough stone slabs toward the vestry. Dan held her hand tightly; he was
looking at her.

She turned her gaze toward him. His face was unsmiling, but there was a look in his eyes that she could
only describe as wonder, and in this moment, she

prayed, "God, let me love him, for he deserves to be loved. . . ."

It was over. They were back in the carriage, and Harry, aiming to break the solemnity of what he termed to himself a wedding that had been sadder than any funeral he had ever attended, clapped his hands loudly together as he said, "That church; I've never felt so cold in all me life. How do the poor beggars sit through a service in there? An' him; he looked as if he hadn't thawed out for years."

"You'll have to donate the money for a stove and coal, Dad." Dan smiled wryly now as he looked at his father from the opposite side of the carriage where he sat beside Barbara, still holding her hand.

"What! Me donate a stove and coal you say? Not on your life, lad. From what I know of those fellows they see to number one; big fires for their toes and laced gruel for a nightcap. I know where the coal'd go."

"I couldn't imagine he's seen a good fire in his life."

"Well, whether he has or not, you're not gettin' me to donate any stove. Now, if you had brought it up afore and not rushed at this thing like a bull in a gap, and I'd been given some idea of what I was to go into this mornin', then I would have had two stoves put in there. Anyway, it's done; isn't it, lass?" He leaned forward and put his hand on Barbara's knee, and her voice low, she answered, "Yes, yes, Mister . . ."

"Now look, get over that an' quick. No more Mr. Benshaming; you either call me Harry, or Dad, like the rest; you can have your pick. Now this one here"—he turned his head on his shoulder and looked at Miss Brigmore—"she would sooner go to the gallows than call me Harry, wouldn't you?"

Miss Brigmore looked back into Harry Bensham's eyes. She knew what he was trying to do, but she couldn't assist him by even a smile and was grateful when he returned his attention to Dan and Barbara and said, "What did I tell you? . . . By! I wish they'd get a move on." He looked out of the carriage window, then added, "But I'd better not push him else we'll

256

end up in a snowdrift. Eeh! You're lucky, you know."
He nodded from one to the other. "Going off into the
sun. I wish I were coming with you. I never thought
I'd say I was fed up with the North, but by! lad, these
winters get me down. You know"—he put his head
on one side—"when you're settled someplace you drop
me a card. Just put on it *Sun shining, spare bed,* and
I'll be over like a shot."

"We'll do that." Dan nodded at his father. He
too knew what he was trying to do, and his gratitude
to him was gathering as a pressure under his smart
pearl-buttoned waistcoat, a pressure that could find no
release.

Of a sudden Harry sat back against the leather
upholstery of the carriage and let out a deep breath.
He felt tired, almost exhausted. This business of trying
to say the right thing, of aiming to pass off the occasion as if it were ordinary, of wishing he could do
something about Brigie's face, was more wearing than
hard labor. Aye, but he had never seen any woman look
so hurt in his life as she had looked these last few days.
He hoped devoutly that his new daughter-in-law would
show more concern for her husband, should he ever
need it, than she had done for the woman who had
brought her up and given her life to her.

There was a funny streak in that lass. They talked
of the Mallen streak; he was beginning to think there
was more in it than just market gossip and old wives'
tales. She was beautiful, there was no doubt about that,
but he would have thought a man would have wanted
more than beauty. Aye, a man did want more than
beauty, he wanted warmth, and if there was any in
her, Dan would be lucky if he ever warmed his hands
at it.

He had taken on something had Dan; but there,
it was his life. You bred sons and daughters and what
did you know of them? To think that Dan had loved
that lass all his life and he hadn't had an inkling of it
until lately. Then there was Katie who had the same
warmth in her that had been in her mother; but she was

257

freezing it, damping it down by piling the stack of causes on it; and now she was saying she wanted to marry Willy. Funny, but the more he thought of that match the more he was against it. It was odd but somehow he thought it would have less chance of survival than the one sitting opposite to him. Aw, to hell! He had himself to think about, and he was going to think about it, he had done enough thinking for others. Matilda had told him: "Don't worry about me, lad," she had said; "don't wear black at breakfast, dinner, an' tea. And get yourself some comfort, but with the right one, you know what I mean?"

Aye, he had known what she meant. There had been depths in Matilda he had never reached. He had been a blind man in some ways, ignorant and blind. Still, he'd put a stop to that, and very shortly.

The wedding breakfast was held in the cottage; Miss Brigmore had stood out against Harry's protests. The meal was plain, almost ordinary, although Mary had done her best; as Harry and Dan were doing now in an effort to keep the conversation going. Even Barbara was forced to help them in defense against Miss Brigmore's muteness.

The meal over, the healths having been drunk, they rose and went into the sitting room, and there Harry, pulling out a heavy gold watch from his waistcoat pocket, said, "Well now, I don't want to hurry anybody, but if you want to catch that train an' the state the roads are in you should give yourself an extra hour, I think you should be making a move."

"Every . . . everything is ready, I have only to put on my outer things; would . . . would you excuse me?" Barbara actually ran from the room, and Dan and Harry were left looking at Miss Brigmore where she stood supporting herself with her two hands gripping the back of the couch.

Going to her, Dan put his hands gently on her

258

shoulders and said, "Try not to worry, Brigie; I'll . . . I'll look after her. And I promise you that if . . . I mean when we settle someplace I will write to you and make arrangements for your coming."

She could not speak, she could only stare at him and pray inwardly that she would not collapse, not yet awhile.

When Dan turned her gently about and went to press her toward the door, saying, "Go up and have a word with her," she shook her head, for all the words that had to be said had been said, she could bear no more.

Dan now asked quietly, "Won't you come to the station with us?"

Again she shook her head.

"Leave her be. Leave her be, lad."

Dan turned and looked at his father, and Harry made a sharp motion with his head.

When Mary's loud sobbing came to them from the hall they went out, Dan holding the door open for Miss Brigmore, and they looked at Mary and Barbara enfolded in each other's arms. They were both crying, but Barbara was making no sound.

And now Dan, going forward, took hold of Mary's arm and drew her away and toward the kitchen, and Harry followed them, and so for a moment Miss Brigmore and her beloved child were alone. Her beloved child who was now a married woman and who was going out of her life never to return into it again.

"Brigie. Oh! Brigie darling. I'm . . . I'm sorry for all I've done."

They were clasped tightly together. "I'll . . . I'll never forgive myself for all the trouble I've brought on you. Will . . . will you forgive me? Please, please, say you forgive me. And . . . and as Dan says, you must come to us. Brigie, Brigie, speak to me, say something."

They were standing, still joined but only by their hands now, but Miss Brigmore did not speak, she could not. Releasing her hands, she cupped the beloved face for the last time, then leaned forward and kissed

259

Barbara, gently turned her about and pressed her toward the door before turning hastily back into the sitting room.

When the men returned to the hall it was to find Barbara standing with her head bowed deeply on her chest, the sobs shaking her body.

A few minutes later they were in the carriage. The coachmen had put the two valises on the rack; this was the only luggage they were taking with them. Barbara did not raise her head to give a last look toward the cottage, nor did Harry look out of the window; it was Dan who waved good-bye to the solitary figure of Mary standing at the gate.

Mary stood and watched the carriage rumbling over the frozen road, she watched it until it disappeared around the bend, then she turned shivering and went up the path toward the front door, crying bitterly as she muttered, "Eeh! She's gone. I can't believe it. God Almighty! What's to become of Miss?"

It was as she closed the door that the strange sound came to her. Throwing off the coat she had put on against the cold, she hurried to the sitting room and when she thrust the door open she stopped for a moment and gazed down at the figure sitting on the floor in front of the couch, her body half over the seat and her face smothered in one of the cushions, while her two hands clutched and unclutched the upholstery as if she were kneading dough.

"Oh! miss, miss." Mary threw herself down on the floor beside Miss Brigmore, and putting her arms about her she cried, "Don't take on so. Don't take on. Come on, sit up. I'll get you a drink; come on, come on, lass." She so far forgot herself as not to apologize for the slip.

It was some little while before she was able to persuade Miss Brigmore to get up from the floor, and when she had her settled on the couch and had drawn a shawl around her shoulders she said, "Now, now, just stay put for a minute, I'll get you something hot. And I'll lace it. That's what you want down you, a good lacing."

The tears still flowed and, making no effort to dry them, Miss Brigmore sat and stared into the fire. After a while her eyes lifted upwards and came to rest on Thomas's picture. Benign as always, he was smiling at her; the watch chain across his portly figure gleamed and seemed to pick up a light in his eyes. It was as if he were saying, "Come on, come on, it isn't the end of everything. You're no worse off than when you started, in fact you're better off, much better off than when you had me to look after, for have you not got a house that is yours, and three thousand pounds in the bank, and a friend like Harry Bensham?"

A friend like Harry Bensham? Harry Bensham would soon follow his son and Barbara. Like them he would disappear from her life, perhaps to reappear at intervals to give her his good wishes. She looked up into the eyes that seemed alive and for a flashing moment she thought, I wish I had never stepped into High Banks Hall, for then I would never have set eyes on you, and my life might have been my own, not given to this one or that, to be thrown back at me empty, holding nothing worth living for. But the softness in the eyes looking into hers melted the thought away, and the expression on the face appeared to take on a sadness now, and she heard Thomas's voice riding the years, saying, "I've loved you like I've loved no one else; be content with that."

But could one be content to live on a mere memory? Well, she'd have to, wouldn't she? She'd have to gather her forces together and face what life offered to such as she; Miss Brigmore; always Miss Brigmore.

TEN

She had gone to bed and sleep had come to her through a mixture of exhaustion and whiskey, for Mary had, last thing that evening, laced a cup of hot milk to the extent that it had become cool.

It was nine o'clock the following morning when Mary came into the bedroom carrying a breakfast tray. After placing it on a side table she opened the curtains; then bending over the bed, she gently shook Miss Brigmore by the shoulder, saying, "Sit up, miss, and have this."

"What!" Miss Brigmore turned onto her back, opened her eyes, and blinked. Then she glanced toward the window and murmured, "I've . . . I've overslept; what time is it?"

"Going on half nine."

"Half-past nine!" Miss Brigmore drew herself up against the pillows, buttoned the top button of her nightdress, smoothed down the coverlet, then said, "It's . . . it's still very cold."

"Aye, and likely to get colder; there's been another three inches in the night an' it's still coming down. Here, put this round you." She brought a woollen shawl from the chair and placed it around Miss Brigmore's shoulders; then putting the breakfast tray across her knees, she said, "Now get that down you, an' no saying you don't want it. I've been doing a lot of thinking since yesterday and what I thought was, we've got to go on livin'."

Miss Brigmore looked up at Mary, and after a moment she said, "Yes, Mary, you're quite right, we've got to go on living. But . . . but you must not make a practice of this; we won't have any change in our daily arrangements, I shall take breakfast in the dining room at half-past eight each morning as usual. But . . . but I thank you."

Mary's face crumpled. She turned quickly from the bed, saying, "Oh! miss," and as she went out of the door she repeated, "Oh! miss."

Miss Brigmore could not face the breakfast of bacon, fried bread, and white pudding, and so, after she had drunk two cups of tea, she carefully scraped the breakfast onto a napkin and put it in a drawer for disposal later. But first she made sure that the knife and fork showed signs of being used.

Half an hour later, dressed and trim as usual, she carried the tray downstairs; and Mary, looking at it, smiled and said, "Well! That's it now; that's a good start. You can face any day if you've got somethin' in your stomach. That's what I say. Now the fire's blazin' and if you're going to do the accounts, it being Friday, don't you sit in that office but bring the books into the sitting room and make yourself comfortable."

"Thank you, Mary."

As she turned to go out, Mary said, "You didn't say what you wanted for dinner; I could make a meat pudding which would be warmer, or there's the cold pie and odds and ends from yesterday."

"I think we'll just have the odds and ends, Mary."

"Well, all right, please yourself, but the puddin' would have been more warmin' for you. Still, as I said, please yourself."

Miss Brigmore crossed the hall to the sitting room. The day had started normally, except for her having breakfast in bed, and from now on she must keep it normal, but she would, as Mary sensibly suggested, bring her books from the office into the sitting room.

When she had done this and had set up the table some distance from the fire, she picked up her pen; then her hand dropped onto the open page of the

263

household ledger and her head fell forward. This was loneliness, and no amount of routine was going to ease it, for the routine affected only the surface. Inside was a waste, as wide and frozen as the fells outside, and like the snow falling thickly beyond the window, she saw the years falling into it, yet not filling it but eroding it until there was nothing but the shell of her left.

As the tears welled up into her eyes she brought her head sharply up and her hand into a writing position, telling herself as she did so that she must practice what she had preached all these years, self-control, under all circumstances self-control. But her preaching hadn't borne much fruit, had it? Little more than a week ago her beloved Barbara had thrown self-control to the winds and told her what she thought. She had stood just there. She looked toward the window, then closed her eyes, saying sharply to herself, "Enough, enough." Then she bent over the account book.

2 lb sugar	1s.6d.
¼ lb best Indian tea	2s.6d.
¼ lb ordinary tea	1s.8d.
¼ lb China tea	2s.9d.

She paused. The China tea would be unnecessary in the future, it was Barbara who had liked China tea, and she herself sometimes offered the preference to visitors, but that would be unnecessary now. She scratched out the last item.

½ lb cheese	8d.

She went on adding items such as oatmeal, flour, yeast, and finally ended up with lamp oil, half a dozen tallow candles, and half a dozen wax candles.

Accounting for one person less in the household, the accounts should be one third less, but they didn't work out like that, for the same amount of coal, wood, candles, and oil were needed. Yet she could cut down on oil; Barbara had kept her lamp alight well into the night.

The accounts finished, the bill for the groceries made out to give the carrier, when he could get through, she turned and looked toward the fire and asked herself what she should do now. Well, what did she do other mornings? She had for the past few months been attending Barbara's personal wants; prior to that period she would, at this time, have been in the Hall most week days certainly; weekends she reserved for a little leisure for quiet reading and such, and she hadn't the slightest desire to pick up a book.

At eleven o'clock Mary bustled in with a bowl of soup, saying, "Ah, there now; I'm glad to see you sitting quiet for a minute."

"You . . . you haven't put anything extra in the soup, Mary?"

"No, no." Mary shook her head from side to side. "I wouldn't think about lacin' soup, now would I?" She smiled, then went to the scuttle, and as she lifted it to throw more coals on the fire Miss Brigmore said, "It is quite all right, it is quite big enough for the time being. I'll attend to it when it needs it."

Strange, she even thought so herself, that now when she had more money to spend on herself and the house than ever before, the frugal habits still held.

"Well, don't let it go too low."

On this admonition Mary went out, and she was left alone again. She looked at the soup. She had no appetite for it, but there was no way of getting rid of it unless she opened the window. And that was impossible. Slowly she sipped at it and she had drunk only about a quarter of it when she heard the dull thumping against the outer wall, then the banging on the front door. She put the bowl down as she heard Mary go to the door; then Harry Bensham's voice came to her from the hall, saying, "No, I'm not stayin', so I'll keep me coat on."

When the sitting room door opened she rose slowly from the couch, and he came straight toward her, saying, "What a day! 'Tisn't fit for a dog to be out. Come on, get your things on."

"Why?"

" 'Cos you're coming back with me, you're not staying here on your own moping."

"I'm . . . I'm not moping, and I'm perfectly all right, and . . ."

"Now look, I'm frozen to the marrow, I've committed a sort of crime getting those beasts out of the stables, I don't want to keep them standin' out there until they freeze to death. And another thing"—he came close to her now and looked down into her face—"I'm lonely. There's times when I hate me own company, and it looks like I'll not get to the station for some days; they only just made it yesterday, an' by the skin of their teeth. By! That was a ride and a half. I don't know how we got back, near on ten o'clock when we got in. So come on, do me a good turn, and come and have a bite with me. An' bring Mary along. I'll tell her."

Before she could say anything he had turned from her, opened the door, and called into the hall, "Mary! You, Mary!"

When Mary appeared from the kitchen he said, "Get into your things, you're coming back with us."

"Oh! Oh! Are we? Oh, that's good, that's good, Mr. Bensham. I won't be a tick."

He turned back into the room saying, "No trouble in that quarter." He was standing near her again. "Come on," he said gently, "do this for me."

He watched her head droop to the side, he watched her bite on her lip, then he watched her move slowly past him with lowered gaze and go out of the room. Turning to the fire, he patted his coat tails to let the blaze warm his buttocks while he said to himself, "Aye! Aye! Well now, here we go!"

It was almost an hour later when the carriage stopped within a hundred yards of the Hall gates and Harry, opening the window and letting in a fierce icy blast, cried, "What's it now?"

"It's the incline, sir, they can't make it, the wheels are skidding all the time."

"Blast! Do you want help to push?"

"I . . . I doubt it would be very little use, sir, just the three of us, it'll need half a dozen or more. The back wheel looks as if it's gone into a rut."

"Well"—Harry turned to Miss Brigmore—"are you up to shanking it? Once we're off the road the drive isn't too bad, they cleared it yesterday."

"Yes, yes, of course; we'll walk."

Miss Brigmore had said they would walk, but even walking in the deep cart ruts, which had almost been filled again with the overnight snow, she found it impossible without the support of Harry's arm, and he, walking in the deeper snow in the middle of the ruts, lurched and slithered and several times fell against her, almost overbalancing them both. Mary, coming behind, was assisted by the second coachman.

When at last they reached the drive where there were but three or four inches of snow Harry did not relinquish his hold on Miss Brigmore, but linked his arm in hers until they entered the vestibule, and there, pressing her forward into the hall, and Mary too, he cried, "Now off with those wet boots and stockings the pair of you, and put your feet in hot water. I'll see it's upstairs afore you are. Brooks, see to that, will you? Get some cans of hot water up to Miss Brigmore's room. An' sharp now!"

Then in answer to a question that Brooks put to him he shouted back across the hall, "No, no! Not for me; the snow hasn't been made that'll get through these boots."

He mounted the stairs behind Miss Brigmore and Mary and as they were about to disappear toward the gallery he called, "As soon as you're ready, there'll be something hot downstairs. Don't make it too long."

When Miss Brigmore reached the sitting room in the nursery wing she was gasping. She thought the walk through the snow had taken it out of her; she must be overtired for in the ordinary way it would have had no effect on her, she would have enjoyed it. She refused Mary's aid in helping her off with her outer clothes, saying, "Get your own things off, your feet look sodden."

Mary was two years younger than herself but she always treated her as if she were so much older.

When the first and second housemaids entered the room, both carrying large copper cans of hot water, she thanked them, and to Jenny Dring's remark, "What a day for you to come out, miss!" she answered, "Yes, it is rather wild."

"Some bet the coach wouldn't get to the cottage when the master left, never mind him getting you back here." Jenny poured the water into the china dish. "But they lost their bets as I knew they would; when the master makes up his mind to do a thing he does it, I said. Like Mr. Dan, they're both the same. . . ."

"Thank you, Jenny; we can manage."

They had bet that the carriage wouldn't get to the cottage, and the master wouldn't get her back here. There was nothing servants didn't know, the slightest nuance in the temper of the house was registered by them. No doubt they knew much more of what was in Harry Bensham's mind than she did with regards to what he intended to do with the Hall, yet she was certain in her own mind that he'd already decided to leave it, and his action today in bringing them from the cottage, considerate as it might appear, proved to her that he could not possibly tolerate living here alone. A man such as he, who had been used to noise and bustle all his life, would find living alone intolerable; and so, as she saw it, he would retire to Manchester and the company of Mrs. Talbot, who undoubtedly would suit his requirements in many ways. She had promised Matilda that she would do her best in an advisory capacity to prevent such a liaison, but what could she do? And with a man like Mr. Bensham! For she agreed with Jenny, if he made up his mind to do something the devil in . . . Really! Really! Mary's sayings infiltrated one's mind, especially when one was low and off one's guard.

"Thank you, Mary; I can see to my own feet, you see to yours. But if you wouldn't mind handing me my house shoes from the cupboard and a pair of gray stockings from the second shelf, I'd be obliged. It's as well I didn't take them away before."

Ten minutes later Miss Brigmore, looking entirely herself except that there was no color in her cheeks, stroked her hair from its center parting and with both hands tucked a wayward tendril that was always escaping from a point near her temple to its place behind her ear; then turning to Mary, she said, "When you're ready come down to Mrs. Kenley's room, I will see her and arrange that you spend the day with her. You are not to stay up here alone."

"Don't you worry about me, I can see to myself. I'll be down later on when I'm ready, you get yourself warmed, and food into you an' made comfortable."

"Yes, yes, I will, Mary."

She went out and down the nursery stairs, and then hesitated before she crossed the landing, debating whether to go down the main staircase and into the office and send for Mrs. Kenley to come to her, or to go through the gallery and down the back staircase and to the housekeeper's room. She decided on the latter course because she knew Mrs. Kenley would appreciate this; Mrs. Kenley was a very good house-keeper and knew her place, but it was a good thing to recognize her position by an occasional small gesture of this kind. She'd be sorry to part company with Mrs. Kenley, for since the day she had chosen her from a number of applicants there had been mutual respect between them, and she herself had enough vanity to hope that wherever Mrs. Kenley went after leaving this position, she would remember her with favor and as someone who knew the correct procedure in the maintenance of a large establishment.

She went through the gallery and her steps slowed before she came to the end of it. She loved the gallery. Years ago she had thought it a very romantic place; now she put the name stately to it. The deep windows were set at short intervals along one wall each with its cushioned seat. When she was twenty-four she had likened them to lovers' seats, but then, when she was twenty-four she had been very young and silly. No, never silly. She had never been a silly person, she abhorred silly women.

She opened the far doors of the gallery, crossed the small landing, went through a green-baized door and into a passage, from where to the right a flight of stairs led down to the wide corridor from which doors gave off to the housekeeper's sitting room, the upper staff dining room, the servants' hall, the butler's pantry, the doors to the cellars, the door to the kitchen, and at the extreme end, the gun room.

The stairs leading to the passage were part spiral and before she rounded the curve which would have brought her in sight of the passage below and those in it, she heard Harry Bensham's voice raised in anger.

She paused with her foot halfway toward another step, withdrew it, and stood undecided for a moment whether to descend or to return the way she had come. But she remained standing where she was when she heard Harry say, "Now look here, Brooks! I've stood enough of this. You've had it coming to you for a long time, but this is the finish. I won't cut your pension 'cos I'm not a man who goes back on me word, but as soon as this snow clears you can get yourself back to Manchester. You've taken advantage of me over the years, more so of late since you've got the idea that your Willy's coming into the family. Well, that isn't clinched yet, not by a long chalk. And if he was in it already I'd still say this to you, you mind your own bloody business. I'm master in this house and when I give an order I expect it to be carried out the same as I would at the mill, an' if I was to tell you that hot water had to be carried up to Lily Rossiter's room I'd expect it to be done, and no back-chat or bloody innuendoes."

From her place around the curve in the stairs Miss Brigmore was not surprised to hear Mr. Bensham use the word bloody, but she was definitely surprised

270

that he should use innuendo. It was as she had thought for a long time, there was more in his head than he'd let out. It pleased him to play the rough, ignorant individual. He had also called the butler by his surname. His next words startled her.

"You and her never got on 'cos you, like all your tribe, you don't recognize class when it's under your nose, unless it's stinkin' with money. Well now, I'm going to tell you somethin', and you're privileged in a way 'cos you're the first one I've voiced it to, an' it's this. If I get my way she's here for life. Now put that in your pipe and smoke it, and give all the others a whiff of it. And I don't think there'll be one that won't welcome it except yourself, because as I've known from the first it was a mistake to bring you here, you were never cut out for the job. An' what's more I'll tell you this when you're on, you haven't hoodwinked me all these years. You might have been going to have consumption in the first place, but there's many worse off than you who carried on workin'. Because we ran the streets together when we were nippers, you played on me, at least you thought you did, but I've had your measure, an' what I overheard you saying a few minutes ago proved I've been right in me surmise of you all along. Now, now, don't come back with anything, Brooks, 'cos I won't listen. As I said, as soon as it's cleared up you get back to your beginnings. You won't be badly off, I'll see to that, or Willy will, that's if he hasn't got too big for his boots and doesn't recognize you. And mind, I'm tellin' you this, that's something you've got to look out for an' all."

Silently but hastily, Miss Brigmore retraced her steps back to the next landing; then quietly she let herself into the gallery again, and after walking a little way down it she stopped near one of the tall windows and lowered herself onto the velvet seat. She was here for life; he was putting her in charge, he was going to keep the place on after all and let her manage it. He had never mentioned Mrs. Talbot. It didn't sound as if he were going to marry. Some of the weight lifted from her heart. Oh, this was kind of him, indeed it was. Oh

271

yes, indeed. Doubtless he had been swayed by pity for her loneliness knowing how devastated she was at the loss of Barbara. He was a kind man; she'd always had proof of that, but now she knew he was also a compassionate man.

She looked out over the frozen landscape, and it did not appear quite so bleak and desolate now. What had Brooks said about her that had brought his master to her defense? Something from her past life doubtless, for there was nothing about it that wasn't common knowledge.

When she heard a movement outside the far door she rose swiftly to her feet, smoothed the front of her gown, and walked sedately along the gallery. As she neared the door it was opened by Armstrong, and he stood hastily to the side and held it well back in order that she might pass through; and she inclined her head toward him and said, "Thank you, Armstrong."

Emerson, who was crossing the hall, observed her descending the main staircase and he turned sharply about and went toward the drawing room door, and there he waited until she approached, when he opened it for her.

The servants had always been civil in their manner toward her, but in these two last encounters there had been a subtle change leading to deference. She thought wryly that lightning had no edge on the communications in a servant's hall.

"Ah! There you are. Feel warmer?"

"Yes, thank you."

"Come and sit yourself down and drink some of this hot toddy; perhaps it'll bring some of the color back into your cheeks, you look as white as a sheet.

"There you are." She had settled herself in the corner of the couch opposite the roaring fire, and before handing her the steaming mug from the tray he pushed a foot stool toward her, using his own foot in the process. "Put your feet up; you might as well make yourself comfortable for it looks as if you're set for a few days."

He now sat down on the couch, not in the far

corner from her but in the middle, within arm's distance of her, and after drinking the steaming sweetened whiskey and water, he lay back and exclaimed on a sigh, "Ah! That's better. How about you?"

"It's . . . it's very warming."

"Well, don't make a meal of it, drink it up. Talkin' about a meal, I had a word with Mrs. Kenley; she thought you might like to start with hare soup, she says you're fond of that, and then some sweetbreads. For me own choice, I picked a saddle of mutton; to my mind nothin' beats a saddle of mutton, with plenty of carrots. Then she suggested almond pudding. I'm not one for puddin's as you know, give me some cheese. But will that be all right?"

"Yes, yes, indeed."

"I thought we'd have it early, say about two o'clock. You know I'm used to having me meal around midday, habit I suppose. I never fell in with this three o'clock business 'cos around five I like me tea, and when I say tea I mean tea, not just a cup you know, like we have here, but a good spread with muffins, oh aye! toasted muffins in the winter, there's nothing like them, and a granny loaf. I'm not very fond of your fancy cakes but I like breads, you know, currant or spiced, or with caraway seeds, any kind of bread. But when you have a big tuck-in around three you've got no room for anything more till supper, have you?"

"No, that's correct."

He edged himself round on the couch now until he was looking at her squarely, and he repeated softly, "That's correct."

Then as she looked at him and blinked he waited a moment before saying, "Miss Brigmore, do you think we could stop being correct just for the day, as a trial like?"

"You are laughing at me, Mr. Bensham."

He bent slightly toward her now and, his voice low, he said, "No lass, I'm not laughin' at you, I'm asking something of you. You know, we've known each other a long, long time, a lifetime you could say, and you've never unbent once, not in my presence

273

anyway. Do you know that? You've never even been Brigie to me. You would be Brigie to the bairns, and act like Brigie I suppose, but to me you've always acted like Miss Brigmore, and nothing seemed to alter you. I've chaffed you about, I've even bullied you a bit, but nothing I did could make you unbend. Matilda used to say you weren't starchy with her, so why couldn't you treat me in the same way?"

Miss Brigmore drew in a short sharp breath before she said, "Because of our respective positions."

"Respective positions be damned! Aw"—he tossed his head to one side—"I'm not going to apologize for swearin'. You'll hear more than that afore you're finished. Anyway, you should be used to it by now, you've heard me at it long enough. And I say again, respective positions be damned! I wasn't a Thomas Mallen. . . . And now-now-now"—his hand came out suddenly and gripped hers—"don't stiffen up 'cos I mention his name, 'cos I'm casting no aspersions, because from what I can gather he seemed to be a bloke more sinned against than sinning; bit too generous in all ways I should have said. If he had his fling he paid for it. And I pity any man who goes bankrupt, and I've seen a few. I've been scared of it meself in me time. So look at it this way, if I can talk about Matilda surely you can bear that he be spoken of, because he was, in a way, your husband. Now"— he lifted up one finger and sternly wagged it at her, and his face was equally stern as he said, "I'm goin' to get something straight, I've been wanting to put it straight for a long time. You thought I insulted you once, didn't you, because I said I couldn't understand how you'd been his mistress? Well, you didn't let me finish what I was going to say that time. It was no insult I was handing you, because having come to know you I thought this much, you weren't the kind of woman to give yourself lightly to anybody, and it wasn't your fault if you weren't married to him. He was a widower and I don't know why he didn't give you his name. But there it is; that's your business and I'm not probing into it, now, or at any other time. But what I wanted to say that time, and

274

what you stopped me saying, but what I'm determined to say now, is that I'm not asking you to be me mistress, I'm asking you to be me wife."

His voice had dropped low in his throat. He was holding her hand; they were staring at each other, and when she didn't speak he went on, "You mightn't know it but I've cared for you for a long time, oh aye, long afore I lost Matilda. Matilda knew it. At least, looking back on the things she said, I think she had a pretty good idea. You see, I'd never met anybody like you in me life afore. Oh, I'd mixed with the up and ups an' their wives in Manchester, and when I say the up and ups, I mean the up and ups, from the Mayor onward. But what were their women? If they were good looking they had nowt in their heads, and some of them were no better than well-dressed trollops. It was just to show them what I could do that I bought this place; I intended to bring them here in their cart-loads when I first set up. I did bring two parties but somehow it didn't work out. Matilda, as you know, never had the touch, an' they looked down their noses at her. By God! They did that, the snots!"

She did not wince, and he went on: "It was at that point that I thought, well, I'll have me bairns so trained that nobody'll look down their noses at them. And so you came on the scene; an' you know, it was from then that I began to have a different slant on life, at least what I mean is I saw there was another way to living it. But I knew it was too late for me, I was no longer pliable. I'd been brought up in the rough. And then the Manchester lot, money, money, money; that's all anybody could think about, or talk about. And it isn't a bad thing either, I'm not despising it, mind; but I found it had a place, and it was only of value when you could use it to make you and them about you happy. I wanted to talk about these things. I wanted to have things explained to me, then to argue about them, and being me, to deny them while at bottom believing they were right. And I wanted to do all this with you. But you would have none of it, or me. You know, you used to look at me sometimes

275

as if I wasn't worth three pennorth of copper. And I wasn't in your eyes, and I resented it. Very likely that's why I showed you me worst side. Loosen your stays, I used to say, remember? And I could have kicked meself when you went out of the room.

"Oh, Miss Brigmore"—he nodded at her now, a smile creeping over his face—"you've given me a lot of food for thought. Anyway, there it is, I've had me say, or nearly. One thing more. You might not think it's fittin' that I should talk like this and Matilda not being gone a year, but Matilda would have been the first one to understand, and if the subject had come up she would have said, 'Do it right away, lad; there's only one thing I don't want you to do,' she would have said, 'and that's let Florrie get her claws into you.' Oh, she hated Florrie. An' so did you, didn't you?" He bent his face closer toward hers.

"Oh, Mr. Bensham."

"Aw! For God sake, lass, drop the Mr. Bensham." He flung one arm outwards. "Me name's Harry. Can't you call me Harry? Now look; I can see I've startled you; we'll leave it for a time, we'll have a meal, eh? And then a game of cards, I like a game of cards. There's something else I like, an' I bet this'll surprise you, I like to be read to. You know, when I used to sit in the bedroom, supposedly reading the paper while you read to Matilda, I used to lap it up. I never had time to read; I've never read a book in me life; and that's not sayin' I don't want to, or I don't like to hear a good story. Sounds as if I'm going into me second childhood, doesn't it? But no, I think there's lots of blokes like me; looking back from my age they're full of regrets at not having learned a little about things. But it's not too late, is it? Is it?"

He waited, and when her head fell forward and she covered her eyes with one hand, while her voice breaking, she murmured, "No, no, it's n . . . not too late," he hitched himself rapidly toward her, and, putting his arms about her, he said, "There, lass. There. Don't cry. I'm sorry. It must have come as a shock to you. But in any case let me tell you this." He dared to put his hand up onto her hair and stroke it. "If you can't see your way clear to becomin' Mrs. Bensham I'd still want you to run this house, take over sort of permanent like, live here. You could let Mary have the cottage. You'd be doing me a favor in that way if nothing else, 'cos I can't bear coming here and eating alone; sittin' by meself in this barracks nearly drives me mad. I could sell it. I've told meself over and over again that if you turn me down that's what I'll do, I'll sell it, but at bottom I know it would go against the grain, selling it I mean. I would sort of lose prestige; and you know fellows in my position cling like limpets to prestige; self-made men have to have something to to show for their efforts, or else what'd be the use of it all? Aw, come on. I'm sorry, I'm sorry I've made you bubble. You've never heard that word afore, have you?" He pushed her gently from him, and putting his hand under her chin, lifted her tear-stained face upwards. "Me grandma came from the northeast, Shields way. She was always using the word. 'Stop your bubblin',' she would say, 'else I'll skelp the hunger off ya.' . . . I can't make you laugh, can I?"

Miss Brigmore hastily sought in the pocket of her gray woolen dress for a handkerchief; when she found it she dabbed her eyes and gently blew her nose. Then she looked at the man sitting opposite her. His face was rugged, his hair was gray, his eyes were a clear blue; unlike Thomas's body, his was flat and, if the flesh of his hands and face were anything to go by, firm. He was a much younger-looking man than Thomas, but he was the antithesis of Thomas. Thomas had been a gentleman, this man was rough; yet he was not coarse, there was a difference; and he had confessed an eagerness for some kind of culture. Yet she knew that nothing she or anyone else could do would put a veneer on him, not at this stage of his life. Yet perhaps she could feed the inward need in him, as he would help fill up the great void in her.

But as yet she could not take in the real import of his offer. He had asked her to marry him . . . *marry him*. She would no longer be Miss Brigmore, she would be Mrs. Bensham, and she'd be mistress of this house. It all had the quality of a dream. She who had come into this house as a governess thirty-six years ago, and had worked in the nursery for six years before Thomas went bankrupt, but not once during these early years had she been invited to a meal or function downstairs, never had she sat in the dining room until the man sitting opposite to her had invited her to his table. During the ten years or more she had spent in the cottage with Thomas, she had never received a penny in wages and times without number she had pretended loss of appetite in order that Thomas and the girls should have better helpings. She had suffered humiliation and not a little privation in serving the Mallens, and what had been her reward?

Now there was this man offering to make her mistress of the Hall. Had it come as a surprise to her? Yes, yes. Oh, yes, it had. She was not unaware of her accomplishments, but she had little personal vanity, and had never, never imagined that she had been in Mr. Bensham's thoughts all these years. It was something she must get used to and she would get used to it, and she would repay him for the honor he was doing her. Oh yes, yes, she would; and she began to say this.

"You are doing me a great honor in . . ."

He cut her short. "Now, now, Brigie, don't go into any polite palaver, not at this point. If you want to tell me now, just say yes or no, an' let's have it.

She blinked rapidly, blew her nose gently again, then said, "I am honored to accept your proposal, Mr. Bensham."

She watched the muscles of his face drop, she watched his mouth spread into a wide smile, she watched his hand come up and cover his brows and then his eyes. She watched his shoulder shake, and then he began to laugh.

"Aw! Lass, lass, you're the limit. Look"— he was gripping her hands tightly now—"repeat after me: Harry, I'll take you."

Her chin dropped slightly, her eyes closed for a

second, a smile hovered around her mouth and she repeated, in a voice little above a whisper, "Harry, I'll take you."

"There! There!" His voice was no longer quiet, it was like a bellow, and the next moment she was enveloped in a hug that jerked the breath out of her. And then his lips were on hers, right on her mouth, and his kiss was hard and warming, so warm that it seemed to melt her body right through to the void. And she was as surprised as he was when she relaxed against him and her hand touched the back of his neck.

It was some minutes before he released her. Then holding her at arm's length and with his head to one side, he said, "There's some good years ahead of us yet, lass. And you'll be surprised to know one of the things I'm looking forward to is the things you can learn me."

As she looked back into his face her gaze was soft, her mind gentle toward him, and she did not correct him and say, "There is nothing I can learn you, I can only teach, it is you who must learn." But what she said, and with a smile in her eyes, and on her lips, was, "I'll be delighted to learn you . . . Mr. Bensham."

And at this he again pulled her into his arms and close to him, and what he said was, "I'll Mr. Bensham you afore I'm finished, Anna Brigmore, by lad! I will."

ABOUT THE AUTHOR

CATHERINE COOKSON is one of the most widely read contemporary woman novelists. Her background, which she so vividly recreates in many of her novels, was the north of England at Tyne Dock. Since her first book in 1950, she has been acclaimed both as a regional writer and as the author of exciting historical fiction. Two of her books have been filmed and others translated into as many as eight languages. American readers will remember her for *The Dwelling Place, The Glass Virgin, Kate Hannigan, Katie Mulholland, Feathers in the Fire, The Fifteen Streets, Fenwick Houses, The Mallen Streak* and *Pure as the Lily*. THE MALLEN GIRL is the second volume of a trilogy, following *The Mallen Streak*. Mrs. Cookson and her husband, a schoolmaster, now live in Hastings, England.

CATHERINE COOKSON NOVELS IN CORGI

WHILE EVERY EFFORT IS MADE TO KEEP PRICES LOW, IT IS SOMETIMES NECESSARY TO INCREASE PRICES AT SHORT NOTICE. CORGI BOOKS RESERVE THE RIGHT TO SHOW AND CHARGE NEW RETAIL PRICES ON COVERS WHICH MAY DIFFER FROM THOSE ADVERTISED IN THE TEXT OR ELSEWHERE.

THE PRICES SHOWN BELOW WERE CORRECT AT THE TIME OF GOING TO PRESS (JULY '80)

☐	11160 0	The Cinder Path	£1.25
☐	10916 9	The Girl	£1.50
☐	11202 X	The Tide of Life	£1.50
☐	11374 3	The Gambling Man	£1.25
☐	11204 6	Fanny McBride	95p
☐	11261 5	The Invisible Cord	£1.25
☐	11571 1	The Mallen Litter	£1.50
☐	11570 3	The Mallen Girl	£1.50
☐	11569 X	The Mallen Streak	£1.50
☐	09894 9	Rooney	95p
☐	11391 3	Pure as the Lily	£1.25
☐	09373 4	Our Kate	£1.00
☐	09318 1	Feathers in the Fire	£1.25
☐	11203 8	The Dwelling Place	£1.25
☐	11260 7	The Invitation	£1.25
☐	11365 4	The Nice Bloke	95p
☐	08849 8	The Glass Virgin	£1.25
☐	11366 2	The Blind Miller	£1.25
☐	11434 0	The Menagerie	£1.00
☐	11367 0	Colour Blind	£1.25
☐	11448 0	The Unbaited Trap	£1.00
☐	11335 2	Katie Mulholland	£1.50
☐	11447 2	The Long Corridor	95p
☐	11449 9	Maggie Rowan	£1.25
☐	11368 9	The Fifteen Streets	£1.00
☐	11336 0	Fenwick Houses	£1.00
☐	11369 7	The Round Tower	£1.25
☐	11370 0	Kate Hannigan	£1.00
☐	08821 8	A Grand Man	85p
☐	08822 6	The Lord and Mary Ann	85p
☐	08823 4	The Devil and Mary Ann	95p
☐	09074 3	Love and Mary Ann	95p
☐	09075 1	Life and Mary Ann	95p
☐	09076 X	Marriage and Mary Ann	95p
☐	09254 1	Mary Ann's Angels	85p
☐	09397 1	Mary Ann and Bill	85p

All these books are available at your bookshop or newsagent, or can be ordered direct from the publisher. Just tick the titles you want and fill in the form below.

....

CORGI BOOKS, Cash Sales Department, P.O. Box 11, Falmouth, Cornwall.
Please send cheque or postal order, no currency.

U.K. Please allow 30p for the first book, 15p for the second book and 12p for each additional book ordered to a maximum charge of £1.29.

B.F.P.O. & EIRE allow 30p for the first book, 15p for the second book plus 12p per copy for the next 7 books, thereafter 6p per book.

Overseas customers. Please allow 50p for the first book plus 15p per copy for each additional book.

NAME (Block letters) ....

ADDRESS ....

....